D0683731

ALSO BY JEFFREY LAYTON

The Good Spy

Vortex One

Warhead

Blowout

THE FOREVER SPY

A YURI KIROV THRILLER

JEFFREY LAYTON

PINNACLE BOOKS
Kensington Publishing Corp.
www.kensingtonbooks.com

PINNACLE BOOKS are published by

Kensington Publishing Corp.
119 West 40th Street
New York, NY 10018

All Kensington titles, imprints, and distributed lines are available at special quantity discounts for bulk purchases for sales promotions, premiums, fund-raising, educational, or institutional use. Special book excerpts or customized printings can also be created to fit specific needs. For details, write or phone the office of the Kensington sales manager: Kensington Publishing Corp., 119 West 40th Street, New York, NY 10018, attn: Sales Department; phone 1-800-221-2647.

PINNACLE BOOKS and the Pinnacle logo are Reg. U.S. Pat. & TM Off.

ISBN-13: 978-0-7860-3715-5
ISBN-10: 0-7860-3715-6

First printing: May 2017

10 9 8 7 6 5 4 3 2 1

Printed in the United States of America

First electronic edition: May 2017

ISBN-13: 978-0-7860-3716-2
ISBN-10: 0-7860-3716-4

To my daughters, Kerry and Kimberly

CHAPTER 1

It was an ideal time to work on the ice—no wind, clear skies, and just minus fifteen degrees Fahrenheit. The two researchers from the University of Alaska stood on the frozen sea. Alaska's Icy Cape was about a hundred nautical miles to the southeast. The international boundary with the Russian Federation lay forty-eight miles to the west.

The sheer white slab supporting the men appeared to extend to infinity in all directions. To the north, the Arctic Ocean stretched to its polar cap. To the south, the Chukchi Sea connected to the Bering Sea, which abutted the immense North Pacific Ocean.

The staff physical oceanographer and the moorings technician from the School of Fisheries and Ocean Sciences had just over two hours to install the equipment before returning to Barrow. Their ride sat on the ice twenty yards to the east. The helo pilot dozed inside the cockpit. Although it was 1:20 P.M., the early February sun barely rose above the southern horizon. In a few hours, it would disappear entirely. The charter pilot refused to fly during Arctic dark.

Designed to measure and record the speed and direction of currents flowing under the ice sheet, the array when deployed would extend 130 feet down, terminating twenty feet above the seabed. Real-time data from the current meters along with the GPS coordinates of the drifting ice pack supporting the array would be transmitted to a satellite and relayed to the chief scientist's office at the Fairbanks campus.

Although not expected to survive more than a week due to shifting ice floes, the instruments would provide data that would be used to help verify a mathematical model of late-winter water exchange between the Pacific and Arctic Oceans. The study was part of a larger effort to document climate change. The polar ice cap was in an unprecedented retreat. By the end of the coming summer, sea-ice extent would likely shrink to a new record minimum.

The investigators were dressed to battle the cold. Each wore a base layer of thermal long johns and vest, a fleece tracksuit for a mid-layer, and an outer layer consisting of an arctic parka and insulated leggings. Wool hats and thin micro-fleece balaclavas covered their heads. Large mittens with thin inner gloves protected their hands. Long arctic boots with removable liners encased their feet.

It took the two men an hour to assemble the current meter array, laying it out in a straight line along the ice. Their next task called for boring an eighteen-inch-diameter hole through the seven-foot-thick ice sheet.

The technician fired up the heavy-duty gasoline-powered auger, referred to as "Icenado" for its tendency to toss operators pell-mell when concrete-hard multiyear sea ice jammed the bit. As the tech let the engine warm up, the racket of the auger's top-mounted engine polluted the otherwise tranquil environment.

Half a minute passed when the technician shouted, "All set, boss."

"Okay, Bill."

The oceanographer grabbed the handle on the opposite side of the auger and the tech goosed the throttle. The bit tore into the first-year ice, advancing three feet in about half a minute. A cone of splintered ice mounded around the borehole.

As the auger continued to penetrate the ice, the operator backed off the throttle, expecting the bit to break through in seconds. That's when he spotted the change.

"What's that?" he said, peering down at the black material disgorging from the hole.

Just then, the bit pierced the ice keel and a torrent of blackish seawater erupted, pumped onto the ice surface by the still spinning auger. The tech switched off the engine and both men extracted the auger from the borehole. More black fluid surged inside the puncture.

The scientist dropped to his knees and removed a mitten. He reached into the hole with his right forearm. When he pulled up his hand, the fingertips of the inner glove were blackened. He raised them to his nose.

"Son of a bitch!"

"What?" asked the technician.

"It's oil!"

"How can that be? We're out in the middle of frigging nowhere."

"I don't know—something's not right."

The oceanographer stood. Dismayed, he wiped the soiled glove on the side of his leggings and said, "I've got to report this right now."

He reached into his parka and removed an Iridium satellite phone. Forty seconds later, he connected with the chief scientist in Fairbanks.

Within an hour, a transcript of the field report would reach the desk of the president of the United States.

CHAPTER 2

Day 1—Monday

Laura Newman cradled the coffee mug, embracing the warmth radiating from the porcelain. She stood on the spacious deck of her home, overlooking the serene waters of Lake Sammamish. It was a few minutes before eight o'clock in the morning. She'd already run for half an hour, following her usual route of narrow lanes and streets that snaked up and down and across the hillside of her affluent suburban neighborhood. Downtown Seattle was a dozen miles to the west.

A snow-white terrycloth robe concealed her slender frame from neck to ankles; she'd just showered and shampooed. Her damp hair remained bundled in a towel, turban-style. Clogs housed her feet.

An exotic blend of Scandinavia and equatorial Africa, Laura had inherited her Nordic mother's high cheekbones, full ripe lips, azure eyes, and russet hair. Her father's tall willowy frame, broad nose, and cocoa skin, all linked to his distant Bantu ancestors, complemented her mother's genes.

In her early thirties, she had little need for makeup. Nevertheless, she would complete the ritual before heading to work, touching up her chocolate complexion.

Always a morning person, Laura prized the solitude of the early hours. She used the quiet time to think and plan. Once she stepped into her office building, it would be a whirlwind for the next eight to ten hours.

Laura sipped from the mug, savoring the gourmet blend. Yuri ground the premium beans and brewed a pot, something he did every morning.

They had been together for over a year—lovers, best friends, and recently business partners.

Leaning against the guardrail, Laura spent the next few minutes strategizing, preparing for a teleconference she would lead at ten this morning with at least a dozen participants from Palo Alto, Denver, and Boston. She would serve as ringmaster for the launch of a new project that she hoped would further enrich her company.

Laura drained the mug—she limited herself to just half a cup a day. She turned and walked back into the living room. Half a dozen steps later, she entered the nursery; it was just off the master bedroom. Madelyn remained fast asleep in her crib.

Laura beamed as she gazed at her divine daughter. Born eight months earlier, Maddy had finally started sleeping through the night, which was a relief to both Laura and Yuri. Several days earlier, however, Maddy's first tooth had erupted through her lower gum, reinstating the nightly disorder. Awakened around three o'clock this morning, Yuri held Madelyn for half an hour as she chewed on the teething ring before falling back asleep.

Laura reached down and gently stroked Maddy's angel-soft ash-blond hair. She stirred but did not wake. Laura's ex was the biological father, but Yuri treated Madelyn as his own—a blessing Laura cherished.

"See you in a little while, sweetie," Laura whispered. Before driving to work, she would nurse Madelyn.

Laura walked into the kitchen.

Yuri stood at the island, his lean six-foot-plus frame propped against the granite countertop and his arms crossed across his chest. A couple of years younger than Laura, he wore a trim beard that accentuated his slate gray eyes and jet-black hair. As he stared at a nearby wall-mounted television, his forehead contorted. Laura had observed that look before and was instantly on alert.

"What's going on, honey?" she asked.

Yuri pointed to the TV—a Fox News Channel logo hovered in the lower left corner of the screen. "Oil spill in Alaska. A big one." Just a trace of his Russian accent remained.

"Where?"

"Chukchi Sea."

"Oh no—isn't that near where you're supposed to work?"

"Yes."

Laura focused on the television screen. A ringed seal encased in thick gooey oil lay lifeless on a sheet of ice.

"Do they know what happened?"

"No, just that some researchers found the first oil far

offshore over the weekend. Then someone else found the seal near Barrow."

"How many wells did Aurora drill?"

"Four."

"This is going to change everything."

"Yes, it is."

CHAPTER 3

Yuri Kirov sat behind a desk in the office section of a twelve-year-old concrete tilt-up building in Redmond, Washington. It was a quarter past two in the afternoon at Northwest Subsea Dynamics. Yuri had just finished a twenty-minute call with an airfreight company, arranging for a charter flight.

Yuri stood, walked out of his office and passed through NSD's engineering division—a collection of four cubicles each equipped with the latest CAD/CAM computer systems. He greeted one of the engineers, a twentysomething East Indian woman with a freshly minted master's degree in mechanical engineering from MIT. Yuri opened a door and stepped into the warehouse section of the building—the heart of NSD's operations.

Along the nearest wall were three computer-aided manufacturing workstations. Two 3-D printer units, a lathe, and a laser-cutting table occupied floor space along the far wall. Shelving lined another wall, the bins filled with hundreds of assorted electronic and mechanical devices. The assembly area, about three thousand square feet, took up the center of the warehouse.

Yuri approached the three men standing beside a canary yellow cylinder that was twenty feet long and three feet in diameter. The autonomous underwater vehicle was mounted on a steel cradle, its crown chest high.

The men loitered near the AUV's bow, its bullet-shaped fiberglass hull covering removed. They stared at the exposed internal steel pressure casing that housed the AI computer system—*Deep Explorer*'s brain.

NSD's senior engineer and eldest employee at forty-eight turned to face Yuri. "What did they have to say?" he asked.

"You're all set, Bill. Wheels up at eight tomorrow morning at Boeing Field. You guys are on the same flight. The freighter has half a dozen passenger seats behind the cockpit—so you'll have it to yourselves."

"Awesome," Bill Winters said. He turned and with a beaming smile fist-bumped his two assistant engineers, both in their mid-twenties. Winters was the shortest of those assembled, a hair over five and a half feet, and rotund.

"Is she ready?" Yuri asked.

"Yep. We just ran a system check, she's perfect."

"Okay, let's get her crated up along with the support gear. I've got a truck on its way. It should be here by four o'clock." Yuri gazed at his charges. "A few words of advice. It's the end of the world up there, so take everything that you might conceivably need—tools, extra parts, spare batteries . . . even duct tape."

The men chuckled.

"Got it, boss," Winters said. He ran a hand through

his thick graying-blond hair. "When are you coming to Barrow?"

"Probably in a couple of days, but don't worry about me. You're in charge. Just make Aurora happy and I'll be happy."

"Will do."

Yuri returned to his office and again sat behind the desk. He leaned back in his chair and stared at a nearby wall. A color map depicting the top of the world filled most of the wall's surface. He focused on the offshore waters near Alaska's North Slope. Bill Winters and his crew were bound for Barrow.

Yuri reached for his desk phone, dialed, and waited.

The receptionist on the other end of the line in Anchorage routed Yuri's call to NSD's most important customer.

"Good afternoon," Jim Bauer said.

Bauer was the Alaska operations manager for Aurora Offshore Systems.

"Hi, Jim," Yuri said. "I just wanted to let you know we're on schedule down here. Barring weather issues, *Deep Explorer* and my crew will be in Barrow tomorrow afternoon."

"That's great news."

They had communicated numerous times by phone and e-mail but had not yet met in person.

"We're really counting on you guys," Bauer continued. "Houston is already getting bombarded by the media and attacked online by every environmental whack job out there."

"How about you?"

"Nothing here yet, but it will come. The greens hate us."

Houston-based AOS cut its teeth drilling in the Gulf of Mexico, having accumulated enormous cash reserves from over a dozen spectacularly successful well fields developed offshore of Texas and Louisiana. After Shell Oil retreated from its Chukchi Sea exploration program due to poor test well results, the federal government banned future Arctic offshore leases. But new trouble in the Middle East and Russia's stranglehold over Western Europe's natural gas supply prompted the White House to reverse policy. Alaska's northern continental shelf was reopened for development. Aurora elected to expand into Alaska, submitting the winning bid for a lease of ten thousand acres east of the Shell site.

"Have you been able to get a crew out to the field to check for oil?" Yuri asked.

"No. Weather turned shitty. Too dangerous for a chopper that far offshore. Maybe tomorrow."

In spite of fierce out-of-state environmental opposition, AOS won approval to drill four exploratory wells in the Chukchi Sea. The State of Alaska welcomed Aurora warmly and the feds were unusually cooperative; they played strictly by the rules, minimizing regulatory politics as directed by the president. All four bores hit commercial quantities of oil and gas—an unprecedented accomplishment. Aurora planned to drill additional test wells the coming summer in preparation for development of the field.

"Were there any problems cementing in the wells?" Yuri asked, referring to the safety measure of filling the test bores with cement to temporarily plug the drill casing.

"None. It was all textbook. The feds signed off on everything."

"It must be coming from a seep or an abandoned well."

"That's our take on it, too."

Northwest Subsea Dynamic's original assignment for *Aurora* was for a second Chukchi Sea venture. AOS had recently leased an additional twenty thousand acres from the federal government. NSD was under contract to provide precision bathymetry for the new tract.

Preliminary geophysical surveys hinted that the Chukchi Plateau, located in deep waters near the limit of the United States' Arctic Ocean continental shelf claim, held enormous hydrocarbon reserves—several times those of Prudhoe Bay. *Deep Explorer*'s innovative sonar and photographic systems coupled with its speed and extended under-ice endurance capability were all well suited for surveying the site. But that work was now on hold. *Deep Explorer* had a new mission.

"How long do you think the survey will take?" Bauer asked.

"At least forty-eight hours, maybe longer."

"You'll check the test wells first, correct?"

"Yes—that'll be our first task."

Fallout from BP's *Deepwater Horizon* blowout in the Gulf required *Aurora* to prove its existing Chukchi Sea exploration wells were not the cause of the pollution.

Conventional survey and photographic surveillance of the seabed from ship-deployed remotely operated vehicles—ROVs—would not be possible until the summer, when the pack ice retreated. That left only one option—under-the-ice observation.

Deep Explorer's new mission was to produce HD video recordings and photographs of the bottom-mounted equipment for Aurora's Chukchi Sea wells. A companion mission was to survey and video-map the entire development field of its leasehold to search for natural oil seeps or seabed ruptures that might be the source of the oil.

"When will you be coming up?" Bauer asked.

"I'm not sure yet. I'll know more once my crew is in Barrow."

"Well, Matheson is flying in tomorrow. I'm sure he'll want to meet you."

"Okay, we'll work something out."

"Great, nice hearing from you."

Yuri hung up and again leaned back in his chair. Northwest Subsea Dynamics had a terrific opportunity ahead. He had enormous confidence in his crew, especially Bill Winters.

Winters was one of the founding partners when the company was launched five years earlier. The four partners, all former NOAA engineers and scientists, created a remarkable underwater robot—*Deep Explorer*. But like so many start-ups, NSD burned through its cash reserves. After exhausting personal savings and repeatedly striking out with angel investors, NSD was about to fold when rescued.

Laura Newman purchased NSD—for Yuri. Bill Winters remained, keeping his 25 percent interest while his partners cashed out. Laura appointed Yuri as general manager and Winters kept his chief engineer position.

Yuri did not draw a salary or any form of compensation from the company; he functioned as Laura's representative without pay. It was simpler that way, and it provided Laura with a layer of protection.

Yuri did not have a Social Security number, a must for employment, nor did he possess a Green Card or even an expired Visitor's Visa. Yuri had entered the United States over a year earlier on a clandestine mission for the Russian government that had soured. He had been hiding in plain sight ever since, using an alias and supported by Laura. But he now worried that his ruse might be exposed.

Jim Bauer's strong hint about the need to meet with Aurora's CEO weighed heavily on Yuri. His plan all along was for Bill Winters to take the limelight while he remained in the shadows. But with Bill on his way to Barrow, Yuri had no choice but to represent NSD in Anchorage.

The press would soon be hounding Aurora's Alaska operations office. Somehow Yuri needed to avoid being photographed or videoed.

Nearly halfway around the globe from Washington State and sixteen time zones ahead, the two men met in a luxurious suite on the twenty-eighth floor of the hotel. The brownish stain of smog marred the otherwise spectacular view of the sprawling cityscape this morning.

The subject matter called for a face-to-face, but secrecy dictated that they meet at a neutral venue. Both in their early fifties, the deputy directors of the brother intelligence agencies sat across from each other at a teak conference table. The waiter had just departed, leaving a pot of steaming green tea. They were now alone; their aides waited below in the lobby.

"I thought we would have more time," the taller of the pair said as he picked up his cup from the tabletop. He was a major general in the Army but today he wore a plain gray suit.

"We were supposed to have another month before it was discovered—when the ice starts to break up," the civilian said. He wore a custom-tailored Savile Row wool suit over his squat, thick frame.

The general took a sip and said, "Should we advance the schedule?"

The foreign operations spy chief nursed his teacup and took his time responding. "I don't think that is warranted—yet. All they know is there's a leak. My people estimate it will be months before it is plugged. The oil will continue to spread during that time."

"Just the same, I think it would be prudent to plan ahead in case we need to advance the schedule."

"What do you have in mind?"

The military spymaster reached into the chest pocket of his suit jacket and removed a folded document. He unfolded the single sheet of paper and placed it on the table. "This is our most current estimate of the American Navy's deployment timetable."

The intelligence chief studied the document before glancing back at his counterpart. "The next one departs in six weeks—that's not much time. Can you be ready that soon?"

"I've already dispatched a team. They're on-site now. I'll know in a few days."

CHAPTER 4

DAY 2—TUESDAY

Laura Newman was in the middle of composing an e-mail when the intercom on her office phone handset came to life. It was the receptionist. "Laura, you have a visitor."

Laura glanced at the open Outlook calendar on her PC; she had nothing scheduled for the afternoon. "Who is it?" she asked.

"Ah, Mr. Hamilton. He says you don't know him but it's about your former husband. He's working for Mr. Newman's mother and says he only needs a few minutes of your time."

Lawyer, was Laura's instant thought. "Okay. Please show him to conference room C. I'll be there soon."

"Okay."

Tom Hamilton was in his late fifties, slim with almost skeletal features. His blue blazer, starched white shirt, and silk tie fit the mold of an attorney's attire, but Laura's intuition was wrong.

Laura and the visitor sat at a circular table in an interior conference room.

"Thank you for meeting with me," Hamilton said.

"The receptionist said this is about Ken."

"Yes, I'm a private investigator. Mr. Newman's mother, Deborah, hired me to look into his disappearance."

"I assume you've talked with the police."

"Oh yes. I've read the reports from Redmond, Bellevue, and Whatcom County."

"Then you know there's been no hint as to where he might be now."

"That's right. The official files have gone cold. That's why Mrs. Newman hired me. You know, give everything a fresh look." Hamilton retrieved a file from his briefcase and thumbed through the contents. He pulled out an eight-by-ten color photograph and slid it across the tabletop.

Laura picked up the photo of a waterfront home. The image released an instant blizzard of memories.

"That was the place you were staying at in Point Roberts, correct?"

"Yes." She looked away from the photo, meeting Hamilton's eye. "On the advice of my attorney, I rented it to get away from Ken because he was going to be served with divorce papers. I assume you know about why I filed for divorce."

"I do." Hamilton's brow narrowed. "Still, he ended up following you there . . . to Point Roberts."

"That's right."

"And then he had the trouble with the DUI."

"I don't know what happened. We met briefly at the house I was renting and then he left."

"And you didn't see him after that time?"

"I had a restraining order against him. I told him if he contacted me again I'd call the police and have him arrested."

The PI nodded. "Do you know what happened to his car?"

"What?"

"His Corvette. It was impounded in Point Roberts but disappeared."

Hamilton removed another photo—Ken with his shaggy blond hair standing next to his cherry red sports car. "Deborah let me borrow this photo of the car." Hamilton placed the print on the tabletop.

"I don't know anything about that."

"Do you know if he came back to Point Roberts after his release in Bellingham?"

"I suppose he could have . . . but I didn't see the car."

As Hamilton again glanced at his file folder, Laura launched her own inquiry. "What have you found out so far?"

"Very little. Mrs. Newman hasn't heard anything from Ken—it's been well over a year now. Nor has anyone at the real estate company he worked at or any of his friends. And you, I assume you haven't heard from him."

"You know I haven't."

Hamilton removed a multipage document from the folder. "Were you aware that Mrs. Newman pledged a certificate of deposit as security for Ken's bail—a hundred thousand?" He displayed the first sheet of the bail bond form.

"No. And why so much for a DUI? That doesn't sound right."

"He resisted arrest. He clobbered a deputy sheriff, broke his jaw."

Laura glanced away, shaking her head. This she believed, having also been on the receiving end of Ken's rage when he was plastered.

"When Ken failed to show up for his trial, the bond was forfeited and Mrs. Newman lost her money," said Hamilton. "It was part of her retirement portfolio."

"I'm sorry to hear that, but what has it to do with me?"

"Mrs. Newman is convinced that Ken is dead. She would have heard from him by now if he were alive. They were close."

"This is about the divorce, isn't it?"

"I understand that you went ahead and since Ken did not make an appearance, the divorce was eventually granted."

"That's all in the record."

"Right. And since Mr. Newman did not contest the divorce he came out of it with just a pittance."

Laura's annoyance surged. "The court awarded him what he was due based on the prenup."

"But just half a million? That seems like nothing in comparison to your resources."

"I purchased that home before we married—for cash. He never contributed a dime toward it. And my stock ownership in the company, most of those awards were made before we got married. The court took all of that into consideration."

"Yes it did. But since Ken wasn't there to argue otherwise, you certainly benefited."

Laura had had enough. "What do you want, Mr. Hamilton?"

"Mrs. Newman plans to petition the state to have her son declared dead. As his only remaining family, she would then receive the divorce proceeds that were placed in trust for Ken."

"I don't have a problem with that."

"There is still the question of life insurance."

"What are you talking about?"

"It was through Ken's work. He had a quarter million term policy; his mother was named as the primary beneficiary."

This was news to Laura. "Okay, but what does this have to do with me?"

"The problem is the policy expired last December— before she found out it existed. He'd paid his premium annually."

"So it's no longer in effect?"

"Correct, but if it can be proved that Ken died before the policy lapsed, Mrs. Newman would receive the benefit." He met Laura's eyes. "My job is to make the case to the court that Ken died and that his death most likely occurred before the policy expired. And I need your help to do that."

"How?"

"From my research, I'm convinced that something happened to Ken at Point Roberts."

"You think I was involved?" Laura said, raising her voice an octave.

"No, of course not. But Ken had that run-in with a deputy sheriff, and I know he has a problem with alcohol. If he returned to Point Roberts to get his car and ended up in a bar again, just about anything could have happened to him."

Laura remained mute, not sure where Hamilton was headed.

"What would really help me—and Deborah—is that once we make our case to the court you would support it."

"You want me to testify?"

"I think just an affidavit would work. I'll have to check with Mrs. Newman's attorney to make sure."

"When do you need it?"

"It'll be a month or so. I'm heading back to Point Roberts next week. I'm planning on staying there for several days, really hitting it hard—interviewing anyone I can find that remembers Ken."

"You can tell Deborah that I will help."

"Thank you."

Laura returned to her office. With the door locked, she sat at her desk nursing Madelyn.

After meeting with Hamilton, she'd picked up Maddy from her company's day care center, four levels below Laura's penthouse office. Not yet ready to hire a nanny, Laura preferred to keep her daughter close by while at work.

Located near the center of Bellevue's downtown core, Cognition Consultants occupied most of the twenty-five-story tower. As senior vice president of operations, Laura owned 35 percent of the closely held company.

While Madelyn suckled, Laura turned away from the window wall, ignoring the twilight view of Lake

Washington and the distant Seattle skyline. She leaned back in the chair, and with her eyes closed, rehashed the trauma from a year earlier. The nightmares had finally abated, but she would never forget the revulsion of that night.

Laura knew exactly what had happened to her husband.

CHAPTER 5

"How long will you be gone?" Laura asked.

"At least a couple of days, maybe as long as a week."

Laura and Yuri were home, sitting at the kitchen table. Four months earlier, they had moved into the new custom-built tri-level contemporary that overlooked the eastern shore of Lake Sammamish. Laura purchased the City of Sammamish hillside spec home after vacating her Redmond residence. The haunting memories of Ken at her former home were unbearable.

Yuri sipped a glass of merlot while Laura drank chilled apple juice. Their dinner was simmering on the gas range, a pot roast Yuri had prepared. Laura had just arrived; he'd been home for two hours. Maddy was in the adjacent living room, still asleep inside the detachable car seat.

"Are Bill and his team okay?" Laura asked.

"Yes. I talked to Bill this afternoon. The crew arrived without incident. They plan to get everything set up tomorrow and then head out on the ice the next day."

Laura smiled. "This is what you've been waiting for."

Yuri returned the smile and took another sip of Fourteen Hands. "Aurora already wired us the mobilization fee—a hundred fifty thousand."

"Great. That certainly helps with cash flow."

He offered nothing additional.

Laura sensed something was off. "You seem a little down, honey. What's the matter?"

"The oil spill is a huge story. It was all over the TV news again tonight."

Laura tensed up, recognizing Yuri's concern. "Maybe you shouldn't go. Let Bill Winters take the lead on everything."

"I can't. Aurora wants my direct involvement. I have to brief the CEO and his key people tomorrow in Anchorage."

"That's not a public meeting. You should be okay."

"Probably."

Laura sipped the last of the juice. "I don't think you have anything to worry about. Just tell Bill and his crew that Aurora wants NSD to remain low profile and that they are not to speak with the press. If you stay in the background you should be fine."

"That's what I told Bill."

"Good." Laura grinned. "Besides, with your lovely beard and longer hair no one will recognize you."

"Maybe I should try wearing some fake glasses."

"Sure, why not?"

Dinner was over. Yuri was in the bedroom, packing. Laura sat on a sofa in the living room. Maddy was crawling on the carpet near her feet—exploring. As Laura sipped from a mug of decaffeinated tea, she worried.

The risk was real. If Yuri were spotted, it would place everything in jeopardy. They needed more time to make the transition.

Laura had a specialty law firm in D.C. working on the problem, but it was a delicate subject. In the end, it would likely reach Secretary level at both Departments of State and Defense, and maybe even the White House.

Laura loved Yuri deeply and would do everything in her power to protect him. But he would be on his own in Alaska.

He can do it! Laura thought, knowing Yuri had already been tested to the extreme. Alaska would be a cakewalk. *Just stay in the shadows and no one will know*.

Laura drained the mug and was about to pick up Maddy and join Yuri when another loose thread tugged at her conscience. She had intended to tell Yuri about her meeting with the private investigator but then thought better of it. Yuri had too much on his mind already. She didn't want him to worry about the PI dredging up old wounds. She would take that burden alone.

Besides, her ex was the root of that problem.

CHAPTER 6

The Alaska Air 737 departed Seattle fifteen minutes earlier. Bound for Anchorage, it was over the southern end of Vancouver Island nearing its cruising altitude of thirty-four thousand feet. The morning was cloudless. The view from the right side of the fuselage was exceptional. In the far distance, the Cascades were in full bloom, their jagged peaks icy white. The mega-metropolis of Vancouver lay at the northerly base of the mountain range. In the foreground, the emerald waters of the Strait of Georgia—the north arm of the Salish Sea—filled the viewport.

Yuri Kirov leaned toward the porthole. South of Vancouver, a long narrow peninsula jutted several miles into the Strait of Georgia. Yuri focused on the vast inland sea. It was right there, he thought, eyeing a patch of water south of Point Roberts.

Yuri turned away, leaning back in his seat, eyes shuttered. Sweat beaded on his forehead. He gripped the armrests with both hands, heart pounding.

It had happened fifteen months earlier. Fifty-three lives snuffed out in just minutes.

The *Neva* was deep inside hostile waters—it was Yuri's mission—spying on American and Canadian naval installations. An accident sent the Russian submarine to the bottom over seven hundred feet down. Using high-tech diving equipment from his espionage operations, Yuri escaped the underwater tomb—barely.

Suffering from decompression sickness, alone, and a hundred miles inside enemy lines, Yuri's new mission was to rescue the *Neva*'s remaining three dozen survivors before the U.S. Navy discovered the marooned spy sub. He never could have done it without Laura's help.

Yuri took a deep breath and opened his eyes. He leaned forward and pulled up his briefcase from under the forward seat. He opened it and removed a copy of NSD's contract with Aurora Offshore Systems.

The boring reading would help flush the lingering effects of the flashback.

The two men stood near the shoreline and peered at the Chukchi Sea. It was noon, yet the sun hovered just above the horizon. There was enough light to make out the distant ice ridges. The nearest fold jutted a dozen feet above the sheet of ice that stretched to the horizon.

"It looks bleak out there," offered the taller man.

"No kidding," said his companion. A head shorter and in his bulky white ice suit that amplified his ample belly, he mimicked a walking snowball.

"How far do we have to go?"

"At least a mile, maybe two." Bill Winters squinted, probing deeper into the dimness. "We need to be able to get beyond the grounded ice to launch but at the same time remain on the landfast ice for retrieval."

"How thick is the ice out there?"

"The University of Alaska people said it should be about a meter at the launch site."

"That should be easy to get through with the chain-saws."

"Right."

The men stood in silence, both thinking about the work that lay ahead. The assistant finally said, "This place looks much tougher than I expected."

"Once she gets under the ice, she'll be fine."

"I don't know, Bill, it just seems extreme to me."

Winters turned to face his companion. "Don't worry about it. *Deep Explorer* can do it." He grinned. "Believe me, this project is going to put us on the map."

"Are you really going to do that interview with that TV reporter?"

The previous evening, Winters had treated the NSD team to pizza and beer. They sat next to a table with a network television crew.

"Sure, it'll be great publicity for the company."

"But I thought we were supposed to keep a low profile."

"This oil spill is going to be the company's ticket to the big times."

"Okay, but I'd be careful. You can't predict what those people will do."

"It'll be okay."

* * *

The helicopter patrolled the shoreline, although it was difficult to determine just where the land and the ice met. The smoothness of the snow covering both the ground and adjacent frozen Chukchi Sea obscured the interface. The pilot and his observer worked for the U.S. Fish and Wildlife Service. Their task was to monitor polar bear activity between Point Hope and Barrow. It was winter and the prime hunting season for the apex predators. But *Ursus maritimus* was in peril. Thinning ice sheets and extended ice-free summers had sharply reduced populations, forcing the Service to list polar bears as threatened under the Endangered Species Act.

The MD-500 was twenty miles south of Barrow, heading southward. So far there had been no sightings, but that was about to change.

"Wow, look at that," the pilot said.

"What?" asked the biologist. In her early twenties, she was a recent graduate from the University of Washington.

"Two o'clock, fifteen hundred yards."

She spotted the distant target: a black splotch on a field of white. "What is that?"

"I don't know. Let's take a closer look."

The helicopter landed on the ice about a hundred feet from the sighting. The passenger exited and worked her way under the still whirling rotors. She carried the 12-gauge but it wasn't needed.

The boar was huge—easily twelve hundred pounds. He'd had his fill of seals but was frozen solid.

The biologist knelt next to the carcass and ran her gloved hand over the fur. It had once been snow white but was now coal black. She raised the glove to her nose. Despite the harsh conditions, the stench of crude oil remained potent. "Oh dear God," she mumbled.

Soon the chopper was airborne. The biologist-observer couldn't wait. She was on her portable VHF radio, speaking with her supervisor in Barrow over a public channel.

"It's just awful, Mike."

"Are you sure it's oil?"

"Absolutely, he was drenched in the stuff. I took samples as well as a ton of photos."

"Injuries?"

"Nothing obvious, and he certainly wasn't starving."

"He probably ingested the stuff. We'll know more after the necropsy."

"Can you get a team out here soon?"

"Tomorrow, weather permitting."

"Good," said the biologist. "Mike, there must be more of them out there like him."

"I'm afraid so."

"Holy shit! Tell me you got that!"

"I got it, boss."

The network TV crew was in a hotel room in Barrow. The producer, her soundman, and cameraman were running equipment checks. The correspondent was in the bathroom working on her makeup. Out of habit from a twenty-plus-year career at an NYC affiliate, the producer brought along her police scanner. The receiver had just picked up the public radio conversation between the wildlife biologist and her supervisor.

"They must have been talking about a polar bear," the soundman said as he cued up the recording.

"I'm certain of it. Somehow that bear managed to get into the stuff."

"What do you want to do?"

"I need to call New York. Upload that recording ASAP."

"Will do."

The producer turned to the cameraman. "Get ahold of that chopper pilot you were talking with. I want to be airborne in half an hour."

"I'm on it."

CHAPTER 7

Yuri Kirov walked into the restaurant. A comely brunette in her mid-twenties standing by the reservation desk greeted him. "Good evening, sir. May I help you?"

"I'm John Kirkwood," Yuri said, using his alias. "I'm looking for Chuck Matheson."

"Oh yes. He's expecting you. Right this way."

Yuri followed the hostess through the four-star Anchorage restaurant. About half the tables were occupied, mostly couples with a few singles. Directed to a table in a far corner of the dining room, Yuri approached the two men occupying it.

"John, so nice to finally meet you," said Charles "Chuck" Matheson as he stood with an extended right hand. The CEO of Aurora Offshore Systems was in his early fifties, a fit and trim six-footer with all of his hair. His tailored wool suit, silk shirt, and Armani tie clearly identified his station.

Yuri shook his client's hand.

"Good flight?"

"Great, the weather was clear nearly the entire way up. The Chugach Range was spectacular."

"That it is. All checked in?"

"Yeah. At the Captain Cook. Very nice."

"Indeed." Matheson turned to his side and introduced his other guest. "John, this is Jim Bauer."

"It's a pleasure to meet you in person, Jim," Yuri said as he gripped the offered hand of AOS's Alaska operations manager.

"Likewise."

Bauer was about forty-five and a tad heavy for his five-foot-nine frame. He wore a blue blazer with an open collar shirt.

Yuri also hadn't bothered with a tie. He slipped out of his parka, laying it on an adjacent chair.

Yuri ordered a glass of Riesling. Matheson was on his second. Bauer preferred bourbon.

"I understand your crew is on-site in Barrow," Matheson said.

"Yes. They arrived yesterday. I spoke with the project manager just after landing. They plan to launch tomorrow, weather permitting."

"Excellent. I assume you have all of the location information."

"Right. Jim provided coordinates for the entire field. They have been preprogrammed into *Deep Explorer*'s CPU."

"How long will it take for the survey?"

"About forty-eight hours."

"What about seeps?"

"Once the wellheads have been checked, *Deep Explorer* will start the tract survey looking for seeps. Because of the size of the lease, that's what will take the most time."

"That oil has to be coming from a seep," said Bauer. He referred to an opening in the earth where natural hydrocarbons escape.

"It's vital that we find the source of the oil to prove it is not coming from our operations," added Matheson. "We're just getting killed in the press over this thing."

"Right," said Bauer. "Guilty until proven innocent."

They were halfway through the meal, all enjoying the Alaska king crab special. The restaurant had filled up. A young couple was seated nearby. The stunning blonde in a short, tight red skirt caught all of their eyes when she walked by.

The table conversation morphed from the offshore oil business to the new superyacht Matheson had commissioned. It was under construction in Seattle. The 180-footer was about a year away from launch.

"You must be planning to take a long cruise once it's completed," Yuri said.

"Eventually, but until I retire I plan to keep it close by—in the Gulf or Caribbean so I can get to it without a lot of flying. It'll have a complete office with all the latest communication toys so I can continue to run the company from just about anywhere."

"Sounds great."

"I'm really looking forward to it. Delta Marine is doing a fabulous job."

Yuri was about to ask another question when the blonde in the crimson dress at the next table stood up and approached their table. She was five-foot-eight, slim, with all the right curves. She held a black leather purse in her hands.

She smiled and said, "Mr. Matheson?"

"Yes," Chuck replied.

"I have something for you." She opened her purse and in a flash withdrew a soup can–size container and hurled its liquid contents at Matheson.

The charge of used motor oil splattered the front of his suit. Black stinky goo streamed down his jacket, shirt, and tie. Splatter peppered his face.

Yuri steered clear of the spill zone but Jim Bauer caught blowback.

Speechless, Chuck stood up.

"This is just a sample of what you are doing to our environment, you miserable polar bear killer!" said the blonde, turning away.

Yuri noticed her companion standing at the table. He held a smartphone in his right hand; it was aimed at Matheson.

"*Govnó!*"—Shit.

Laura Newman was home. She'd showered, slipped on her pajamas, and climbed into the bed. With Yuri not at her side, the huge bed swallowed her slim form. Maddy slept in a second crib she kept in the master.

Laura spent most of the evening in her home office, editing a report that was due in a couple of days. Although exhausted, she was not yet ready for sleep. After placing a pair of headphones over her ears, she keyed a remote, turning on the wide-screen television mounted to the wall at the opposite end of the bed. She clicked through a couple of channels, settling on the late evening news from a local Seattle station. The male newsreader's voice broadcast through the mini–ear speakers:

"Breaking News from Alaska. We now bring you a live report from our affiliate in Anchorage."

The screen changed to an attractive female reporter dressed in a heavy parka with her station's logo stenciled on it. She stood on a downtown Anchorage street next to the entry of a building. She made her report:

"About an hour ago, the CEO of Aurora Offshore, Mr. Charles Matheson, was ambushed by an eco activist while at dinner in this restaurant. The attacker tossed what appeared to be oil onto Mr. Matheson as he sat at a table, apparently in response to the oil spill offshore of Barrow. The incident was captured by cell phone video and then went viral on YouTube. Here is a clip of the assault."

Laura watched in horror as the rerun of the sneak attack played out in vivid color and full sound. Matheson was clearly the center of attention, but Yuri was also videoed.

Stunned, Laura sat up and reached for the bedside phone. She dialed Yuri's cell. It went to voice mail.

"Oh dear Lord," she whispered. "What do we do now?"

CHAPTER 8

DAY 4—THURSDAY

The view of Hong Kong's harbor was beyond spectacular, but Elena Krestyanova remained the center of attention. A dozen people were seated around the teak conference table on the pinnacle floor of the thirty-story office building. They spoke in English, a common second tongue for all in attendance.

She had arrived twenty-five minutes earlier with the other four members of the Russian trade delegation. The greeting rituals were over and her team had just concluded their PowerPoint presentation. It was now Q&A, always a challenge with the Chinese.

As the lead delegate, Elena was the designated chief responder.

"Ms. Krestyanova, regarding salmon output, what can we expect on an annual basis?" Elena's counterpart from Beijing sat across the table. Like Elena, she was in her early thirties—and equally beautiful.

Elena met Yu Lin's ebony eyes and said, "We can guarantee you forty thousand metric tons."

"And the species distribution?"

Elena expected the question. "Fifty percent Kamchatka sockeye, thirty percent coho, and the balance Chinook."

Ms. Yu kept her poker face, but several of her assistants, all males, nodded approvingly at Elena's response.

The next series of questions centered on price and quality issues. Then the discussion proceeded to timber exports—and eventually oil and gas, which everyone had been anticipating.

"I'm sorry, but our Sakhalin Island facilities are already fully committed," Elena said.

"To the Japanese?" asked Yu.

"Yes, we have long-standing supply contracts."

"There is no surplus?"

"Not at this time. But we are developing additional resources on the Island and will be starting production in the Kuril Island chain soon."

"What about the Arctic?"

"Eastern Siberia?"

"Yes."

"We are just getting under way there and hope to conduct new exploration operations in the near future."

"We would like the opportunity to joint venture with your oil and gas enterprises. We have much to offer."

Elena understood Yu's probe. China Inc.'s Achilles' heel was energy—it continued to thirst for hydrocarbons. Oil and gas imports had fueled its meteoric growth. If China didn't continue to grow, Yu's superiors in Beijing—the Politburo Standing Committee of the Communist Party—could lose their grip on the country. No army or police force could hope to contain half a billion pissed-off peasants.

Oil and gas was also Russia's bane. Blessed with

hydrocarbon resources that were abundant but for decades mismanaged and pilfered, Russia had become so dependent on the export market that over half of its national income came from the sale of oil and natural gas. The recent crash in the price of crude had revealed Russia's vulnerability to the entire world.

"We of course welcome your interest in our petroleum operations," Elena offered. "I will convey your interest to both Gazprom and Rosneft."

"Yes, please do that."

The discussion concluded with coal and rare earth exports. Servants then brought in bowls and trays of traditional Chinese fare. All used chopsticks; Elena had insisted that her staff become proficient with the implement prior to the trip.

Elena was on her second cup of tea when a young woman entered the conference room and whispered to Yu Lin, handing her a thumb drive.

Ms. Yu then turned to face Elena. "It appears that there has been an interesting development regarding the oil spill in the Arctic."

"The one in Alaska?"

"Yes." Yu turned to an assistant with a laptop. She handed over the drive and issued instructions in Mandarin. He attacked the keyboard. Half a minute later the huge wall-mounted plasma screen on a nearby wall blinked on.

"I think we'll all find this video interesting," said Yu. "It's from a U.S. television broadcast, just recorded."

Elena watched, more than curious, as the narrator introduced the story. The female reporter was aboard a helicopter, flying along the Alaska coastline in twilight conditions. The camera focused on the frozen sea; the sheer whiteness stretched to the North Pole. But as the aircraft descended, the focus of attention crystallized. An enormous black animal lay on the ice, obviously injured; its head rotated toward the chattering helo. The narrator explained that another polar bear was near death after encountering the black-stained waters.

The reporter ended the story with a recap of the YouTube clip of the eco attack in the Anchorage restaurant.

All those gathered around the table laughed when Aurora Offshore's CEO took the direct hit. The United States was a common adversary to both Russia and China. Whenever it got what it deserved there was cause for celebration.

Yu ordered champagne.

After the glasses were filled and the toasts made, Elena graciously thanked her hosts and invited Yu and her entourage to visit Vladivostok.

While Elena's staff chatted with the Chinese, she remained mute, still not quite sure what she had seen in the video.

It can't be him, she thought.

CHAPTER 9

"Hey, boss."

"Hi, Bill," Yuri said as he approached Bill Winters. They were inside a warehouse in Barrow. Winters stood next to *Deep Explorer*, which rested on its cradle.

"I heard Aurora flew you up in that fancy bird of theirs."

Yuri smiled. "It was a nice ride all right." Yuri and two other AOS employees had made the six-hundred-mile trip from Anchorage aboard a Hawker 850XP jet. They had touched down twenty-five minutes earlier.

Yuri scanned the rest of the warehouse. "Where's the crew?"

"Breakfast. I told 'em to load up. No telling how long we'll be out on the ice today."

"Good idea. The *Explorer* ready to go?"

"Yep, everything checks out five by five. I'm giving the batteries a final charge. As soon as we get some light, we'll shove off."

It was still black outside. Sunrise was in two and a half hours—a few minutes after ten o'clock.

"I saw the caravan of snow machines out front. You got room for me?"

"Sure do, but you'll need to suit up. Forecast is minus thirty with a twenty-knot northerly. It's going to be a real bitch out there today."

"Okay. My gear is in the truck."

Yuri had started for the door when Winters said, "We heard about what happened last night."

Yuri turned. "You see the video?"

"Yep. Looked like an obvious setup to me." Winters rubbed an ear. "You manage to stay out of the line of fire?"

"Yeah, I lucked out, not even a drop."

"How'd Matheson take it?"

"Remarkably well, more embarrassed than anything else. But you can be certain that he'll have security around him now. They could just have easily thrown acid or had a gun."

"What happened to those fruitcakes?"

"They got away. Everyone in the restaurant was just as bewildered as we were. They flew out the front door. A car was waiting for 'em."

"Is Matheson coming up to observe?"

"No, he's headed back to Houston—he's a very busy fellow." Yuri yawned. "It'll just be us up here on our own."

"Fine by me. Besides, I can just about guarantee he would not enjoy the trip today."

Yuri didn't take the bait. "You're probably right. Anyway, I'm going to get my gear."

"Great."

As Yuri tracked across the concrete floor, he couldn't help but think that Bill was trying to discourage him from tagging along on today's trip. He and Winters co-existed, but Yuri still detected resentment. Laura had acquired controlling interest in NSD and Yuri represented her ownership, which meant he was in charge. Winters, as one of the founders, still considered NSD his creation.

The bay was sloppy this morning, three-foot swells rolling in from under the Golden Gate. The boat swayed in response, upsetting more than a few bellies. But Nicolai Orlov was used to it, just part of the commute.

Under way for about ten minutes, the passenger ferry from Sausalito would dock at the Ferry Building in another fifteen. He would hustle up to California and Drumm and catch the cross-town cable car to Van Ness. He would then hoof it the rest of the way to his office. On average, his commute from the floating home he rented in Sausalito to the consulate general of Russia in downtown San Francisco took over an hour.

Orlov loved San Francisco. It was hands down the best duty station of his seventeen-year career in the SVR—*Sluzhba Vneshney Razvedki*. As the successor to the former first chief directorate of the KGB, the SVR served as Russia's CIA.

Orlov had a full day ahead. A general staff meeting was set for ten o'clock; the SVR *rezident* would be expecting progress reports from the various case officers on their recruitment efforts. As assistant *rezident* and head of Special Projects, Orlov would only need to listen. He'd already submitted his report in writing; it was for the *rezident*'s eyes only and for a select few back in Moscow.

Over the noon hour, Orlov and a colleague planned to lunch at the Oakland Rotary Club. The consulate general was the featured speaker. The title of his talk, "Improving Trade between Russia and the USA." He and his associate would mingle with the club's business and community leaders, spreading goodwill as best they could. But they also would provide security for the consulate general. Relations between the United States and the Russian Federation remained sour due in part to the nasty business in Ukraine and elsewhere. Although there had been no direct threats to the consulate, public opinion in the United States was decidedly negative toward Russia's adventurism with its neighbors. The fear was not of the Rotarians; it was concern about others who might try to "crash" the luncheon. The Bay Area was loaded with potential troublemakers.

As the ferry charged ahead, Orlov took out his iPhone and called up the morning national news on SFGate— a digital version of the *San Francisco Chronicle*. In the middle of the headlined story, he clicked on the link to the referenced YouTube video. He watched the sneak attack on the CEO in Anchorage; it was just the type of event he worried about for the consulate general.

Near the end of video, he muttered, "*Kakógo chërta!*"—What the hell.

Orlov replayed the video. He increased the magnification and moved the screen closer to his eyes.

"*Tvoyú mat'!*"—Son of a bitch. "It's Yuri!"

CHAPTER 10

It was a bone-chilling minus thirty-eight degrees Fahrenheit, but the wind remained tolerable, just a ten-knot breeze from the north. There was enough light to work but it was waning; the sun would drop below the horizon in another hour.

Yuri stood next to the pit. Carved out of ice, the four-foot-deep by eight-foot-wide and twenty-five-foot-long hole had been a Herculean effort. Chainsaws had efficiently ripped through the ice, but removing the twenty-three-ton block of frozen seawater was the problem. Bill Winters's crew sliced the slab into sections, wrapped each unit with a nylon lifting strap, and yanked it out of the water with a snowmobile.

Deep Explorer remained on its sled at the edge of the launching pit. Intense yellow, twenty feet long, and three feet in diameter with a bullet-shaped nose cone, stubby tailfins, and a ducted propeller, the autonomous underwater vehicle looked like an apparatus of war. Stenciled in black paint on both sides of the fuselage, RESEARCH identified its true purpose.

One of the techs ran a final check. Despite the brutal cold, all systems were go.

"Okay, gents, it's showtime," Bill announced.

"Lower the cradle?" asked a technician.

"Yep, crank her down."

The man used both gloved hands to rotate a handle that lowered the forward end of the cradle. About a minute later, *Deep Explorer*'s bow was aligned with the end of the pit. A cable on the opposite end of the cradle restrained the AUV, preventing it from sliding.

Winters turned toward two others who knelt on the ice at the forward end of the cradle. "Go ahead and connect the ramp."

"Will do," answered one of the men. The techs connected a rounded aluminum sheet about four feet wide and ten feet long to the end of the cradle and lowered it into the ice fissure.

Bill walked over to Yuri, who stood next to *Deep Explorer*'s propulsor, a ducted fiberglass propeller. "We're ready to launch. You okay with that?"

"Absolutely."

"All right." Winters turned to face his chief tech. "Let's get her wet."

"Yes, sir."

Within half a minute, the autonomous underwater vehicle was free-floating in the ice pit; already the exposed seawater had begun to freeze, forming a pencil-thick sheet that shattered when *Deep Explorer* slid gracefully into the hole.

Bill and Yuri stood at the trench edge opposite *Deep Explorer*'s midsection. Winters held an insulated freeze-protected laptop; both men studied the display. The wireless transmitter antenna projecting six inches above the hull communicated with the Apple.

"Everything's in the green," Winters announced.

"Excellent. Let's proceed."

The fore and aft ballast tanks soon flooded, submerging the AUV. When the *Deep Explorer* sank below the ice keel, the propulsor engaged and it sprinted forward. The yellow hull of the submersible swam out of view after traversing the ice pit.

"She's on her way," Bill said.

"Let's check the hydrophone," Yuri said.

"Okay."

Bill and Yuri walked to the opposite side of the launching pit, stopping next to a stainless box about the size of a cooler. Bill squatted to open the lid. He removed a softball-sized device with its connecting black cable. He lowered the hydrophone into the ice pit and let it submerge about five feet below the underside of the ice. Bill next extracted a pair of Bose headphones from the container and handed them to Yuri.

"Can you hear it?" Bill asked.

The soft swishing tone of *Deep Explorer*'s propeller broadcast into Yuri's ears from the noise-canceling mini-speakers. "Sounds normal." Yuri removed the headphones and handed them to Winters.

Bill listened for about half a minute before smiling. "She's running perfect."

"When's the first check-in?"

Bill rolled the sleeve back on the left arm of his parka, exposing the wristwatch. "We should get our first ping in about five minutes."

"And after that?"

"Every hour."

"Okay. Assuming she makes her first check-in, we should start getting ready to head back to shore. I don't like the look of what's coming in from the north."

Winters turned around and eyeballed the mass of black vapor surging from the pole zone. "We'll be back on shore before that shit hits."

Deep Explorer's initial sonar ping arrived on schedule, which was a relief to both Yuri and Bill. The next underwater check-in, and those following, would be transmitted to NSD's shore station via a short-range radio connected to the hydrophone. Mounted on a cable-stayed aluminum antenna pole that jutted twelve feet above the ice surface, the radio signal represented NSD's sole means of tracking the AUV. Because the entire surface under which *Deep Explorer* would be operating was encased by ice sheets anywhere from four to eight feet thick, and up to sixty feet plus at ice ridges, underwater sound was the only viable communication method. But that link would be tenuous at best. The Chukchi Sea and the connecting Arctic Ocean resonated with sound energy, ranging from grounding ice keels and colliding planes of pack ice to tectonic plate movements and erupting subsea volcanoes. The natural racket could dampen the minuscule sound pulse broadcast from the AUV.

Even more worrisome were topside conditions. A curious polar bear just might decide to wage war on the radio tower.

Laura Newman was in Cognition's main conference room this afternoon. With over two thousand employees and six offices, the software company that specialized in generating insight from Big Data generated big profits.

One of Laura's project managers wrapped up his presentation, allowing Laura to call for a ten-minute break. While sitting at the head of the table, she took the opportunity to check messages on her cell phone. Since the meeting had started, a dozen e-mails and four text messages had accumulated. Hoping to hear from Yuri, she raced through the e-mails, his preferred method of digital communication. Nothing. She checked the texts. The third message astounded her; it was from a 415 area code with a one-word message: NEVA.

Oh dear Lord, Laura thought.

After the conference, Laura walked along the sidewalk in front of the downtown Bellevue midrise that served as Cognition's headquarters. She informed her secretary that she needed to run an errand and would return in an hour.

She hurried to the library. Once there, she took a seat in front of a public computer and logged onto a Gmail account. She checked the draft folder. Her pulse quickened as she opened the message. It was from Nick: YURI MAY BE COMPROMISED. RECOMMEND PLAN B.

After stopping at the day care center to pick up Maddy, Laura returned to her office. She closed the door and instructed her secretary to hold all calls, except from Yuri.

Laura sat at her desk, cradling her daughter in her arms. Maddy was awake, her chubby cheeks dimpling as she smiled and her navy blue eyes following her mother's every movement. Laura smiled back, but her mind was elsewhere. She remained shaken to her core.

While she sat at the library computer, dread had overwhelmed Laura's well-being with the suddenness of a mountain avalanche, burying her alive with the awful memory of Ken, struck dead by a single blow to the temple, blood everywhere.

Months had passed since her last attack. She had barely made it to the library bathroom when she vomited. The therapist warned her that flashbacks could erupt at any time, triggered by myriad precursors.

For the past year, she and Yuri kept in touch with Nicolai Orlov, but carefully. They used the Gmail account to pass messages, always from public computers. When they needed more interaction, they met face-to-face.

Nick's warning confirmed Laura's suspicions.

Yuri's real identity might have been exposed.

CHAPTER 11

Yuri and Bill had a table to themselves in the corner of the surf-and-turf establishment. The rest of Northwest Subsea Dynamics' crew opted for the teriyaki place. They all made it off the ice as the leading edge of the storm roared into Barrow. Howling winds chilled to minus forty-five now buffeted the town of forty-five hundred.

Yuri was especially grateful to be indoors. The arctic chill pierced his ice armor, and the last few minutes of his ride on the snowmobile were brutal. He'd been chilled to his core once before during a deepwater dive mission. The hours of in-water decompression during that ascent triggered hypothermia; it nearly killed him.

Yuri was halfway through the tasty halibut. Bill Winters had inhaled the porterhouse and was now working on the remnants. Yuri checked his wristwatch and looking toward Bill said, "She should be checking in in about ten minutes."

Bill polished off the last morsel of steak. He pulled

out a cell phone from his coat pocket and placed it on the table. "I'll get a text when she checks in."

"I just hope we get a signal."

"Don't worry, she's in fine form. You'll see."

But Yuri was worried. The company's future was currently miles offshore, deep under the ice, prowling in utter darkness—all on its own. From Yuri's experience of working underwater, he envisioned countless glitches, every one a potential mission killer.

"If we end up needing the backup, how long will it take to get it ready to ship?" asked Yuri.

"*Deep Adventurer* is in excellent shape. No more than a day to run diagnostics and charge the batteries."

"Good. I have a feeling we're going to need it."

Bill frowned. "I know you're looking out for Laura's interests. Of all people, I'm the most grateful that she rescued the company. But you don't yet have the hands-on experience I have with this technology. It really does work. Just wait a few minutes." He tapped the cell phone with his right index finger.

"Okay." Yuri stood. "I need to use the head first."

"I'm going to have another beer, you want one?"

"Sure."

As Yuri stepped away, Bill picked up his cell and checked the text tab. Nothing. But it was still early. He peered through a nearby window, which faced the frozen sea. Other than a distant streetlight, it was ink-black outside. The occasional gust rattled the window-pane. It's shitty out there all right, Bill thought. *But she should be just fine, doing her thing.*

Bill Winters was a brilliant electrical engineer, and his coding skills were equally exceptional. *Deep Ex-*

plorer's brain was cutting edge; no other commercial autonomous underwater vehicle could match her performance. Maybe one or two military AUVs could come close.

He believed in his creation. *Deep Explorer*'s current mission was straightforward: swim to the coordinates using the onboard inertial navigation system, run side-scan survey tracts, and take videos of the infrastructure. It had already conducted dozens of similar surveys.

Piece of cake!

But something else about *Deep Explorer*'s mission gave him angst—not that it wouldn't work. No, he was confident of success. It was something that he had not told Yuri.

He would never have approved it. I had no choice but to keep quiet.

After completing the contractual obligations, Bill had programmed *Deep Explorer* to conduct another task, one that might take it farther offshore into the real unknown.

Yuri walked back to the table and sat down. Bill sipped a fresh Redhook and Yuri started on his own. Bill's cell phone chimed. He reached down and picked it up. He smiled and then turned the screen toward Yuri. "We got another sonar pulse. She's just fine."

Yuri raised his bottle, tipping it toward Winters. "Nice going, Bill. I'm going to sleep well tonight."

"Me too."

CHAPTER 12

DAY 5—FRIDAY

The leggy blonde with the luscious curves mingled with the legions of shoppers that crowded the five-level shopping center. The largest mall in Hong Kong, Harbour City offered over seven hundred shops, fifty-plus food and drinking establishments, several movie theaters, and a couple of supermarkets. Complementing the retail outlets were three hotels and a world-class cruise ship terminal.

Elena Krestyanova took her time, visiting Gucci, Chanel, Joyce, and Lane Crawford, where she purchased a pair of Stella McCartney sunglasses for $300 U.S. She didn't need the shades, but she had to buy something to justify the visit. It was late afternoon. The rest of the trade delegation was happily parked in a bar at their hotel, slugging back vodka shots. She would join her team later for dinner.

Elena surveyed her surroundings. So far, she had not detected a tail. But with so much activity around, she could be under surveillance and not know it.

Hong Kong was China's bright and shining face for

the world's eyes. The unapologetic capitalistic fever for wealth continued, but the rulers in Beijing had cunningly changed the rules. Big Brother now had its fingers deep into the pie, just taking tidbits at first, but every year a little more. The Internet was filtered and monitored, not as oppressive as in the mainland but certainly a notch down from what it been. And operatives from China's Ministry of State Security were everywhere. Hong Kong remained China's principal incubator for dissent, and the Beijing elite was determined to squash all troublemakers.

The MSS did not concern Elena. It was her own security forces that she feared, the SVR and worse yet, the bastards from the FSB—*Federal'naya Sluzhba Bezopasnosti*. The FSB served as Russia's FBI and then some.

Elena Krestyanova was not an official trade delegate but she played the role convincingly, having auditioned for the part during a previous assignment in Vancouver. Her current role as trade envoy was cover only. Elena's real employer was the SVR. Moscow tasked her with wooing a wealthy Chinese businessman with the hope of turning him.

They had met before, first in Sydney during an East Asian business conference and then again in Tokyo. Both times, the sex was terrific; he was an accomplished lover, not like the last target she'd seduced— an overweight, balding CEO who focused solely on his own release.

Elena's heart beat faster now as she neared the teashop, tucked away in a far corner of the mega shopping empire. Her longing was legitimate, but it was the money that truly turned her on.

* * *

He was waiting for her, seated at a discreet table in the quaint teahouse with few patrons. He stood as Elena approached. Tall for his race, just shy of six feet, his superbly tailored silk suit highlighted his athletic build.

Kwan Chi extended his right hand and Elena accepted; his touch electrified her.

"You look fabulous," he said with a smile that revealed his perfect teeth. His long, luminously thick black hair and tan skin tone completed the pleasing face.

"Thank you, Chi." They spoke in English, again the dialect they had in common.

He stepped to the side of the table, pulled the chair back for Elena, and then gestured for her to sit, always the gentleman. Elena cherished the attention. Russian men were uncouth pigs when it came to chivalry.

The green tea was served, a special house blend with a hint of cinnamon.

"How long will you be here?" he asked, sipping the steaming brew.

"We're off to Singapore tomorrow."

"Too bad. I was hoping that we might be able to spend more time together."

Elena shared his disappointment. The schedule was too tight. She was due back at the hotel within an hour to accompany the delegation to a reception and dinner in their honor at Hong Kong's equivalent of the Chamber of Commerce. There just was not enough time, even for a quickie. Skipping the event was an impossibility—she was one of the honorees.

Kwan took another sip. "Your last contribution was most useful. Thank you again."

"You're welcome," she said, beaming. His word choice amused Elena. The current deployment of nuclear submarines at the Rybachiy Naval Base at Petropavlovsk-Kamchatskiy represented her latest "contribution."

She'd used her cell phone's camera to photograph the report; she found the classified document buried under several file folders and magazines stacked on a desk in the apartment of a naval officer stationed in Vladivostok. She'd met the submarine squadron commander at a party; both single, they hooked up on occasion. That early morning several months earlier, Georgii was nonresponsive when Elena had opted for round four. Unable to perform any longer and still half-blitzed, the captain first rank rolled over and resumed snoring.

Kwan wired five hundred thousand dollars U.S. to her anonymous account in the Cayman Islands. From there, Elena transferred the funds to another secret account she maintained in a Luxembourg bank. So far, the People's Republic of China, through the MSS, had paid Elena just over four million dollars U.S.

They exchanged small talk and then Kwan mentioned that he would be visiting Los Angeles soon and hoped they might meet again there.

"LA," Elena responded. "That does sound like fun. I might be able to swing that."

"Excellent. I will look forward to it."

Elena reached into her purse and removed a small gift-wrapped box; it had a ribbon on top.

"For your birthday," she said, sliding it across the table.

"May I?"

"Please."

He untied the ribbon, removed the wrapping paper, and opened the box. He withdrew the pair of gold, diamond-studded cuff links.

"Thank you, Elena, these are wonderful."

"I hope you like them."

"I do," he said, continuing to admire the craftsmanship.

She'd paid a thousand dollars for the man jewelry at a shop in her hotel, but it wasn't Kwan's birthday. It was just part of the game. The real gift was under the setting at the bottom of the box. The thumb drive held complete dossiers on two dozen SVR agents working in East Asia.

It was the final contribution for their initial agreement. The balance of one million would be waiting in her Caribbean account before she returned to Vladivostok.

They were standing, about to depart, when Elena said, "I may have something new for you soon."

"Really—can you give me a hint?"

"Something that you have wanted for a long time."

"Sounds interesting."

"I'll know more by the time we meet in Los Angeles."

"I can't wait."

"Neither can I."

Elena headed back to the hotel in a taxi. Her mind raced at mach speed. She couldn't help but think about the video she'd watched the previous day at the trade meeting.

Yuri Kirov, if he's really alive, that could be it!

Elena's goal was ten million. With the Kirov contribution, she'd be there and then some. Elena would then disappear. No one would ever find her.

CHAPTER 13

After methodically inspecting Aurora's four subsea wells, *Deep Explorer* had just completed the last transect of its survey of the ten-thousand-acre leased tract. While the side-scan sonar probed the seabed for surface anomalies, acoustic sensors listened for any venting, hissing, or surging that might reveal a bottom rupture. No fluid plumes were detected by sonar, and the sound sensors found nothing suspicious, just biologics and colliding ice sheets. During the grid search, aka mowing the lawn, the sniffer unit probed for waterborne hydrocarbons but likewise detected nothing. These arctic waters were as pure as it gets. But that was not the case earlier in the AUV's voyage.

As the vessel tracked westward along the descending seabed, *Deep Explorer*'s sniffer detected oil. It wasn't much, just slightly above background. It lost the scent two hours later but duly recorded the finding.

Deep Explorer's primary mission was complete, but it was not yet ready to return to Barrow. The underwater robot had a second task, coded by Bill Winters. If oil was not discovered inside Aurora's lease boundaries but was detected elsewhere, *Deep Explorer* was to proceed to the coordinates of the original spill sighting logged by the UA-Fairbanks current meter team where it would start a new search. Before executing the secondary mission, however, Winters had pre-instructed *Deep Explorer* to conduct a provisioning duty.

After probing the overhead ice cover for twenty minutes, the AUV's upward ranging sonar found a suitable opening in the five-foot-thick floe. The diameter of the breathing hole was about fifteen inches, just enough for a ringed seal to slither into and out of the water.

Deep Explorer hovered under the fissure and extended its telescopic mast upward from inside its hull until the snorkel projected a foot above the water surface. The mini–diesel generator inside the pressure casing ignited, powering the generator. Exhaust vented to the sea from a hull port.

While the batteries charged, *Deep Explorer* broadcast a "Here I Am" radio signal heavenward via a UHF radio antenna cabled to the snorkel. It also verified its earth coordinates with a GPS fix.

It took just over an hour to top off the batteries. After retracting the mast, *Deep Explorer* calculated the parameters for its second mission. It then turned to the southwest and accelerated to ten knots.

CHAPTER 14

DAY 6—SATURDAY

Elena Krestyanova sat on the bed, her back supported by a stack of pillows. It was late evening in Singapore. She keyed her laptop, working through websites. She accessed the Web through the hotel's Wi-Fi network, paying an excessive daily surcharge. But it was worth it.

She tried to research U.S. sites from Hong Kong. However, the crackdown by Beijing on dissident student bloggers, who during her visit had again lambasted the PRC's aggressive policy of cutting back on Hong Kong's autonomy, bogged down the Web and even blocked access to many outside news outlets. Frustrated, she'd given up.

Singapore also censored the Internet, but at least Elena could access American business sites without interruption.

Elena was hot on the trail, closing in fast.

The first lead came from an Anchorage newspaper article about the sneak attack on the chief executive officer of Aurora Offshore. A screenshot from the infamous YouTube video was featured; it showed Charles Matheson, splattered with oil, reacting in complete shock. His two table companions were visible and identified.

John Kirkwood, so that's what he's using, Elena had thought after reading the article. Still, she wasn't certain that it was really Yuri.

Next she researched Northwest Subsea Dynamics. The company's website was no help. John Kirkwood was listed as the general manager, with no background, photo, or experience record provided. The NSD person featured was someone named Bill Winters.

When Elena ran a Web search on John Kirkwood, none of the individuals with that name remotely fitted the profile she was expecting.

Suspicious, Elena kept mining. Following threads from Bill Winters, she found a six-month-old article in a Puget Sound business journal that featured Northwest Subsea Dynamics. The article noted that LLWN Investments LLC, another Washington State corporation, had acquired controlling interest in the company. The article noted that Bill Winters remained as chief engineer.

Further digging through the Washington Secretary of State website revealed that a Bellevue, Washington, law firm represented LLWN Investments. Expecting a brick wall of client confidentiality, Elena opted out from calling the registered agent.

Elena again tackled the Washington State website, this time accessing a statewide public data extract that she downloaded. And now, after acquiring and downloading database software, she'd just opened the corporation file. It didn't take long to find the real owner of LLWN. Laura Lynn Wilson Newman was listed as owning 100 percent of the limited liability company.

Elena was ecstatic.

No one knew what had happened to Yuri, least of all Elena. She'd endured almost two weeks of the submerged transpacific crossing, completely out of the loop. When she returned to Vancouver, Moscow had already closed the mission file.

The briefing report from the two FSB operators sent to find Yuri and his accomplice tracked the workboat to a dock in Seattle, but then the trail turned to ice. The vessel was vacant and the owner absent. The photographs in the file revealed that Laura was aboard the *Hercules* when it headed back to Seattle. But where did she go . . . and where was Kirov?

Why didn't he return to Russia? Elena wondered. *He's a hero.*

Yuri's actions had earned him untold praise from the Russian military. Although officially still listed as Away without Leave, he was not pursued. It was unthinkable that he would desert after attaining legendary heroic status. Instead, it was widely feared that Yuri had succumbed to his injuries and was buried somewhere in the Seattle area under an assumed alias.

He must be living with her—yes, that's got to be it!

Elena's mind raced with the possibilities.

This could be the key to everything.

CHAPTER 15

"I don't hear it," Yuri announced. He knelt next to the ice pit, headphones covering his ears. The hydrophone dangled ten feet below the underside of the ice sheet.

Bill Winters stood at his right side. "It's early. Give it a while longer."

Yuri stood and removed the headgear, handing it to Winters. "I thought we might hear something by now."

"There's a lot of background racket today."

"There sure is."

"Pack ice farther offshore is moving around. It's like a demolition derby out there."

Bill's idiom was unknown to Yuri, but he got the gist.

Yuri scanned the sky. The sun tracked low across the horizon. It was half past two o'clock. The storm had moved on. Tranquil air with crystal skies followed in its wake. Even the air temperature had improved—a mild minus ten.

Yuri and crew arrived at "Ice Station Laura" an

hour earlier. Bill had so designated the site in honor of NSD's savior. Yuri let it go, not certain if Bill's intention was legitimate or a subtle jab in Yuri's back. Although Yuri was the boss, he also slept with the company's real owner.

Deep Explorer was due to return in forty minutes. Yuri expected to hear the hum of its propeller as it retraced its path to the launch site. The homing beacon, cabled to another hydrophone suspended below the ice, broadcast a low-frequency signal. A receiver in *Deep Explorer*'s nose cone and linked to its CPU would seek the homing signal during the last leg of the voyage. The AUV's computer would also compare digital bottom soundings recorded during the outbound voyage to current sonar readings to help guide itself home.

Yuri had heard not a chirp from the robotic sub for nearly two days. As the range steadily increased, the every-hour "Here I Am" sonar pulses faded into the background noise after the first day. As far as the NSD team knew, their showpiece was gone for good. The risks were legion, from springing a leak and sinking to simply losing its way and running default search tracts until the juice ran out.

Despite loss of contact, Bill Winters continued to profess his faith in *Deep Explorer*.

But that trust would soon be tested.

An hour later, Yuri again listened with headphones. His frown said everything.

"Nothing?" Bill asked.

Yuri shook his head.

"Hmm."

Yuri walked away with his back to Winters, reached into a pocket of his parka, and removed a portable sat-phone. He keyed the dial pad.

"What are you doing?" Bill asked.

"Calling the office. I'm having them ship the back-up unit."

"But it's not ready."

"I know. We'll have to cobble it together here."

"It's too early for that. We should wait another day."

"Another day! It was supposed to pop up in this ice hole half an hour ago, and there's nothing to indicate it's anywhere nearby."

"I think she's busy elsewhere."

"What?"

Bill dreaded the next few minutes. "I programmed in a second mission, if certain criteria were met."

Yuri almost blurted a Russian expletive but caught himself. "What are you talking about?"

"If she didn't find the hydrocarbon source during the survey of Aurora's facilities but detected background levels of oil in the water, she was supposed to head out to the coordinates of the original U of A sighting."

"And do what?"

"Conduct a search for the source, limited to twelve hours max."

"Why didn't you tell me?"

"You wouldn't have approved it."

"That's right!"

Bill lowered his head. He eyed the ice for a long moment before looking back at Yuri. "She checked in yesterday via satellite."

"Checked in—how?"

"I programmed her to find an opening in the ice for the snorkel to top off the batteries. That's when she sent the confirming message."

Yuri shook his head, stunned at the news. "We never tested recharging under ice."

"I know, but it worked. The key was finding an opening—there are plenty of breathing holes for seals out there."

Yuri remained silent as he struggled to repress his fury.

Bill continued. "I actually think it's really good news that she didn't show up today. *Deep Explorer* has more than enough power for the extended search. Just think about what it will mean for us if we can find the source."

"You don't know where it is right now."

Bill checked his wristwatch. "My take is that she's completed the secondary search and is now making a beeline back to us—you know how well she executes her missions."

"What about the batteries—will it need to recharge?"

"No. With the one charge, she'll have plenty of reserves to get home."

Yuri sighed heavily, checkmated. "How long before we know?"

"She should be here about this time tomorrow at the latest, possibly earlier."

Yuri sighed. "Since we have good weather, I want to keep the homing beacon alive and the recovery hole ice free."

"Good idea. I'll take the first shift with Don and Mark. You and the other guys head back into town and get some rest."

Yuri uttered a reluctant "Okay."

He started to walk toward the parked snow machines when Bill called out, "Leave us the shotgun . . . in case we have a visitor again."

Yuri raised his hand in acknowledgment while eyeing the crumpled radio antenna. A roaming polar bear had objected to its presence.

CHAPTER 16

Yuri flew across the open reach of ice, gunning the snowmobile. Every fifty meters or so, a plastic rod topped with fluorescent orange flagging jutted above the ice. This section of the shorefast ice was stable, which allowed marking the pathway from Barrow to Ice Station Laura. Today the flagging hung limp in the chilled cloudless Arctic air. The low arc sun was about to dip below the horizon, extinguishing the waning daylight into utter darkness.

The collection of equipment and snow machines was just ahead. Yuri roared into the site, followed by two techs on their own Yamahas. It was their second shift. Eight hours earlier, when they'd departed in the dark for R & R in Barrow, *Deep Explorer* was a no-show.

They parked the machines, removed their helmets, and with Yuri in the lead walked toward the open ice pit. Bill Winters and his crew huddled along the far side of the opening. Bill had the headphones on. His face wrinkled as if straining to hear.

"Anything?" Yuri said.

Bill raised his hands, signaling quiet.

Yuri peered into the ice hole. A floodlight powered by a portable Honda generator illuminated the cavity. A thin crust of fresh ice covered the entire opening, binding the slushy remnants of previously broken ice into a solid sheet. Through the opaque lens, he detected movement—a blurred yellowish icon.

Bill stood up, his face beaming. "She's home!" he announced.

Deep Explorer's nose cone cracked through the half-inch-thick ice sheet, jutting a foot above the surface.

One of the techs grabbed an aluminum rod with a hooked end and slipped it over the nose cone's tow ring. "I've got it," he yelled. He pulled the AUV to the side of the hole, where another man reached down with a half-inch Dacron line and tied a bowline knot to the ring.

Yuri stood speechless beside the ice hole as the NSD crew hooted and hollered, high-fived each other, and then back-slapped Bill Winters.

Yuri was ready for Bill's expected "*I told you so*" retort.

Instead, Bill rushed to Yuri and hugged him.

"Thanks for having faith in us. We couldn't have done it without you."

CHAPTER 17

DAY 8—MONDAY

Yuri was in Anchorage at Aurora Offshore Systems' office. It was almost noon. He was in the media conference room with Alaska operations manager Jim Bauer. They both sat in front of the video wall. Four ultra-wide plasma screens covered the wall. The image of Chuck Matheson filled the upper right display. He was in the Houston office, sitting alone in a similar videoconference facility.

Yuri was near the end of his briefing. The screen next to the Houston feed displayed video playback from *Deep Explorer*'s voyage, edited to highlight key findings.

"And this is the last observation for Well Four. Like the other wells and the rest of the entire tract, there was no sign of leakage."

For the past twenty minutes, CEO Matheson had suppressed the elation of Yuri's initial summary. He wanted to view the videos and side-scan sonar data for each well of Aurora's Chukchi prospect before allowing himself to believe the nightmare was over.

"This is wonderful news. I just knew we had the right company for this challenge."

"Thanks," Yuri said.

Jim Bauer piped in, "Chuck, that leak must be coming from one of our competitors."

"Not our problem anymore." Matheson leaned back in his chair. "Jim, I want to get this information to the feds today. I'm going to call the director right now and let him—"

"You might want to wait a little on that," Yuri interrupted.

"What do you mean?" Matheson asked, his brow wrinkling. Jim Bauer flashed a questioning look Yuri's way.

"*Deep Explorer* had a default mission—at our expense. After completing the survey of the overall tract, it conducted a second survey starting from the original spill sighting made by the University of Alaska research team. Nothing was found there, however."

"I'm not surprised," Bauer said. "The oil could be coming from just about anywhere. The pack ice at that location moves a lot, plus there's a strong current moving northward from the Bering Strait."

"What about the wind?" asked Matheson. "That blows the ice around, too."

"Yes, but the Bering current often overrides wind stress."

Yuri reentered the conversation. "*Deep Explorer* did find a trail of oil." He keyed his laptop, cabled to the video wall. A new still image appeared on the monitor: black viscous fluid pooled under ice. "This photo was taken ten miles west of the original sighting coordinates." Yuri adjusted the view and continued, "*Deep*

Explorer kept following the trail; it was sporadic but consistently westward." He typed again. Another image appeared, this one in motion as the AUV's video camera recorded a stream of oil flowing under the ice.

"Where's this at?" asked Matheson.

"About sixteen miles west."

"I'll be damned," muttered Matheson.

"*Deep Explorer* followed the trail to the source and here's what it found."

A new video clip of a pipe stub projecting from the seabed filled the screen. A steady flow of brownish black fluid jetted from the jagged opening.

"It's a blowout—where the hell is that well?" demanded Matheson.

"It's in Russian territorial waters—about twenty-five nautical miles west of the border and a hundred and forty miles east of Wrangel Island. Water depth is a hundred and eighty feet." Yuri recited the earth coordinates.

"Son of a bitch," Bauer blurted.

"The Russians explored in that area last summer," Matheson said. "But I never heard anything about hitting pay."

Neither had Yuri nor Jim Bauer.

Matheson took half a minute to collect his thoughts before eyeing Yuri through the video screen. "This is incredible news," he said. "We're indebted to you and your team. Please express my sincere gratitude to your staff."

Yuri was about to respond when Matheson continued. "Jim, I'm calling the BSEE director as soon as we hang up. Upload everything you've got to our server and then call both regional directors of BSEE and

BOEM and let them know what's going on." Matheson hesitated. "And be prepared to be swamped by the press—this is going to hit like a tsunami. I'm alerting our PR department. We'll need to get a press release together as soon as Legal says it's okay. I want to get out in front of this thing and stay there."

"Will do, Chuck."

Matheson looked to Yuri. "Your company is really going to be in the spotlight, so get ready. And thanks again." He terminated the connection.

"My lord," Jim Bauer said, smiling at Yuri. "What a day."

"Indeed."

Yuri had already anticipated the coming events. Bill Winters would serve as NSD's one and only spokesperson while Yuri remained in the shadows. It was a role that Bill was well suited for and had earned.

Yuri sensed that NSD had just turned a crucial corner. That pleased him because it meant Laura had not squandered her resources on a lark to keep him occupied.

Still, Yuri sensed the threat. More than ever, he would keep his guard up. And at all costs, he was determined to keep his face out of the papers and off the TV.

CHAPTER 18

Kwan Chi knew about the story several hours before it hit the American networks and cable channels. An MSS mole strategically placed in the U.S. government a dozen years earlier had ascended steadily in the Department of the Interior, first with the Minerals and Management Service and then in a successor co-agency, the Bureau of Ocean Energy Management. Another asset in the Bureau of Safety and Environmental Enforcement, eagerly paid by the MSS for information to feed her ongoing gambling addiction, confirmed the report.

Kwan sat on a sofa in the living room of his fifty-third-floor Kowloon condominium. It was evening. The nightly spectacle of embellished city lights from the ten-thousand-square-foot penthouse apartment was a highly sought commodity. But his attention focused on the wide-screen television. Tuned to the BBC, the evening news was under way. The female announcer read the lead story:

"The United States government announced today that the source of the spilled oil discovered in the

Chukchi Sea near the Alaska town of Barrow is not from any of the drilling operations that are located in U.S. territory. Instead, the source of the crude oil that is believed to have contaminated large swaths of ice-covered waters offshore of Alaska's northwest coast-line has been traced to an oil well drilled in Russian waters. An American company, Northwest Subsea Dynamics, under contract with the Aurora Offshore Systems, discovered the leaking oil well. Our Alaska correspondent, Clive Johnson, spoke with Bill Winters, designer of the underwater autonomous vehicle that made the discovery."

The high-def television display changed to a split screen. Oil surging from the well blowout rolled on the left side while a video of Bill Winters played on the right. Winters was speaking:

"Our unit, Deep Explorer, *traced the source of the oil by following its chemical footprint. Special sensors in the vehicle sampled the seawater and when hydro-carbons were detected, it homed in on the scent like a bloodhound searching for . . ."*

Kwan muted the television and picked up his cell phone from the nearby coffee table. He hit a speed dial number. It was answered on the second ring.

"Did you watch it?" Kwan asked in his native Mandarin.

He listened to the expected response and said, "Should I proceed?"

Another short wait. "I'll leave immediately."

Kwan hung up and keyed another number, issuing new orders. His Gulfstream with a flight crew of three would be ready to depart in ninety minutes.

Kwan stood and walked to the bar. A glass of whiskey was in order.

An American whiskey, he thought. *Yes, how appropriate.*

Yuri was relieved to be home after taking an afternoon flight from Anchorage. After a shower and fresh change of clothes, he was in the kitchen enjoying a bottle of Redhook ale. Laura and Madelyn had returned from work ten minutes earlier. Madelyn was in a playpen in the adjacent dining room, just a few steps away and visible from the kitchen. She crawled on the mat, engaging with her favorite toy—a stuffed elephant twice her size named Oscar.

On the way home, Laura stopped at their favorite Thai restaurant for an order of takeout. The aroma of pad Thai, panang curry, and golden fried spring rolls permeated the air.

Yuri sat at a table in a kitchen alcove that overlooked the deck and the lake beyond. Lights from homes on the opposite shore of Lake Sammamish blinked on as residents arrived home.

Laura dished out the fare, passing a plate to Yuri and then sitting down herself.

"Smells wonderful," he said.

"I know, and I'm famished."

"No lunch today?"

"Wall-to-wall meetings. I'm exhausted."

Yuri's eyebrows arched. "You need to take better care of yourself."

She smiled back. "I know. I plan to run in the morning."

"No, I mean you should eat lunch."

"I'm okay, Yuri, don't worry about me."

But he would. He couldn't help it. She was everything to him.

Laura took in a forkful of pad Thai and Yuri followed. She briefed him on her day.

Now it was his turn. They'd talked the night before on the phone, so she knew the highlights.

"Did the Coast Guard authorize the work?" she asked.

"Yep, we're good to go. Time and expenses for now."

"That's wonderful." Laura remembered a potential glitch. "Aurora must have been okay with it."

"No problem. In fact, Chuck Matheson told the Coast Guard admiral in charge of Alaska that he'd be a fool not to hire NSD."

"When do you start?"

"Wednesday. Bill and the crew are going to spend tomorrow checking over *Deep Explorer.*"

Laura was proud that Yuri and NSD had landed a lucrative contract with the federal government. *Deep Explorer* would soon start mapping the oil spill. The contamination continued to spread, yet the winter cover of ice hid the horrible reality of what would be in store for the Arctic when the spring breakup occurred.

"Do they really think they can corral that oil while it's under the ice?"

"No one knows yet. But that well has to be plugged first."

"I heard on the news that might take a while."

"Months," he said as he scooped up a heaping spoonful of the panang curry.

Russia had given no indication of how it planned to rein in the runaway well. It was almost impossible to do anything with the ice cover over the site. It might take six months before a drilling rig could sail into the area to drill a relief well. By then untold millions of barrels of oil would have flowed into the Chukchi Sea. The resulting consequences to the pristine Arctic environment in Russia, Alaska, and Canada could be catastrophic. It would dwarf BP's *Deepwater Horizon* blowout and spill.

Laura and Yuri finished their meal. She sipped a chilled glass of orange juice; he nursed a second Redhook.

Laura briefed Yuri on a new project she was about to launch. As usual, he enthusiastically supported her work, praising her technical skills and people skills, which Laura appreciated.

But now Laura had to broach something that had been gnawing on her for several days. While Yuri took another draw on the beer bottle she said, "I heard from Nick this week."

Yuri placed the bottle on the tabletop, startled. "What about?"

"He saw the YouTube video. He's worried that others will see it, too."

Yuri's eyes narrowed. He wanted to blurt out a couple of choice Russian curses but refrained, knowing Laura would dislike hearing them. She'd learned enough Russian to know.

"I was worried that might happen," he said.

"What should we do, honey?"

"I don't know."

"Do you think they'd come after you—us?"

"Technically, I'm still in the Navy."

"Do they really care, after all of this time?"

"They care—I know too many secrets for them not to care."

"This is not a good situation for us."

"No, it is not."

CHAPTER 19

The remotely operated vehicle swam just above the seafloor in the western Chukchi Sea. It approached the objective with caution, its floodlight illuminating the jagged pipe end that continued to spew crude oil and methane. The buoyant plume ascended out of the light cone.

One hundred eighty feet above the bottom, the ROV's pilot sat at a control station inside a tent staked out on the ice. It was bitterly cold this afternoon, approaching minus forty degrees Fahrenheit with a twenty-knot wind from the north. The helicopter that transported the team from the Russian naval base on Wrangel Island sat two hundred feet away, its engines idling to prevent freezing. The din of the whirling rotors masked the whine of the gas-powered generator parked on the ice near the tent.

A pencil-diameter tether transmitting power and communications connected the pilot to the ROV. He worked the joystick, maneuvering the robot to within twenty feet of the ruptured wellhead.

The pilot turned away from the video monitor, facing his assistant seated on a wood crate to his right. "Is the camera recording?"

"Yes, everything is up and running."

"Good."

The ROV operators were Russian government biological oceanographers. They were conducting under-ice research in Chaun Bay near Pevek when they were pressed into new service the previous evening.

The ROV pilot turned to address the observer who stood behind his assistant. "What would you like us to do now?"

The captain-lieutenant replied, "I'd like you to run a perimeter survey first. Say, fifty meters. I'm interested in debris."

"Three-hundred-sixty-degree orbit?"

"Yes, that will be a good start."

"Okay."

The ROV was about a third of the way through the search when the assistant spotted something. "What's that?" he asked, pointing to the display with his right hand.

The pilot eased the submersible into a hover about twenty feet above the bottom, high enough to minimize wake effects from the thrusters on the silt-coated bottom. He peered at the screen. "I don't see anything."

"There was something there. Try reversing."

"Okay."

A new image materialized in the monitor. A thin line running along the bottom was visible in the illuminated zone, extending to the limit of the light cone.

"What is it?" asked the pilot.

"Looks like a wire to me."

The naval officer scooted forward between the two scientists. He studied the video image. "Can you increase magnification?"

"Yes," the pilot said.

It took a moment for the resolution to improve, and then the officer muttered, "What the hell?"

"Do you know what it is?" asked the pilot.

The captain-lieutenant ignored the question. Instead, he said, "Can you get a sample of it?"

"The wire?"

"Yes."

"We should be able to use the manipulator arm to grab it."

"Good . . . please proceed."

An hour later, the ROV completed its work, retrieving multiple samples of the wire and other debris. It ascended, following the tether back to the oil-filled eight-foot-square hole carved in the ice.

Drenched in crude, the underwater vehicle with its cargo was loaded aboard the helicopter. The evidence would be delivered to the Kremlin within twenty-four hours.

Yuri didn't bother with using a public computer like Laura. Instead, he accessed the anonymous Gmail account from his desktop PC at work. He typed the message and posted it in the Draft folder. Then, using a throwaway cell phone he kept just for this purpose, he texted the code words: LITTLE MAC SAYS HELLO.

Yuri hoped to receive a response later in the day, probably in the evening.

Nicolai Orlov could not risk accessing the Gmail account from inside or near the Russian consulate in San Francisco. Like Laura, he would use a public computer, maybe at a library or Internet café. The consulate maintained excellent internal electronic security—that wasn't the worry. Eavesdropping by the FBI and other federal snoops created the concern.

Nick would also need to check for any tails that he might attract after leaving the consulate, which Yuri knew Nick was expert at shaking.

Yuri at first resisted contacting Nick. It would be risky for him, still an active SVR officer conducting operations. But Yuri had no one else to call on.

Yuri would ask for advice and nothing more. He wanted to protect his friend. Besides, Yuri was forever indebted to his fellow spy. Nick had saved his life—and Laura's, too.

CHAPTER 20

DAY 10—WEDNESDAY

Yangzi was a stately vessel, worthy of her namesake—China's epic Yangzi River, third largest in the world. At ninety-three meters with six decks including a helipad, *Yangzi* was one of the world's most elegant and costly superyachts. Today the ship occupied a side-tie slip along the guest dock of a marina in Long Beach, California. Kwan Chi had arrived in LA earlier aboard his own Gulfstream.

One of Kwan's companies had purchased the yacht a year earlier, for millions less than it cost to build; the previous owner had gone bankrupt. Kwan could not resist such a bargain. Besides, the *Yangzi* provided a convenient home away from home for his foreign operations, especially in the United States. Awarded a Green Card after investing nearly a billion in real estate from San Diego to Seattle, he could come and go aboard his floating palace as he pleased.

On paper, Kwan Chi owned the *Yangzi*, but the Chinese government, through its Ministry of State Security, supplied the acquisition funds. Responsible for foreign intelligence and counter-intelligence, the MSS was the People's Republic of China's equivalent of the CIA and the FBI.

A twenty-year veteran of the MSS, Kwan Chi, and his masters in Beijing, had carefully established his role as an astute businessman. It was the perfect cover. Who would ever expect a billionaire to be a spy?

Kwan Chi sat in the salon on the yacht's fourth level—his personal deck. The Asian artwork decorating the room was from the Ming dynasty. He wore a polo shirt, khakis, and deck shoes. Sitting across the white marble coffee table was Elena Krestyanova. Her flight from Singapore had landed at LAX ninety minutes earlier. Dressed in a sleek knee-length skirt and sheer blouse, she looked radiant despite the long transpacific flight.

It was late afternoon and they both sipped a chilled Napa Valley chardonnay. They chatted for ten minutes, catching up on each other's travels. Subconsciously, both anticipated the playtime they would have later in the evening in Kwan's palatial cabin, where Elena had spent time before. But for now it was all business.

"Tell me," Kwan said, meeting Elena's electric blue eyes, "has the new opportunity that you hinted at evolved?"

Elena smiled. "It has, and I think you will find it very interesting, possibly quite valuable."

"Please, continue."

Elena removed an iPad from the handbag that she'd carried aboard the yacht. She activated the screen and called up a video file.

"I'm sure you remember the oil spill in Alaska and

the oil company executive that was splattered by oil from the eco nuts."

"How could I forget that?"

"I know." Elena played the clip. Near the very end, she froze the video and increased the magnification. She passed the tablet to Kwan.

He stared at the image of Yuri Kirov. Puzzled, he asked, "So who is this fellow?"

"He's my five-million-dollar man."

"Hmm. Tell me more."

CHAPTER 21

Nick Orlov sat at a desk in his third-floor office of the consulate, leaning back in his chair. At six-foot-two and 180 pounds with stylish dark hair and chiseled face, he had good looks that were received well by females and males alike.

It was early afternoon. His thoughts focused on Yuri. After communicating via the Gmail account, they talked by phone.

Nick had called Yuri's disposable cell this morning, using a throwaway he'd purchased. He called while on the ferry from Sausalito, confident that the chances of a tail with a mobile electronic eavesdropping device intercepting the call were minimal. After two years, he recognized just about every commuter on the boat.

The threat was genuine. Despite Yuri's beard and longer hair, Nick had recognized his friend. Others back in Russia might also make the connection.

The original plan had been for Yuri to fake his death. Nick's verification that Yuri had died on the south-bound boat trip, succumbing to decompression sickness, would close the book on the issue. But events changed their scheme. The nasty business with Laura's estranged husband forced them all to rethink their next moves, especially Yuri.

There were too many at the marina and the hospital in Vancouver that saw them. It would be impossible to hide the fact that Yuri had survived the voyage. Besides, Laura had insisted that Yuri receive treatment at a specialty hyperbaric facility in Seattle, another venue that Yuri could be traced to even with a bogus name.

In the end, Yuri nixed the phony death plan. He'd argued that it would be too risky for Nick should the ruse be discovered. Willing to take the chance, Nick relented. In his official post-mission briefing to SVR headquarters and to his boss at the consulate, he reported that Yuri had disappeared with his female accomplice after they returned to Seattle with the workboat.

Nick was now thankful for Yuri's foresight. If the SVR, FSB, or Russian Navy made the connection in the YouTube video, Nick would be in the clear.

But Nick still fretted. His admiration of Yuri Kirov was genuine. He often recalled what Yuri had done to save his crewmates, suffering grievous injury while trapped behind enemy lines but never giving up.

"He's a good man," Nick muttered to himself. "I need to help him—somehow."

The *Yangzi* was thirty-five nautical miles offshore of the southern California coastline, cruising northward at sixteen knots. Despite the six-foot-high swells rolling in from the southwest, the yacht's ride was silky. The horizontal hull stabilizers and the antiroll gyros located in the forward and aft compartments of the steel hull dampened the nausea-inducing motion that habitually plagued those without "sea legs."

Today there were no landlubbers aboard the 305-foot-long ship; it was just Kwan Chi and his seasoned crew. Kwan was in the operations center, a spacious compartment located near the bow on level three—the main deck. Equipped with the latest electronic communication devices, it allowed Kwan to stay connected with the homeland wherever his travels might take him.

This early evening he was speaking over an encrypted telephone link to the MSS's deputy minister of operations in Beijing. A Chinese military communications satellite facilitated the conversation.

"Do you trust this Russian?" asked the deputy director.

"No, sir. Not at all. She was trained by the SVR and is still in its employ."

"Are we getting played?"

"It's always a possibility, but I believe her motives are strictly monetary."

"What do we know about this person she's offering up?"

"I made a request to the Second Department for verification. The subject, Yuri Kirov, is in fact missing—for over a year now. The Department's operative at the naval base in Vladivostok reported he was aboard a submarine on a clandestine mission somewhere in North America but did not return with the submarine. He is officially listed as missing."

"What's his background?"

"Intelligence officer, a captain-lieutenant. Thirty years old."

"GRU?" asked the MSS spymaster, referring to the *Glavnoye Razvedovatel'noye Upravlenie*, Russia's military intelligence service.

"Yes, sir. He's with fleet intelligence."

"His mission?"

"He was assigned to a submarine based out of Petropavlovsk-Kamchatskiy."

"Interesting."

"Yes, sir."

The deputy minister asked, "What else did this woman say?"

"If we had interest, she would make him available to us."

"For what price?"

"Five million American."

"What's the quality of her prior information?"

"Excellent. We have learned much about Russian defenses in the Far East. All of her information has proven to be first rate."

"Very well, you are authorized to proceed to the next step."

"Thank you, sir."

Kwan hung up, terminating the satellite link. He leaned back in his chair and closed his eyes. He remained drained; it was Elena's fault.

The previous night they'd spent together in his stateroom was one he would long remember. Elena's appetite was insatiable. He loved it.

While Elena and Kwan played, the fact-checking that he'd ordered his assistants to undertake proceeded full throttle. When *Yangzi* cleared the outer breakwater at the Long Beach Harbor, the report from the PRC's Military Intelligence Department, aka the Second Department, was downloaded, decrypted, printed, and then set out on his desk in the operations center.

Kwan thought ahead to the mission. If what Elena hinted the Russian submarine officer could provide was even half-true, it was a game changer. Nevertheless, he remained cautious.

The Russians were just as devious as his own countrymen—and women.

CHAPTER 22

Day 12—Friday

Yuri watched the video from his office computer. It was a live broadcast of the Russian Federation president's address to parliament. Yuri heard about the pending speech from a Russian-language cable television channel he'd watched at home the previous evening. He made a habit of listening to the channel to keep his Russian fresh and to stay abreast of homeland politics.

Yuri accessed the live broadcast through a Russian government website.

The Russian president reported that the seabed oil well in the Western Chukchi Sea was sabotaged. He blamed the United States of America, providing evidence collected from the well site to validate the accusation. A wire-guided torpedo destroyed the wellhead, causing the blowout and ongoing spill. During the speech, he held up a one-meter length of a paper-thin fiber-optic cable to the cameras, claiming it was retrieved from the bottom near the well and further stating that the other end of the wire had extended over two kilometers to the east.

The president also pointed to debris displayed on a nearby table. The metal fragments and electronic components were parts from the weapon. He concluded his speech by calling the sabotage an act of war and threatening retaliation.

Yuri didn't believe for a moment that the USA was behind the attack. There was nothing for America to gain. The spilled oil was apolitical; it would contaminate the Arctic regardless of international boundary lines.

He's hiding something. Someone probably made a mistake, causing the accident, and now he's covering it up.

Yuri had observed it before while in the Russian Navy. Accidents aboard nuclear submarines were legion. Invariably, the causes resulted from poor manufacturing processes, minimal maintenance, or inadequate crew training. Rarely would the Navy or its government-run shipyards take responsibility. Usually, the accidents were blamed on human error with officers at the bottom of the totem pole taking the heat.

They're obviously hiding something. I bet someone screwed up big-time regarding the oil well and now the Kremlin is trying to pin the blame on Uncle Sam.

Russia will never change.

Kwan Chi finished reading the translated text of the Russian president's speech, compliments of the MSS's Technical Support Department. It was all beginning to fall in place. Compared to the others he was just a cog in Operation Sea Dragon, but his contribution would be critical, possibly even the inciting element. That thought both thrilled and vexed Kwan. Success would bolster his already stellar career. Failure would dethrone him, allowing a rival—and there were several—to take over his coveted role.

No! I will not allow that to happen. The mission will succeed—whatever it costs.

The *Yangzi* continued its northerly advance. Now offshore of the Oregon coast, approaching the mouth of the Columbia River, the superyacht would arrive in Seattle the following afternoon. Kwan looked forward to that port of call. Elena would be just a few hours away by automobile.

He had called her after receiving approval from Beijing. Ecstatic, Elena promised to move forward with her plan at once.

Recruited during his third year at the Tsinghua University School of Economics and Management in Beijing, Kwan Chi was the ideal candidate for the Ministry of State Security's burgeoning Foreign Affairs Bureau. Fluent in English and highly regarded by his SEM professors as one of the school's best students ever, the twenty-year-old Kwan was wooed by several state-owned businesses with promises of a fat salary, a prestigious office, and international travel.

Born four years before China implemented its one-child-per-family mandate, Kwan was the youngest of three siblings. He grew up in an affluent section of Hangzhou in Eastern China's Zhejiang Province. His father was a mid-level Communist Party bureaucrat who provided well for his family. Both of his brothers ran successful businesses in Hangzhou. But Kwan was special—his test scores were off the charts and unlike many of the academically gifted, he had a gregarious personality that opened untold doors of opportunity.

After graduation, the MSS allowed Kwan to earn an MBA degree from Tsinghua University's SEM, which included a semester at MIT's Sloan School of Management for which he also earned a certificate and bragging rights.

At twenty-three, Kwan entered China's business world just as the Party embraced capitalism as its savior. For the next twenty years, China rode a tsunami of economic growth that catapulted the world's most populous nation into a global financial juggernaut. Kwan rode that wave of prosperity at its crest, coached and spurred on by his masters from the Ministry of State Security.

Successful execution of Kwan's role in Operation Sea Dragon would supercharge his already stellar career. Failure would result in the curtailment of the perks he took for granted, and might even earn him a bullet in the head.

CHAPTER 23

The *Norsk Voyager* hovered thirty feet from the well site. The mini-sub had arrived two hours earlier, transported by a Russian Federation nuclear-powered attack submarine. The *Barrakuda* loitered about a thousand feet to the south, sandwiched by overhead ice floes and the shallow mud bottom.

About the size of a heavy-duty pickup truck, the submersible was chockfull of equipment, leaving a cramped cockpit for the three-man crew. Upon arriving at the Petropavlovsk-Kamchatskiy naval base aboard a Russian cargo jet, the Norwegian mini-sub mated to the *Barrakuda*'s aft escape hatch. The sub then made a speed run, transiting the Bering Sea through the Bering Strait into the Chukchi Sea.

The submersible's crew deployed the cryogenic unit, using *Norsk Voyager*'s onboard ROV to transport the pre-assembled copper coiling and install it around and inside the well's steel casing. The torn end of the approximately twenty-inch-diameter pipe jutted six feet above the bottom. A steady flow of brownish-black oil mixed with dissolved natural gas poured from the conduit.

The Norwegian pilot turned to face the customer's representative, who occupied the observer's seat behind the cockpit. "We're ready. Permission to start flowing?" he asked in English, the crew's common tongue.

"Yes, proceed," answered the Russian petroleum engineer.

The pilot nodded to the copilot-navigator sitting to his right, who typed a series of commands onto a laptop keyboard.

"We're flowing," announced the copilot.

"How long before we see anything?" asked the observer.

"Hard to know," the pilot said. "According to our engineers, the model tests suggest that the hydrates should start precipitating once the temperature drops eighty degrees below ambient."

"I don't know about this. The flow out of the bore may be too high for this to work."

"We'll just have to wait and see."

The plan to shut in the runaway well was a long shot, implemented the same day the Americans announced the discovery of the blowout. It was Russia's only option. In theory, the liquid nitrogen circulating within the coil of tubes wrapped around the exterior and interior of the exposed steel casing would freeze the wall surface of the pipe, dropping the steel's temperature to at least minus one hundred fifty degrees Fahrenheit. The reduced temperature coupled with the hydrostatic pressure of the water depth would then encourage the formation of methane clathrate in the escaping fluid. Crystals of methane and water within the escaping flow would form. The ice-like crystals would adhere to the interior pipe wall surface and the cryo-tubing placed inside the bore. As the crystals grew, they would eventually choke off the flow and hope-fully seal the well.

Everyone aboard the *Norsk Voyager* recognized that the risk of failure was sky-high. Such a procedure had never been attempted. But it was the only method available. It would be months before the ice melted enough to allow a drilling rig to return to the site. And then it would take another couple of months to drill deep below the seabed to intercept the well's casing and plug it with cement.

As expected, the exterior surface of the exposed pipe casing froze into a rock-solid block of ice about a foot thick. The liquid nitrogen circulating from the cryogenic plant in the submersible's cargo hold to the copper tubing in the well bore readily froze the seawa-ter surrounding the pipe casing.

The copilot noticed the change. "It looks like some-thing's happening," he said, pointing to the video mon-itor in the center of the cockpit display. Trained on the open end of the pipe, the camera revealed that the steady stream of fluids pouring from the pipe opening had evolved into spurts and pulses.

"I see it," said the pilot. "Looks like the flow is slowing. Maybe it's starting to work." There was hope in his voice.

The Russian observer said a silent prayer.

The crew continued to watch the battle. As the hy-drate crystals grew inside the pipe casing, they par-tially choked the flow, which increased the fluid velocity. The higher speed eroded the crystals, peeling chunks of the hydrates away, which reduced the flow velocity, allowing the crystals to again reform. The see-saw action persisted for nearly an hour until finally the expanding hydrate formation choked the flow to a dribble. Ten minutes later, the flow stopped completely.

"Fantastic—it worked!" the pilot cheered.

"I just knew it would work," the copilot echoed.

"Thank you, God," whispered the Russian engineer.

CHAPTER 24

DAY 14—SUNDAY

The CNN broadcast of the White House speech had just concluded. Normally, Yuri would not have bothered to watch the live presentation while at work. He preferred to catch up at home with the evening news. But the Kremlin's bombshell announcement earlier in the morning that the runaway oil well in the Chukchi Sea had been shut in was the subject of the president's presentation.

Yuri was at NSD in his office. He leaned back in his chair, reflecting on the eight-minute speech. He expected a chilly reception from the Kremlin to the president's offer to put aside their differences to concentrate on the cleanup. The president also repeated that the United States had nothing to do with sabotaging the oil well and would cooperate fully with the Russian government to determine the cause of the accident.

Yuri wanted to believe the American president. However, *Deep Explorer* provided proof that an explosion had destroyed the Russian subsea well. Color screenshots from the AUV's digital videos littered his desktop. The bottom debris cited by the Russian government as components from a U.S. Navy torpedo was visible in the recordings. The evidence was damning. Still, Yuri could not bring himself to believe the USA had destroyed the well. What advantage would there be with such action?

Yuri dismissed his misgivings, knowing it would be up to others to determine what had happened. Besides, he had other concerns to address. Another glitch had developed, requiring his attention. He picked up his desktop phone and dialed.

"Hi, Bill," he said, connecting with Bill Winters in Barrow.

"Did you get the bearing?" Winters asked.

"It's on the way. Tom came in and helped me remove it from *Deep Adventurer* this morning. He's on his way to Alaska Air Cargo as we speak. You should have it by noon tomorrow."

"Terrific, that'll work out fine."

"How's the rest of the unit look?" Yuri asked.

"Remarkably good. The worn bearing was the only issue." Winters had called Yuri at home earlier in the morning. Bill and crew had removed *Deep Explorer* from the ice and ferried it back to Barrow for routine maintenance.

Yuri said, "I just listened to the president's speech about the blowout. What's your take on the U.S. and Russia working together to clean up the spill?"

"Ain't gonna happen. They blame us."

"I think you might be right."

*   *   *

The *Yangzi* had arrived in Seattle the previous day. Moored at the Elliott Bay Marina's guest dock, the superyacht dwarfed the other boats in the marina. Located in Seattle's Magnolia District, the spectacular marina provided premium moorage facilities for over a thousand boats and splendid views of downtown skyscrapers.

Kwan Chi always enjoyed his visits to Seattle. With a thriving economy, magnificent scenic surroundings, and ample open space, Seattle was a city he could envision calling one of his homes. Maybe someday, he thought. But for now, it was business as usual.

It was early evening. Kwan was in the yacht's operations center, phone to his ear, waiting for the conference call to start. The Minister of State Security overseer and his counterpart at the Military Intelligence Department requested his participation. The two intelligence chiefs, each in their own Beijing office complex, were currently conferring on a separate line. While Kwan waited, he wondered who else might be listening. He preferred videoconferences where all of the participants were visible. But today it was audio only.

"Kwan, you still there?" The voice was flat, almost monotone. It was the result of the encryption process.

"Yes, sir."

"Good, we're ready to proceed," the MSS deputy minister of operations said. "I assume you heard that the Russians capped the oil well."

"I did."

"As you can imagine this was a surprise to all of us.

Our technical people assured us that the well could not be sealed until the summer."

Kwan was privy to key elements of Operation Sea Dragon. Critical to the venture was the continual release of oil for months. "A festering boil that would antagonize both parties," his boss had told him during an earlier briefing.

"Because the Americans are holding out an olive branch to the Russians, requesting that they jointly work together to clean up the oil spill, we must now advance the schedule."

"Yes, sir."

"The second phase will commence soon. We're still working out the details but expect to authorize action in the next day or so. We will then follow up with the third phase."

"The schedule has really accelerated."

"Yes, due to the premature plugging of the well," the MSS chief said. "That brings us to your part. We are intrigued with what you reported about this Russian naval officer and believe what you suggested has merit. How soon will you know if that approach will be a viable option?"

"Within the next forty-eight hours."

"Very well. I need to know, one way or the other, by that time."

"I understand, sir."

"You are excused, Kwan. The general and I have other business."

"Yes, sir," Kwan said, and the line went dead.

Kwan understood the need for the change in plans. Nevertheless, his worry quotient just ratcheted up another notch. Always a careful planner, he was not a fan of last-minute alterations. His angst expanded when he thought about the minister's final comments.

They're seriously considering my suggestion about the Russian officer. But if that doesn't work out, what then?

CHAPTER 25

DAY 15—MONDAY

It was mid-afternoon at Northwest Subsea Dynamics. Yuri sat at his desk and dialed Bill Winters's cell.

"Did you get it?" asked Yuri.

"We did, and it's already installed."

"Great."

"Thanks for the quick turnaround. We should be good for the time being, but I'd sure like to have another bearing for backup."

"We're on it. We ordered three spares today. Should arrive in a couple of days. I'll ship two of 'em to you when they arrive."

"Perfect."

Yuri swiveled his chair, glancing at a printout of the project schedule taped to the wall behind his desk. "Are you still on schedule?" he asked.

"Yep, we relaunch tomorrow morning."

Bill and Yuri spoke for a few more minutes before hanging up.

Yuri was thinking of heading home when the intercom speaker on his office phone activated. It was the receptionist. "John, you have a visitor in the lobby—an old friend."

"Who is it?"

"Elena . . . from Vancouver."

Yuri's spine stiffened. He muttered, "*Tvoyú mat*"—Dammit.

"What?"

"Nothing. I'll be out there in a couple minutes. Please show her to the conference room."

"Okay."

It can't be!

Yuri remained seated in his chair, half-paralyzed.

Elena, shit! I knew this would happen. What the hell is she doing here?

Yuri stood and walked out of his office.

Calm down. Don't let her get to you!

Yuri opened the conference room door.

Elena Krestyanova stood beside the conference table, her back to the door. She spun around and with a beaming smile walked toward him with her right hand extended. "Nice to see you, John," she said. Adorned in a tight knee-length black leather skirt with matching coat, she appeared dazzling as ever.

Yuri shook her hand. "Good to see you," he reciprocated. He shut the door and gestured for her to sit down.

"*Alë, garázh!*" she said. Hello, citizen.

"Please, English only."

"As you wish."

"Elena, what are you doing here?"

"I should be the one asking that question."

"What?"

She cracked a weak smile. "Yuri, everyone back

home thinks you're dead—from the bends or whatever that nasty condition was called."

"I survived."

"Obviously." She scanned the conference room. Displayed on the wall were several photos of *Deep Explorer* and a couple of other NSD vehicles. "I see you are still working with underwater machines. Very impressive."

Yuri did not respond, unsure what this she-devil was up to.

"How's Laura?"

Shit! "She's fine."

"So she bought this company . . . for you, correct?"

"What do you want?"

"I don't want anything. I'm just the messenger."

I bet. "So what's the message?"

"You're wanted back home."

"I have a new life here. I'm not going anywhere."

"You're still officially in the Navy."

"I'll resign my commission."

"I don't think it works that way."

"Just tell them I'm fine and I have no plans to return to Russia. The United States is now my home."

"So, you're going to marry her and live happily ever after, especially with all of her money?"

Yuri bristled but refused the bait. "I know you want something, so tell me."

"There is a request. Again, I'm just the messenger. It comes from the Defense Ministry, not the SVR or FSB."

"Yes."

"It's about your mission from last year."

"What about it?"

"The Navy would like you to retrieve the monitoring pods that you planted."

"They don't need me for that. They can do it themselves."

Elena cocked her head to her side, eyes narrowed. "Sorry, but no, they can't. After what happened with the *Neva*, it is now impossible for our submarines to return."

"Then the Americans probably found the pods."

"We don't think so. Our agents in the Pentagon have not reported anything remotely close to that scenario." She shifted position in her chair. "We certainly want the data, but it is paramount that the pods be removed before they are discovered. As you know, there is much tension between Russia and America now. The Kremlin fears that if the recording pods are discovered, the U.S. will use it as an excuse to retaliate."

"I don't think so. Their subs spy on the homeland ten times as much as we do on theirs."

"Again, I'm just repeating what I was told to tell you."

Yuri glared. "I'm not interested."

"Okay. I'll let them know. However, there will be consequences—but not just for you."

Yuri's stomach flip-flopped.

"Should you decide not to cooperate," continued Elena, "I was instructed to tell you that a file will be delivered to the FBI detailing Laura Newman's involvement with the *Neva*."

Yuri turned away, engulfed by a wave of nausea. He waited for nearly half a minute before turning back to face Elena. "What exactly do you want me to do?"

Elena laid it all out for him.

"If I do this," Yuri asked after she finished, "what assurances do I have that you're not going to continue to blackmail me?"

"Remember, it's not me—"

"Yeah, yeah you're just the messenger. I get that but you know what I mean."

"With the monitoring equipment removed, there will no longer be any need for your services. You can stay here or if you wish return home. Your choice."

"You've dumped a lot on me. I need some time to think about this."

"I need an answer no later than twenty-four hours from now."

"How do I contact you?"

After Elena left, Yuri returned to his office. With the office lights switched off, he sat in the dark.

That damn video—I should have never gone to Alaska.

No, it was bound to happen sometime.

Laura. Once again, I've put her in jeopardy.

I've got no choice!

CHAPTER 26

Laura was later than usual. It was 8:35 P.M. when she walked into the kitchen, carrying Maddy. Laura noted that the table in the nook had been set for two. The aroma of salmon baking in the oven caught her attention. *Fantastic, he's such a great cook.*

She walked into the darkened living room; a single table lamp glowed in a corner. "Oh, there you are," she announced.

Yuri smiled as he sat in his favorite chair by the lake windows.

Laura noticed the vodka bottle on the coffee table. She walked forward, sitting in the chair next to his, catching a whiff of booze.

Yuri held a shot glass in his right hand. "*Dobryj večer!*" he said just before tossing back the slug of chilled vodka.

"Good evening to you, too." By now, Laura had picked up basic Russian greetings.

"How's sweet pea?" Yuri said, leaning forward to make eye contact, displaying his goofy grin. Maddy instantly responded with her beaming smile and a tiny chuckle.

Yuri cooed and Madelyn reciprocated.

The interplay warmed Laura's heart. "She's hungry and probably needs a diaper change."

Yuri settled back into his chair. He said, "So, how was your day?"

"Long, too many meetings. I'm worn out. And you?"

"Same old stuff."

Something's wrong. She sensed it when she first walked into the living room. Yuri would occasionally crack open a bottle of vodka but typically preferred a single beer before dinner. This was the second evening this week she had come home to find him tossing back vodka shots. Acutely aware of the warning signs from her addicted ex, Laura's angst skyrocketed.

"Where did you get the salmon?" she asked.

"One of the engineers at work gave me two fat fillets. Apparently, someone told him that I love salmon. He also handed out some to a couple of others. He caught 'em last fall and has a freezer full at home."

"That was certainly nice of him."

"It was. He's new and wants to fit in."

Laura ran a hand through Maddy's hair. She wanted to find out what was bothering Yuri but decided to hold off. If she probed too early, he would clam up. "When will it be ready?"

Yuri consulted his wristwatch. "Fifteen minutes."

"Great, I'm going to feed Maddy."

"Okay, I'll have a plate ready for you." Yuri stood and headed for the kitchen. He left the vodka bottle behind.

Good, Laura thought as she headed to the nursery.

* * *

Garnished with vegetables, the salmon was scrumptious, as was the green salad Yuri had cobbled together. Yuri had also returned the vodka bottle to the fridge, saying he'd had enough. *Thank you, God,* Laura said to herself.

They returned to the living room, both sitting on the sofa. Maddy was asleep in her crib.

It was time for Laura to probe a little deeper. "You seem a bit off tonight, honey. Is there something wrong at work?"

"I'm that transparent?"

"No, but I know you've been under enormous pressure lately."

"So have you."

"But not quite like you."

He gave her a smile. "I love you for caring about me, Laura. You know that, don't you?"

"Yes, and I love you, too." *Something is wrong!*

"I got some bad news today."

"What?"

"Elena—she walked into my office this afternoon."

Laura's right hand flew to her mouth. "Oh dear Lord," she groaned, her heart racing.

She was horrified by Yuri's unfolding story. Yuri downplayed the threat, telling Laura that he was the target—not Laura.

"I don't trust that woman one iota. She's devious," Laura said.

"Yes, I feel the same."

"Why would they send her? If Russia really wanted you back, wouldn't they send another naval officer, or maybe even Nick?"

"She knows her way around the Pacific Northwest. She's still part of the Vancouver trade mission, so returning to Seattle fits in with her work profile."

"I don't know. I still have a bad feeling about her."

It had been over a year since Laura had encountered Elena Krestyanova, yet it seemed like yesterday to her.

"Elena's the messenger," Yuri said. "Don't work yourself up about it. She's following orders, that's all."

Laura reclined into the folds of the sofa. The rush had receded; weariness now set in. "Can you do what they want . . . find those recording devices?"

"Probably, if they're still there."

Laura considered the situation. "I think it's time to have the attorney make formal contact with the State Department. You need to request asylum."

"We've been over this before. I won't do that. The attorney said that you could be prosecuted."

"I know, but I'm willing to take that chance." Laura reached forward with her hands and gently clasped Yuri's right wrist. "Honey, you just can't continue in limbo like this. You're too vulnerable."

Yuri met her eyes. "You've done so much for me. I can't ask you to sacrifice anymore."

"But I want to help you."

"I'm going to tell Elena I will cooperate. Besides, it's time for me to return to Russia and get closure."

"But your government turned its back on you and your crew—you were all expendable. Remember what Nick said."

"I know, but it's time for me to put that aside. I need to clean up my affairs at home and then somehow find a way to return to you."

Laura's heart sank. Her chief horror was now playing out in real time.

"I don't want you to leave—it's too risky."

"It's time. I have to take care of this—to remove the cloud over you that I caused."

"Before you respond to Elena, please talk with Nick," pled Laura. "Ask for his advice. He's always been a friend, and he knows the situation better than anyone else."

"That's a good idea. I'll do that."

"Thank you."

Yuri moved next to Laura's side and whispered, "I love you so much. You are my life." And then he kissed her.

CHAPTER 27

DAY 16—TUESDAY

The crude carrier slipped into its berth at the Valdez Marine Terminal well before dawn. Loading operations commenced as the early sun glinted off its decks and towers. After verifying all landside pumping and shipboard receiving systems were functioning properly, the crew increased its flow rate to 120,000 barrels an hour. By seven o'clock in the evening, 1.3 million barrels of North Slope crude would occupy the eighteen separate cavernous holds of the tanker. Scheduled to depart at ten, the *Alaskan Star* would then begin its two-thousand-nautical-mile southbound voyage to Los Angeles.

Captain Mike Martin stood in the dark wheelhouse of the colossal ship. A hefty six-footer with a thick russet mane sprinkled with streaks of silvery gray, he peered through the bridge windows. Shipboard and terminal lighting illuminated the steel deck that stretched out nearly three football fields in front of Mike. Packed with a vast and confusing maze of piping, valves, and

pumps, the mechanical and electrical systems aboard
the tank-ship rivaled those found on an aircraft carrier.

Mike had made the round-trip between LA and
Valdez over fifty times. Pushing sixty, he expected to
finish out his three-decade maritime career aboard the
Star. With retirement looming he wasn't quite sure
what he would do to keep busy, but for damn sure he
wasn't going to buy a boat. Janet had made that clear.
After being away at sea for almost half of their twenty-
eight-year marriage, Mike knew it was time to be a
grounded full-time husband. He was okay with that
prospect, especially since his oldest daughter and her
husband had announced before he departed they were
"expecting" in late September.

Grandpa Mike! He liked that thought.

"Captain, I have a report from Engineering."

Mike turned to face his third mate. The twenty-nine-
year-old Merchant Marine Academy graduate monitored loading operations. She also worked through the
pre-voyage checklist.

"What's up, Wendy?"

"One of the generators has an output problem. The
engineer wants to take it offline to run a couple of diagnostics. He suspects a faulty voltage regulator."

"Can it be replaced before departure?"

"Yes. He estimated two hours."

"Very well, tell him to proceed, but I want an update in an hour, one way or the other."

"Aye, aye, sir."

Mike was a stickler about maintaining sailing sched-
ules. Any significant delay would have a cascading
impact on offloading operations at the refinery in LA.

Besides, his wife's fifty-fifth birthday was a week away. His three daughters had a blowout party planned for their mother and there was no way in hell he was going to miss it.

The meeting called for a head-to-head. Yuri took a mid-morning Alaska Air flight. Nick drove, taking evasive steps to shake any trailing vehicles. They entered a restaurant on the outskirts of Sacramento, selecting a quiet booth away from the developing lunch crowd.

During the drive from the airport, Yuri briefed Nick on the basics. The discussion continued to center on Elena Krestyanova. They spoke in English.

"Can you do this work that she's requested—recover the recording pods?" Nick asked while rubbing his forehead. He shared Yuri's concern. The unveiled threat to "out" Laura was right in line with SVR/FSB tactics. Hold a cocked pistol to the head of a subject's loved one and you'll always get what you want.

"Probably. I know the approximate locations from memory. It will take some searching, but that's what our equipment is good at."

"Your underwater robot?"

"Autonomous underwater vehicle—AUV. It's designed to conduct underwater surveys."

Nick recalled part of their earlier conversation. "But I thought your machine was in Alaska and that it would be working up there monitoring the oil spill through the spring."

"That's right. *Deep Explorer* is on a surveying mission in the Chukchi Sea right now. Her sister vehicle,

Deep Adventurer, is in our warehouse in Redmond. She's on standby should we need her in the Arctic."

"I see." Nick took a sip from his water glass. "Once you locate the devices, how would you recover them?"

"I'll send down a ROV to attach a line and then haul 'em up."

"Like what you used with the *Neva—Little Mac*."

"Yes."

"So you won't have to dive yourself."

"Not if I can help it."

That rekindled a memory for Nick. "Your leg, I didn't notice a limp. Has it mended?"

"Yes, finally. I still have residual numbness in parts of my calf but have learned to adapt."

After half a dozen hyperbaric chamber treatments and then four months of daily physical therapy—all paid by Laura without insurance—Yuri regained use of his once paralyzed lower left leg. The doctors warned Yuri that he should avoid future deep dives. He had suffered severe damage from his dual bouts with decompression sickness. Another exposure could kill him.

Their meals arrived. They took a break from the Elena problem while eating.

Yuri said, "So, how are things at the consulate?"

"Busy. I'm spending more of my time as a liaison with the Chinese delegation."

"How's that going?" The Russia-China pact was now out in the open. Six months earlier, both countries had announced the enhanced joint economic and military alliance.

"Good. I'm heading to Beijing next month for a couple of meetings. Should be interesting."

Yuri didn't bother asking about Nick's real mission

with China, knowing that Nick would have to lie. Instead, he changed subjects.

"Your Forty-Niners had a tough year."

Nick's face rolled into a scowl. "Yeah—very disappointing."

Nick was a fanatic 49ers fan. Yuri had not yet caught the fire, but Laura had. Her Seattle Seahawks had been in contention for another NFC title but were edged out in the playoffs.

Nick returned to his chicken enchilada while Yuri reflected on his colleague and friend. He was forever indebted to Nick. He'd stood by Yuri, risking his career and his life. No one else other than Laura had helped.

Elena was the wild card. Although she had worked with Nick, she was not an ally. But it was all complicated. Nick and Elena had been lovers. Yuri decided to find out if that spark was still alive.

"Have you seen Elena since Vancouver?"

"No. We've talked on the phone a couple of times. She's still pissed about what happened."

"Does she suspect it was a setup?"

"I don't think so. She just blames me for not waiting for her."

Yuri, Nick, and the sub's captain had conspired to trick Elena to board the *Neva*. It was to protect Laura. Moscow ordered Elena and Nick to "clean up" the loose ends of the mission that had gone awry. One of those ends was Laura. Nick refused the orders but Elena had not.

Forced to endure a two-week voyage across the Pacific, first aboard the crippled spy sub and then in a rescue submarine, Elena was left in the cold.

"What is she doing now?"

"I checked after you called. She remains with the trade delegation but has been working on the Asian circuit."

"Still based in Vancouver?"

"Officially, yes. But she spends much of her time in Vladivostok. It's a short commute to China. Apparently, she has some type of op going on there."

Yuri did not like the thought that Elena remained in his backyard, even part-time. Seattle was just a couple of hours' drive from Vancouver.

Yuri considered Nick's revelation and said, "Why would they assign her to make contact with me? If anyone, it should have been you. You accompanied us to Seattle while she was stuck on the *Neva*."

"I don't know. I wondered about that, too." Nick took another sip of water. "When are you supposed to get back to her?" he asked.

Yuri glanced at his watch. It was almost two o'clock. "By six tonight."

"Hmm, I'm not sure how to advise you. Maybe you should hold off and let me do a little more digging."

"That's what I was hoping you'd say."

CHAPTER 28

DAY 17—WEDNESDAY

The *Alaskan Star* departed from the Valdez Marine Terminal on schedule at ten o'clock. For the next two and a half hours, Captain Mike Martin and the Valdez pilot guided the 940-foot-long fully laden behemoth through the Valdez Narrows and the Valdez Arm. Escorting the tank-ship were two Prevention and Response Tugs. Should the *Alaskan Star* lose power or suffer a navigation control casualty, the PRTs were there to keep her off the rocks.

It was now 12:38 A.M. The *Alaskan Star* had just passed Bligh Reef to the port, where the infamous *Exxon Valdez* ran aground in 1989. Nearly eleven million gallons of crude poured into Prince William Sound after rocks ripped open the bottom plates of the single-hull tanker. The spill cost billions to clean up and remained a decaying sore with local fishermen and environmental groups.

Although the *Alaskan Star* had a double hull, the latest navigation equipment, and two PRTs that would escort her all the way to the Pacific, Captain Martin always breathed a little easier after passing Bligh Reef. Not one gallon of product or fuel had ever spilled from a vessel he commanded, and he intended to maintain that record.

The pilot disembarked for a return trip to the Emerald Isle base in Valdez. Captain Mike had complete control of his ship. The tanker was in the southbound lane of the Prince William Sound Vessel Traffic Service running at ten knots. The escort tugs trailed on either side of the *Star*. The U.S. Coast Guard Vessel Traffic Center in Valdez tracked all three vessels by radar.

It was a clear night. Moonlight illuminated the waterway while a dazzling display of northern lights lit up the heavens. The seas were calm with just a faint breeze from the south. And there had been no reports of icebergs from the Columbia glacier. Faultless sailing conditions.

The warship patrolled a hundred meters below the surface. The sonar watch started tracking the tank-ship and its escorts once the convoy passed into Valdez Arm. The attack center had working solutions on all three contacts, but the captain focused on just one target.

"Sonar, range to target," he said.

"Fifteen point three kilometers. Target maintaining ten knots, sir."

The captain continued with his checklist. "Attack, what's your status?"

"Firing solution locked in, sir."

"Weapons, status."

"All systems hot."

The captain turned to face his weapons officer. "Stand by for attack order."

"Aye aye, Captain."

The skipper of the *Guardian* sipped from a fresh mug of coffee as he piloted the 140-foot PRT. With Bligh Reef behind them, it was now a relaxing voyage as *Guardian*, her sister tug *Vigilant*, and the *Alaskan Star* cruised across the broad reach of Prince William Sound.

The tug captain was alone in the pilothouse, standing at the helm. His crew was below in the galley on a coffee break. He turned to the port to check his charge. The gigantic tanker remained abeam two hundred yards away. Fully illuminated with racks of floodlights running fore and aft, it looked like a floating factory.

The captain had completed a radio check with *Alaskan Star* and *Vigilant* when something caught his eye in the reflected moonlight. "What the hell?" he muttered.

The aberration ripped across the water surface at an incredible speed, kicking up a wake that shot a hundred feet into the air. Within three heartbeats, it punctured the *Alaskan Star*'s hull. The tank-ship erupted into a colossal fireball.

Then the pressure wave from the blast slammed into the *Guardian* with the impact of a freight train.

With ears ringing and completely stunned, the tug captain pulled himself from the deck to peer through the now windowless windscreen. "Mother of God," he muttered.

Ripped diagonally from just aft of the starboard bow to near amidships on the port side, the *Alaskan Star* had cleaved into two sections. The bow's deck was already nearly awash. The aft hull section remained afloat but burned fiercely.

The captain reached for his radio.

"Valdez Traffic, this is PRT *Guardian*. Tanker *Alaskan Star* has exploded and is burning. I repeat, the *Alaskan Star* has exploded and is burning. Get everyone out here NOW!"

It was chaos inside the *Alaskan Star*'s bridge. Multiple alarms and annunciators blared throughout the compartment. Captain Mike Martin gripped the handrail at the base of the windscreen with his left hand. As in the *Guardian*, the explosion blew out all of the tempered glass panels in the pilothouse.

Bleeding profusely from glass shrapnel, Mike pressed his hand against his forehead. He was unsteady on his feet. No other watch standers were standing. He heard a weak groan from behind. At least someone else is alive, he thought.

Searing waves of heat from the inferno surged into the bridge. Mike stepped back several feet and stared at his command in shock. *What happened?*

It took nearly a minute before the enormity of the event registered. "She's lost," he muttered.

* * *

After notifying Valdez Vessel Traffic Center and Alyeska's shore-based traffic control center of the explosion and fire, *Guardian*'s captain tried to hail both the *Alaskan Star* and the *Vigilant*. But there was no response.

By now, the *Guardian*'s four-man crew was huddled in the pilothouse. The chief mate asked, "Skipper, what happened?"

"Just before she went up I saw something streak across the water, incredibly fast. And then it hit, blowing the *Star* sky-high."

"Jesus," muttered someone.

"The Coast Guard is on the way," the captain continued. "Valdez Traffic has notified the spill-response team and they're mobbing right now. *Thor* is under way and should be here soon."

"Where's *Vigilant*?" asked another crewman.

"No response yet."

"Hey, look at that!" shouted one of the men, pointing toward *Alaskan Star*'s stern.

"Looks like they're getting ready to launch a lifeboat," announced the first mate.

The captain turned to face his crew. "Prepare to take on survivors."

After making a head count, Captain Martin ordered his crew to abandon ship. Three men were missing, all workers in the forward section of the ship that had already sunk. Of the remaining fifteen survivors, not including Mike, eight had suffered assorted injuries ranging from broken limbs and concussions to third-degree burns and deep lacerations.

They had all mustered at the starboard lifeboat station located just aft of the bridge. For the moment, the superstructure shielded the survivors from the thermal radiation of the broiling hydrocarbons. The overwhelming stink of crude oil polluted the air.

Mike ordered everyone to board the lifeboat. As he waited, a cloud of guilt consumed him.

What did I do wrong?

The warship cruised just below the surface, its periscope mast piercing the interface. The captain and the others in the attack center viewed the main color video display. Magnified a dozen times, the target continued to burn but its main deck was almost awash. One of the sentinel tugs had just powered to a lifeboat launched from the stricken ship. There was no sign of the other tug.

The captain turned to his weapons officer. "Excellent work," he said.

"Thank you, sir."

The captain addressed the watch officer. "Submerge the boat to one hundred meters and turn to a heading of one seven zero. Make turns for five knots."

The officer repeated the order.

The captain turned toward the chief sonar technician. "Start the transmission," he ordered.

"Aye, aye, Captain."

The submarine began its retreat, masking its real acoustic sound print. It was the same cloaking technique employed two months earlier when it sabotaged the Russian subsea oil well in the Chukchi Sea. After employing an AUV to place a demolition charge on the exposed wellhead and then scattering evidence on the seafloor that would implicate the United States, the sub retraced its path through the Bering Strait and Bering Sea to the North Pacific.

CHAPTER 29

It was noon. Yuri sat at his office desk surfing the Web. He checked MSN for the latest news on the Prince William Sound oil spill.

The *Alaskan Star* was on the bottom in 1,400 feet of water—in two pieces. A least 200,000 barrels of crude oil—8,400,000 gallons—had already been released. Oil continued to surface over the wreck site, confirming fears that the submerged tank compartments holding the remaining 1.1 million barrels of crude were leaking. A massive armada of spill-response vessels and aircraft were attacking the spilled oil in a warlike manner.

Yuri turned away from his monitor in disbelief. What were the odds of having two huge oil spills so close together?

Bill Winters and his crew remained in Barrow, monitoring *Deep Explorer* as it mapped the extent of spilled oil from the Russian subsea well blowout.

Thank God for cryogenics. Using methane hydrates to plug the well. What a clever idea! Those Vikings are amazing.

The Russian government–owned oil exploration company claimed the credit. However, those in the business knew the Norwegian contractor developed the radical procedure for shutting in the runaway well. With the flow of hydrocarbons temporarily halted by high-tech freezing, the submersible crew installed a valve over the severed pipe that mechanically sealed the well.

Bill and his guys are doing a great job, too.

Preliminary survey results from *Deep Explorer* were encouraging. The bulk of the spilled oil from the blowout remained in Russian territorial waters, pooled under the ice cap. Surface currents appeared to be slowly carrying the bulk of the oil northward, away from Alaska. However, the tendrils that made their way into the eastern Chukchi Sea and then offshore of Barrow remained. The U.S. Coast Guard estimated that ten thousand barrels had migrated into U.S. waters.

Maybe we can do something about that.

Spurred on by Yuri's brainstorm, NSD engineers in Redmond, assisted by Bill Winters and his staff in Alaska, were working on a plan to use AUVs like *Deep Explorer* to help extract the trapped oil in both U.S. and Russian waters before the spring breakup.

To make it work, we need workstations on the ice to—

Yuri's thought line stopped when his secretary walked into the office.

"John, a messenger just dropped this off. It's marked urgent." The forty-two-year-old mother of three handed over the large envelope.

"Who's it from?" Yuri asked, looking for a sender label.

"I don't know. All it has is your name and address on the front."

"Okay, thanks."

After the secretary exited his office, Yuri opened the package.

"*Govnó!*" he muttered as he extracted the contents.

He spread the half dozen eight-by-ten color photographs on the desktop. All were of Laura aboard a boat.

This is Elena's work!

Yuri had ignored her deadline, waiting for Nick's report, which he had not yet received.

The guilt would never disappear—confining Laura and then manipulating her into aiding and abetting his covert activities; it was always in the background, a specter waiting to haunt him again when provoked. Today it was the photographs.

Damn her! Elena knew just the right buttons to push. *Where did she get these?*

Most of the photos were of Laura as she moved around the decks of the ninety-six-foot workboat. Yuri knew the vessel and its location when photographed. The *Hercules* was in a navigation channel, exiting a small craft harbor near Vancouver, British Columbia.

It took a minute to notice the anomaly. The port door to the pilothouse was wide open, as were several other portside cabin windows. And then in a shot of the aft end of the cabin and its connection to the main deck, he observed that the cabin door was also open. Yuri put it together.

The gasoline! These were taken when we left Point Roberts, still airing out the cabin.

But who took them? Elena? No way. She was on her way across the . . .

And then it registered.

Someone else was watching us. But who?

It didn't take long for Yuri to weed out the possibilities. Either the SVR or FSB provided Elena the recon photos.

Yuri cupped his forehead with both hands.

CHAPTER 30

Kwan Chi was alone in the operations center. The *Yangzi* remained moored at the private marina near downtown Seattle. He initiated the call at 7:00 P.M., employing the vessel's satellite transceiver to contact MSS headquarters in Beijing. The deputy director of operations was on the other end of the encrypted call. It was 11:00 A.M. the next day in China.

"That is very good news, Kwan. When will the survey work begin?"

"A schedule is being developed now. I will probably know in a day or so."

"You need to push the Russian. This must not drag on if we are to use intel from it."

"I understand, sir." Kwan hesitated. "If possible, could you tell me how much time we have?"

"Maybe a week. Phase three will occur soon and then it will be your turn."

Kwan had pushed Elena on the schedule but she pushed back, noting that Kirov would need time to mobilize his equipment.

"Thank you. I plan to stay here and personally monitor the situation."

"Good. But under no circumstances are you to compromise yourself or your team. If the Americans get even a whiff of what is planned, the operation will fail."

"I understand."

"Very well. Send me the schedule when you have it."

"Yes, sir." The satellite feed clicked off, severed in Beijing.

Kwan relaxed, settling back into his chair. He thought of Elena, wondering what leverage she had over the Russian naval officer. She had called Kwan an hour earlier, reporting that Yuri Kirov was cooperating.

Elena would be driving to Seattle later this week. Kwan looked forward to her visit. The memory of their last hookup in LA remained vivid. He was ready and willing for round two—no, that's not quite the right descriptor.

Kwan was ravenous, and this time he would play the aggressor.

Yuri walked into the great room at 7:35 P.M. Laura sat in her favorite chair by the window wall, typing on her laptop. She looked up. "Hi there," she said, smiling.

"*Dobryj večer!*"—Good evening.

Yuri parked himself in a leather couch near Laura. He kicked off his shoes, stretched out his arms, and yawned.

Laura said, "You must be tired."

"Long day. How about you?"

"Same."

"Maddy asleep?"

"Yep, hopefully for the night. She was fussy this afternoon—teething again."

Yuri stretched his arms. "What are you working on?" he asked.

"Implementation memo for our Power Pulse program."

Cognition Consultants had captured a niche market that continued to expand. Having developed artificial intelligence algorithms running on a deep neural network, Cognition had become a wizard at analyzing huge blocks of digital information—Big Data. The company remained in high demand by oil and gas exploration companies for its capacity to draw insights from unbelievable volumes of seismic test data. Building on that expertise, the firm was also taking on the power industry, applying its innovative software that models the human brain to increase the efficiency of the nation's electrical grid.

"Hmm," Yuri mumbled while nodding off.

Yuri woke with a start. He shook his head, trying to focus. Finally awake, he noticed that Laura was gone.

He soon found her.

"I fell asleep," he said, walking into the kitchen.

"I noticed."

He had not slept well the night before, after his one-day trip to Sacramento.

"What are you making?" he asked, sniffing the pleasant aroma wafting from the oven.

"Lasagna—from Costco."

"Great." There would be plenty of leftovers for another dinner and a lunch, too.

They sat at the table. He elected to forgo his usual beer. In his fatigued state, alcohol would finish him off.

While eating they talked about the mysterious sinking of the oil tanker in Prince William Sound—it continued to dominate the broadcast news. Laura asked if NSD might be involved in the investigation; Yuri doubted that it would—the company was already overcommitted. That conversation rolled into what Yuri had been holding off all evening.

"I've decided to do what Elena wants," he announced.

That took Laura by surprise. She returned her fork to the plate and said, "Did you hear back from Nick already?"

"No, not yet, but that doesn't matter. I couldn't wait any longer."

Laura wrinkled her brow. "She's pressuring you."

"Yes, I just want to get it over."

Laura sat silently, fuming.

"I need you to do something for me," Yuri said.

"What?"

"It's going to take me a week or so to do the work. There's a chance that I could be discovered. If that happens, I don't want you anywhere near me, so that you're not implicated."

"What do you have in mind?"

"Take Maddy and go to Hawaii or Mexico—someplace a long way from here."

Laura fidgeted in her chair. "Whatever happens, it won't take long for the FBI to link me to you. You know that. Now, what are you really trying to tell me?"

Laura was so sharp. Yuri should have expected that she would see through his ruse.

"Elena's threatening to expose you if I don't cooperate."

Laura lowered her head. "She's everything I thought she was—and more."

"She's a blackmailing bitch."

"Yes, that, too."

CHAPTER 31

DAY 18—THURSDAY

The President of the United States—POTUS—sat in a high-back leather chair behind his Oval Office desk. It was mid-afternoon. Facing him across the tabletop was his national security advisor. They were alone, the president's usual entourage not invited.

Both men were in their late fifties and showing it. President Tyler Magnuson's paunch had expanded a couple of inches since taking office, but he'd managed to keep his hair. National Security Advisor Peter Brindle had lost his locks years earlier, and his face had leathered from three decades of smoking that finally ceased after a heart attack scare.

Both were veterans. The president had served as an infantry platoon leader after graduating from Texas A&M with a degree in political science and a commission as a second lieutenant earned during his four years in ROTC. Brindle was a graduate of the Naval Academy. He spent thirty-two years as a surface warfare officer before retiring as a vice admiral.

Today the only subject on the agenda was the oil

spill in Prince William Sound. NOAA chart 16700 stretched across the president's desktop.

"Are they absolutely certain about this?" POTUS asked.

"I've seen the data and listened to the recording. It was a submarine all right."

"Russian?"

"Yes, *Akula*-class, very quiet and lethal."

"But not that quiet—those sensors picked it up."

"They may have not been aware of the hydrophones on the buoy arrays."

"My God, the balls on that son of a bitch."

The Hinchinbrook Entrance, a seven-mile-wide waterway between Montague and Hinchinbrook Islands, provided the southern access to and from Prince William Sound. To reach the Gulf of Alaska and the North Pacific Ocean beyond, the *Alaskan Star* was bound for the passage; it sank twenty miles short.

Spanning the Hinchinbrook Entrance were fifteen submerged buoys. The buoys contained underwater instruments associated with monitoring water quality, tidal currents, tsunamis, and biological activity. Several of the buoy arrays contained hydrophones, which provided real-time monitoring of whale activity and other biologics. One of the hydrophones, owned by the U.S. Navy's Integrated Undersea Surveillance System, also listened for the faint acoustic signature of submarines entering or exiting the channel.

"When it came in, it must have been detected."

"The analysts went back eight weeks. There was no trace of it passing through the Hinchinbrook Entrance into Prince William Sound."

The president placed his right index finger on the chart. "What about this other entrance?"

"There are buoy arrays there, too. They checked and found nothing."

"How about this other channel?" POTUS said, again pointing to the chart.

"They're narrow and shallow channels to the west. It's possible it entered that way—probably on the surface, running at night during slack tides."

"Why not exit the same way?"

"We don't know. They may have decided to risk the Hinchinbrook Entrance to get out of Dodge quick."

"Okay, what about the sinking? Did the hydrophone pick it up?"

"Yes."

"Torpedo?"

"Yes, but not what you would expect."

President Magnuson tilted his head.

"The weapon used appears to be some form of a rocket torpedo. It was fired near the—"

"I don't follow you—rocket torpedo?"

"Instead of using batteries or a liquid-fueled engine, like conventional torpedoes, a rocket motor is employed."

"It fires underwater?"

"Yes, they generate enormous thrust and typically have a special nose cone that is designed to create a super-cavitation bubble around the hull, which allows it to—"

The president frowned, but Brindle continued, "Super-cavitation bubble—a small portion of the exhaust gases from the rocket are channeled to the nose cone and injected into the slipstream formed by a disk mounted at the tip of the weapon."

Brindle opened a file folder and removed a single sheet, placing it on the tabletop. "This is a photo of what it looks like. This is the disk," he said, pointing to it.

The president studied the photograph.

"The combination of the deflector and the injected gases keeps water away from the surface of the torpedo. That really reduces drag. The result is one frigging fast underwater weapon."

"How fast?"

"Two hundred fifty to three hundred knots plus."

Magnuson gasped. "Wow . . . I don't know that much about torpedoes, but that seems extreme."

"It is. Our top-of-the-line torpedo has a max speed of around sixty knots."

The president picked up the photo for a closer look. "Go on," he said.

"The weapon appears to have been fired near the surface. There are eyewitness reports of something speeding across the water surface just before the explosion. It's possible they observed the exhaust wake from the rocket motor."

"So it hit the tanker and the warhead exploded."

"It hit the hull, all right, but we don't think it had a warhead."

"What?"

"It was designed to penetrate, punch a hole clear through the hull from one side to the other." Brindle shifted in his chair. "A warhead wasn't needed. The exhaust flames vaporized the crude, causing a hell of an explosion that split the hull apart."

"A hot knife through butter."

"Yes. An efficient way to sink it while releasing the maximum amount of oil. Three center compartments were ripped opened in a heartbeat."

"What about the missing tugboat?" POTUS asked, returning the photo to the table.

The NSA grimaced. "Sunk. We think it was hit by the torpedo after it took out the tanker."

"My God."

President Magnuson mulled over what he'd learned and then said, "Let me guess, the Russians use this type of torpedo."

"They do but primarily as a defensive measure for their subs."

"How so?"

"If attacked by another submarine or surface vessel, they instantly return fire with what they call a *Shkval*, firing it down the reverse path of the attacking torpedo. It's designed to scare the crap out of the aggressor—to break off the attack."

"That would do it."

"Yes, sir."

"Anyone else have these things?"

"Iran."

"Jesus, you don't think they were behind this?"

"No, sir. They don't have the capability. Plus we have a positive ID on the boat as it exited. Definitely Russian-made."

"Could they have sold it to somebody?"

"Possibly, but this particular boat is still in their inventory."

"Then we've got them."

"Yes, sir. We have sufficient evidence to point the finger right back at the Kremlin."

"They've already denied any involvement and continue to blame us for the blowout of their well." POTUS leaned back in his chair. "He's a damn hothead, reacting like this with no cause."

"I agree."

"Let's sit on this for the next day or so. I'm not ready to do anything yet. Things are dicey and I don't trust that SOB. We need to really think this situation through."

"Very good, sir. If it is permissible, I would like to work on some contingency plans."

"That's fine, but keep it in-house with your key staff. Need to know only."

"Will do, sir."

CHAPTER 32

Elena set up the meeting, insisting Yuri attend. They sat at a conference table high up in the downtown Seattle tower. Designed to impress, the meeting room faced an extraordinary view of Elliott Bay. An international law firm occupied the office space, taking up three floors.

Yuri at first wondered how Elena had procured such a lavish venue but then decided the law firm must represent Russian government interests.

After placing a chart of the Strait of Juan de Fuca on the tabletop, Elena made the introductions. Expecting Russian operatives, Yuri was half-right. The man sitting to his right fit the profile of a typical SVR or GRU officer assigned to North American activities. In his early thirties, Tim Dixon—his cover name—was a medium-height Caucasian with a lean build and stylish brown hair.

The man sitting opposite Yuri next to Elena was the wild card. Of Asian origin, David Wang—a partial alias—spoke better English than Yuri, and Yuri was fluent. The trim mustache helped disguise his age, which Yuri guessed to be around his own—thirty years plus or minus. Wang's close-cut hair, the well-tailored suit that fit his trim physique, and his erect posture in the chair all pointed to one conclusion—military.

After making the introductions, Elena addressed Yuri. "I expect you're wondering why Mr. Wang is joining us today."

"Yes."

"For this assignment, we are working with our ally the People's Republic of China. Accordingly, Mr. Wang is representing the PRC's interest in the project."

"You should have told me about this." Yuri faced Wang. "No offense is intended to you personally, Mr. Wang, but I am not comfortable with an outsider on this mission. I want our own people."

Wang Park kept his poker face.

Elena reacted. "Mr. Dixon is here and he will assist you, along with Mr. Wang. There is no compromise on this—it comes straight from the top. We are to share all intelligence information obtained with our Chinese friends."

Yuri again addressed Wang. "What is your background?"

"I'm an officer in the People's Liberation Army-Navy, a lieutenant commander."

"Your specialty?"

"Anti-submarine warfare."

"Sea duty?"

"Multiple deployments on destroyers. One cross-training deployment with a submarine."

That got Yuri's interest. "Tell me about the sub deployment."

"I received training in submarine tactics used to evade surface ships. It was enlightening."

"I bet it was." *And a damn smart move by your superiors. Russia should do the same thing.*

Yuri continued, "What's your experience with the Russian Navy?"

"I was attached to a destroyer that made a port call to Vladivostok. We attended a banquet hosted by the base commander."

"When did that occur?"

"Four years ago—in July, as I recall."

Yuri tilted his head at Elena. "Sounds like he knows what he's doing. That'll be important out on the water." He focused on Dixon. "Have you had any sea duty?"

"Ah no . . . other than taking ferries across the English Channel a couple of times and boating on the Black Sea during a vacation."

Yuri grinned. "Better make sure you take anti-motion sickness pills. It can get rough out there," he said, pointing to the chart. "You'll be no good to us if you're puking your guts out all day long."

That lifted the icy tone of the meeting. Smiles broke out on both Wang's and Dixon's faces.

Yuri looked toward Elena. "You want to come with us? I know you've had plenty of time on the water before."

"No thank you. I'll let you gentlemen do the honors."

Facing Wang, Yuri pointed to the chart. "We'll need to transport *Deep Adventurer* by truck to the Duwamish Waterway and transfer it to the workboat."

Yuri and Wang spent the next forty minutes planning the mission.

* * *

Yuri took the elevator to the lobby solo. Elena remained in the conference room with her two associates "to coordinate," as she'd said to Yuri after the meeting concluded.

The Chinese connection was a concern. Yuri could not imagine the Fleet Intelligence Directorate going along with such an operation. Russia's penetration of the U.S. Navy's strategic crown jewel, the Trident ballistic missile submarine force, represented the pinnacle of a military intelligence operation that had been in play for years. Yuri had been right at the tip of that op.

As he took another elevator to the garage, his apprehension expanded.

There's something else going on here.

By the time he slipped into the seat of his Highlander, he had made up his mind.

I need to run this past Nick.

CHAPTER 33

DAY 20—SATURDAY

"You have a lovely home, Ms. Newman."

"Please, just Laura. And thank you, we're very comfortable here."

"Okay, Laura."

Laura just completed the house tour. It was late afternoon. Her guest was in her early forties. Slim like Laura, Sarah Compton was an inch taller. She wore a professional pantsuit with a matching tailored jacket. There was just a slight bulge under the left armpit. To the layperson, the Sig Sauer semiautomatic nine-millimeter she carried was invisible. The only reason Laura noticed was because Yuri had insisted her bodyguard be armed at all times.

"I understand you're a runner," Sarah said. Yuri had supplied background information on Laura and Madelyn.

"I like to run in the mornings before heading to the office." Laura hesitated. "Is that going to be a problem?"

"No, not at all. I'm also a runner."

"It will be nice to have company. Since Yuri will be gone, I'll be pushing Maddy in her jogging stroller, so it will be the three of us."

"Great."

"I typically leave around eight thirty. The office is about twenty minutes away—if the traffic isn't backed up on five-twenty."

"While at your office, where can I hang out—without being too conspicuous?"

"I'll set you up in an office across the hall from mine. We'll bring in a couch so you can sleep if you like."

"Thank you." Sarah would remain on duty during the late evening and early morning hours—the high threat times for home intrusions—resting only during daylight.

Laura considered the personal protection overkill. Nevertheless, she promised to abide by Yuri's request, at least for the next few days.

Sarah Compton worked for a Seattle area–based security firm that specialized in executive protection. A former U.S. Army Military Police officer, she'd been lured from her military career with a compensation package that nearly tripled her annual service pay. Her specialty was female protectorates. Sarah's services were in high demand in Silicon Valley as well as the Pacific Northwest.

"Will John be home this evening?"

"No. He's already left. He'll be away—at least a couple of days."

"Can you provide me with any additional information on the threat?"

"Nothing specific, only that an anonymous caller

warned John at his office. The caller made it clear that I was the target."

"Have you reported the call to the police?"

"No, not yet." Laura glanced down at the floor. "If we make a formal report, there will be a public record of it. The press could get hold of it—we cherish our privacy. Besides, I think it was a crank call."

"Are you sure? You have a large company, and I suspect there are one or more disgruntled ex-employees out there."

Laura met Sarah's eyes. "I suppose it's possible but Yur . . ." Laura corrected herself. "John tends to be overcautious at times. I'm sure this is nothing."

"Well, just the same, my job is to protect you and your daughter."

"I understand," Laura said, now growing weary of mixing truths with fabrications. She checked her wristwatch. "I don't feel like cooking, so I'm going to order out. Do you like Thai?"

"Very much."

Laura reached for her cell phone and called up the speed dial menu.

"Will you be ordering from a restaurant you've used before?"

"Yes. Why do you ask?"

Sarah removed an iPhone from her jacket pocket. "Please, use my phone—just in case someone is monitoring your phone. That will minimize the risk. And I'll answer the door when the delivery is made."

"Okay," Laura said, impressed with Sarah's vigilance.

CHAPTER 34

DAY 21—SUNDAY

It was an abysmal morning—just a few degrees above freezing, with negligible visibility and sporadic downpours approaching monsoon status. Swells running down the hundred-mile-long Strait of Juan de Fuca agitated the local waters.

The last gusher petered out, leaving a whisper of vapor in its wake. But somehow, the chill of the drizzle penetrated Yuri's rain gear and underlying parka. As he stood on the starboard bridge wing of the 120-foot workboat, eyes peering through the binoculars, he shivered. Although more than a year had passed since his last bout of hypothermia and decompression sickness, he wondered if his body's memory was sending him a warning.

"See anything?" asked the man standing next to Yuri.

Yuri lowered the binocs while turning to face David Wang, aka, Lieutenant Commander Wang Park. "No, it looks clear."

"Good. I didn't see anything nearby on radar, so I

think we should get started." The PRC naval officer, similarly outfitted in rubber boots and yellow rain gear, appeared unaffected by the cold.

"Let's proceed."

They had been under way since late the previous evening. After employing a dockside crane to transfer *Deep Adventurer* onto the aft main deck of the *Ella Kay*, Yuri and crew departed from the Duwamish Waterway pier and headed into Elliott Bay. The workboat headed north. They arrived at the launch site at sunrise.

Yuri and Wang, and one of Wang's assistants encased in a black neoprene wetsuit, stood on the *Ella Kay*'s deck near the stern. By their side, *Deep Adventurer* remained nestled in its cradle. Bright yellow with a twenty-foot-long by three-foot-diameter cylindrical hull, the autonomous underwater vehicle was a twin to the *Deep Explorer*, which continued its work in the Chukchi Sea.

As part of Yuri's negotiations with Elena, he had insisted that she supply the vessel. In addition to deploying the AUV, the workboat would be needed later to recover the underwater spy pods, assuming Yuri could locate them.

Commander Wang and Tim Dixon procured the *Ella Kay*, managing to charter the vessel bare-bones—without an owner-supplied crew. Dixon and the workboat's skipper, another Asian and presumed by Yuri to also be a PLAN operative, remained in the pilothouse. Despite the anti–motion sickness medication he'd taken, Dixon's belly had rebelled earlier in the morning. Still queasy and with his stomach emptied, he continued to function, impressing Yuri with his grit.

Ella Kay jogged in a wide orbit two miles northwest

of Protection Island. It was a few minutes before eight o'clock. The mile-thick mat of saturated clouds hung just five hundred feet above the water surface. The overcast concealed the steep slopes of the Olympic Mountain Range to the south. As a new near-shore shower cut loose, the shoreline several miles south-ward was a blurry smear of green and brown. To the north, across the twenty-mile-wide western limit of the Strait of Juan de Fuca, Vancouver Island and the adja-cent San Juan Islands were similarly obscured.

Yuri had been adamant with Elena about manpower. No NSD staff would be involved in the operation. Yuri emphasized security as the reason for exclusion. But his real purpose was to protect his employees. If the op went sour, no one other than Yuri would be in jeopardy with the feds.

Yuri's excuse to the NSD staff for taking *Deep Adventurer* unaccompanied was also security-based. A potential new client requested a secret demonstration dive in the Strait of Juan de Fuca. Yuri let the staff work on that morsel as they prepared the AUV. By the time *Deep Adventurer* was fine-tuned and loaded onto the semitrailer truck along with all of its ancillary gear, NSD employees were convinced that Yuri was meeting with the U.S. Navy. How ironic, Yuri had thought.

Yuri stepped to the base of the boom crane and slipped into the operator's seat. He engaged the winch and slowly reeled in the steel cable, tensioning the fore and aft nylon lifting slings wrapped under the AUV's hull.

"Ready?" he called out.

Wang gave a thumbs-up.

Deep Adventurer was afloat about ten feet from the *Ella Kay*, still attached to the lifting slings. Wang and his assistant stood by, each holding a mooring line attached to a sling strap.

Yuri stepped away from the crane and called out to Wang, "Keep holding it there! I want to run a quick check!"

Wang nodded.

Yuri now occupied a covered workstation on the main deck next to a bulkhead connecting with the cabin superstructure. He keyed the laptop, initiating a wireless transmission to *Deep Adventurer*. The diagnostic test took fifty seconds with the results displayed on the laptop's screen. The pressure hull was watertight and all systems were go.

Yuri returned to Wang's side. "Tell your man to get wet."

Within two minutes, the assistant was treading water next to *Deep Adventurer*'s bow; he worked on the forward lifting strap. He'd already released the aft connection, and Yuri had retrieved the mooring line. The forward strap disconnected and Wang reeled in his line.

Yuri faced Wang. "Tell him to swim away. I'm going to let her go now."

Wang repeated the request.

Yuri returned to the workstation and with a two-stroke keyboard command sent *Deep Adventurer* on its way.

He walked back to the port bulwark and watched the AUV surge northward, its propeller biting into the water. About half a minute later, it submerged, leaving a faint bubble trail that soon dissolved.

Satisfied with the launch, Yuri addressed Wang. "Let's get your man aboard."

"All right." Wang hesitated. "How long do you think we'll have to wait?"

"It's going to take a while. Since I don't have the exact coordinates, I've programmed *Deep Adventurer* to execute a search in the general area. The nearest pod is about twelve miles from here—that assumes the Americans never discovered it." Yuri checked his wristwatch. It was 8:22 A.M. "We might have something around sixteen hundred."

"So we wait here?"

"Yes, unless it gets really rough. Then we might need to shelter in Port Townsend."

"Okay."

It was now early afternoon. Yuri was the first to notice the jet; it was several miles away, but it flew abnormally low, especially for such a large aircraft. He picked up the binoculars and peered through the pilothouse windscreen. "Trouble," he muttered.

"What?" Wang said. He sat on the bench seat behind the helm.

Yuri pointed northward. "U.S. Navy patrol aircraft—one of their new ASW platforms."

Wang stepped forward and Yuri handed him the binoculars.

"You're right—it's a Poseidon. Must be from the naval air station."

"No doubt."

Yuri had warned both Elena and Wang about the Naval Air Station Whidbey Island. Located at the eastern end of the Strait of Juan de Fuca, it was the home to several squadrons of elite naval aircraft including P-8 Poseidon sub hunters and EA-18 Growler electronic attack jets.

"Maybe it's on a training mission," Wang offered.

"Maybe."

Yuri and Wang watched the P-8 as it turned southward and then looped eastward, heading back toward Whidbey Island. Based on the Boeing 737 airframe, the Poseidon skimmed the low-cloud ceiling, still about five hundred feet above the water surface. Then an object dropped from the fuselage. It floated downward suspended from a white parachute.

Wang uttered something in Mandarin.

Yuri didn't need a translation. "This is a huge problem. I was afraid of this."

"They must have detected your craft."

"It looks like it."

"Can they actually find it?"

"Possibly. *Deep Adventurer* is quiet, but they must have placed new sensors in the area . . ." Yuri almost added, *after we defeated their sensors the previous year.*

"If they manage to track it, what would they do?"

"*Deep Adventurer* is running a standard series of transects—mowing the lawn. Assuming they heard it—its electric drive is much quieter than any nuke— they would eventually develop a plot that would indicate a grid search." Yuri paused. "Remember seeing the word *research* that was stenciled in red paint on the hull?"

"I do."

"That was done in case there's a malfunction and it

pops to the surface. I don't want it scaring a recreational boater—thinking it's a torpedo or mine. That's also why NSD's phone number and reward notice are painted on the hull—they'll get some money if they tell us where it is. Now, if the U.S. Navy manages to snag *Deep Adventurer* and brings it to the surface, they'll likely chalk it up to a general mapping project. I'll probably get a nasty phone call but probably nothing will come of it."

"But we can't be connected to it."

"That's right. None of our legends will hold up."

"So what do we do?"

"Head to Port Townsend—slowly. I don't want to call any undue attention to ourselves while the U.S. Navy is operating in this area. We can wait there until whatever they are doing is complete. Hopefully, it's an exercise and has nothing to do with us—just our bad luck."

"That's too much of a coincidence. They must have detected your machine."

"I warned you about this scenario."

"I know." Wang was silent for half a minute before responding. "What about retrieving your craft?"

"We'll have to come back later—after dark. We can't risk being seen during recovery."

"What will the AUV do if we aren't at the coordinates when its survey is complete—you said it would return at sixteen hundred hours?"

"If we're not there at the end of its mission, *Deep Adventurer* will submerge. It will sit on the bottom and wait to be recalled."

"What about batteries—how long will they last?"

"She has very long legs, at least a week."

"Good, then we'll get it back."

"Damn right, I've got a fortune tied up in it. It's going to be recovered, one way or the other."

"Let's go."

It was now 8:35 P.M. aboard the *Ella Kay*. The workboat was eastbound in the channel between Protection Island and Cape George on the mainland. *Deep Adventurer* reoccupied its cradle, hauled out of the water fifteen minutes earlier. Under a rack of overhead floodlights, Yuri stood on the cradle's steel framing, leaning over the AUV's cylindrical hull near its forward section. He'd just opened the main access hatch and reached inside.

David Wang loitered nearby waiting for Yuri's report.

Yuri turned toward Wang. "Got it." He held up a portable hard drive, extracted from *Deep Adventurer*'s CPU.

Yuri climbed down from the cradle and stood on the desk beside Wang. "Everything should be on this drive. Let's go check it out."

Yuri and Wang went inside the cabin and sat at the galley table. Yuri inserted the data cable from the two-terabyte portable hard drive into a USB port on his Dell laptop. They waited as a proprietary program analyzed the raw data.

"How does this code work?" Wang asked.

"It's running a search for seabed rock formations that project above the bottom."

"Rocks—why?"

"The device we planted in this area of the Strait was configured as a boulder, about two meters long and just under a meter in diameter—it barely fit through the escape hatch. It was made of fiberglass. Once outside the hull we attached lead weights to it and then used a water jet to embed it into the bottom about half its diameter. From a visual perspective, you'd never know it was fake."

"Clever."

Yuri studied the output summary on the laptop's screen. He then faced Wang. "I was afraid of this. There are a hundred forty contacts in the search area, so this is going to take a while. I'm going to have to review every image."

"Fine."

Yuri opened up the photo file and began to study the color images, frame shots from the digital video stream.

He was about half through the image file when he stopped. "Well, what do we have here?"

Wang leaned forward and eyed the image. "What's that?"

"It's a listening device, but it's not one of ours."

Both men examined the mechanical apparatus. Constructed like a tripod, it jutted above the seabed about two meters. A large stainless-steel box was welded to its base plate. Greenish slime coated the entire device.

"The American Navy?" Wang asked.

"Yes. I've seen these before. This is a new one."

"Could it detect your robot?"

"Absolutely. For *Adventurer* to record this image means it was just a few meters away." Yuri paused. "Besides ASW aircraft, that naval air station on Whidbey Island is home to the U.S. Navy's sonar surveillance group. It monitors the Pacific Northwest for submarine activity. This sensor is literally in its backyard. Probably has a direct cable connection to shore."

Wang swore in Mandarin. "What do we do now?"

"Stay away from that damn thing."

"But how will you conduct the search?"

"Can't—not the way *Adventurer* is currently configured." He pointed to the image on his laptop. "That thing will pick up everything it does. This might have triggered the P-eight air search."

Wang looked away, clearly disappointed. "Can you modify your machine to improve its stealth?"

"Probably."

"How long would that take?"

Yuri raised his hands. "I don't know. A week or so."

"What?"

"It would need to be disassembled and every mechanical system tested. That can only be done at our Redmond facility."

"That's out of the question. We must proceed without the upgrade."

"No. That's not going to happen—it's too risky."

Wang stood up. Without further comment, he walked forward and passed through a hatch onto the main deck.

Yuri smiled. *It worked*.

In addition to the rock formations, Yuri had programmed *Deep Adventurer* to seek out the U.S. Navy underwater listening post. He'd found the same unit the year before during his spy mission. The Russian surveillance probe he had planted was twenty miles west of the American device and not within today's survey grid for *Deep Adventurer*.

CHAPTER 35

DAY 22—MONDAY

Yuri continued to insist they return *Deep Adventurer* to NSD's Redmond facility to make the stealth upgrades. Wang argued for conducting the search without the modifications. In the end, they compromised, settling on Anacortes.

Tim Dixon found the moorage facility. Located about seventy-five miles north of Seattle, Anacortes was famous for its commercial fishing heritage and for being the gateway to the San Juan Islands. *Ella Kay* currently occupied the seaward end of a heavy-duty floating pier that jutted over three hundred feet into Fidalgo Bay. Near Anacortes' downtown core, the privately owned moorage facility provided the security that both Yuri and Wang required.

They arrived in Anacortes early in the morning. After sleeping and having a late lunch ashore, Yuri and the others aboard rigged a plastic canvas awning over *Deep Adventurer*, sheltering it from the rain. Yuri then spent the afternoon dismantling and inspecting the AUV. Wang waited patiently.

With the assessment now complete, Yuri addressed Wang. "There's a problem with a bearing for the propeller shaft—some excessive wear that's probably generating extra noise. I'll need to replace it."

Yuri lied. The bearing was brand new, replaced before departing Redmond. Yuri shipped *Adventurer*'s original unit to Barrow as a replacement for *Deep Explorer*.

Wang responded, "Have your people get it up here. It's only a couple of hours' drive."

"I know, but that's not the problem. There are no spares in Redmond." Yuri had taken the spare bearing along with other parts for *Deep Adventurer* but tossed it overboard on the run to Anacortes.

A skeptic Wang frowned.

"We shipped all of our spares to Alaska—to Barrow. We have a huge contract up there mapping the Arctic oil spill with our other AUV."

"Surely you can get a spare from the manufacturer."

"Yes, but it's probably going to take a day or so. They're located in Germany—Hamburg."

"*Shǐ dàn!*"—Shit.

"I'll have them ship it overnight via FedEx."

"This is taking too damn long, Kirov."

"While we're waiting I can upgrade some other systems and then when the bearing gets here, she'll be ready to go—with at least a fifty percent reduction in acoustic signature. That will really help with avoiding detection."

"Just get it ordered."

"I will, but everything's closed back there now, so I'll call first thing tomorrow morning—Hamburg time."

Disgusted, Wang threw up his hands, turned, and walked forward. When he passed through the watertight door into the cabin, Yuri climbed over the workboat's starboard bulwark and stepped onto the floating dock. He worked his way shoreward.

After walking up the aluminum gangway Yuri stood in the parking area. Floodlights illuminated the uplands; dozens of large yachts were stored in the gravel yard, secured by chain-link fencing along the property lines. He checked his wristwatch: 5:26 P.M. *He should be on his way home now.*

Yuri reached into a coat pocket and removed his cell. He hit the speed dial. After the third ring he heard, "Hello."

"Can you talk?"

"Yes," Nick Orlov said. He was sitting on a San Francisco cable car eastbound on California.

Switching to Russian, Yuri said, "What have you got for me?"

Yuri had checked in with Nick just prior to leaving Seattle for the voyage north.

"You were right. She's up to something."

"What?"

"I don't know. I made a couple of inquiries in Vancouver and Vladivostok. I confirmed she's on some type of op concerning the Chinese, but none of my contacts had any details. That's not surprising because everything's compartmentalized regarding our so-called new alliance with the PRC."

"Then what she's doing up here could be legit?"

"That's the issue. She shouldn't be in Seattle. My Vancouver contact told me that when Elena left the trade mission she was supposed to head back to Vladivostok and then on to China for more trade talks. But she never showed up."

"She came here instead."

"So it seems."

"I don't like this. Something's off."

"I agree. So what are you doing?"

"Trying to stall Wang, but he's getting suspicious." Yuri remembered something else. "What about Dixon, you find anything on him?"

"Nothing under that name, even as a cover. But that's not unusual if he's operating in the States—he could have a very deep legend."

"Yeah, I thought so. He seems okay but I can't trust him."

"How's Laura?"

"She's fine. I talked with her earlier today. The bodyguard shadows her at all times, even while at work."

"That's good." Nick hesitated for an instant. "Maybe Elena's op is real and she's been ordered to pressure you into cooperating. You know how our system works."

"Maybe, but threatening Laura to get to me is too much."

"Yes, that is concerning . . ." Nick had a memory flash. "That reminds me. There's been absolutely no chatter about you in our system. Nothing about you being spotted. You're still officially listed as missing."

"Somebody high up must know, otherwise who would have authorized Elena's op?"

"True. Still I find it odd that there's nothing in our system about it."

"Please keep digging, Nick. I don't like Wang, and our so-called joint mission with PRC doesn't feel right to me. And Elena—you know she and Laura didn't get along. I think that might be affecting her judgment."

"I'm staying on it. We're trying to track down Wang, and a colleague in Moscow is discreetly checking on Elena for me."

"Call me when you have something."

"I will."

"Thank you, my friend."

When the cable car reached the end of the line, Nick Orlov stepped onto the street. As he made his way toward the ferry terminal, his discussion with Yuri remained fresh.

Nick's two-week fling with Elena Krestyanova the year before was something he was unlikely to forget. The sex was simply astounding; Elena was an accomplished lover, no doubt part of her training in the SVR.

Nick had genuinely enjoyed Elena's company but there was another side to her character that had vexed him. She followed orders explicitly with ruthless efficiency and no mercy. There was no question in Nick's mind that if he had not intervened, Elena would have disposed of Laura as mandated by Moscow.

Now, considering the current circumstances, Nick wondered if the orders from a year earlier had been reissued.

CHAPTER 36

"Why do you believe he's stalling?" asked Kwan Chi.

"He keeps delaying. I don't trust him."

Kwan noticed the frustration in Commander Wang's voice as he stood alone on the *Yangzi*'s port bridge wing. It was a brisk forty-two degrees Fahrenheit on the exterior deck. "He's Russian. Of course you can't trust him."

Both men employed portable encrypted satellite phones to communicate with each other. A team of cryptanalysts at the MSS's Beijing Communications Bureau developed the encryption algorithms, which remained unbreakable so far.

Kwan continued. "However, he did deploy his underwater machine and it located the American listening device. That's certainly helpful."

"Yes, it is. But we're no closer to recovering the monitoring pods. They are critical to our needs." Wang remained in Anacortes.

"When will you restart the survey?"

"It will probably be at least two days, maybe three."

"Why so long?"

"Kirov says it's too risky to deploy the AUV without reducing its acoustic signature."

Wang spent the next couple of minutes repeating Yuri's storyline.

"Hamburg—can't they get it from someplace closer?" Kwan asked.

"He claims no. The propulsion unit is German-made, so I can see the need to use the same manufacturer for the bearing."

"Perhaps he's just being cautious about the Americans. They did send out one of their patrol aircraft. The sensor must have detected the AUV."

"It's possible, but I don't think replacing the bearing is going to reduce its signature. My assistant told me the machine is already quite stealthy. He's operated our own units and indicated Kirov's vehicle is vastly superior. Besides, he also examined the propeller assembly and the bearing—they appeared undamaged to him."

"Can you operate the machine without his assistance?"

"Not yet. My assistant needs more time with the unit to figure out its control and monitoring functions. Plus, Kirov has a proprietary program that he uses to analyze the data. That alone will take time to understand."

"All right. I'll work on it from here."

"Thank you, sir."

"One more thing, Wang."

"Sir?"

"Keep Kirov under surveillance. If he is up to something, I want to know about it."

"Yes, sir."

Kwan Chi switched off the satphone and slipped it into his jacket pocket. It was late evening in Seattle. He peered forward into the shadows. A sentry manned the bow station, about twenty-five meters away.

Standing next to the anchor capstan, the MSS operator monitored the adjacent floating pier for the occasional marina patron that hoofed down the pier to eye the *Yangzi*. He also watched the bay for any waterborne interlopers. Clipped to the left side of his belt was a .40-caliber semiautomatic pistol. A similarly armed guard occupied a post at the yacht's stern.

Kwan turned toward the south. The view of the Space Needle, bathed in floodlights, and Seattle's mountain range of radiant high-rises was notable. But it was a mere sideshow compared to his hometown's skyline. At night, Hong Kong's core was ultra electric.

Kwan pulled out a cigarette pack and lit up. Addicted as a teenager like millions of other Chinese mainlanders, he enjoyed smoking. It helped with stress. And this mission was particularly stressful.

The report from Lieutenant Commander Wang ratcheted up Kwan's anxiety another notch. Despite Wang's youthful looks, he was a seasoned military intelligence officer with an untarnished record of successful foreign operations. Because Wang worried the Russian naval officer might be playing them, Kwan now worried, too. But what should he do?

When the cigarette's smoldering tip neared the filter, Kwan made the decision. *Yes, that should get his attention.* He flipped the butt, watching it arc into the water.

Kwan checked his wristwatch. *They should be just*

about done by now. He returned to the bridge and stepped aft into another compartment that connected with the elevator.

On the lower deck, he walked into the yacht's garage. The aft compartment housed the yacht's watercraft—jet skis, runabout, tender, and other toys. But this afternoon it took delivery of a massive timber crate from a harbor workboat.

Several technicians milled around the open lid of the shipping box. Inside was a black steel cylinder three quarters of a meter in diameter and seven meters long. When it was airfreighted to Seattle from Shanghai two days earlier, the U.S. Customs and Border Patrol inspector approved entry of the high-pressure containment vessel with just a cursory examination. The bill of lading listed a refinery in Ferndale, Washington, as the recipient.

Kwan approached the engineer in charge. "What's the status?" he asked.

"We ran a preliminary diagnostic check on the propulsion unit. It checks out. We'll be making additional tests on the navigation and sensor units."

The engineer held a thick wad of papers.

"That the manual?" Kwan asked.

"Yes, sir." He handed over the bound report. The text was in Cyrillic and there were dozens of diagrams.

"You must be fluent in Russian?"

"I am, sir."

Kwan returned the report.

"The warhead is on its way. You'll have it tomorrow morning."

"Very good, sir."

"Carry on."

"Yes, sir."

The PLAN mission planners judged it too risky to ship the warhead with the unit. CBP sniffers might detect the explosives. Instead, it was sent to the PRC's San Francisco consulate under diplomatic seal aboard an Air China charter. Two security officers were currently northbound on Interstate Five in a Ford van. A single crate four feet square occupied the cargo compartment.

Once the warhead was mated with the delivery body, the torpedo mine would be reassembled. It had been purchased from the Russian mafia for $2 million. The MSS considered the acquisition of the Mark 12 *Gadjúka*—Viper—a bargain.

Kwan Chi returned to his stateroom on the upper deck. There was nothing more he could do this evening. The mission had its own momentum. The best he could do was to nudge it along.

He relaxed in the elegant bathroom's soaking tub, where multiple jets needled and massaged his spine and shoulders. The previous evening, he and Elena had spent time together in the same chamber. That was nice, Wang thought, recalling how inventive Elena could be, especially after three glasses of wine.

He looked forward to their next hookup.

With a voracious appetite, Kwan had a stable of sex partners to call upon when he traveled throughout China and East Asia. In Hong Kong, his corporate center and his principal residence, Zhu Jia was his favorite lover. Just thirty-three, Ms. Zhu ran her own advertising agency, which thrived as mainland China's evolving middle class clamored to catch up with the West's insatiable demand for consumer goods.

Introduced by the wife of a business associate at a party, Chi took an instant liking to the beautiful and gracious Jia. She was equally attracted and they soon became regular partners. In concert with the sex, Kwan genuinely enjoyed Jia's company. She was both "lovely and good," embodying the meaning of her given name.

Kwan had considered marriage before he learned Jia was barren. Rendered sterile after a battle with uterine cancer as a college student, survivor Jia had focused all of her energy on building her business rather than a family.

Kwan had plenty of time to wed should the opportunity arise. Both of his older brothers had families—with sons, which satisfied generational pressures. Nevertheless, his mother remained relentless in her campaign for her youngest to produce offspring.

Kwan smiled as he envisioned the reaction he would receive from his mother if he brought Elena Krestyanova to Hangzhou for a family visit.

CHAPTER 37

DAY 23—TUESDAY

"That's great news, Bill. Tell the boys I'm proud of 'em."

"Will do, boss."

Yuri was on his cell phone in Anacortes, standing on a floating pier near the *Ella Kay* in the early afternoon. Bill Winters was on the other end of the circuit in Barrow. Bill had just provided Yuri with a progress report.

"By the way, when will you be coming up?" asked Bill.

"Maybe next week, once I get through this test program."

"Great, I could use your help." Bill shifted gears. "When will you be able to tell us more about this mysterious prospective customer?"

Yuri detested lying but continued the deceit. "I had to sign a confidentiality agreement, so I'm hamstrung. If it comes together I can reveal what's going on."

"Can you at least tell me how the *Adventurer* is doing . . . she holding up?"

"Except for the bearing, she's fine."

Yuri had mentioned the bogus bearing issue to Bill, perpetuating the charade.

"That just doesn't make sense to me . . . going out so quickly like that. Must have been a flawed bearing."

"I agree. I chewed on the manufacturer's rep this morning about it. Lucky for me he spoke English."

"I hope it doesn't screw up your test demo."

"As long as it gets here in the next day or so, we should be okay." Yuri hesitated. "I assume the bearing we sent you is working out."

"Yes, it's fine, and our spares are perfect, too."

"Great."

"Okay, good luck with your trial run. Talk to you later."

"See you."

Yuri ended the call and began walking back to the workboat. Thankfully, the rain had stopped. He'd already completed tinkering with *Deep Adventurer*, making minor adjustments to improve its stealth. None of the changes were necessary; they were part of his other charade to buy more time.

Having been summoned to Seattle for a meeting, Wang took off around ten o'clock. He provided no details, only that he would return the following morning. Dixon and Wang's assistant remained aboard the *Ella Kay* to support Yuri with the repairs. Yuri figured they were watchdogs.

Laura and Madelyn were fine; he'd chatted with Laura at noon. That was a relief. Even so, he remained antsy. Yuri had not yet heard back from Nick, and he could only bluff Wang so far and then he'd have to resume the search.

* * *

With Laura Newman in the passenger seat, Sarah Compton guided the jet-black GMC Yukon Denali down the asphalt driveway and into the parking court of Laura's hillside home. Other than the perimeter lights, it was black outside.

Laura had wanted to take her BMW when they left in the mornings for work, but Sarah insisted on driving her vehicle. The modified four-door SUV had bullet-resistant windows all around, Kevlar-lined doors, body panels, and roof, and tires that if punctured could run on solid rubber cores. Powered by an enhanced V-8 generating over five hundred horsepower and equipped with a beefed-up suspension, "the Beast," as Sarah referred to the Denali, could accelerate like a rocket ship and turn on a whim.

The Beast belonged to the company that employed Sarah. It came as part of the complete Executive Protection Package, set up by Yuri with the firm's owner.

With Laura remaining inside, Sarah stepped out of the Denali onto the parking court's concrete pavers. She used her smart key to lock the SUV's doors. The engine idled but was barely audible due to the armoring. She heard a dog yelping to her left down the hill. She made a quick three-sixty. Nothing.

Sarah now faced the driveway. When arriving, she drove the SUV around the circular court to align it with the asphalt drive. The headlights illuminated the road; it led back to the public street about a hundred feet away. If a threat developed, Sarah could jump in and blast off.

Sarah took her time surveying the perimeter, looking for trouble. Finally, she walked back to the Denali and opened the driver's door. "All clear," she announced.

"Great."

As Laura stepped out, Sarah activated the Denali's automatic rear door-hatch opener and shut down the engine.

Once in the kitchen, Laura parked Maddy in her carrier on the table; she was awake, her eyes following her mother's movements. Half a dozen grocery bags from Whole Foods were stacked on a counter. Laura needed to restock the fridge and pantry.

Laura was busy unpacking supplies when she removed the carton of gourmet hot cocoa mix. She turned toward Sarah, who stood nearby helping to empty the bags. Holding up the box, Laura said, "I'm going to have a cup of cocoa. Would you like one?"

"That would be wonderful."

Acting on orders issued by Kwan Chi, the four-man team huddled together in the back of the heavy-duty Ford van. Parked two blocks away from the Newman residence, they all wore headphones and stared at twin side-by-side thirty-inch computer monitors. The screens displayed live video feeds from ten cameras. Earlier in the afternoon, two from the team spent almost an hour inside the residence installing and concealing six audio-video bugs. Four additional cameras, each with infrared capability, were positioned around the exterior of the home.

They observed Laura offer Sarah a cup of cocoa. So far, Lieutenant Commander Wang Park was favorably impressed with the bodyguard. They would need to take exceptional care when dealing with her.

Yuri and Nick connected a few minutes before ten o'clock. Nick called from his floating home in Sausalito. Yuri remained in Anacortes. With the wireless connection still live, Yuri exited the workboat's main cabin. He stood on the floating dock, near the shore. His watchers remained aboard the *Ella Kay*. Dixon was in the cabin watching television, but Wang's assistant had relocated to the pilothouse. It was high enough above the water to allow the PLAN operative to keep an eye on Yuri.

"All right, I can talk," Yuri said, speaking in Russian.

"Sorry to be getting back to you so late." Yuri had left three voice mail messages for Nick. "But I was in meetings all afternoon and then a cocktail reception with the consulate general." Too tired to bother with his normal commute, Nick commandeered a pool car and drove across the Golden Gate into Marin County and then home.

"I understand." Yuri tried to calm himself. His angst had swelled all evening. "Have you learned anything new?"

"Nothing concrete at this point. I can't find anything about Elena's specific operation, but I did confirm with a second source that she's working the China Desk."

"How about my cover—any changes there?"

"No. There's still nothing about your resurrection." Nick hesitated. "Believe me, if that got out, someone would leak it. They'd earn a fat paycheck from the Western press."

Yuri could see the headlines too: RUSSIAN SPY SUB HERO HIDING IN USA. And then the media vultures would pounce on Laura: MILLIONAIRE LOVER PROTECTS SPY.

"Okay," Yuri said, "at least I don't have to worry about that—yet. Any news on Dixon or the PLAN officer?"

"Still nothing on Dixon, but I did get a hit on this David Wang character. First of all, you wouldn't believe how many Wangs there are. But when you told me his ship supposedly made a port visit to Vladivostok in July four years ago, I checked. A PLAN ship did visit the port and there was in fact a banquet."

"So he was there?"

"Someone named Wang Park with the rank of lieutenant was aboard. I got a copy of a souvenir photo taken of the event. It's decent quality. I'm texting it to you now."

Yuri waited until the image flashed onto the screen of his cell. He zoomed in and examined the faces. "That's him."

"I took a chance it was the right guy and ran him through our system. The GRU has a file on him. He's Navy but for the last three years, he's had shore duty. He's attached to a special naval operations unit based out of Shanghai."

"What kind of unit?"

"*Zhongdui*—similar to our naval Spetsnaz."

Yuri moaned. "He's not just a sailor, is he?"

"I'm afraid not. You need to watch out for him."

"*Govnó!*"

CHAPTER 38

DAY 24—WEDNESDAY

They waited until 0345 hours before making entry. The high-end security system was nothing more than a nuisance to the team. During the first penetration in the afternoon, they disabled the system within just twenty seconds. The name of the alarm monitoring company was prominently displayed on placards placed around the house. Using a smartphone, they consulted a cloud-stored file that listed various types of equipment used by the alarm company and a host of other security-alarm providers. The People's Republic of China manufactured the electronic monitoring components for many alarm systems, including the target residence. To remain operating, those mainland manufacturers "voluntarily" provided the bypass codes to the MSS. The secret practice had been in place for decades.

Commander Wang and his two companions reentered on the ground floor—a daylight basement—picking the lock of a door that opened to the backyard. Already familiar with the house, they headed up the stairway to the first floor. Black-clad in assault gear with POLICE stenciled in reflective letters on the jacket back, each man carried a suppressed compact submachine gun.

The fourth *zhongdui* team member remained in the van monitoring the spy cameras. He was in direct voice contact with Wang and the others, employing an encrypted short-range radio system.

"Status report," Wang whispered in Mandarin into his voice-activated boom microphone.

His earbud activated. "Primary remains in room six. Secondary is active but remains in room three."

"What activity?" Wang asked.

"Reading."

Doesn't she ever sleep? Wang knew the second target was the immediate concern. They had been waiting for the bodyguard to climb into her bed. Yet she remained fully clothed, except for her shoes. For most of the night, she'd circulated throughout the vast home, checking door locks and windows, and monitoring the alarm system. About twenty minutes earlier, she'd relocated to the bedroom, where she currently sat in a chair by the window reading. Running out of darkness, Wang elected to proceed.

They were on the main floor next to an elegant stairway that led to the second floor and all of the bedrooms.

Wang hand-signaled to his men.

The two gunmen advanced up the stairway, one after the other.

They were now huddled outside the doorway to room three, both squatting. The man nearest the room trained his weapon on the closed door. His companion was busy studying the screen on his smartphone.

Wang, still at the base of the stairway, monitored the same video image. The secondary sat in a chair by the bed reading. "Proceed," he whispered.

Sarah Compton heard the click of the doorknob as it turned. Startled, she launched herself out of her chair in a flash. She reached for her pistol just as the door swung open.

The first hollow-point hit with sledgehammer impact. The nine-millimeter round blossomed to twice its diameter after smashing through a rib under the right breast. The mushroomed mass of copper and lead shredded a lung before embedding itself in the spine. The next missile plowed into the belly, obliterating the spleen and part of the colon. The third bullet from the sound-suppressed burst clipped a kidney and exited through her back, smacking into a dresser packed with linen and spare blankets.

Sarah buckled to the floor.

Wang rejoined his companions. The secondary remained on the floor, huddled into a fetal position on her right side. She moaned. Her tortured rasp was the product of the shattered lung and the unmitigated agony erupting from the lacerated bowel. Blood continued to drain from the wounds, leaking onto the oak flooring. A pungent coppery scent mixed with the stink of gunpowder flooded the room.

Wang stared at the hapless victim. The bodyguard was a worthy opponent, but she'd had no chance—by Wang's design. She might survive if they provided first aid; all three were trained medics. However, his orders were unequivocal.

Wang stepped next to Sarah Compton's side, taking care to avoid the pooling blood. He lowered the barrel of his weapon to her temple. He ended her misery with a single round.

Wang looked up, facing his charges. "Time for the primary," he whispered.

Laura lay on her left side with knees slightly bent. Madelyn was in a crib next to the bed, just a few feet away. In the dimness, she could see Maddy bundled in her pajamas. Her daughter's breathing was steady, a soft reassuring purr to Laura's ears.

With Yuri gone, she wanted Maddy close by. He slept with a light ear, always the first to wake when Madelyn fussed. Yuri would rise and check Madelyn, changing a diaper and warming a bottle as needed—a true blessing to Laura.

Laura had been awakened five minutes earlier, but not by Maddy. For what seemed like hours, she was back at Caltech inside a crowded classroom struggling with a physics test she had not prepared for. Just as the proctor's cell phone alarm went off, announcing "time's up," Laura woke. She'd relived the same dream dozens of times since graduating.

Reassured to be back in the present world and knowing she'd actually aced the exam, Laura closed her eyes and took a deep breath, hoping for another hour or two of sleep.

Still conscious, she heard the single creak. One of the bedroom's oak floorboards by the doorway had delaminated. It was scheduled to be repaired later in the month.

Laura turned to her right and started to sit up.

Before she could utter a word, a black hulk smothered her body, clamping her mouth shut and pinning her gyrating form to the mattress with its bulk. Almost instantaneously, something lanced her neck, an arctic spike that surged to her brain in a lightning burst.

And then nothing.

CHAPTER 39

Standing beside the bed, Wang scrutinized the primary as the assault team stood nearby. She lay unconscious, knocked out with a syringe-delivered sedative laced with ketamine and other downers.

He trained the barrel-mounted light from his SMG on Laura Newman. Her predominant Nordic facial features and shoulder-length auburn hair caught Wang's eye. Clad in a pajama top and panties, her long, lean, and curvy form was a stirring sight. Her chocolate complexion came as a surprise. He was not aware of Laura's biracial heritage.

Wang addressed his charges, "Bind her and then take her downstairs."

"What about the child?" asked one of the *zhongduis*.

"I'll take care of it."

The two men leaned over the bed and slipped a pair of plastic flex cuffs over Laura's wrists and ankles, tugging both sets of cable ties tight. They hauled her to their side of the bed. One of the operators grasped Laura's torso with his arms and in a fluid motion pulled her up, placing her abdomen across a shoulder. With

Laura's head and arms hanging over his back, he gripped her thighs with an arm. He carried her downstairs, his partner following.

Wang remained in the bedroom, relocating to the crib. The child continued to sleep. The decision was his; Kwan did not care either way.

The Ford van was waiting in the darkened carport. Laura was loaded into the cargo bay, a blanket used to conceal her presence. Standing beside the open rear door of the van, Wang handed the portable carrier to the man who had hauled Laura downstairs.

Wang said, "She remains asleep, but will likely awaken soon."

The commando stared at Madelyn, unsure of his orders. His nose flared, catching a ripe odor.

Wang smiled. "She needs a diaper change."

The commando's jaw dropped in horror.

Wang opened an oversize maternity bag he carried with his other hand. "I found this in the bedroom. It has diapers and other items for the child." He unzipped the top of the container and pointed to a pair of bottles filled with an off-white fluid. "These were in the refrigerator in the kitchen. Probably her mother's milk."

The operator's eyes blossomed. "But what do I do . . . I've never—"

Wang cut him off. "Relax. When you arrive, just give these to Zu Peng. She will take over."

He shifted his stance, obviously relieved.

"Go ahead and take off."

"Yes, sir."

As the van pulled away, Wang used his cell phone

to check on the standby recovery unit. The janitors were ten minutes out.

With the other remaining *zhongdui* standing watch in the carport, Wang returned to the secondary's room. He rifled through a compact purse he found on the bedroom dresser. Besides the driver's license and the usual credit cards and cash, he discovered a color snapshot of a fortyish male with two young children—boys—sitting in his lap.

Wang wondered if they were the secondary's family. Although the ruthless nature of his business had become commonplace, the photograph did not sit well with Wang. He wished that he'd left the wallet alone.

Wang removed Sarah Compton's pistol and her other gear and personal effects from the room, stuffing them inside a canvas bag he always carried on ops.

The two-man recovery team arrived as scheduled in another Ford van. They slipped the corpse inside a black heavy-duty plastic body bag and zipped it shut. The men dragged the container down the stairs to the first floor and loaded it into the van.

After recovering the victim, the janitors attacked the kill zone with practiced efficiency. They used a mini-vacuum to extract the partially congealed blood from the hardwood flooring. Wang and the other shooter had already policed their spent casings.

The cleanup crew extracted a slug from an oak strip in the bedroom floor, left over from Wang's kill shot. They injected a fast-setting epoxy resin into the cavity. A color additive in the resin, mixed on the spot by one of the janitors to match the floorboard color, partially concealed the bullet hole.

After recovering the spent bullet inside a blanket in

the dresser, the janitors repaired the entry penetration. They also removed the blanket and other linen torn by the errant round.

None of the repairs or cleanup procedures would defeat a determined forensic team. Their sole purpose was to buy time.

When the cleanup team completed its work, just before dawn, Wang released them. The janitors' next task was to drive the van to a mortuary in Seattle. The owner, already alerted, would be waiting alone for their arrival. The Chinese immigrant was on call for special duty like today. The welfare of his family members still in China guaranteed his cooperation. He would cremate the corpse on arrival.

After the janitors departed, Wang and the remaining operator removed the monitoring cameras and completed one last check of the house. One of the janitors had disabled the GMC's GPS tracking unit, rendering the vehicle's onboard navigation and digital communication system electronically impotent.

Satisfied, they drove away in the Denali, using Compton's smart key to start the vehicle.

CHAPTER 40

"We were forced to accelerate matters. I need your assistance now."

"You want me to come to Seattle—today?"

"Yes, this can't be done over the phone."

Elena Krestyanova was astounded that Kwan Chi had risked calling her at the trade mission. Russia's increasing belligerence over tensions in the Arctic had sparked a new round of electronic communications snooping by the RCMP.

Elena glanced at the digital clock on her cell phone: 8:25 A.M. Her meeting with the chief of mission was about to start. She sat in the conference room alone waiting for his arrival and the other staff members to show up for the meeting.

"I can leave at noon," Elena said.

"You can't leave now?"

"No, that's impossible."

"Very well, come to me."

"Same place?"

"Yes, we're still there."

Elena switched off her cell. She took half a minute

to think through the significance of the call and then it jelled.

Yuri Kirov—he's up to something!

"I know something's wrong," Yuri said. He stood on *Ella Kay*'s aft deck, staring at the waters of Fidalgo Bay. It was 10:35 A.M. in Anacortes. "I've called the house and both of their cell phones all morning long but all I get is voice mail. They never made it to the office. I just spoke with Laura's assistant. She's heard nothing from her this morning. Laura had a staff meeting scheduled for ten, which she missed. And that never happens!"

"I understand your concern, Mr. Kirkwood," said the CEO of the security firm. "I'm going to dispatch two of our operatives to the house right now."

"When will they get there?"

"Half an hour."

"Tell them to call me direct—on this line."

"I will."

Yuri returned the smartphone to his pants pocket. *Something's wrong, I just know it.*

His stomach roiled as a deep veil of despair engulfed his being.

This is Elena's work!

Lieutenant Commander Wang Park and his driver were northbound on Interstate Five in a Toyota 4Runner at 1:50 P.M. They were about an hour away from Anacortes. The rush of the op had long since dissolved, but he still fretted about an esoteric detail.

By now, Wang expected that the armored SUV had been loaded into a steel shipping container and was probably stacked up in one of the Port of Seattle's terminals ready to be loaded aboard the ship. The Chinese shipping company's website reported the ship would sail for Shanghai tomorrow morning at seven.

Wang wondered how the recipient in the MSS's Beijing headquarters would react to the gift. Kwan Chi had made the arrangements. If it had been up to Wang, he would have shipped the "Beast" to South America.

Wang Park shifted his thoughts from the predawn assault to Yuri Kirov. The Russian intelligence officer remained elusive and unpredictable. Wang worried that Kwan Chi might have been too aggressive with the immediate action. Kidnapping the man's lover and her child would without doubt gain his attention. But would that extreme measure also result in his improved cooperation?

Wang wondered if he had been too rash in his judgment that Kirov was stalling. Maybe he'd missed something and the underwater machine really needed repairs. But then he remembered the technician's report. There was nothing wrong with the AUV.

Wang dismissed his misgivings. He would follow his orders as trained.

Born thirty-two years earlier in a village two hundred miles northwest of Beijing, Wang Park was the product of China's grand experiment—the one-child family. Doted on by his proud peasant parents—especially his mother—Park performed exceptionally well in elementary school. Alerted by his teacher, the local Communist Party official began following young Park's progress.

Most of Wang's graduating senior middle school classmates were destined for the farms. A lucky minority received permission to move to the burgeoning urban centers to take construction and manufacturing jobs. The elite attended colleges and universities with the requirement that they would fill Party-controlled positions in business, government, and military.

The Party official selected the People's Liberation Army-Navy for Wang Park. After four years of academy-level training, Wang graduated as an ensign in the PLAN. For several years, he served as a line officer with sea duty aboard several combat vessels before earning a command position with China's naval special forces—*zhongdui*.

For the past several years, Lieutenant Commander Wang and his detachment of seaborne commandos had conducted numerous clandestine operations throughout the Pacific Rim. Sea Dragon was his most complex and dangerous assignment by a wide margin.

Wang embraced the challenge with gusto and fierce determination—following the lead set by his mentors, instructors, and commanding officers. War with America was coming. Sea Dragon would provide the time China needed to prepare for and win that war.

CHAPTER 41

Laura woke up lying on her right side atop a bed. She tried to prop herself up with an arm but discovered her wrists were bound in front; ditto for the ankles.

"What's going on?" she muttered, still lying on her side. Laura had no concept of how long she was unconscious or how she ended up in the bed.

Then the nightmare replayed in a memory burst. Barely able to move under the attacker's bulk, Laura had just started to twist her torso in an attempt to break his grip when a searing sting erupted in the side of her neck.

Maddy, where's Maddy?

Laura struggled to sit up, using her bound arms as a strut. She surveyed the windowless enclosure. About ten feet square, it was a sterile white environment with a single overhead light fixture. The bunk butted against one wall. Several feet from the foot of the bed was a half-open door to what appeared to be a compact bathroom. Along the wall opposite the bed was a built-in desk with an empty bookshelf above and a single chair in front. At the far end of that wall was a closed door with a digital keypad above the lock.

Laura slipped her legs over the edge. She stood, leaning against the bunk—her ankles tied together. Still groggy, she took a deep breath before bunny-hopping across the hardwood floor to the door. She pulled on the handle with her lashed hands, but the door remained locked. That's when she put it together. *This is some kind of a lockup.*

Laura slammed the palms of her wrists against steel door. She shouted, "Open this door! What have you done with my baby!?"

Yuri watched the Cessna 180 as it taxied across the placid waters of Fidalgo Bay. The seaplane powered up to the floating dock and the engine stopped. The pilot opened a door on the fuselage's left side and stepped down onto the aluminum flotation pontoon. After securing the pontoon to the floating pier, the pilot stepped up onto the pier. She wore khaki trousers and a stylish blouse with captain epaulets on the shoulders.

"Hello," Yuri said.

"Mr. Kirkwood?"

"Yes."

"Hi. I'm Jennifer." The thirty-four-year-old charter pilot offered her right hand.

Yuri accepted the handshake.

"Do you have any luggage?"

"No, it's just me."

"Great, then why don't we get started?"

"Okay."

Just as Yuri stepped onto the pontoon, Tim Dixon

rushed down the dock. "Where are you going?" he called out.

"Seattle—I have business to take care of."

"David Wang's on his way. He'll be here in half an hour."

"Tell him to call me on my cell." Yuri turned and climbed into the cabin.

Dixon remained on the dock, clearly annoyed.

Jennifer released the mooring lines, reclaimed the command seat, and started the engine.

As the floatplane cruised away from the dock at high idle, Jennifer turned to face her passenger in the adjacent seat. "Please make sure your lap and shoulder belts are fastened. Feel free to use the headphones if you like—it can get loud in here. There are also earplugs in the side pocket."

Jennifer next went over additional safety items.

Yuri buckled up. He raised his voice over the din and said, "How long will this take?"

"About fifty minutes."

"Great."

Yuri stared through the windshield as the Cessna passed over the town of La Conner, headed southward across Skagit Bay. He avoided the headphones, not wanting the distraction of listening to the radio traffic chatter. The earplugs helped attenuate the power plant's persistent drone.

Yuri ignored the scenery. Instead, he weighed his options.

Sarah Compton's supervisor called Yuri from the Sammamish residence. With all doors locked and windows closed, there were no visible break-in points. The Yukon Denali was missing. Yuri told the supervisor where Laura hid the spare key for the front door. He also provided the code to disarm the security alarm.

After checking every room, the supervisor reported to Yuri that all appeared normal inside the home and Laura's BMW remained in the garage.

Later the security company implemented a GPS search for the Yukon but came up short. That was an ominous sign. It meant that the automatic interrogation system installed on the company-owned vehicle was purposely disabled or the Yukon had suffered catastrophic damage.

A car crash would explain everything. With the vehicle's electronics smashed, the GPS system would be out of commission. If Laura and her bodyguard were injured, they might not be able to use their cell phones. That scenario terrified Yuri.

But the security company quashed that horror later in the afternoon. A check with the Washington State Patrol and every emergency room along the I-5 corridor from Bellingham to Olympia revealed no serious vehicle accidents.

That's when Yuri finally put it together—his ultimate nightmare. Elena's allies had discovered his stall tactics. To bring him back on mission, they kidnapped Laura and the bodyguard—and Maddy!

The unannounced departure in the floatplane was the first element of his rescue plan.

Laura held Maddy as she suckled. Sitting on the bunk, Laura leaned against the wall with her legs stretched out. Her hands were free, but her ankles remained lashed together.

Reunited with her child just minutes earlier, Laura was so relieved that she wanted to cry. Yet she held the tears. Instead, she had demanded answers from the woman who'd carried Madelyn into the room but learned nothing.

The guard sat in the chair opposite the bed staring at the screen of a smartphone. Just an inch or so over five feet tall with a petite build, Laura's minder wore a cobalt blue jumpsuit and a pair of deck shoes. A black ski mask covered her head from neck to crown. Through the slits, Laura noted the woman's dark eyes and un-madeup lips.

"What do you want from me?" Laura said. She'd asked this before.

The guard ignored Laura.

She was about to ask another question when there was a loud rap from outside. The guard stood up, walked to the door, and entered a code into the electronic key lock. She pulled open the door.

A male entered, wearing a similar uniform with a ski mask. He carried the current edition of the *Seattle Times* in his right hand.

The two spoke, but not in English.

Chinese! Laura thought, recognizing the dialect.

CHAPTER 42

"She's here—aboard the *Yangzi*?"

"Yes, in a cabin below."

"What about her child?"

"She's here, too."

It was 3:40 P.M. Elena Krestyanova had just arrived. She and Kwan Chi were in the main deck's plush salon sitting on side-by-side sofas. The lounge was spacious with an unassuming Asian design that employed contrasting azure and earth tones to create a welcoming environment.

They were alone. Kwan had ordered all staff not to enter the compartment until his meeting was over.

"Does he know?" Elena asked.

"Not officially, but I'm sure he suspects something."

"Why?"

"He took off this afternoon in a floatplane, left his machine and our people without any explanation."

"Where is he?"

"We don't know. He chartered the plane and it headed south. The charter company would not release any information on the flight. We expect it landed on the lake near here."

"Have you tried his cell?" Elena said, reaching for a glass of water on an adjacent side table.

"Yes, we thought we might be able to track him, but he's turned it off."

"Or he has another phone." She took a sip.

"Yes, that, too."

"So you have no way of contacting him other than his cell."

"Correct."

"What can I do?"

"First call his cell and leave a voice mail that it is urgent you speak with him tonight. Then call his company and leave the same message with his secretary."

"They don't know me there, so why—"

Kwan cut her off. "All you have to say is that it concerns Laura Newman. He will call you back."

Elena shifted her legs. "What do you want me to say to him? And keep in mind that whatever I say he's going to be hostile."

"Follow the same script you've been using. Blame the SVR and the FSB, say they are running the operation and you're just the messenger."

"Yes, he'll believe that but he's still going to blame me—I found him and I threatened to expose Newman." She took another sip and returned the glass to the tabletop.

"All you have to say is that if he gives up his stalling tactics and completes the mission, he and his woman will be left alone—Russia will never bother him again, his duty as an officer would be complete. You can also stress that once the recording pods are retrieved his unique services would no longer be required so there would be no incentive for Russia to try to pull him back in again. If he wants, tell him he can return to Russia at any time to a hero's welcome."

Elena sat quietly on the sofa, taking in Kwan's script. It made sense. One last push and she'd secure the balance of her fee. Still, there were things to tie up.

"What does Laura Newman know about the current situation?"

"Nothing. My operatives removed her and her child from the residence early this morning."

"Any problems?"

"None." He neglected to mention the bodyguard's fate.

"You know he's going to want proof that they're okay."

"Of course. You can send him proof." Kwan produced his cell phone and activated the screen. He handed it to Elena.

The photograph was in color; Laura Newman sat on a bed, her legs bare but her torso covered in a pajama top. A strip of duct tape sealed her mouth and plastic cable ties bound her wrists. She cradled Madelyn in her lap, wrapped in a baby blanket. The front-page headline of the current edition of the *Seattle Times* was on display next to Madelyn.

What struck Elena was Laura's sorrowful downward gaze.

Elena met Kwan's eyes. "This will work."

Where did they take Maddy?

After the male guard used a cell phone to take several photos of Laura and Maddy and the newspaper, he and the female watcher moved Laura onto the chair where they bound her arms, torso, and legs to its frame with rope. Laura protested but the strip of duct tape muffled her demands. When they opened the door and walked out, the female carrying Maddy away in her arms, Laura struggled with the bindings but gained nothing.

And what happened to Sarah?

So worried about her daughter, Laura had forgotten about the bodyguard. *She must be around here somewhere, too!*

Laura again surveyed her habitat.

What is this place?

And then she felt it, a slight tremor in her bare feet on the teak flooring. Earlier, while lying in the bunk, she'd felt a similar shudder. It was a familiar sensation to Laura.

This is a boat!

The wake of a watercraft passing by had just bounced off the superyacht, rocking the hull with a tiny tremor.

As Laura thought about the situation, she was sure the boat was not under way or anchored but instead tied to a pier or dock. *But moored where?*

Laura once again arched her spine, testing the restraints but soon relaxed her strained muscles, frustrated. Her captors were efficient with the lashings, leaving nothing for her to work.

Stay focused—there's got to be a way out of here.

Bound and gagged was not a new ordeal for Laura. A year had passed since her last confinement, which led to three weeks of tribulations that forever changed her—and Yuri. But Laura set aside those trials. She now faced the current crisis head-on.

Elena's behind this—I just know it.

This is exactly what Yuri feared. She's using me to get to him.

I should have listened to him and left as he asked.

And where is Maddy—and Sarah?

Guilt racked Laura's spirit. She closed her eyes, seeking solace.

"Dear Lord," she whispered, "please protect Maddy and Sarah—and me."

Yuri sat inside the SUV at Sea-Tac Airport's cell phone parking lot. It was 8:05 P.M. Nick Orlov's flight from San Francisco was due to land in seven minutes.

It was a tumultuous afternoon. After bolting from Anacortes aboard the chartered seaplane, Yuri landed in Lake Union. He took a short cab ride to the downtown Seattle branch of Enterprise Rent-A-Car, where he rented a Ford Expedition.

During the southbound flight, he'd churned through half a dozen action plans. Yuri's first impulse was to return to Sammamish to check the house for any clues about what happened to Laura and her bodyguard. But he nixed that plan. The SVR might be waiting for him to make an idiotic move like that, same for visiting NSD's office. He even thought of calling the lawyer who had assisted him with his immigration status— that is, his lack of any status whatsoever. He punted on that plan, too, knowing there was nothing the attorney could do to help. In the end, Yuri settled on the security company.

He drove to the company headquarters on Mercer Island unannounced and requested a briefing. The CEO and two senior case officers met with Yuri for over half an hour. There were no new developments. Laura, Maddy, and Sarah remained missing and there'd been no sign of the Yukon. The company continued its search, initiating an All Hands On Deck response. The CEO urged Yuri to notify the City of Sammamish Police and maybe the FBI if they did not turn up soon. Yuri agreed that notifying the local police made sense but was fuzzy on just when that would occur. But talking to the FBI, how he could ever do that?

At the end of the meeting, Yuri requested the use of a room with a phone. He had kept his cell turned off all afternoon and continued that practice. From the privacy of the office, Yuri called Nick on a landline and briefed him. Nick insisted on the face-to-face.

Yuri checked the wristwatch. *He should be landing now.*

He reached into a jacket pocket and removed his cell phone. He needed a new mobile ASAP but for now risked using it. Nick would be calling soon to let him know he'd arrived.

Yuri turned on the cell and scanned through the stack of calls and voice mails but chose not to listen to them. However, there was one text that caught his immediate attention. The thread display read LAURA. He tapped on the thread. An instant later, a color photograph flashed onto the screen.

Dread gripped Yuri as he stared at Laura's forlorn image.

My God—this is my fault!

CHAPTER 43

Nicolai Orlov studied the photograph of Laura and Madelyn. "Is that today's paper?"

"Yes," answered Yuri.

Nick and Yuri sat inside the rented Ford SUV in a Denny's Restaurant parking lot north of the airport.

"Did you call yet?" Nick asked, still peering at the cell phone screen. Embedded at the bottom of the texted photo was a ten-digit telephone number.

"No. I wanted you here first." Yuri shifted in his seat. "I also need to get another phone. They're probably trying to track this one."

"Is it live now?"

"No. It's on airplane mode."

Nick returned the phone to Yuri.

"There might be a pay phone in there," Yuri said, gesturing with his head.

"Don't bother. I've got one you can use."

"No, I can't use your cell. That would implicate you."

"No problem." Nick turned to his left and reached into the backseat, pulling up his carry-on bag. He unzipped a pocket, slipped a hand inside, and removed a small plastic container. He opened it and held up the cell phone. "Throwaway. Activated with a thousand minutes of airtime. Untraceable. I never leave home without one." He grinned. "Everyone in my group at the consulate uses them as backups."

Nick handed over the disposable phone.

Yuri flipped it open, turning on the screen. "Does it have speaker mode? I want you to listen in."

"Should be there. Scroll down the screen."

"There it is."

Yuri next glanced at the display on his own phone. He entered a number on the throwaway's keypad and tapped the Dial icon.

Elena Krestyanova answered on the third ring. "*Allo?*"

"Where are Laura and Madelyn?" Yuri demanded in Russian.

"Yuri, you finally decided to call."

"I want to speak with Laura right now."

"Just calm down. She's fine. And yes, you will get to speak to her soon. But we have business first."

"What business?"

"First, I want you to know that I had nothing to do with their abduction. It was carried out by others without my knowledge or approval."

"Who took her?"

"The FSB."

"*Fignjá!*"—Bullshit.

"It was not the SVR. I'm just the messenger here. The FSB is running the op, assisted by the GRU. Your Navy wants those recording pods back at all costs."

"Why do they want them now—what's so important?"

"I don't know."

Yuri turned to face Nick, looking for a response. Nick held up his palms.

"I want to speak to Laura now."

"Hold on—not quite yet. We need to get something straight first."

Yuri took a deep breath, trying to retain control. "What?"

"Our Chinese allies are convinced that you are stalling the recovery process. They tell me that there is nothing wrong with your underwater machine and that the mission should have been completed by now."

"They don't know what they're talking about. That bearing was worn and—"

"Yuri, stop it. I don't care about the details. It doesn't matter. The Chinese have convinced the Ministry of Defense that you are dragging your feet. The FSB took Laura to motivate you, nothing more, nothing less."

Yuri closed his eyes. "The upgrades have been made and the new bearing will arrive in the morning."

"Excellent. So when will you proceed?"

"Are you in communication with Wang?"

"I should be able to contact him."

"All right, here's want I want you to do."

Yuri and Nick remained in the Ford, still parked at the Denny's. The conversation with Elena just ended.

"I don't trust her," Yuri announced. "I think she's behind this whole thing."

Still digesting Elena's comments, Nick took his time

before commenting. "It doesn't make sense to me that she's calling the shots. Other than her connection with the *Neva*, she's never been involved in military ops before—why now?"

"To get to me, of course."

"Obviously, the GRU and the FSB would both enlist her help, but that would be only to contact you—because of the personal connection. She wouldn't run the mission. That would be someone senior."

"It's a foreign intelligence op, right?"

"Of course."

"So, shouldn't the SVR be involved, at least on a consultation basis?"

"Not necessarily. If the GRU has control they would run it solo."

"What did the GRU liaison at the consulate have to say?"

"I inquired discreetly, as you asked. He indicated that they have nothing going on in the Pacific Northwest at this time, only in California."

"Well, isn't that interesting."

"I know what you're getting at, but he may not be in the loop or was ordered not to share. You know how it is with our system."

Yuri did, and that knowledge continued to haunt him. "There's something else that's really been bothering me."

"What?" Nick said, taking the bait.

"Shouldn't you as the deputy *rezident* for the consulate—our only official outpost on the West Coast of the U.S.—have knowledge of the new mission? The GRU and FSB both know that you and I were involved together with the *Neva*. Why would they use an underling like Elena for such a vital mission? If anyone, it should have been you that contacted me."

Yuri's bombshell hit home with the impact of a Category-5 hurricane. Nick said, "You're right. We—I—have been left totally in the dark about this whole affair."

"Are you somehow compromised—under suspicion for something that would make them gun-shy about using you?"

"No, of course not. In fact, my section is coordinating joint intelligence ops with the PRC's MSS, targeting both the U.S. and Canada."

"Kind of like what's going on up here, but you've been kept in the black, right?"

Yuri let Nick ponder the latest revelation. "Here's something else to think about. How would the GRU or FSB know about me now? Earlier, you told me there was nothing in your system about my 'resurrection,' as I recall you phrasing it. Remember?"

"Yes, but—"

Yuri interrupted, "Am I still off the official radar?"

"I checked this morning—there's nothing new in the system about you."

"Don't you think that's odd? That YouTube video went public three weeks ago. If someone other than you or Elena made the connection, it would have leaked by now."

"Maybe."

"And Elena, what about her? Didn't you say she was supposed to be in Asia someplace?"

"I did get an update. She returned to Vancouver for meetings with the trade mission."

"How convenient. So why is she down here threatening me through Laura? If this were a GRU or FSB, or even an SVR operation, Elena would be the last person to use. A trained intimidator would be hounding me, not a honeypot temptress like Elena."

Nick just nodded. Elena's initial SVR training had focused on using her looks to steal secrets.

"I think this entire operation has not been sanctioned by the GRU or FSB, let alone the SVR," surmised Yuri.

"What are you getting at?"

"Elena's been turned, she's working for the Chinese."

"*Chërt voz'mi!*"—Dammit.

CHAPTER 44

Laura remained locked inside the cabin, confined to the chair but now clothed in cobalt blue coveralls—the same type the crew wore.

An hour earlier, a masked male guard joined the female watcher. They untied Laura's chair lashings, allowing her to use the cabin's compact bathroom and change her clothing. During the changeover, Laura asked several times about Maddy but was ignored. After retying Laura to the chair and taping her mouth, both guards exited the cabin.

Her isolation had lasted about forty-five minutes when a new player entered the cabin.

Laura turned toward the door as it opened.

Like her counterparts, the female visitor wore a balaclava, which concealed most of her face and all of her hair. About the same height as Laura, the woman had a bulky frame and at least thirty pounds on Laura.

The new woman stepped to Laura's side and peeled the duct tape from her lips.

Laura took a deep breath and ran her tongue over dried lips.

The visitor produced a cell phone. "You are going to make a call to verify that you and your daughter are well and—"

"Where's Maddy!" Laura demanded.

The woman tilted her head to the side, meeting Laura's eyes. "Your lovely daughter is nearby. She's asleep. When it's time for another feeding I will bring her to you." Her English was perfect, without a hint of accent. And through the slits, Laura noted the oval eyes—kind eyes, Laura hoped.

The visitor punched a speed dial number on the phone and engaged the speakerphone mode. She then held the cell next to Laura's head. The call rang for just one ring.

"Hello."

"It's me, honey," Laura said, energized by Yuri's voice.

"Are you okay?"

"They've got me tied up, but I'm okay."

"Where's Maddy?"

"Here someplace."

"She's not with you?"

"No, not at the moment."

"I'm going to get you and Maddy out of this situation. Just be patient. I will do what they want and then they will release both of you."

"Do what?"

"A search using the *Deep Adventurer*."

"Be careful on the water—it's not safe."

"Don't worry, I'll be all right."

"You should get to Dan Miller and the *Hercules* to help."

There was a slight hesitation before Yuri replied, "I'll have plenty of help so don't—"

The female guard started to pull the phone away when Laura shouted, "I love you. Be safe!"

After switching off the phone, the visitor resealed Laura's mouth and left.

Laura gambled with the call; it was all she could think to do. The code was subtle and she hoped her captors wouldn't notice.

She was certain, however, that Yuri would pick it up. They both knew full well that Dan Miller was dead.

After Laura's call, Yuri and Nick relocated from the Ford to a quiet booth in the back section of the Denny's. Both sipped coffee. Their isolation allowed them to speak in Russian.

"What do you think she was hinting at?" Nicolai asked.

"I'm not sure."

Laura's clue perplexed both men.

Nick said, "It must have something to do with the water."

"Or boats?"

"Right."

They speculated for a few more minutes before switching emphasis.

"I don't think that's a good idea," Nick offered.

"But I don't have any choice. I've got to buy time and that's the only option."

Nick took another sip from his mug. "Who knows what they're really up to with that underwater gear?"

"They obviously want the intel on the American

submarines—that was the focus of my mission last year."

"Just what does that stuff you planted on the bottom really do?"

"They're acoustic recording devices. They record just about every underwater sound within their particular monitoring zone. From whales and fornicating shrimp to tankers, fishing boats, and military craft."

"So they record the submarines that pass by?"

"Yes, and because the *Ohios* are incredibly quiet, anything that can be recorded helps with detection."

"What do you mean by 'Ohio'?"

"That's a classification the U.S. Navy uses. They're also referred to as Trident subs, for the ballistic missiles they carry."

"Yeah, I've heard that name before." Nick shifted position on the bench seat. "So the Chinese must be trying to come up with a way to detect the Tridents."

"That's right, but they've been going at it backward as far as I can tell."

"Why do you say that?"

"The PLAN contact, Wang, insisted that we first recover the listening pod that was placed the farthest inside, not in the deeper waters. That's backward to me."

Nick's eyebrows narrowed.

Yuri continued, "The problem with the *Ohios* is that they're like a hole in the water sound-wise. We've never really been able to track them while they're on patrol, so any type of recording while they're submerged is gold."

"So, what's wrong with the area you mentioned?"

"The *Ohios* run on the surface there. They don't submerge until much farther into the Strait."

"They make different sounds on the surface?"

"They're still quiet, but they're not running on ultra-quiet deepwater conditions. There's turbulence noise generated by the sea surface interaction with the hull and racket generated by the wake."

Nick mulled Yuri's comments. "So why did you place a pod there if it's not of use?"

"It adds to our overall acoustic profile on the submarines, and there's always a chance they might try to sneak one out by submerging much closer to the base. We've heard rumors to that effect but no evidence yet."

"I see what you are getting at. They should be going after the listening pods where the submarines would normally be submerged."

"That's right. But they're up to something else, I just feel it."

"What?"

"I don't know."

Nick drained his mug. "So what's the plan now?"

"I drop you off at the airport and then I'll head north."

"Aren't you going to try to get some sleep?"

"I'll find something in Anacortes. I agreed to be at the boat by nine o'clock."

Before driving to Anacortes Yuri would turn in the rental at the airport and then take a cab home where he would pick up his own Toyota Highlander.

"Can I contact you while you're on the water?"

"Yes, I'll use the phone you gave me. They'll be watching me on the boat, so when we talk I may refer to you as someone from my office. Just play along with me."

"Got it. And while you are having fun boating I will be working the other end of this mystery."

"Elena's behind all of this. How will you track her down?"

"I'm not sure yet. I've got a few ideas."

Yuri stretched his stiff arms. "Whatever you dig up will be critical." He met Nick's eyes. "Thank you for coming to my aid. I just want this nightmare over with."

"We're going to get Laura and Madelyn back. You just hang in there."

"Thanks."

CHAPTER 45

Elena Krestyanova and Kwan Chi were aboard the *Yangzi*, alone in the elegant dining room on level four, the owner's deck. With the subdued interior lighting, downtown Seattle's skyline sparkled through the windows.

Kwan dismissed the stewards who had served the late evening snack. Both enjoyed a nightcap as they continued to discuss the events of the evening. Elena drank Imperial Russian vodka, chilled and neat. Chi preferred whiskey—tonight it was Crown Royal XR on the rocks.

Kwan said, "Wang was certain that Kirov was stalling, but we do not know why."

"You certainly have his attention now."

"I do not believe we will have any more trouble from Captain Lieutenant Kirov."

"I think you're right, but you need to keep an eye on him. He's quite inventive and you have the most important people in his life."

"He has my full attention, too."

Kwan took another sip of whiskey. "How did they

meet—Kirov and Newman? You've never told me the full story."

Elena slammed down the vodka shot—her second—and followed with a bite from a slice of bread. She wiped her mouth with a napkin and said, "It was a little over a year ago, after the submarine he was aboard had the accident and then sank . . ."

Elena spent the next fifteen minutes going over the high- and lowlights of Yuri Kirov's exploits to rescue the surviving crew of the Russian spy sub *Neva*.

Kwan was amazed at the tale. "He must be a hero back in Russia."

"Yes, certainly with the Navy."

"Why hasn't he returned home?"

"I've never had a clear explanation and he'll never confide in me, but I'm sure it's Laura Newman. He's obviously in love with her." Elena avoided mentioning that Yuri had disobeyed orders and that at one time the Kremlin had deemed the *Neva* and its crew expendable. She said nothing about her orders to "dispose of" both Yuri and Laura.

"But isn't he working here—in the States—illegally?"

"Correct. Newman protects him with her money. She's wealthy."

"But so young."

"She hit it big-time in the software business."

"Hmm," Kwan said, digesting the tale. "The child—it is his?"

"That was my thought at first, but no. Her former husband. I checked the birth records."

"Too bad. We'd have more leverage if it was his bloodline."

"You have her and it's her child, so I wouldn't worry about that detail."

Kwan reached into his coat pocket and removed his cell. He pulled up the photo of Laura with the newspaper. He studied the image. "What is her race?" he said, turning the display toward Elena.

"Biracial. Her father was African American, her mother Caucasian. She was adopted as an infant by a white couple."

"She's certainly attractive."

"I agree."

Kwan set the phone on the tabletop and then refilled their glasses.

After Elena took her third shot, she decided to bring up a sensitive subject, hoping the timing was right. Compared to several hours earlier, Kwan had mellowed, no doubt aided by the two glasses of wine during dinner, the fine whiskey he now sipped, and the expectation of the fun and games that would soon occur in his stateroom's sex tub.

"Chi, may we discuss our business for a brief moment?"

"Certainly."

"I would like to confirm that once Kirov completes his assignment and delivers the intelligence data, my obligation will be complete and the final payment will be made."

"Yes, that is correct."

"Thank you."

"It is my expectation that we will continue to rely on your services, for a fee of course."

"I very much enjoy our friendship and also wish it to continue."

Kwan stood. Smiling, he offered his hand as Elena rose from her chair. "Shall we?"

"I've been waiting all day for this."

He led the way to his cabin.

As Elena followed in his wake, there was only one thought on her mind: *I'm going to take the money and disappear, maybe someplace in the Caribbean.*

With the upcoming final payment, Elena would have $10 million and change salted away in her secret bank accounts. With that much cash, she could evaporate, escaping forever from the SVR, Russia, and Kwan.

There was no one waiting for Elena in the homeland. Abandoned at two years old, Nastasia Vasileva endured a succession of orphanages until she was rescued at age fourteen. Especially bright, she excelled at her schoolwork but it was her golden mane and blossoming body that attracted the female recruiter.

Moved from the drab institution on the outskirts of Moscow, she took up residence in a special school just a few blocks away from the Kremlin. She had her own cheery room with a television and a closetful of colorful clothing, including six pairs of shoes.

The indoctrination was subtle but persistent. For the next four years, the SVR and FSB instructors mentored the twenty-four girls and ten boys. By the time they were ready for their university studies, all but two girls and a boy were deemed acceptable for future service. Each of the graduates moved to their assigned schools with new cover identities, including fictitious detailed family histories.

Nastasia aka Elena accepted her role as a seductress

without question. Lacking any family foundation to fall back on for moral clarity, she found it natural to use her sex as a tool of her government. She embraced her work, wishing only to please her superiors—just as the training predicted.

After completing her college studies in business, Elena carried out her assignments for eight years without hesitation. But just over a year earlier, her armor of lockstep obedience to the State had cracked. The epiphany occurred during the long voyage home.

Confined to the claustrophobic cabin aboard the submarine for nearly two weeks, she had nothing to do other than read a collection of boring novels or think. Locked away in her memory compartments and those engineered by the State were secrets she rarely visited.

Elena opened them all, one by one.

She had been used her entire life. Abused by both male and female staff and residents in the orphanages and then molded into a sex spy by her government, Elena finally acknowledged the awful truth.

By the time the *Barrakuda* had docked in Petropavlovsk-Kamchatskiy, Elena made her decision.

It was time for revenge—and escape.

CHAPTER 46

DAY 25—THURSDAY

The seven-man team reached shore at 0315 hours local time. They emerged from the sea, weapons at the ready. The one-half-meter-high waves breaking on the gravel beach were a minor nuisance.

The moonless night helped ensure the team's stealth. The persistent drizzle further obscured visibility from the legions of security cameras that ringed the plant. Clad in black neoprene from hood to reinforced booties, the men soon reached the base of the beach berm. The twenty-meter tongue of reddish yellow flame erupting from the nearby forty-story flare tower illuminated the shore side of the mammoth hydrocarbon export facility.

The special ops team, codename Tiger, trekked westward, taking care to stay just below the crest of the beach berm. They passed under a roadway bridge that spanned the mouth of a stream flowing to the sea. Five minutes later, the commandos arrived at their destination. They lay prone on the ground, eyeing their dual targets, some three hundred meters to the east.

The tanks were enormous, 60 meters in diameter and nearly a dozen stories tall. Each tank held 100,000 cubic meters of liquid natural gas—3.5 million cubic feet. Chilled to –260 degrees Fahrenheit, the liquid methane stored in each tank could power a small city for a year.

The team leader ordered his men to divide into two squads. Moon squad moved fifty meters to the north. It remained in contact with the team leader, employing an encrypted short-range radio signal. Sun squad waited with the leader.

It took ten minutes for both squads to assemble and test their equipment.

At 0340 hours, the Tiger team leader queried his counterpart, switching to an alternate encrypted frequency. Another seven-man unit had crawled ashore a couple of kilometers to the east. Serpent Team also had twin targets: mammoth steel tanks with floating roofs that contained a combined total of 1.2 million barrels of crude oil.

Serpent leader reported his unit was in place and ready.

The mission commander monitored his wristwatch, and at 0350 hours, he radioed the execute order to Serpent. He then switched frequencies and issued the same command to Moon and Sun squads.

Sun fired first. Its missile streamed across the grassy uplands, passed over the perimeter road, and smacked into the northerly LNG tank about fifteen meters—fifty feet—above the ground. Its two-stage shaped-charge warhead bored through the meter of reinforced concrete with the efficiency of a blowtorch on steroids.

The second stage ripped through the steel wall of the inner tank, spewing shrapnel into the tank's interior.

Moon squad followed, with the same results for the second tank.

Other than the trauma of the dual impacts, neither tank exploded. Instead, liquidized natural gas began to flow from the half-meter diameter wounds in the outer concrete walls. The liquid spilled onto the asphalt below and instantly vaporized.

The wail of a distant siren pierced the still air. And then another alarm blared closer to Team Tiger.

The mission commander again checked his watch. *Five minutes to go.* He looked up just as a dazzling flash of light illuminated the sky to the east beyond the leaking LNG tanks. The sharp clap of thunder shattered the still air, followed by a mushroom-shaped plume of flames rising into the night sky.

Team Serpent was on time and on target. Half a dozen man-portable anti-tank missiles were launched at the two oil tanks. The shaped-charge warheads had punched one-foot-diameter holes through the steel walls, allowing the crude oil to escape. Multiple streams of oil flowed into the containment basins at the base of each tank.

Team Serpent had waited the mandatory two minutes for enough crude to escape before firing the incendiary rounds. The projectiles detonated inside the hydrocarbon-rich vapors that hovered over the pooled oil.

Tiger commander again checked his wristwatch. He spoke into his lip mike. "Moon and Sun, stand by—thirty seconds."

He waited the prescribed time and said, "Execute . . . Execute . . . Execute."

Simultaneous streaks of yellow-white flames raced toward the twin domes. The missiles smashed into the concrete outer walls six meters—twenty feet—above the ground surface but did not penetrate. Instead, the warheads exploded on contract, spewing a shower of white phosphorus. The tentacles arced downward and outward into the ground-hugging layer of semi-vaporized natural gas.

The dual explosions dwarfed the crude oil attack. The concussion smacked the men in their faces as it radiated outward. The fireball scorched everything within one hundred meters.

Even at their distance from the inferno, the men of Team Tiger feared the heat.

With the mission complete, both assault teams prepared to depart. Tiger's squads collected the spent missile tubes and all other expendable gear used in the op; ditto for Serpent's operators. Nothing could be left behind, except for what the mission commander carried.

As Team Tiger assembled around their leader, he removed a packet from the waterproof pouch attached to the left thigh of his wetsuit. He ripped open the plastic covering and then dropped to his knees. He placed the military field dressing, already pre-saturated with human blood, on the ground and partially buried it in the sandy soil, letting one end of the camouflaged Velcro draw strap protrude.

With the task complete, the commander stood and made a radio check with Team Serpent. It was already on the beach.

The commander took one last look at the carnage he and his men had inflicted on the $5 billion installation. The Russian oil and gas processing plant consumed itself with the fury of a volcanic eruption. Collateral damage from the LNG tank explosions had sparked dozens of secondary explosions and fires. But the sky-high flames from the fifty million gallons of burning crude dominated. It was a scene from hell that none would ever forget.

The commander turned to charges and said, "We're done. Time to go."

Team Tiger reached the water's edge, where they waded into the sea and disappeared.

CHAPTER 47

The president of the Russian Federation was in the War Council Conference Room. The defense minister and a collection of his generals and admirals sat on each side of the president. Aides for the flag officers lined up against the conference room walls, most taking notes on paper pads or working the keypads of their digital equivalents.

The assembled focused on the colossal flat-panel screen that occupied the entire wall fronting the table. It was purposely designed to surpass the big screens in the Pentagon. Live color video was streaming into the Kremlin via a military satellite feed.

On the other end of the electronic link and seven hours ahead, a Russian Army colonel stood facing the camera with a backdrop of smoldering ruins. It was mid-afternoon in his time zone with clear skies, which allowed for exceptional viewing of the meager remains of Sakhalin II Hydrocarbon Export Terminal.

"What are the casualties?" asked the president.

"Sixteen confirmed deaths and two dozen injuries, mostly burns and shrapnel."

The colonel and a brigade of his *Spetsnaz* special operators had landed earlier on the grounds next to the flattened LNG processing plant. A fleet of helicopters ferried the force from an Army base on the mainland.

"So tell us about the plant, Colonel. How bad is it—no *fignjá*!"

"Sir, it's far worse than I expected. The blast from the ruptured LNG tanks and the subsequent fires have destroyed most of that section of the plant. The plant manager confirmed to me that in his opinion it is a total constructive loss."

The president muttered a curse.

"As you can see from behind me, the crude oil terminal is still burning," said the colonel. "The tanks were destroyed but fortunately, the containment basins are intact. No oil has escaped to the water."

"How about the processing equipment for the crude oil?"

"There I have some good news. The damage is minor. The manager estimates it might take a month to make those repairs. But replacing the oil tanks will likely take longer—six to nine months if we are lucky, again according to the manager."

The president leaned forward, his eyes glued to the devastation surrounding the colonel. "I know it's early, but what can you tell us about the attack?"

"Part of my team is currently collecting all of the surveillance videos at the plant, and there are over two hundred cameras. Those videos should help pin down what happened. On the ground, so far it appears it was a two-pronged attack. One unit hit the LNG facility from the west and another targeted the crude oil facility from the east."

The colonel pointed toward the shore. "We discovered footprints on the uplands and the shorelines that suggest the intruders came in from the sea and then returned the same way. Looks like they wore wetsuit booties. So far, we have not found any weapons evidence, not even a shell casing. It would appear the attackers were quite skilled."

"They left nothing behind?" the president asked.

"Not that we've found. I have over a hundred men checking every square meter of the facility for clues. If something was left behind, we will find it."

"Thank you, Colonel. Please keep us posted on any developments."

"Yes, sir."

The video blinked to a blue screen.

The president turned to face the defense minister. "It's the Americans, I'm convinced of it."

The minister nodded. "Classic U.S. Navy SEAL team attack."

"Son of a bitch!"

CHAPTER 48

DAY 26—FRIDAY

"*Allo?*"

"*Dobroe utro, yelenu,*" Nick Orlov said, issuing a good morning greeting over the phone line. He was in his office at the San Francisco General Consulate.

"Nicolai—is that you?" asked Elena Krestyanova. She had left Seattle the day before, driving back to Vancouver. She was in her office at the Russian trade mission.

"It's been a while since we last talked. Are you still mad at me?"

"Well, you did leave me stranded—it took me over two weeks to get home."

"I know, and I'm sorry for the thousandth time. We waited as long as we could but then had to leave because of the tidal conditions. Otherwise we would have been stuck waiting half a day."

Nick and Elena had had this discussion before.

"Nicolai, you owe me big-time."

"I do, and I'm ready to make it right."

"Oh, really!"

"Yes. I have reservations for us tonight at the Four Seasons—eight o'clock."

"You're in Vancouver?"

"I will be. I'm about to head to the airport now."

"I don't know. I'm supposed to attend a reception and a dinner at the—"

"Don't worry about it. I already talked with the chief of mission. He invited me, too. I told him we'd attend the reception, have a couple of drinks, and then bug out. He gave his blessing."

"Hmm, sounds like you've thought this one through carefully."

"Always, my love."

"So, you'll come here first—to the mission and then we'll go to the reception?"

"Right, my plane lands around three. I'll take a cab."

"Well, then, be prepared to spend big-time tonight. You know I love seafood, and I'll be famished by then."

"I'm counting on it." Nick glanced at his watch and said, "Wow, I'm late for a staff meeting. I've got to go."

"Okay."

"*Do vstrechi.*"—See you soon.

"*Poka.*"—Bye for now.

Elena returned the telephone handset to its base. She leaned back in her chair and gazed through the window at the cityscape, a smile blossoming. Of all of her lovers, past and present, private and professional, Nick was near the summit of perfection. Her lust for him was genuine.

Still, she found the timing odd. Why had he waited so long? They'd had several post-mission telephone discussions, always ending with the promise that they'd hook up soon.

He must have broken up with that little bljad'.

Elena had learned about Nick's lover from a female courier who frequented both the consulate and the trade mission. Elena pried the gossip out of the twenty-two-year-old after two glasses of wine at a Vancouver bar. When Nick returned to San Francisco after the *Neva* mission, he and the cyber technician from Saint Petersburg resumed their long-standing bed-sharing arrangement.

Elena's body tingled as she anticipated the events of the evening to come and the hazard that accompanied the pending rendezvous. Nick was second in command of the SVR on the West Coast of North America.

Kwan Chi's promise to wire the final payment when Yuri Kirov delivered the data remained fused into Elena's memory core.

If Nick only knew . . .

"It's okay, honey," whispered Laura as she held Madelyn. The infant finished nursing, feeling full but fussy due to teething pain.

Sitting in the cabin chair with Maddy's head resting on her left shoulder, Laura swayed her torso back and forth, mimicking the rocker at home. She also tapped her daughter's upper back tenderly, helping to expel the gas in her tummy.

Madelyn let out a robust burp.

"There you go! Now you'll feel better."

Reunited an hour earlier, the two women who attended Laura had brought Madelyn into the cabin along with the car carrier and two cardboard boxes chockfull of supplies—disposable diapers, a container of wipes, several fresh baby pajama outfits, formula, and two dozen bottles of assorted Gerber baby foods.

The guards offered no explanations. They continued to conceal their faces.

Still confined to the cabin but no longer bound to the chair, Laura was thankful to have her daughter back.

"It'll be okay, sweetie. Yuri will rescue us."

Nick sat in the backseat of the Uber cab as it sped south on Highway 101, headed for San Francisco International. The stated purpose of his visit to Vancouver station was to evaluate the mission's security protocols. He could have sent one of his minions but chose to make the trip himself.

The principal function of the mission was to promote trade between eastern Russia and western Canada. But it also served as an SVR outpost. Like most of the developed nations—West or East—Russia was always on the lookout for opportunities. Economic espionage was now on par with the military spying.

It was a game that the host nations tolerated—to a point. Blatant spying and/or overt agent recruitment by SVR officers could result in expulsion of the mission from the country. It was Nick's job to make certain that did not happen.

Like Elena, Nick looked forward to the upcoming evening. Elena was an exquisite lover; she had nearly worn him out during their last coupling. And maybe tonight they would rekindle that crazed firestorm.

But Nick also had reservations.

Yuri had insisted that Elena's involvement with Laura Newman's abduction went much further than serving just as an SVR messenger. Yuri suspected that she was working for the PRC. Nick didn't buy it. Elena was a pro; she had a bright future with the SVR.

Elena turned—no way!

Nevertheless, before leaving Seattle Nick had promised Yuri he would check on Elena and report back. He also recommended that Yuri retrieve the underwater intel to secure Laura's release.

Nick had already initiated a backchannel investigation of the Vancouver mission, part of his job. He had detailed profiles on the entire staff from the chief to the lowest clerk. Elena's file revealed that during the past year, she'd taken on a new lover—a submarine squadron commander in Vladivostok. The file also provided a summary of her travels throughout East Asia. There were no reports of her visits to the States, which he found disquieting. Yuri had reported that she'd visited him at his Redmond office and again in a downtown Seattle high-rise.

Even more of a concern was the lack of chatter within the SVR regarding Yuri's so-called resurrection. Nick had again made quiet inquiries to Moscow about Yuri's status; he remained missing and presumed dead.

After reviewing the active case files regarding Elena, he had found nothing to indicate her involvement with a joint SVR and Chinese Intelligence op to retrieve Yuri's underwater recording pods. Nothing in the system related to that operation, which because of its nature was not alarming to Nick. However, Elena's file did reveal that she'd been tasked with recruiting an unnamed Chinese businessman.

Nick's trip to Vancouver would allow him to quiz Elena on her current work while at the same time renewing their intimate friendship. He could hardly wait.

CHAPTER 49

"How do you like Vladivostok?" Nick Orlov asked.
"It's okay. You know, it's a Navy town." Elena
Krestyanova picked up her wineglass and took a sip.

Nick and Elena sat at a cozy table in a quiet corner
of the five-star restaurant in downtown Vancouver.
They'd already ordered dinner. A chilled bottle of a
California sauvignon blanc occupied a corner of the
table.

"I visited there once. I know what you mean—typical seaport."

"Yes, and that place just happens to be loaded with
droves of horny young sailors. This I know from experience."

Nick laughed. With Elena's long and lean figure,
shoulder-length blond hair, and endearing smile, she
must have attracted catcalls and wolf whistles when
walking about in the seaside city.

"Will you be relocating permanently to Vladivostok?"

"No way. I'm still based out of here, thank God. But
I'll report in there now and then while working."

"Your China assignment."

She nodded while taking another taste of wine.

"I'm headed to Beijing next month," Nick said.

"Oh really—anything you can discuss?"

"I'm traveling with the consulate general. Another bullshit goodwill tour. Kind of like what you've been doing for the trade mission."

"The new alliance with our Asian ally?"

"Yep."

Elena smirked and said, "Our bosom buddies."

Nick chuckled. "Like we can really trust them. They'll screw us out of every barrel of oil we've got while smiling at us the whole time."

"You'll get no argument from me on that. They're brutal negotiators. If they believe they have the advantage, they will not compromise. It's take it or leave it."

None of this was news to Nick. The SVR's moles inside the PRC's central government provided accurate intel on China Inc.'s game plan to become the dominant power in the Western Pacific. The Taiwan problem was again heating up, the new leader of the renegade island providence strengthening ties with the United States. Taiwan's insolence needed to be dealt with. Paramount to that goal was Beijing's plan to force the retreat of the United States Navy back to its home waters, which was just fine with the Kremlin.

Nick and Elena chatted for ten more minutes on geopolitics and SVR gossip, both careful not to divulge any pertinent details of their particular operations. Just after the waitstaff served their meals—both ordered grilled Chinook salmon—Nick broached a new subject.

"Elena, I need to apologize again for what happened last year with the boat. It was out of my hands. We just couldn't wait any longer."

Elena was about to munch on a morsel of salmon but instead set her fork back on the plate and looked Nick in the eye. "I forgive you, Nick. Stop worrying about it."

"Thank you."

They made small talk for the next few minutes. Nick carefully orchestrated the discourse back to their previous joint op.

Nick finally said, "What happened to the *Neva* once it made it home?"

After taking a sip of water Elena said, "The last I heard it was going to be decommissioned. It was too damaged to be repaired."

"That's not surprising."

"I agree."

Nick chose his next words cautiously. "Have you heard anything about where Yuri might be?"

Elena ran a hand through her hair. "I have no idea. You would know more than me."

"Laura told me she was going to get him help for decompression sickness. That was the last I heard."

"Have you contacted her?"

"No. She asked that I leave her alone. After all she did to help Yuri and the crew, I decided to honor that request."

Elena drained her wineglass. "He was a good guy all right. I wonder if he survived."

"He was, and I hope he did."

Nick refilled her glass and continued with his meal, having completed the first element of his stealth interrogation.

Elena had lied about contacting Yuri—and Laura. Nick wondered what else she was hiding.

CHAPTER 50

It was 1:35 A.M. aboard the *Ella Kay*. The workboat was about two miles north of Dungeness Spit. The seas were calm this early morning. The flush of luminosity to the north marked the City of Victoria, sixteen miles across the Strait of Juan de Fuca.

In the late afternoon, *Deep Adventurer* located the underwater recording pod that Yuri had planted on the seabed the previous year. The *Ella Kay* was above the pod, headed into the flooding tidal current with just enough thrust to maintain a stationary position. The workboat's diesel engine and the bow and stern thrusters were all in sync with the GPS-linked autopilot. As long as the wind did not exceed twenty knots, the *Ella Kay* could maintain its alignment over the bottom co-ordinates within a twenty-foot circle. Such precision was necessary to deploy the remotely operated vehicle.

Yuri was inside the cabin sitting at the galley table, his eyes fixed on a laptop display. With his right hand, he worked a joystick control. A thin wire encased in black insulation linked the hand controller to a computerized power control module located on the main deck about forty feet aft. That device connected to a nearby deck-mounted reel that housed a thousand feet of quarter-inch-diameter cable. Almost six hundred feet of the cable snaked over the gunwale and descended into the water. The neutrally buoyant tether supplied electrical power and communications to the ROV.

Nicknamed *Barnacle*, the underwater robot hovered over the sandy bottom nearly 450 feet below the sea surface. About the size of a shopping cart, it housed a floodlight-illuminated high-definition video camera that focused on a rock outcrop. The boulder protruded about a half meter above the seabed.

David Wang, aka Lieutenant Commander Wang Park, stood next to Yuri, also eyeing the laptop's screen. "How will you attach that line? There's nothing to tie to."

"Just wait. You'll see."

Yuri twisted the joystick to the side and *Barnacle*'s articulated arm extended into view. He moved the appendage over the partially embedded stone and then rotated the clamp at the end of the arm until it lined up with the rock.

Yuri next swung the arm downward, allowing the blunt end of the clamp to strike the stone. After contact, the top of the boulder peeled back, exposing a stainless steel ring.

Wang swore in Mandarin, amazed at how skillfully the listening device blended into the seabed.

Yuri used *Barnacle*'s artificial arm to attach a steel cable to the lifting ring. He turned to Wang and said, "It's secure. Have your man reel it in—but slowly."

Wang retreated to the workboat's stern, where he issued the orders.

As the crane reeled in the lifting cable, Yuri kept watch with the ROV's video feed. The slack in the wire rope disappeared as the winch retracted the cable. The cable tugged on the lifting ring and the motor struggled against the line tension, broadcasting a low-pitched groan, which Yuri could hear from inside the cabin. He feared the motor would stall out. But the strain lessened as the pod broke free of the bottom. Ten minutes later, the Russian Navy's secret underwater surveillance device lay on *Ella Kay*'s main deck.

Yuri and Wang stood beside the recording pod. Yuri had already removed the boulder-shaped fiberglass housing that had projected above the seabed. The underlying cylinder was about six feet long and slightly over two feet in diameter. Wood blocks placed on the deck along each side of the cylinder prevented it from rolling in response to the low ocean swells that continued to travel eastward along the waterway. *Deep Adventurer* was in its cradle next to the pod.

"How does it look?" asked Wang.

"Okay. I don't see any damage."

"Can you open it—to see if there's data inside?"

"Yes, but very carefully."

"Why?"

"It has an anti-tamper mechanism. Open the unit in the wrong sequence and a small charge will destroy the equipment."

"What do we do?"

"First, I need to disarm it. Then we can check data files." Yuri dropped to his knees and examined the exterior surface of the pod.

Wang squatted next to Yuri. "How can I help?"

Yuri gestured toward a nearby bulkhead. "There's a

toolbox inside the locker. I need the set of Allen wrenches plus socket wrenches."

"I'll get them."

To avoid the commercial traffic in the nearby shipping lanes, the *Ella Kay* retreated southeastward several miles. It jogged a slow orbit in Dungeness Bay, just east of the Dungeness Spit. The predawn skies had clouded and the wind kicked up.

Yuri opened the Russian underwater monitoring device and extracted the one-hundred-terabyte data pack. When he transferred the first five-gigabyte file to his laptop to run a diagnostic test on the acoustic recordings, he discovered a glitch. The data was contaminated. Five additional tests on randomly selected files produced the same results. He and Wang discussed the situation.

"Based on these tests," Yuri said, "I suspect the entire data pack is contaminated."

"What caused this?"

"I'm not sure. There must have been a malfunction with one of the hydrophones, which somehow distorted the ambient acoustic level." Yuri pointed to his Dell. Digital static filled the screen. "I think there's real data in there, but extracting it is going to be a bitch."

"How do you extract the data?"

"I'll have to come up with a filter. We had similar problems with hydrographic data from our AUV projects. We ended up writing a program that filtered out the junk."

"Good, then do the same with this data."

"Not so easy." Again pointing to the screen, Yuri continued, "This is acoustic recording data over a wide spectrum, not a narrow beam echo sounder, which was where the problem with the AUV data occurred. For the monitoring pod, there are magnitudes more of raw data that require analysis."

Wang frowned, peering down at the deck. "We're both running out of time. Can you do this or not?"

The threat remained in the background.

"Yes, but I'll need to take the data pack to my office and use the software we have available."

"How long will that take?"

Yuri raised his hands, signaling his frustration. "I'll need several days."

"You've got forty-eight hours. But that's it."

"Forty-eight hours once I get back to my office—I've got to have at least that much."

Wang sighed. "All right, but we need to head back to Anacortes now."

"Good, but I have a suggestion before we leave."

"What?"

"I'd like to redeploy *Deep Adventurer* now instead of waiting until later."

"Don't you have to recharge the batteries longer?" The AUV was currently charging.

"No. The second pod is only about sixty kilometers west of the one we recovered. It's across the Strait on the Canadian side. *Deep Adventurer* has plenty of juice left for that."

Wang checked his wristwatch. "We need to get this data analyzed first. It can wait."

Yuri frowned. "Look, Wang, I want to get this over with—you know why."

Wang started to protest but Yuri held up his hand. "We may need the second pod as a backup—assuming it's still there. The chances of the recordings on that unit having the same type of contamination as this one should be minimal. One other thing, I know Moscow, and I suspect your people, too, want recordings of submerged American missile subs. We are much more likely to have that data on the second pod because it's located in the region where their subs sound."

Wang was sold. "Okay, let's do it."

The *Ella Kay* powered northward across the Strait of Juan de Fuca, bound for Rosario Strait and then Guemes Channel and Fidalgo Bay. Steady rain was falling; a storm brewed to the south. Yuri stood alone on the workboat's main deck near the stern, staring at the churning wake. It was alive with tiny flashes of purple and crimson as the phosphorous-based sea life reacted to the turbulent flow of the vessel's whirling propeller.

Laura and Maddy were always on his mind. After turning *Deep Adventurer* loose, he had requested to speak with Laura. Wang refused, reminding him that would only occur when he had provided the acoustic recordings of the American submarines.

Yuri remained optimistic that he could recover the contaminated data; it was not an unusual problem with the seabed recorders. But he needed to create doubt in order to convince Wang to allow him to redeploy *Deep Adventurer*. It was to ensure that Wang and company released Laura unharmed.

When Wang took a break to use the head, Yuri removed the self-destruct module from the recording pod and installed it inside the AUV's forward compartment.

Instead of commencing a new search in the western reaches of the Strait of Juan de Fuca, the *Deep Adventurer* headed east and descended. It currently rested on the sand bottom 260 feet down near the main shipping channel of Admiralty Inlet.

Now armed with over ten pounds of military-grade plastic explosive—not the small charge Yuri had alluded to—the autonomous underwater combat vehicle stood by for Yuri's orders.

CHAPTER 51

"Mr. President, I don't think we can afford to keep this situation under wraps much longer. The media jackals smell blood."

"What are you hearing?"

"That we know what happened but are not talking."

"Well, they certainly have that one right for a change." President Tyler Magnuson stared over his desk at his national security advisor. It was mid-morning. The two men were alone in the Oval Office. POTUS grimaced as he asked, "Has the Navy confirmed the initial report?"

"Yes, sir," Peter Brindle said. "The tanker was definitely struck by a rocket torpedo, but there's a complication." The advisor leaned forward a bit. "It might not have been the Russians after all. It turns out the North Koreans have the capability."

"What?"

"The CIA has a credible report that the North Korean Navy has at least half a dozen of the Russian rocket torpedo knockoffs manufactured by Iran. They apparently made some kind of trade—missile parts for the torpedoes."

"Good Lord, when did all of this happen?"

"We don't know when the trade occurred. The agency is rechecking shipping records for the past couple of years. They might find something, but you know how devious both of them are."

"Go on."

"Anyway, a CIA asset in China made the report about the rocket torpedoes a month ago. The individual involved is with the PLA Navy, so the intel's credibility is high. The agency had not yet processed the report, but that all changed after the tanker was blown up."

President Magnuson leaned back in his chair. He gazed at the map mounted on a nearby wall panel. He had taped the NOAA chart of Prince William Sound to the wall himself. After mulling over the situation he turned back to face Brindle.

"What about those recordings? I thought we had hard evidence that the submarine was Russian."

"That's right, sir. What the hydrophones picked up in the Hinchinbrook Entrance was a Russian boat. But in light of the North Korean connection, it's possible that what was picked up might have been the playback of another recording."

"You mean it could have been faked?"

"It's possible. The Navy Department's underwater acoustic experts could not rule it out. Apparently, our submarines have been using false recordings to hide some of their own operations."

POTUS glowered, clearly agitated.

"There's more, sir. The Navy indicated that if the

North Koreans were involved, they would have used a diesel submarine to sneak into Prince William Sound. When operating on batteries, they are incredibly quiet. The monitoring hydrophones would never pick it up if it was operating in stealth mode."

"It wouldn't have to be a nuclear submarine?"

"No. They could have modified one of their diesel boats to make the trip across the North Pacific. Once they reached Prince William Sound, they would switch to battery power. They're much quieter than nuclear plants. No pumps, turbine, or steam plants to worry about."

The president raised his hands in frustration. "This is just great. I've got an environmental disaster on my hands that was the result of an act of war, but I can't pin it on anyone."

"Not yet—at least."

"What about Sakhalin, any news on what happened there?"

"Just what our satellites picked up. The LNG plant appears to be a total loss. The crude oil terminal might be salvageable."

Magnuson stood up, signaling the meeting was over. "You watch, Peter. That son of a bitch in the Kremlin is going to try to blame that mess on us, too."

"I wouldn't be surprised."

"Where is she now?" asked Nick Orlov, speaking in Russian. He was in his Vancouver hotel room. It was 7:40 A.M.

Nick listened to the caller's response and said, "Keep on her at all times but don't let her catch on. She's expert at spotting tails, and she'll have her guard up, even around here."

Nick waited for his subordinate to complete his report. "Very well, keep me posted," he said, and terminated the call.

Nick set his cell phone on the desk by the window wall. His hotel room had a commanding vista of Burrard Inlet with towering Grouse Mountain in the distant background. But the low-pressure front flowing over BC's lower mainland obscured both vistas this morning. Torrents of rain pelted the windowpanes as forty-knot gusts buffeted the high-rise building.

Nick was mildly hung over. He and Elena had killed two bottles of wine during their two-and-a-half-hour dinner. The vodka nightcaps didn't help.

Despite his elevated blood alcohol content, all systems were "go" when they took the elevator to his room. The sex was everything Nick had remembered—and hoped for. Elena was a superb lover.

After two whirlwind round-trips, both fell asleep.

Elena climbed out of Nick's bed two hours earlier. She took a shower, dressed, and after a quick farewell peck to Nick's forehead, she walked out of the hotel room.

Once she'd departed, Nick dialed his cell phone, connecting with the two-man surveillance team from the San Francisco consulate. The SVR officers had followed their boss to Vancouver. Nick ordered the men to trail Elena when she exited the hotel garage in her Mercedes. The team had already installed a GPS tracker on the sedan.

The SVR surveillance team leader called in a progress report. Elena drove straight to her condo apartment, where she remained for an hour before again using her automobile. She headed to the trade mission and went into her office.

Wow, she's already at work—and on Saturday. Nick was amazed at the woman's stamina.

After showering, Nick dressed and walked out of the hotel room, carrying his overnight bag. The top of his skull pulsed. He needed a cup of coffee and a couple of aspirin.

As he headed for the hotel lobby, Nick wondered if he was on a wild-goose chase. He still could not fathom Yuri's assertion that Elena was working for the People's Republic of China. Yet he had heard her make the blackmail demands to Yuri.

It must be part of the operation she's involved with.

Nick also worked with the PRC, part of Russia's new alliance to constrain the USA both economically and militarily.

Nick would return to San Francisco in the afternoon, but he ordered the SVR team to monitor Elena for the next forty-eight hours. If nothing turned up, he would recall the officers and let Yuri know that Elena was a dead end.

It was the least he could do for his friend.

CHAPTER 52

DAY 28—SUNDAY

Yuri Kirov and Commander Wang sat at a large table in the conference room. They were alone this afternoon at Northwest Subsea Dynamics. Occupying half of the tabletop was NOAA chart 18471: *Approaches to Admiralty Inlet*. Scattered across the remainder were dozens of data sheets.

Yuri keyed his laptop, pumping out another color plot of acoustic recordings from a high-speed printer in a corner of the room.

Wang tossed aside a ten-page collection of plots and said, "I had no idea there is so much traffic in that part of the Strait. This is going to take forever to sort out."

"If you could refine the time periods you're interested in, that would help."

Yuri resurrected the acoustic digital recordings from the underwater recorder's memory pack. He adapted code that NSD and Laura's company had developed to analyze raw side-scan sonar imagery and the *in situ* oceanographic data.

"I have a couple of dates that we know for certain it was operating in the Strait. I'll look them up."

"Okay."

Wang removed his iPhone from a coat pocket. He read off the dates from a cloud-based file.

Yuri consulted the Dell, opening a date file. He studied the output for a minute. "What was the time on the first one?" he asked.

"Around fourteen hundred hours, local time."

"Ah ha, got it." Yuri fingered a flurry of commands on the laptop's keyboard and issued the print command over a wireless circuit. The HP spit out half a dozen sheets.

Wang walked to the printer and examined the acoustic recordings, one sheet at a time. After scanning the last sheet, he looked up, a smile breaking out—the first Yuri had observed in several days. "I think we have it. Everything fits." He walked to Yuri and handed him the hard copies.

It only took just an instant for Yuri to make the connection. "This is a surface contact. I thought you were looking for submerged recordings."

"We are, but this particular recording is also useful."

Yuri studied the data before commenting further. "I assume the timing corresponds to the transit of an *Ohio* through the area."

"Yes, it was outbound at that time."

"And it was shadowed?"

"What?"

"Escorts."

"Yes, how can you tell?"

Yuri pointed to the plot. "There are multiple propeller recordings in the recording."

"Ah, yes." Wang consulted his cell phone. "It was escorted by a Coast Guard cutter and two barricade workboats, one on either side."

"Okay. What's next?"

Wang repeated the second date.

Yuri keyed in the request. The new date was seventy-two days later than the first.

Wang reviewed the second data set.

"How does it look?" Yuri asked.

"It's a match."

"So the boat completed its patrol and was returning to Bangor when it was recorded the second time."

"Correct. We have confirmed recordings of its propeller's output for two separate surface passages."

"Are you happy now?"

"Of course."

"Then let's end this op. I've complied with everyone's request. It's time to release my family and let us have our lives back."

"You're not done yet. Both of our navies want the data from the second pod. You know why."

"I don't even know if the recorder is still there," said Yuri. "Besides, we've never managed to record one *Ohio* boat submerged. When in stealth mode, their acoustic fingerprints are like a hole in the water—virtually impossible to detect."

Wang gestured to the color plots scattered across the conference table. "We need all of this data analyzed for both surface and submerged contacts. Plus if your machine finds the other recording pod, we need that data analyzed, too."

"Dammit, Wang, I'm not going to do anything more

until you release Laura and Madelyn. When I'm convinced they're safe I'll finish the work."

"That's not the arrangement we had."

"I don't care. You can go screw yourself." Yuri turned away, staring blindly through the window and the parking lot landscaping beyond.

"You are leaving me no choice but to report your refusal to cooperate to both of our superiors," said Wang.

Still facing the window Yuri said, "You can tell the SVR and the FSB to screw off, too."

Commander Wang retreated, fearing he'd pushed too hard. "Look, I understand the position your government has imposed on you. It is not fair."

Yuri snapped back, facing Wang. "You're damn right about that."

"Try to look at it from my point of view. We're both in the same business. I have an operation to complete, which I suspect is similar to what you have had to do in the past. As the mission commander, I have some leeway. I will speak with my supervisor and make your request known. Perhaps we can make an accommodation without having to involve the SVR."

Yuri perked up. "Good. All I want is to get this over with."

"I know." Wang stood. "I need to leave for a meeting." He reached forward and collected the data sheets scattered across the tabletop. "I will use that opportunity to discuss your request."

"Okay." Yuri also stood and helped gather the remaining sheets. He handed them to Wang and said, "I'll keep working on this stuff. You can reach me on my cell."

CHAPTER 53

"Is he causing trouble again?" Elena Krestyanova asked, speaking into her cell. She was in her high-rise Vancouver apartment this early evening, sitting on a living room sofa. She wore a knee-length bathrobe with a towel wound around her scalp. She'd just walked out of the bathroom after a forty-minute soak when her phone chimed.

"He's stopped cooperating," Kwan Chi said. "There's still much more that he must do."

Kwan was alone in his stateroom aboard the *Yangzi*. Five minutes earlier, Wang had briefed him by satphone while sitting in an SUV in NSD's parking lot.

"What does he want?" Elena asked.

"He's demanding that we release the woman and child. But without them as leverage, how can we expect him to complete the assignment?"

Elena stretched her shapely legs onto the sofa and contemplated her toes. She'd have to find time for a pedicure soon. "Kirov is in a precarious position. He can't go to the American authorities because of the possible repercussions to Newman. He will protect her and the child at all costs. He believes the SVR is part of the operation, so he can't expect any help from Russia. That leaves him only one option—cooperate and hope that the SVR leaves him alone once he's completed the mission."

"So he's bluffing."

"That's the way I see it."

"Do you have any suggestions?"

"Go ahead and release Newman and the child but detain Kirov until he's completed his work. He'll go for that."

"That's my conclusion, too."

"So you plan to release them?"

"Yes, tomorrow. I'd like your assistance with that matter."

"Why?"

"We need to keep the veil of your security services upfront. He has to believe he's really working for Russia and not me."

"I'm sure he knows nothing about you."

"Commander Wang suspects Kirov believes the PRC is involved far more than what he was originally told. And that is dangerous for all of us."

Elena could not fault Kwan's thinking. If Yuri discovered that she had deceived him on behalf of the PRC by holding Laura and her child hostage for a $5 million payout, Elena's head would be first on his chopping block.

Elena calculated the solution. After completing the mission, Yuri simply had to go. Only that would guarantee her and Kwan real peace of mind.

Elena said, "I understand. What would you like me to do?"

* * *

Yuri sat at his desk at 7:20 P.M. He had NSD's offices to himself. Bill Winters was on the phone. He'd left several voice mails for Yuri.

Still working in Barrow with his crew, Bill provided a detailed progress report on NSD's monitoring of the Chukchi Sea oil spill. *Deep Explorer* continued to excel, only requiring routine maintenance during scheduled recharging of the batteries. The constantly shifting sea ice shuttled the trapped oil northward and eastward in response to subsurface currents. *Deep Explorer* kept track of the migrating spill on a daily basis.

Yuri was more than pleased with the report.

"That sounds terrific," Yuri said. "Please convey my thanks to the team. There will be substantial bonuses for everyone."

"I will, and they really have been doing a terrific job." Winters shifted gears. "I'm glad you called me back because we have another opportunity up here I need to talk to you about."

"What's that?"

"Remember that test we did with the microbes?"

"The oil-eating bacteria?"

"Yeah. After the *Explorer* injected the stuff, those little critters ended up consuming ninety-five percent of the oil in the test pockets. The Coast Guard and EPA went ape shit when they got results back. The U. of Alaska Fairbanks is currently brewing up a new batch, scaled up about fifty times from the first run. The Coasties want to start full-scale cleanup operations for trapped oil located on our side of the boundary line with Russia. The Canadians also want in on the action."

"Where do we fit in?"

"They plan to ferry the stuff out to the ice pack on a fleet of choppers, drill holes in the ice, and then inject the bacteria right into the trapped oil. They want us to keep track of the cleanup with *Deep Explorer*."

"That's great, but how can you do that as well as track the overall spread of the spill?"

"If I had the *Adventurer* up here, we'd have it covered. When can you ship her up?"

The request stunned Yuri, who knew he should have anticipated it. All along, *Deep Adventurer* had been held in reserve as a backup.

"I'm almost done with the testing. Maybe in a couple of days I can send her north."

"Great, I'll let the Coast Guard's spill coordinator know. In the meantime I think the *Explorer* can work double duty."

"Okay, sounds good."

Winters changed course again. "How have your test trials been going?"

"Fine."

"Do we have a new customer?"

"Hard to tell. I went over some test results today with the PM. He was closemouthed." Yuri improvised on the spot, knowing NSD's gossip mill remained on full alert. "*Deep Adventurer* has performed to their standards so far."

"Still can't give me a hint about who this mysterious client is?"

"Soon, Bill, soon. Once the testing is complete."

"Okay, good luck then."

"Same to you."

The conversation ended. Yuri stood and walked to a four-drawer file cabinet in the corner of his office. He used a key to open it. Stored in the top drawer along with dozens of confidential company personnel files was a plain cardboard box. Yuri opened the box and removed the bottle.

He returned to his desk and filled his empty coffee mug with a generous shot of Stoli. He swigged it down and followed with a second. He preferred his vodka chilled but dared not store the bottle in the company's refrigerator.

Yuri detested lying; it rasped against his moral grain. He wanted Bill to know the truth, so he could seek his advice and his technical skills. But Yuri could not risk it, especially now. Laura and Maddy's freedom might be just hours away. He would do nothing to jeopardize their release.

Yuri swigged down a third shot of vodka.

The day after Elena showed up at the office he had purchased the bottle and after helping himself to an inaugural triple shot, he hid it in the cabinet. Later, when the anonymous package arrived at his office with the photos of Laura aboard the *Hercules*, he had tapped it again—certain that Elena had served up that mini–heart attack.

Drinking alone at his place of employment was taboo. But tonight the fire in Yuri's belly helped quiet his rage.

Just let it go. All that counts is getting Laura and Maddy back.

CHAPTER 54

It was early evening aboard the *Yangzi*. The super-yacht remained at its berth in the Seattle marina. Madelyn slept in her carrier on top of the bunk. Laura knelt next to the cabin door, working on the lock. It was an electronic mechanism with a ten-digit keypad. On the opposite side of the door in the interior passageway was a duplicate keypad. With the right code, the dual mini keyboards allowed access into and out of the compartment.

About every six hours, one of her watchers would enter the cabin to check on her and Madelyn and bring meals and supplies. Each time a guard departed, Laura zeroed in on the keypad as they punched in the code. Usually, the person's torso blocked Laura's view but not the last time. When the female sentry had left half an hour earlier, Laura had memorized five of the six digits of the authorization code. Unfortunately, she missed the final number when the guard had shifted her stance in anticipation of pulling open the door.

Laura started with 0 and had just keyed in 7 when

the electromagnet inside the lock mechanism released with a muted metallic click.

Gotcha!

Before opening the door, Laura reached to her right and switched off the brig's overhead light, plunging the compartment into blackness. She'd already examined the cabin for a monitoring camera but found nothing. Laura rotated the handle. She opened the door about an inch. A slash of light erupted around the door frame. She pulled open the door, stepped into the passage, and assessed the situation.

Good. No guards.

Now, how do we get off this damn thing?

Kwan Chi and Wang Park sat across from each other at the head of the twelve-seat rosewood dining table on the upper deck. They were alone, the wait-staff dismissed after serving bowls of noodle soup and platters mounded with spicy Kung Pao chicken, *char siu*—barbecue pork—and fried rice.

Both stuffed, the two men sipped tea. Kwan listened as PLA Navy Lieutenant Commander Wang completed his briefing.

"Kirov was able to isolate the signature of the submarine both departing and arriving."

"You're certain it is the same vessel?"

"Yes, the time line of the recordings matched our own tracking data."

An MSS deep cover operative planted years earlier resided in a waterfront residence that overlooked the mouth of Hood Canal from a bluff. The agent's principal task was to monitor submarine traffic into and out of the waterway. The HD video camera he maintained monitored the drawspan section of the Hood Canal Floating Bridge twenty-four/seven. During night or low-light conditions, the camera automatically shifted to infrared mode.

The floating bridge spanned the mile-and-a-half-wide Hood Canal, linking Kitsap and Jefferson Counties. A dozen miles to the south was the U.S. Navy's most highly prized Pacific Coast installation—the Naval Base Kitsap-Bangor. Every ballistic missile–laden submarine homeported at the base navigated through the movable section of the bridge. Located near the center of the bridge, dual sections of the drawspan retracted to create a six-hundred-foot-wide opening. The elaborate maze of underwater cables anchoring the bridge to the bottom impeded submerged crossings by the subs.

"When is it scheduled to depart?" Kwan asked.

"We believe soon. Our agent reports that supplies are now arriving at the wharf and are being loaded aboard."

A civilian contractor responsible for coordinating the delivery of foodstuffs to Bangor routinely provided a female MSS deep cover operative with a summary of his work. Hired for just $500 a month cash, he believed the spy's storyline that she was trying to get a "leg up" on her competitor, who currently had the main supply contract with the Navy base.

"We don't have much time left," Kwan said.

"No, sir."

Kwan took another sip of tea. "When will you know

if Kirov's machine has found the second recording device?"

"Maybe tomorrow. We will need to take the workboat out to the Strait of Juan de Fuca and recover the AUV."

"Let's assume it located the Russian device. How long will it take to recover it and then analyze the data?"

"Even with Kirov cooperating, I expect it will take a couple more days."

"We can't wait that long. I want you to set aside the second recording pod and proceed with your primary mission. With this new acoustic information our chances of success have skyrocketed—we cannot jeopardize that gift." Kwan hesitated. "If we have time later, I'll consider the other pod."

"Yes, sir."

Kwan shifted in his chair. "Can you analyze the data from the second pod without Kirov's assistance?"

"Sir?"

"He's become too much of a liability—we may not be able to count on him."

"I see." Wang considered the change of events and said, "I'll need access to the software he uses. Otherwise, our people will have to reinvent the code. That could be time consuming."

"Where is this software?"

"It's a proprietary program owned by his company."

"Can you get it?"

"Yes, with access to Kirov's company offices I expect we can locate the code and copy it."

"Do it."

*   *   *

Laura made it to the yacht's main deck without detection. She was stunned at the immense size of the *Yangzi* and its opulent furnishings. Maddy continued to sleep in the baby carrier.

After following an interior passageway on the lower deck that led through the crew quarters, she encountered an elegant staircase with Persian carpeting, which she ascended. She walked through another doorway onto an exterior side deck. Hugging the shadows, she surveyed her surroundings. Illuminated by hundreds of dock lights, a sea of sailboats and power yachts stretched to the west as far she could see in the dimness. *What marina is this?*

Laura scanned the shoreline. *There's the Palisades.* The waterfront restaurant was one of Laura's favorites. *This must be the Elliott Bay Marina!*

The *Yangzi* remained moored to the guest float at the marina. The floating pier extended nearly a thousand feet to the shore. The landing platform of the yacht's gangway was a couple of steps aft of Laura's position. The portable aluminum ramp sloped downward to the floating dock.

I need to get down that thing and then run like mad!

Laura had continued aft, stepping softly, when she spotted the sentry. She froze. The guard was just below her perch with his back to Laura. He stood on the floating pier next to the gangway landing enjoying a cigarette. Smoke wafted upward to Laura.

Dammit, now what?

Laura retreated, taking cover by the doorway.

No way can I get past him without being seen.

A new idea coalesced.

I'll just fake it—we'll walk past him, give him a smile, say "good night," and head to shore. Yes, that could work.

But Laura promptly dismissed that thought.

He's probably one of the guards who've been watching me.

Laura switched to plan B. She needed to find a phone to call for help and find a place to hide.

Laura reentered the main deck's superstructure, passing through a passageway that opened into the galley space. A female crew person stood next to the grill, her back to Laura.

Laura backed up and turned to her right. She headed forward, following another interior passage. With Maddy's carrier gripped in her left hand, Laura pulled open a massive mahogany door with the depiction of a dragon carved onto its surface.

She stepped inside. *What is this place?*

Laura surveyed the spacious compartment, looking for a phone. Filled with electronic equipment, several desks, various consoles, file cabinets, a conference table, and other gear, the room extended the full beam of the ship—almost forty-five feet.

There must be a phone in here someplace!

Laura was about to pull open a desk drawer when she noted a collection of documents on the desktop, including several color photos. She retrieved the image that caught her eye.

It was Yuri in his uniform—a captain lieutenant in the Russian Navy.

Taken aback, Laura examined the other papers, when she heard voices from outside the compartment.

Someone's coming!

Trapped, Laura frantically searched for a hiding place. Maddy began to fuss.

Lord, help us!

CHAPTER 55

Kwan Chi pulled open the door to the operations center and stepped inside. Commander Wang followed. They continued chatting in Mandarin.

"Who do you expect to be attending?" asked Wang.

"Most will be from the Second Department plus Guo and his aides. I also expect that Admiral Soo will be attending, so don't be shocked if you see him. This is his brainstorm."

"Thanks for the warning."

Kwan sat at a console near the center of the compartment. Wang took a seat on his right side. Kwan typed at the keyboard. A mammoth deck-to-overhead LCD display flashed to life on the forward bulkhead. The twelve-foot-long by eight-foot-tall screen displayed the flag of the People's Republic of China—an outsized golden star in the upper left corner framed by four smaller stars to its right, all on a crimson field.

Both men waited as the yacht's transceiver antenna synchronized with a People's Liberation Army satellite parked in a geostationary orbit over the North Pacific Ocean. The satellite communication system was housed inside two massive fiberglass white spheres mounted side by side halfway up the ship's radar mast.

The imposing array of communication equipment nested onto the *Yangzi*'s mast fit the stature of the vessel and its owner. But what was not normal—even for a billionaire—was the military grade of the gear. Disguised to appear as top-of-the-line civilian hardware, the yacht's comms system was the same used on the PLA Navy's most modern warships.

A new image materialized on the screen.

Kwan and Wang stared at a conference room with a dozen individuals seated around a semicircle table. All but two wore military uniforms.

It was nine o'clock in the evening in Seattle; noon the next day in Beijing.

Kwan said, "Good day to all."

"And to you," replied the nearly bald and portly fifty-two-year-old man in civilian clothes seated at the center of the table. Guo Wing was the deputy minister of operations for the Ministry of State Security and Kwan's boss. To his right sat a major general in the PLA's General Staff Department, also known as the Second Department (*Er Bu*). A year older and nearly half a foot taller than his MSS counterpart, General Sun Jin had retained his hair but kept it close cut. His uniform displayed his trim, athletic build.

"With your permission, sir," Kwan said, "we are ready to proceed with the briefing."

"Proceed."

Kwan typed in a new command on the keyboard and the screen split into thirds: the live feed from Beijing to the left, a nautical chart of the Strait of Juan de

Fuca in the center, and a color photograph of Yuri Kirov in uniform to the right.

"Sir, I am pleased to announce that we have been successful in obtaining acoustic recordings of an American *Ohio*-class submarine under way in its home waters. The information was obtained from a Russian naval officer."

Laura Newman nearly screamed when Yuri's likeness blinked onto the screen. On her hands and knees with Maddy in the carrier just ahead, she crouched inside an empty storage locker to the left of Kwan and Wang. After climbing in and pulling the door shut, she remained motionless, barely even breathing. Maddy was awake but content. When Laura heard a new foreign tongue respond to Kwan, she pushed the locker door open a bit. That's when she saw the split video screen image of her lover.

Laura could not understand a word of the conversation, but the brilliantly clear images of those assembled at the other end of the video link filled her with dread.

Dear God, what are these people up to?

"How accurate are these recordings?" asked the naval officer sitting to the left of the MSS deputy director. At fifty-eight, Admiral Soo Xiao was the oldest in the room and the highest rank of all the military in attendance. Although balding, he maintained a trim build that reflected regular exercise, healthy eating habits, moderate drinking, and complete disdain for cigarette smoke.

None of the assembled dared light up in his presence, including Kwan and Wang.

Kwan Chi turned to face Wang. "Commander Wang will respond."

"Ah, Admiral Soo, the recordings are of excellent quality. We were able to filter out all extraneous noise including the barricade vessels." He hesitated. "Even operating on the surface, the *Ohio*-class submarines are ultra-quiet. There is minimal propeller cavitation and the hydrodynamic hull flow noise is suppressed."

"But can it be tracked for this condition?"

"Yes, sir. Even as quiet as it is, there are enough markers to isolate it as a unique target."

"Can the Mark Twelve lock in on that signature?"

"It should, sir. The water in the target area is shallow, only fifty to eighty meters deep. That will help preserve the signal."

"What about the escorts?"

"Those acoustic signatures are markedly different from the *Ohio*'s. The Mark Twelve should have no trouble distinguishing the target with multiple escorts."

"Excellent," the admiral said.

Madelyn was squirming—one of her signals for hunger pangs. Laura had seconds to act before Maddy erupted into a full-scale verbal assault.

With just enough light seeping in from the partially opened locker, she rotated the carrier 180 degrees. Laura unzipped the front of the jumpsuit she wore and leaned over Maddy, offering a breast.

* * *

The technical Q&A with Beijing continued for ten minutes and then Kwan summarized the presentation.

"As Commander Wang has discussed, we are now ready to implement the next phase of Sea Dragon. We expect the target will depart from its homeport in the next forty-eight to seventy-two hours. If it meets with your collective approval, we will deploy and prime the weapon for release."

Kwan and Wang waited for a response as Director Guo, General Sun, and Admiral Soo conferred with their microphones muted.

About a minute later Admiral Soo spoke. "What is your estimate on obtaining the intel from the second recording pod?"

Wang responded. "Sir, we are hoping to recover the unit tomorrow or the following day. I will then pressure Kirov to process the data into a usable form."

"If there is the slightest chance that it contains a recording of a submerged *Ohio*, I want you to recover it. Do you understand?"

"Yes, sir."

Kwan Chi reengaged, "But Admiral, the primary mission still takes precedence."

"Correct. However, we may never get a chance like this again. It has now become paramount that if at all possible, the second recording device should be recovered if it does not interfere with Sea Dragon."

"I understand."

General Sun spoke next. "What about the backstory regarding this Russian officer—is it fully in place now?"

"Yes, sir. When the Americans investigate, they will

find a trail leading back to Yuri Kirov and Northwest Subsea Dynamics."

"And what will be the final disposition of this particular individual?"

"He will be disposed of in a manner that will not be traceable to our operation. It will be consistent with his position as a Russian intelligence officer operating under deep cover carrying out the orders of his government."

The three key players again conferred offline.

Spymaster Guo said, "Kwan, you are authorized to proceed. Notify command when the target is under way."

"Yes, sir, we will comply."

The video blinked to a blue screen as the feed from Beijing terminated.

Kwan sighed, thankful the conference was over. He reached into a coat pocket and removed a pack of cigarettes, offering one to Wang.

After jointly lighting up, Wang said, "What about the woman, what's to become of her?"

"Same as Kirov—she will be in the vehicle with him when the accident occurs."

"Hmm, I see."

"You disapprove?"

"No, sir. I was just wondering about how we would take care of . . ." Wang searched for the right words. "What the Americans call *lost endings*." He struggled with his English.

"Loose ends," Kwan corrected him, also in English.

"Yes, that's it."

* * *

Maddy wasn't interested in nursing anymore; she was restless, squirming in her carrier. And Laura knew why. The odor emanating from the stinky diaper permeated the storage compartment.

Oh dear Lord, Laura thought.

Wang summed up the Kirov issue. "They need to be linked together to complete the deception. She will be viewed as a traitor, aiding and abetting a Russian spy. A clear path will be laid out that goes back to the Russian submarine incursions that occurred last year. The CIA and DIA analysts will conclude that the operation was planned well in advance of the current events. The data you collected from the recording pods will be linked to Kirov's company, completing the chain of evidence."

Wang nodded his understanding and then said, "And after the sinking, that will provide the justification for the war."

"Correct. We'll let the U.S. and Russia hammer on each other. The Americans will no doubt win, but it will cost them dearly."

"And then we make our move."

"Yes."

Wang was about to ask a follow-up question when he heard a muffled cry. Kwan heard it, too. They both turned to the left, eyeing the nearby locker.

Commander Wang stood up and stepped to the locker. He squatted and pulled open a door. Startled at what he'd discovered, Wang said, "Well, Ms. Newman, I see that you and your lovely daughter have been busy this evening."

CHAPTER 56

"She must have heard everything," Kwan Chi said. "I'm certain she did, but I doubt that she understood much."

"Maybe, maybe not."

Kwan and Wang were alone in the op center. Two guards had just escorted Laura and Madelyn back to the brig.

Kwan stood next to the locker where Laura had eavesdropped. As Wang watched, he kneeled and crawled inside the compartment, pulling the door shut. A whiff of the dirty diaper remained; it was a tight fit for his six-foot frame. He cracked open the locker door and peered outward. The bulkhead video display, now blacked out, was in his direct line of sight. He swore as he climbed out.

Now standing, Kwan faced Wang. "She may not have understood much, but she would have had an unrestricted view of everything on the screen."

Commander Wang mulled over Kwan's observation. "She would have certainly seen the photograph of Kirov."

"No doubt."

"And our entire command staff was displayed on the screen."

"Yes."

"I had all of those photos of the assembly of the Mark Twelve in the presentation—and photos of the *Ohios*."

"She's a smart woman," Kwan said. "She may not know all the details, but she saw enough to be a severe risk to us. She should never have been able to get out of the compartment. It was purposely designed as a holding cell—in case we ever had a problem with any of the crew."

"She's an engineer and runs a large enterprise. I now see how capable she really is."

Kwan walked the deck from port to starboard and back, considering his options.

While Kwan paced, Wang stood next to a desk, examining half a dozen eight-by-ten color photographs displayed on a desktop—surveillance photos taken at Laura Newman's home and NSD's office building. He picked up one of the photos.

Kwan completed his worry walk and stepped to Wang's side. He pointed to a print of Laura Newman and said, "We can no longer risk returning her and the child to Kirov, even for a brief period."

"I agree, but without them he will not complete the recovery of the second pod." Kwan returned the photo of Sarah Compton to the desk, slipping it under a photograph of the house.

"Then we need to change the plan."

"Sir?"

"With the recording information from the first pod, we now have everything needed to implement the next phase of Sea Dragon. The intel from the second pod is not vital to that mission—so as operation commander I can ignore that element."

"I agree, sir. But if the other seabed pod has recordings of one or more submerged missile boats, that would be of immense value to our anti-submarine forces. That was why Admiral Soo pushed so hard during the briefing."

"It's that important?"

"We still have no defense against them."

"Can you operate the underwater equipment to recover it without Kirov?"

"No, sir. We need his continued cooperation."

"He won't cooperate unless he gets Newman back . . . but if we do that she will tell him everything, and he'll figure it out."

Wang remained silent, unsure of Kwan's direction.

"So the key to this situation is to keep Kirov engaged but without giving in to his demands."

"I agree, sir, but at the very minimum he will demand proof of life again, which I don't think should come from us."

"Why?"

"Kirov must continue to believe this is a joint PRC Russian Federation operation. If he suspects otherwise, he could blow the entire operation." Wang pointed to the photo of Yuri in his uniform. "Remember, sir, he's still an officer in the Russian Navy. From everything I know about him he will not betray his brothers in arms."

Kwan turned to leave. "I need to think about this for a while. I'll be in my cabin."

* * *

Laura was again in the holding cell but without Madelyn. Instead of the original chair restraints, she lay flat on her back on top of the bunk. Her arms and legs were spread-eagle with each limb shackled to the adjacent corner of the oak frame that supported the mattress. Stainless steel handcuffs instead of rope secured her limbs. Heavy-duty steel eyebolts screwed into the frame anchored the companion cuffs that ensnared her wrists and ankles.

Laura could shift her torso an inch or so, but that was it. The cuffs were chafing her skin, especially on her ankles. She stopped struggling, knowing escape was impossible.

Even if Laura managed to pull a Houdini, it would not have gained her anything. A guard occupied the chair by the door to keep her company. Even more alarming, the guard and the other watchers who had bound Laura to the bunk all neglected to wear their masks—an ominous sign. But most vexing of all, every person Laura encountered this evening was Asian. That's when Laura realized she and Maddy were prisoners aboard a foreign vessel. It could be bound for just about anywhere.

Laura's current watcher was a slim female in her early twenties with glossy black hair cut short. Laura tried to engage her in conversation but received no response, not even a glance. The woman busied herself by reading magazines, which from Laura's limited vantage appeared to be in Chinese.

Laura looked upward at the unadorned overhead, her mind busy rehashing what she'd observed earlier in the evening.

The Chinese are up to something—but what?

How is Yuri involved?

What did they mean about "loose ends"?

Laura had been designated a "loose end" the year before. Yuri never mentioned it, but Laura feared she knew too much. To maintain operation security, the SVR had deemed Laura a liability. It had tasked Nick and Elena to eliminate that burden.

Fortunately for Laura—and Yuri—Nick refused to carry out the orders.

What about Elena? Laura wondered. *Could this be payback for what happened last year?*

Yuri had fretted about Elena's recent contact and the threats from Moscow that she'd relayed.

No, she's just the messenger. There's something else going on. Why are the Chinese involved?

Finally, her greatest worry of all. *Where's Maddy?*

It was all too much. She closed her eyes, flushed her wondering thoughts, and relaxed her taut muscles.

"Dear Lord," she whispered, "thank you for watching over Yuri and Maddy and me. Please continue to protect Yuri, and please help Maddy and me. Amen."

The guard looked up from an issue of *Xinmin Weekly*, trying to decipher what the American was muttering. Although she spoke passable English, nothing registered. A native of Shanghai and the daughter of a low-level Communist Party leader, she had never once prayed in her young life.

CHAPTER 57

DAY 29—MONDAY

Nick Orlov was asleep aboard his floating home when his cell phone announced its presence, transmitting from the nightstand next to his bed. He grudgingly reached to his side and picked it up. The display identified the caller.

"Hello, Fredek," he said in Russian.

"Sir, sorry for the early call, but the target is on the move."

Nick lowered the smartphone and glanced at the display: 5:48 A.M. "Where is she?"

"In her car, heading south."

"South . . . where south?"

"We think she's heading to the U.S. border."

Nick was now standing. He slept in a T-shirt and a pair of briefs. "Is she alone?"

"We think so but aren't sure. We're following two hundred meters behind. If we get much closer she could make us."

"Are you tracking her car with the GPS bug?"

"Yes."

"Drop back to about half a kilometer, just far enough to keep a visual on her vehicle."

"Yes, sir."

"What's your story for the U.S. border crossing?"

"We have a meeting in Seattle and then we'll be returning to Vancouver."

"What kind of meeting?"

"We're interested in a real estate investment—an apartment house for sale." Nick's operative continued with real names and places, all generated from a Seattle commercial real estate broker's website.

Creating a backup legend while on the go was standard protocol for SVR officers. Both men carried authentic Canadian passports expertly modified to include each man's photograph and physical description. Even the rental car could be traced to the driver's alias, paid for by a legitimate Visa card in his bogus name.

"Very good," Nick said. "Once you're through the border, keep the same distance behind but don't let her out of your sight, even though you're tracking her with a bug. She still might try to check for tails."

"Got it."

"I suspect she's heading to Seattle. I want you to call me every half hour with a status report."

"Every half hour—yes, sir."

Nick relocated to the shower. As the sizzling water washed over his weary body, Elena remained on his mind. During dinner in Vancouver she had told him she would be leaving on this day for another trip to Vladivostok and then to Beijing.

What is she doing?

* * *

Yuri stood on the timber deck, leaning against the railing while sipping from a coffee mug. He was home—the only real home he'd ever known in his adult life.

Laura had purchased the 5,500-square-foot home for its view. She loved to rise early and wait for the sun to climb over the Cascades, transforming the lake surface from dull gray shadows to brilliant azure hues. The sunsets were equally dazzling. This morning the sky was clear, portending fair weather for the rest of the day.

Yuri arrived home just before one in the morning. The three shots of Stoli he'd downed at NSD took its toll. He'd sacked out in his office, laying on the couch for a quick snooze. He woke up nearly four hours later, still worn out but sober enough to drive.

Returning to the house was a burden, knowing strangers had invaded it and stolen his love and her child.

None of this would ever have happened if I'd just left her alone!

Yuri had needed an ally if he was going to have any chance of the saving the *Neva*'s remaining crew. His manipulation was subtle, the fabrications and half-truths designed to win Laura over.

I'm a fraud; I used her.

She risked everything to help me.

Humbled, Yuri closed his eyes and asked for guidance, a rite he had embraced as a youth but let languish for most of his adult life—until Laura.

Kwan Chi took the elevator from his stateroom to the lower deck where he proceeded aft, entering the sanitary white engine room. Both turbocharged diesels were silent; ditto for the twin generators. The *Yangzi* remained on shore power.

He walked past the portside exhaust manifold, its gleaming stainless steel collector mirroring his distorted image. Finally, he reached his destination, opening a watertight hatchway that led to the tender compartment—also known as the "garage."

Located at the aft end of the lower deck, the huge compartment stored the *Yangzi*'s toys: a couple of paddleboards, four Kawasaki Jet Skis, a twenty-foot rigid-hulled inflatable, and a twenty-eight-foot Grady White tender.

This morning a steel cylinder occupied the deck space typically reserved for the tender. Seven meters long and a meter in diameter, the industrial black tube did not fit in with the other water toys in the super-yacht's garage.

Kwan walked to the midsection of the cylinder where Commander Wang squatted next to a hull opening. Both of his hands were inside the inspection port.

"Trouble?" asked Kwan, now kneeling beside Wang.

Wang turned. "There's some kind of wiring fault. I ran a system test and the fault showed up. It can be by-passed, but I want to see if we can correct it first."

"This won't delay us?"

"No. We could launch right now, if we had to. I just want to get it back to one hundred percent."

"The acoustic information—you've already added it in?"

"Correct. We transferred the digital data file of the submarine's propulsion and propeller sound prints into the unit's targeting computer. I already ran a full course of diagnostics. Everything is as it should be—no faults there."

"Excellent."

Kwan stood and took a few steps to the forward end of the cylinder. Death was inside the canister. The torpedo's warhead housed inside the cylinder contained 250 kilograms of high explosives.

Kwan ran his hand aft over the black substance that covered the Mark 12's skin when Commander Wang joined him. "What is this coating?" Kwan asked. "It feels like rubber."

"It's an anti-sonar coating. Minimizes acoustic reflections."

"Hmm," Kwan said, withdrawing his hand.

"Sir, what do you plan to do about Kirov?" Wang asked.

"The SVR contact will be here soon."

"The woman?"

"Yes. I'm going to use her to deal with Kirov."

Wang expected additional details, but Kwan offered nothing further. He moved on to his second inquiry.

"If we have the time, I would like to recover Kirov's underwater device. It would be a real asset to the Fleet Intelligence Group."

"Where is it now?"

"It should have completed its survey mission for the second listening device. I expect it is currently sitting on the bottom offshore of Whidbey Island, waiting for the recall signal to surface."

"Do you have this recall code?"

"No, Kirov has it."

Kwan wrinkled his brow, the pressure in his gut

building. "I can't promise anything at this time. The mission comes first—you know that."

"Of course."

"If we have time, I'll consider it."

"Very good, sir.

"Good morning, Chi," Elena Krestyanova announced as she entered the reception section of Kwan's personal suite. It was 9:20 A.M. Elena wore a knee-length navy blue pleated skirt with a matching jacket and a beige silk blouse underneath. She had substituted a pair of deck shoes for her usual three-inch heels.

Kwan rose from the leather couch, always delighted to take in the Russian's spectacular looks. "Thank you for coming so quickly. I know you were scheduled to leave for Vladivostok today."

"No problem. I delayed my flight."

Kwan gestured toward the private dining cupola a dozen steps aft. "I have coffee and a light breakfast, if you are hungry. Please join me."

"Wonderful."

Kwan and Elena sat side by side at a round hardwood table that could have easily accommodated a dozen. The southerly view took in downtown Seattle's skyscrapers. The silhouette of towering Mount Rainier was visible in the haze.

Kwan drank coffee while Elena munched on a fruit plate. He rarely ate breakfast.

Kwan waited until his personal steward refilled the coffee cups and departed. He then provided Elena with the basics.

After taking in Kwan's report, Elena picked up her

coffee cup and took a sip. "Kirov is not going to like the change in plans," she said.

"He's the one who changed the plan. All along, he was tasked with retrieving both underwater recording pods. It's vital that he finish the assignment. We need the acoustic data from the second unit."

"But didn't you say he wouldn't do anything else until Newman and the child are released?"

"Yes, that's what he told Wang yesterday."

"He's stubborn, believe me."

"That's why I asked you to come here. I need you to convince him to complete his work and then we'll release his woman and the baby."

"They are still aboard?"

"Yes."

"And where is Kirov?"

"At his home."

"Under surveillance?"

"Yes."

"And the workboat that he and Wang have been using, where is it right now?"

Kwan said, "Anna . . . Anna-something."

"Anacortes?"

"Yes, that's the place."

Elena looked away as she rehashed Kwan's request. The idea jelled half a minute later. She turned back to face Kwan. "Okay, here's what I think."

"Yuri, Nick."

"*Dobroe utro!*"—Good morning.

Yuri remained at home; Nick called from the consulate in San Francisco using a secure phone. Yuri used the cell Nick had provided. They spoke in Russian.

Nick said, "I have an update on Elena."

"What's she up to?"

"Trouble, I suspect. She left Vancouver early this morning and drove to Seattle. I had her tailed. She ended up at a private marina near downtown. She just boarded a huge yacht tied up to the visitor's dock. My team following her reported that the damn thing is a football field long."

"What do you know about it?"

"The boat is at the far end of a dock and the gate to the dock is locked. We should have more info soon— my guys will figure out a way to get an ID on it."

"Could her trip be related to official SVR business?"

"Right now, she's supposed to be on an Air Canada flight to South Korea. From there she's scheduled to connect with another flight to Vladivostok."

"So we have a sudden change in plans."

"Apparently."

"Have you been able to check with her supervisor?"

"That's part of the problem. The op she's involved with in China is run from Moscow. We're totally out of the loop here at the consulate. Without making waves, I can't get past the security protocols. I don't want to tip my hand until we know more."

Yuri digested Nick's report. "It sounds like you think there could be a problem with her."

"Maybe. There's still nothing that I could find in our system that indicates she was recalled to deal with you regarding the seabed recorders—or Laura's situation."

"Nick, she's working on her own. None of what she's doing with me has been sanctioned."

"I don't know. It's possible that what's going on is related to her China operations."

"Do you really believe that?"

"I know you have suspected her all along but—"

"She's turned, Nick. That's the only thing that makes sense."

"But why would she go rogue? I don't understand that."

"If I had to guess, I'd say money."

"I don't know . . ."

Yuri moved on. "Last night, I told my PRC contact I wasn't going to provide any additional intel on the seabed recorders until Laura and Maddy are released. That didn't go over very well. He's been pressing me hard to finish the work, claiming that both China and Russia need all of the underwater data in order to counter the U.S. missile subs. I know that's bullshit— at least for our own uses."

"I don't understand."

"I'm convinced the GRU knows nothing about this operation, same for the SVR." Yuri hesitated, recalling an open issue. "And remember the so-called liaison— Tim Dixon. He has to be a shill. I bet he's not even Russian."

"I haven't found anything on him."

"And you won't because he's a fake," Yuri said. "The risks that we're now taking, searching for and re-covering the seabed pods, are insane. Russia's rela-tions with the U.S. are at near crisis point because of the problems in the Arctic plus what happened to their oil tanker and then the attack on Sakhalin. Think about that. The Kremlin would never sanction an operation to recover the pods at a time like now."

"It would be a perfect excuse for the Americans to start a war."

"Exactly. We were lucky last year with the *Neva*. But now, if the American Navy discovered the pods—or me—it might be enough to push them over the cliff."

"You're right," said Nick. "There's something wrong here."

"And guess who's mixed up right in the middle of it?"

"I get it, Yuri."

"Elena's in Seattle to deal with me. Whoever she's working for wants me to finish the recovery. She's going to continue to use Laura and Maddy as leverage to force me to comply. And when I do that, you know what's going to happen to us."

"How can I help?"

"I need you here again—now!"

CHAPTER 58

When Yuri drove into Northwest Subsea Dynamic's parking lot at 10:12 A.M., the cell in his coat pocket chimed; it was Nick's throwaway. His company phone remained silent and its GPS tracker turned off. Yuri parked his Highlander in an open stall, switched off the engine, and reached for the ringing mobile. Only two people knew its calling number, Nick Orlov and Elena Krestyanova. The screen displayed "Unknown Caller."

"Hello," he answered.

"Privet, Yuri."

"I wondered when you would call," Yuri said, switching to match Elena's dialect.

"Yes, it seems that I have been tasked once more with coordinating this operation. Our Chinese partners claim you are being unreasonable—again!"

"You're wasting your time. I'm not doing anything more until Laura and Madelyn are released."

"Come on, Yuri. You're almost done."

"I don't care—this has gone on too damn long."

"We need you to recover your underwater machine today and then process the data. That's it—then you'll be done and your lovely partner and her infant will be returned to you."

"No."

"Captain Lieutenant Kirov, this comes straight from the Ministry of Defense." Elena's voice stiffened. "You are directed to complete the operation and cooperate fully with our Chinese allies."

"Not until they're released."

Yuri waited for the expected reply but heard nothing. "Elena, are you still there?"

A new voice responded in English. "Yuri, honey, it's me."

Laura! Yuri was energized as a flood of endorphins surged into his bloodstream.

"Are you okay?" he asked.

"Yes, I'm fine. They've been treating us well. Elena's here, too."

"Where are you?"

"I can't say anything about that. The people holding us will only allow me to say that if you finish whatever it is you're supposed to do today they will release Maddy and me tonight."

She seemed to be listening to another voice in the background, then continued. "They promised me that if you finish the assignment and we remain silent about what's happened, you can stay here—in the United States. You will be officially retired from the Navy in good standing and the Russian government will not object to your immigration to the U.S."

"Who promised this?"

Yuri's question met another round of silence.

Elena spoke, this time in English. "As Laura just said, you'll be a free man once you complete the assignment. No strings attached."

"What do you want me to do?"

"That's more like it."

Yuri remained seated in the SUV, thinking about what had just happened. He picked up the same cell and dialed.

Nick answered on the third ring.

"It's me again," Yuri said. "I just heard from Laura."

"She and Maddy okay?"

"Yes, and guess who's with her?"

"No?"

"Elena claimed that the FSB and GRU again recalled her to convince me to cooperate."

Nick cursed. "That means Laura is in Seattle with Elena."

"Yes. Is Elena still on that yacht?"

"As of twenty minutes ago, when my guys phoned in a status report."

"That's where they've been holding them. Remember what Laura first told me about asking Dan Miller and the *Hercules* for help to find the pods? We knew it was a clue, but I didn't make the connection until now."

"You're right!"

"What has your surveillance team found out about the boat?"

"It's named the *Yangzi*. Registered in the Cayman

Islands. Supposed to belong to some Hong Kong billionaire named Kwan."

Yuri cursed.

"There's more—it's all fitting together now."

"What?"

"When I ran Kwan's name through our system, he was flagged. Turns out he's MSS."

"She's working for this guy, Nick. He turned her somehow."

"I agree. She's a double."

"I'm running out of time. I've got to get Laura and Maddy off that boat before everything implodes. When will you be here?"

"My flight leaves at one fifteen."

"I'll pick you up."

The MSS operatives stalking Yuri Kirov parked their Honda Accord on the street about fifty meters from Northwest Subsea Dynamics. The GPS tracker attached to the frame of Yuri's Highlander allowed them to follow discreetly. The two men had an unobstructed view of the SUV. Aided by a pair of binoculars, the MSS team leader kept watch as the target remained inside the vehicle.

When Yuri exited the Toyota and walked in the front door of the office building, the senior operative decided to phone in a status report. He connected with Commander Wang.

"The subject drove straight from his residence, arriving at his business approximately twelve minutes ago."

"No stops?" asked Wang.

"That's correct, sir. But when he parked, he sat inside the vehicle for ten minutes. He appeared to be talking on a cell phone."

"But he's inside the building now?"

"Yes, about two minutes ago."

"Keep monitoring. I expect he will be on the move soon. When he does leave, continue your surveillance but at safe distance. Call me the minute he leaves."

"Yes, sir."

Yuri ignored the first three calls from Nick's throwaway phone as he sat at his office desk working. He suspected either Elena or Wang, but the caller left no voice mail messages. The NSD receptionist also held all of his landline calls.

It was half past noon. Knowing he could not delay any further, Yuri answered the fourth call. "Hello," he said.

"What are you doing?" demanded Wang. "You're supposed to be in Anacortes now."

"Something's come up."

"I don't care. You need to leave now."

"No, I don't."

Wang said, "Look, Kirov, if you ever want to see—"

Yuri cut him off. "I already have what you want."

"What do you mean?"

"This morning I took a second look at the data from the recording pod we recovered. Remember the background noise that I filtered out to help capture the surface contacts?"

"What about it?"

"I ran an analysis this morning on the raw background sounds—unfiltered."

"Why?"

"I didn't have the time, or the energy last night, plus it's a hassle to set up. Anyway, we—the Russian Navy—always analyze every byte of the data recorded by the pods, even background. Sometimes you get lucky."

"You found something!"

"I did."

"A submerged contact?"

"Yes."

"Is it an *Ohio*?"

"I don't know yet, but it certainly is not a *Los Angeles-* or *Virginia*-class. I know those sound prints."

"What then?"

"Possibly a *Seawolf*. The prototype is based here." Yuri paused. "But what I really suspect is that it's one of the two converted *Ohios* that are based at Bangor."

As part of the Strategic Arms Reduction Treaty with Russia, the U.S. Navy removed all nuclear-tipped Trident missiles from four *Ohio*-class SSBN submarines. The missile silos were converted to carry conventional armed cruise missiles and the subs reclassified as SSGNs. Two of the converted boats homeported at Bangor with each sub carrying up to 166 Tomahawks.

Wang considered Yuri's revelation. "Why would the American Navy allow it to run submerged so close to its base?"

"The risks are lower—no nukes aboard, other than the reactor. Plus they carry another very special cargo that demands absolute secrecy."

Wang picked up instantly on Yuri's lead-in. "SEALs."

"Correct."

In addition to carrying cruise missiles, the *Ohio* SSGNs were equipped with an advanced SEAL delivery system that allowed for the clandestine insertion of a SEAL force up to sixty-six strong onto a hostile shore.

Wang said, "We've heard rumors that those boats simply disappear."

He referred to the MSS illegal who monitored submarine traffic into and out of Hood Canal. On several occasions, the spy had reported the unexplained and unobserved departure of an SSGN. In contrast, the missile subs—SSBNs—were always noticed. As an apparent safety requirement for submarines carrying nuclear weapons, the Trident boats would navigate on the surface when passing through the drawspan opening of the Hood Canal Bridge. Traffic backs up on both sides of the opening, allowing unobstructed public views of the warships as they cruise to and from the Bangor base.

"That fits," Yuri said. "I think the converted ones must be allowed to navigate under the floating bridge rather than use the surface opening. That way they could reach the Pacific submerged and avoid satellite tracking."

"That explains a lot," Wang offered.

"Piece of cake for the U.S. Navy."

"What?"

Yuri didn't try to enlighten Wang on the meaning of the America idiom, one that he had picked up from Laura. Instead, he said, "With the sonar capability of an *Ohio*, they could easily sail under the floating bridge, even with its anchor lines."

"This is very good news, Kirov," said Wang. "We

may no longer need to recover the second pod. I need to review your analysis of the submerged recording to make that determination."

"There's no need to waste time with the other pod. I have what you want. The complete analyses along with the raw data files are stored on a portable drive sitting on my desk."

"I'll send a messenger—he can be at your office in minutes."

"Not so fast. We have other business first."

"I know what you want, but you must produce the data first."

"No. We're going to make an exchange on neutral grounds."

Wang rubbed his chin. "What do you propose?"

"I will only deal with my people, specifically Elena Krestyanova. I know her and trust her."

"That might be possible, assuming the Kremlin sanctions the trade."

"It will. Our Navy wants this data just as much as yours. Why do you think we risked placing the recording pods in the Americans' backyard? It's been a priority for years."

"All right, what else?"

"We make the exchange tonight; I want Ms. Krestyanova to handle it." Yuri dictated the details of the swap.

After taking in Yuri's demand, Wang said, "What you propose is feasible, assuming Krestyanova receives clearance from Moscow."

"She will, but what about you—what clearances do you need?"

"None. This is my operation."

"Good. Then you need to find Elena and have her call me."

"I will work on it as soon as we hang up."

"One final item, Wang." Yuri raised his voice. "If you double-cross me, I will blow the entire operation. I don't care that you're partnering with Russia. Both of you have used my family as pawns."

"Calm down, Kirov. This is going to work out."

"You know I only care about one thing?"

"Yes."

"Just make sure they're safe."

"Do you believe his story?"

"Technically, yes. What he said about the submerged recording is possible. But I still don't trust him."

Kwan Chi and Wang Park relocated to the operations center, sitting across from each other at the conference table. Elena remained in the upper-deck salon. Wang had just briefed Kwan on his conversation with Yuri Kirov.

"So he flatly refused to recover the second recording pod?"

"He claims it's no longer needed."

"We have no way to know if he is playing us or not."

"Not until we get access to the raw data and conduct an independent analysis."

Kwan looked away, thinking. Half a minute later, he faced Wang. "I agree that it is wise to remain cautious regarding Kirov. However, we have backed him into a corner, which is dangerous for us as well as him. We must now use finesse to complete the process. He needs the illusion of hope, and that has to come from you."

Illusion of hope, Wang thought, knowing it was code. "I understand, sir."

"Do you still have him under surveillance?"

"Yes, he remains at his office."

"Very well, your request to abandon recovery of the second pod is approved. You may recall your team from Anacortes. I will have Ms. Krestyanova set up what Kirov wants."

"Thank you. I'll get right on it."

"Commander, there's something else." He met Wang's eyes.

"Sir?"

"I know the importance of the information Kirov says he has, but it's now secondary to our mission. Kirov's threat to expose us is something I cannot take lightly. He could screw up everything."

"I understand, sir."

"I want you to plan for the exchange as he outlined, but your primary task is to take him out during or immediately after it is completed—do you understand?"

"Terminate Kirov."

"Correct. He needs to be removed tonight."

"And his companion?"

"The woman needs to be disposed of with Kirov."

"And the child . . . ?"

"We are not monsters, Wang."

Wang looked concerned. "It could get messy, sir. He'll no doubt be armed . . . and in a public place."

"I'm sure you can work it out."

Wang started to stand but Kwan waved him back. "One last item," he said.

"Sir?"

"You will have a third target tonight."

Wang frowned, uncertain about Kwan's reference.

"Our Russian liaison, Ms. Krestyanova. She cannot be trusted. Nothing can be traced back to us through her."

CHAPTER 59

Yuri paced the carpet in his office. His stomach broiled, a dull ache over his forehead was in its infancy, and he'd started limping earlier in the morning, the nerves in his lower left leg misfiring—remnant damage from the bends triggered by anxiety.

He had outmaneuvered Wang. But at what cost?

There was no sound print of a submerged U.S. submarine hidden within the background clatter of the underwater recordings, just a mishmash of static.

Yuri had made it up.

The thought had come to him in the morning back at the house while sipping coffee. He needed his own leverage if he was going to save Laura and Maddy. And now he had it, at least for a while.

Just the hint of what Yuri had promised about the acoustic data would catapult Wang to superstar status in the People's Liberation Army-Navy. An unambiguous recording of a submerged *Ohio*-class sub would represent the crown jewel in Red China's program to suppress U.S. power in the Pacific. The recording would allow the PLAN to engineer methods to track and sink America's most secret strategic weapon system.

But it was all a lie.

Yuri had one chance to pull it off. Elena was his key. Her role would make sense to Wang and his controllers. To succeed, however, Yuri needed help. Nick was on the way and two of his operatives were already on-site keeping tabs on Elena. But that wasn't enough.

Yuri walked to the window and peered at the parking lot. The Honda Accord remained parked in the same spot.

He checked his wristwatch.

Soon, he thought.

The cavalry was five minutes out.

"He was adamant about you. He told Wang you are the only one he trusts."

"We did work together over a year ago, but we're hardly friends."

"Nevertheless, he wants you to make the exchange."

Aboard the *Yangzi* at 1:25 P.M., Kwan Chi and Elena Krestyanova were in Kwan's personal salon on the upper deck. They sat on leather sofas facing each other.

"Where is this exchange supposed to take place?" Elena asked.

"At the airport—Alaska Airlines check-in section."

"Very clever. That's about as public a place as you can get."

"Yes, and it's full of security."

"Trade Newman and her baby for this new underwater intel he has?"

"Yes. We really need the data—and so do you, for your final payment."

That grabbed Elena's attention. "I sense there is a new issue with Ms. Newman."

"There is. We can't possibly let her free—she knows far too much now."

Elena's eyebrows narrowed. She was unsure of where Kwan was leading her. "Then you—we have a problem. If there's one thing I know about Kirov, it's that he never gives up. And he is incredibly resourceful."

"He's already told Wang that he'll blow the operation if we turn on him."

"You should believe him, Chi. His life revolves around Newman. If she's gone he has nothing to lose."

"I take his threat seriously. We must continue to maintain operational security at all costs."

"That's fine, and like I've said before, I don't want to know what your op is."

"Understood. But still, he has thrust you back into the fray."

"He will not release the data until Newman and the child are free, and you can't let her go because she knows too much. Do I have it right?"

"Yes."

"Then it's all a matter of timing. When will your op here be over?"

"Two to three days, maybe four."

"All right. That gives me something to work with."

Laura remained locked up in the holding cell but no longer shackled to the bedframe. She lay on her side on the bunk facing a bulkhead. Her ankles and wrists were still cuffed. Her watcher, another young Asian female, sat in a chair by the door. She held a tablet, reading.

Earlier, Elena Krestyanova paid a visit, informing Laura that her release was imminent provided she cooperated.

Laura's few words with Yuri had boosted her spirits, but the euphoria soon eroded.

Laura had never once trusted Elena. From her first encounter the year before, Laura's radar penetrated the Russian's veneer of charm and beauty, sensing an underlying core of ruthless deception. Yuri had eventually caught on and outmaneuvered Elena.

But here they were again—mixed up with Medusa herself.

Lord, please help us.

CHAPTER 60

"What did they do?" asked Yuri.

"Took off like rabbits."

"Good."

Yuri was in his office at Northwest Subsea Dynamics. The African American sitting in the chair fronting his desk was mammoth—six-seven and a well-muscled 260. His all-black ensemble was military quality. Although no weapons were visible, Yuri was certain he was armed.

"How long were they there?" asked the senior security consultant.

"I spotted them when I drove to work this morning, just after ten o'clock. They've been parked there the whole time."

"Can you provide me with some additional background on the situation?"

"It's complicated. They're associated with the people holding my partner and her child."

"What about Sarah Compton?"

"I don't know, but I suspect she's also with Laura."

"You've spoken with your partner—today?"

"Yes, a couple of hours ago."

"Ransom demand?"

"I'm putting it together now."

"I know you have talked with my boss about this, but we still recommend that you notify the local police and the FBI. This is serious shit."

"I understand but I can't—at least not yet."

"Okay, Mr. Kirkwood, I understand your situation." The former U.S. Army Ranger shifted position in his chair. "I want to assure you that your case has highest priority."

"Thank you. You've already helped by getting rid of my tail. I don't think they'll be back, but I'd like some of your men to stay behind to protect my employees. The staff here has no idea what is going on, and I want to keep it that way."

"Certainly."

"Do you have the capability to locate transmitters?"

"Electronic bugs?"

"Yes."

"We sure do—I can have a debug team here within an hour."

"I'd like the entire office swept plus my vehicle—it's the silver Highlander." Yuri pointed at the nearby window and the parking lot beyond.

"No problem. I'll set it up right now." He reached into a jacket pocket and removed a cell phone.

"One other thing?" Yuri said, glancing at his wristwatch.

"Sure."

"I need a ride to the airport—and a handgun."

*   *   *

"Kirov's taking precautions," Wang said.

"What?"

"He has reinforcements—they compromised the surveillance team at his office. I just found out."

Wang called Kwan on the ship's phone system. Wang was on the lower deck in the *Yangzi*'s garage. Kwan was three decks above on the bridge. Elena remained in the upper-deck salon.

"The authorities?" asked Kwan, his voice strained.

"No, private security with at least six operatives in three vehicles. Probably the same company he hired for Newman."

"Where is Kirov?"

"My men believe he's still at his office. They were forced to break off monitoring and no longer have eyes on the building, but his vehicle remains at the office. We have a GPS tracker on it, which means he's probably there."

"He's obviously up to something."

"Being careful, I suspect. He's an intelligence officer and has the same skill sets we use."

"So, it would seem there is no way we can get to him directly."

"No, sir. Not with the hired guns. It would be a bloodbath at the airport. There are local and federal police, plus cameras everywhere."

"He knows that—smart move on his part."

"I agree."

Kwan processed the new information, probing for a path out of the labyrinth he had created and Kirov now exploited.

"We must postpone the exchange until our mission is complete," Kwan said.

"But, sir, Kirov is expecting to make the exchange tonight. I don't know what he'll do if I delay it."

"Commander, he will do nothing—we still have what he wants."

"You're right."

"I will have Ms. Krestyanova make the call to Kirov. And about that other item we spoke about earlier, that, too, will need to be postponed. Understand?"

"Krestyanova?"

"Yes. Where are all of your people right now?"

"I have two teams ashore—one attempting to re-establish surveillance of Kirov and the other casing the airport in case we need to follow through there."

"Recall them. Without this exchange business to deal with, we can depart early."

"Yes, sir. I'll take care of it."

CHAPTER 61

"This place is amazing," Nicolai Orlov said as he stared through the SUV's windshield.

"It is." Yuri sat behind the steering wheel of a Jeep Cherokee. They had just driven into the parking lot of the Elliott Bay Marina. Located north of downtown Seattle, the privately owned twelve-hundred-slip marina offered world-class moorage for boats ranging from thirty-foot sailboats to one-hundred-foot-plus mega yachts.

Yuri pulled into a vacant stall near the center of the marina and switched off the engine. He had rented the Jeep at the airport after meeting Nick.

"That must be it," Yuri said, peering over the dashboard and gesturing toward the distant water.

"Wow, that thing's a monster."

The *Yangzi* remained moored to the marina's guest dock along the eastern end of the moorage basin. Its football-field length and six deck levels overwhelmed the other craft in the marina.

"Where are your men located?"

Nick removed a small notebook from his coat jacket

and opened it. "Near the gate that serves docks at the east end of the marina. The yacht is tied up to the seaward end of the last dock."

Yuri rested his hands on the steering wheel. "You need to talk to them without me present. I don't want any more exposure, especially to SVR case officers. That could get complicated for both of us."

"Agreed. I'll get an update and then turn 'em loose to find a hotel and crash. They've been on the go all day plus tracking her before that."

"What do they know about Elena?"

"Just what I told them—monitor the subject's movements and report only to me."

"You know these guys?"

"They're young but have been trained well. I have confidence in them."

"Good. Hopefully, we can pull this off without their help, but it's encouraging to know they are close by."

"You're still convinced that Laura's aboard that boat?"

"Yes, and we should know soon if I'm right or not."

"Okay, got it. I'm going to talk to them now. I'll be back soon." Nick opened his door and stepped out.

Yuri watched Nick work his way through the sea of parked vehicles. He reached under his seat and extracted the handgun. The Colt Mark IV Series 80 fit comfortably in his hand. The compact semiautomatic's magazine held six .45 ACP cartridges. Its aluminum alloy frame and short barrel resulted in a lightweight concealable weapon that delivered a round with persuasive killing power. After driving Yuri to Sea-Tac Airport, the security company's supervisor lent him the pistol and spare magazine.

Yuri studied the weapon before returning it to the hideaway.

Overwhelmed by fatigue, Yuri yawned and leaned back in the bucket seat. He'd barely slept the previous evening. Within seconds his eyes closed against his will.

Then he jolted awake.

Nick pulled open the Jeep's passenger door and reclaimed his seat.

"Elena's still on the boat," he announced.

Yuri said, "You're certain?"

"Yes. The only way in or out of the dock is from the access pier. It has a gated entrance. They've had eyes on it the entire time. Someone let her in in the morning. That's the last time they saw her."

"Could she have left on another boat?"

"It's possible, but unlikely. They've been watching for boat traffic around the yacht, too. But I didn't notice anything like that."

"Okay, that's good news. Laura must still be on board, too."

"That's my take."

"Where are your men now?"

"Still watching. I told to 'em to wait until I called to relieve them."

Yuri checked his watch: 4:50 P.M. He'd scheduled the exchange for 7:00 P.M. Four operatives from the security company were already at the airport, waiting.

"Elena and her goons should be leaving soon to get to the airport with Laura. Go ahead and turn your men loose and we'll take over." Yuri's plan was to follow Elena and Laura to the airport and then make the exchange. The portable drive with bogus data was in the backseat inside a cardboard box.

"Okay, sounds good." Nick reached into a jacket pocket and removed his phone. Before he could dial, however, Yuri's disposable cell rang. It was stored in the Jeep's center console.

Yuri retrieved the phone and checked the screen. "It's Elena," he said.

"Were you expecting a call this early?"

"No. Something's up."

Yuri hit the speakerphone key. "Hello," he said in English.

"Yuri, Elena here."

"Yes."

"A problem has come up—not related to you, but it concerns what's planned for tonight. We need to reschedule."

"What do you mean?"

"I don't have any details, only that they can't make the exchange tonight."

"I want to speak to Wang. Put him on the line."

"I don't know where he is."

"If you are double-crossing me I'm going to—"

"Back off, Yuri! This is out of my control. I only know what I've been told—the principals are not available tonight."

"When, then?"

"Maybe tomorrow. I'll call you."

"I want to speak with Laura right now."

"Just a moment."

Frowning, Yuri faced Nick.

Nick also grimaced.

"Yuri, is that you?" Laura announced over the speaker. "Are you okay?"

"I'm all right—what's going on?"

"There's some kind of delay."

"That's what Elena said."

"Is she with you?"

"Yes."

"And Maddy?"

"She's with me."

"Have they—"

Elena interrupted Yuri. "Sorry, but we need to end this conversation. As you heard, she and Madelyn are fine. I will call you tomorrow for a new time."

The call ended with a click.

Yuri tossed the phone back into the console. "What the hell are they doing?"

"Maybe they suspect something."

"What?"

"If I had to guess, I'd say it's the airport—a brilliant location for your end of the bargain but dangerous for them."

"Not if they're upfront and make the—" Yuri stopped, the revelation striking like an avalanche. "They have no intention of honoring the deal."

"That's the way I see it," Nick agreed. "You're the target, but there's no way they can get to you at the airport. They probably had operators there this afternoon trying to figure out how but realized it wasn't going to work."

"Shit, what have I done?" Yuri's threats to blow the operation now haunted him.

"You've still got leverage, but when Elena or Wang or whoever calls back to reschedule, there's going to be a new venue, one that's much more favorable for their goals."

Yuri reached under the seat and grabbed the Colt. He racked the slide, chambering a round. He slipped the pistol into a coat pocket and reached for the door release.

"Hang on, Yuri Ivanovich. Not yet."

"I know they're aboard that thing. I can't wait any longer."

Nick placed his hand on Yuri's right wrist. "We need to think this through. Remember now, we've been through a lot more than this. We're going to get them back."

Yuri closed his eyes and inhaled. "You're right. We need a new plan."

"Good. First we need to figure out how to get past the gate on the dock and then—"

Nick stopped when his cell phone chimed. He retrieved the phone and checked the screen. "It's my guys." After listening, Nick announced, "Elena just walked through the gate and is heading for her car."

"My God—are Laura and Maddy with her?"

"No, she's alone."

Yuri started the engine and reached for the gearshift.

"What are you doing?"

"We're going to have a little chat with that bitch."

"Stop. You could blow everything. My guys will follow her."

"But she's going to get away."

"That's not going to happen—I guarantee you that."

"I don't care. I've got to get to her now." He shifted into drive.

"No, Yuri. Think about the situation. What did we just find out?"

"What?"

"Calm down, get your head back in order."

Yuri followed Nick's advice, switching off the Jeep's engine. And then it registered. "They really are on that boat!"

CHAPTER 62

The sun sank behind the Olympics. Yuri and Nick were on the guest dock about a hundred feet from the *Yangzi*. They stood in the shadows, avoiding the dock lights. A friendly boater exiting the dock had let them through the gate.

"Do you see any sentries?" Yuri asked as he studied the superyacht's stern. The *Yangzi* radiated with a dazzling display of shipboard lighting, including underwater hull illumination.

"I don't see anyone obvious, but I'm sure some of those characters are security."

"There seems to be a lot of activity on the decks."

"Yes, it's like they're getting ready for something."

Yuri and Nick watched as crew members scurried about the lower and main decks. Two men walked down the yacht's gangway onto the floating pier. One headed toward the bow and the other to the stern.

"What are they up to?" Nick asked.

"I don't know."

When the man at the stern knelt onto the concrete dock, Yuri figured it out.

"They're releasing the mooring lines from the cleats."

Nick cursed. "It must be leaving."

The two crewmen returned to the gangway and stepped up to the main deck landing.

Yuri yanked the Colt from his coat pocket and moved forward, but Nick grabbed his left arm. "No, Yuri."

Yuri turned to face Nick, enraged. "They're getting away. I've got to go now."

"Not like this. They'll cut you down before you get aboard."

Yuri relaxed, his blind fury checked. Nick released his grip.

Both men watched as a crewman on the main deck activated a hydraulic drive that raised the gangway. Once it was secure in its hull mounting, potent surges of water jetted from the stern and the bow, propelling the 3,300-ton vessel sideways from the dock.

About a minute later, the *Yangzi*'s twin propellers thrust the yacht past the southern end of the marina's offshore rock breakwater. She then proceeded on a northwestward heading across Elliott Bay.

Deflated, Yuri lowered his head and stared at the concrete dock.

Nick put his arm around his friend's shoulder. "Don't give up. We're going to get Laura and Maddy back."

The *Yangzi* ran northbound in mid-channel at twelve knots. Under way on Puget Sound for nearly an hour, the yacht was abeam of Point Wells near the City of Edmonds. The captain stood at the center of the control console, monitoring the autopilot. The navigator manned his station on the right side of the captain.

The ship's control console rivaled that of a jumbo jet, with myriad LED screen displays facing the captain and navigator. Although both men wore civilian garb, they were commissioned officers in the People's Liberation Army-Navy.

The crimson lighting inside the wheelhouse helped with the night conditions; it minimized glare and aided in the identification of objects on the blackened water surface. The rising fractional moon further enhanced sea visibility.

Kwan Chi and Wang Park sat side by side on a bench seat at the starboard side of the pilothouse. A steward brought a fresh pot of tea and two porcelain mugs and placed them on the compact table that fronted the bench. They quietly observed as the ship headed north. After a textbook departure, the *Yangzi* and its crew remained in sync. The ship's crew members were just hours away from executing the most important mission of their careers.

Unlike other superyachts, the *Yangzi* required a minimal complement. Normally, a crew of thirty would staff a vessel of her size. The *Yangzi* required just eighteen. Like the captain and navigator, the crew were handpicked from the PLAN's officers' corps and the NCO ranks. Although military, they carried civilian passports and were never in uniform while aboard. Kwan Chi, his personal steward, and two MSS security officers were the only nonmilitary staff on the ship.

"How long will it take to deploy the device?" Kwan asked after taking a sip from the stinging hot green tea.

"Once we're on station, the entire operation should take no more than five to ten minutes."

"I suppose there is no way for us to remain incognito at that time."

"No, sir. Because of our size, we will have eyes on us during the entire trip. The U.S. Coast Guard is tracking us now. Later, when we enter the Strait of Georgia, the Canadians will take over."

"What happens when we stop for deployment?"

"If we were to stop for more than the planned five minutes, the Coast Guard might notice and we would likely be queried by radio, especially if there is other vessel traffic in the area. I have spoken to the captain about this contingency. If questioned, he will report a minor issue with an electrical generator that resulted in the need for a short engine shutdown. Once we resume normal cruising operations, the Coast Guard's concern will cease." Wang took a quick sip from his mug. "So, it's best that we make the deployment quickly."

"Perhaps we shouldn't stop. Can you do it while the ship is moving?"

"No. With the tender door open, there won't be much freeboard left. It's best to operate the overhead gantry system without the boat moving. Besides, the anchor is heavy and awkward to work with. By stopping, it will be manageable with the equipment we have aboard."

"Just how critical is the location?"

"For the Mark Twelve, it won't matter that much. As long as it is within a one-kilometer radius of the bottom coordinates, it will be fine."

"That's excellent, Commander. Let's hope it all goes as planned."

* * *

Yuri and Nick stood on the edge of the shore and watched the *Yangzi* as it powered across Elliott Bay, its upper decks still lit up like a Broadway musical. When the hull lighting muted, they followed the yacht's progress by watching its running lights. Once the *Yangzi* cruised past West Point, they lost track. That's when they returned to the Jeep, parked near the western edge of the marina's parking lot.

"I bet they're not going far," Nick said.

"That's a world-class boat. It could be going just about anywhere." Yuri, behind the wheel, stared at Elliott Bay through the opening of his rolled-down window. The water was as black as his spirit.

Nick took a hit from a Winston and exhaled through his open window. "It doesn't make sense to me that they would abandon all that work you were doing for them. I think something did come up."

"Why did Elena take off like she did? If they really planned to reschedule the exchange, she's out of the picture. She's been the intermediary since day one."

Nick took a final puff and crushed the butt in the ashtray. "I agree; that's a concern. She should have remained behind in Seattle or stayed aboard the yacht."

Yuri faced Nick. "But she's on her way to Vancouver."

"It does appear that's where she's headed."

The two SVR officers following Elena had phoned in ten minutes earlier. Elena's Mercedes was northbound on I-5 passing through Everett, making what appeared to be a beeline for the BC border at Blaine.

"I've screwed this up so badly . . . dear God, I don't know what to do now."

"Don't give up, Yuri. We're going to get them back."

"So where the hell is that boat going and why?" Yuri turned away.

Nick was at a loss on how to comfort his friend, when a thought flashed. *The boat, where is it going? That's the key.* He reached into his pocket and retrieved his iPhone, the one he used for official consulate business. He called up Bing and entered a search request. He tapped on the link. A minute later, he struck gold.

"I've got it!"

"What?" Yuri said, turning back.

"The boat—the *Yangzi*. Here, look."

Nick held up the phone's screen. It displayed a tiny map of Puget Sound.

Nick pointed with his right index finger. "That, my friend, is the *Yangzi*. It's near Edmonds heading north."

"What is this?"

"It's a public tracking system for marine traffic. I learned about it last year when we were on the *Hercules*—from Miller. Boats over a certain length are required to have a special transmitter on board that broadcasts its real-time GPS coordinates. It's to help prevent collisions, kind of like what they do for airplanes."

"That's fantastic. What other information does it have?"

"Just a sec."

Yuri waited, his heart thundering.

"Son of a bitch." Nick met Yuri's eyes. "It's headed to Vancouver."

"Are you sure?"

Nick expanded the screen. "See right there under *Destination*."

"Vancouver—what are they up to there?"

After Laura nursed Maddy, her watchers re-anchored her to the bunk by each outstretched limb. The metal restraints locked onto her wrists and ankles again chafed her skin. Before leaving with Maddy, the female guard checked each manacle, ensuring there would be no repeat escape.

Laura lay alone on her back in the dark. The only visible light was a turquoise glow emitted from the fire and smoke detector mounted in the overhead.

The yacht was still under way, its ride silky smooth and vibration free. The last vessel Laura had sailed on—a commercial workboat—rode like a freight train compared to the *Yangzi*. She could hear the occasional wave slap the side of the steel hull as the yacht plowed ahead.

Laura closed her eyes, wishing that she would fall asleep. But it was useless. Her mind was a whirlwind of thoughts. *What happened—why was the exchange called off? Who are these people? Where's this damn boat going?*

She had no answers.

Laura flushed the questions, concentrating instead on the positive.

They have not hurt me and are taking good care of Maddy.

I just need to hang on.

I've been through worse.

Born chocolate in a black-and-white world, traumatized by an abusive husband, and thrust into an international incident that nearly resulted in a war and her demise, Laura Newman was a survivor—she never gave up. Central to Laura's tenacity was faith—faith in her God and faith in her lover.

I can do this.

Yuri will find us!

Please help him, Lord!

CHAPTER 63

It was half past ten in the evening. Yuri and Nick were in the rented Jeep Cherokee, headed north on I-5. Vancouver was ninety minutes away. Yuri had the wheel.

"I'm worried about the border crossing," Yuri said.

"You shouldn't have any trouble."

"The passport is Canadian, but my Washington driver's license is in another name. That could be a problem. Plus this is a rental car."

"I doubt the Canadians will care. All they'll be interested in is if you're bringing back any merchandise purchased in the States—to collect an import tax. But you'll have nothing to declare, so that won't be an issue." Nick recalled another concern. "If they ask about weapons in the car, just say no." Nick stuffed Yuri's Colt semiautomatic deep inside the Jeep's dashboard.

"I guess that will work, but still the mismatch in names . . ."

"If it comes up tell them you lost your BC license and you borrowed the car from a colleague."

"But what if they decide to run a check on my passport?" Yuri had grabbed his Canadian passport this morning at the house, alone with Laura's U.S. passport and Maddy's birth certificate. He also liberated the five thousand dollars in cash that Laura kept in their bedroom safe. "For contingencies," he had reasoned.

Nick said, "It should be fine. I still use a Canadian passport for travel between the States and Canada—like what we did last year. I used it last week when I flew to Vancouver. I didn't have any problems and you won't, either."

Nick had procured the passport for Yuri the year before. Manufactured by a special unit in the SVR's Illegals Directorate, the passport booklet was authentic. Two hundred blanks were purchased from an agent recruited at a Canadian government office in Ottawa. The mid-level manager was paid $400,000, which the SVR considered a bargain.

"Why do you use a fake passport to get into Canada?" Yuri asked.

"It's a huge hassle to get visa clearance to come back into the States with my Russian passport. No problem if you're Canadian."

"Okay, I guess it will work out." Yuri was still not convinced.

Nick said, "Maybe I should be in the driver's seat when we cross the border."

"Yes, that sounds good. You're much better at that stuff than I am."

They drove in silence until Yuri thought of another issue. "What about coming back into the States? I've heard that the Blaine station can be difficult."

"You're worrying too much, my friend. We'll work it out at that time." Nick shifted in his seat, stretching his back. "At the next exit we come to, why don't you take it? We can switch and I'll get us through the border. Besides, you need to rest."

"Thank you."

Elena Krestyanova returned to her condominium apartment at 10:40 P.M. Worn out from the drive, she reclined in the tub. While savoring the sizzling therapeutic fluid that pulsed from the bathtub's half dozen jet nozzles, she sipped from a glass of California merlot.

It was a whirlwind day. Elena had yet to close her deal with Kwan Chi; her $5 million payday remained just beyond her grasp. Somehow, Yuri Kirov had screwed up the exchange to get Laura and the infant back. But Kwan provided no details, only that it had been postponed.

Kwan told Elena to return to Vancouver, promising to call her after the *Yangzi* arrived.

Elena thought it was odd that he did not ask if she would like to remain aboard the yacht as it cruised to Vancouver. Instead, he politely but firmly requested that she disembark.

Kwan was up to something, but what?

Yuri Kirov could not be trusted, this Elena knew from her history with him.

While on the drive north, Elena was tempted to call Kirov to get his side of the story. But she decided against it. This was Kwan Chi's op. The less she was privy to the dirty details, the better it would be for her if the mission tanked. Besides, Yuri would never level with her. The distrust between each other was mutual.

And what about the SVR and FSB?

The threat from the homeland's intelligence services was always on Elena's mind. Unlike traitors in the United States or other Western nations, Russian Federation turncoats were not locked up in prison or given work release. Instead, they were disposed of with a bullet to the base of the skull, just as in the old Soviet Union.

So far, Elena remained confident that her treachery had not been detected. Still, her sixth sense instilled insecurity and trepidation.

Maybe it was time to kiss off the big payday and bug out.

Elena had already prepared for a quick exit. Her collection of passports, credit cards, and cash was stored inside a high-tech wall safe in the bedroom closet. She kept a "go bag" in the same closet. Within minutes, she could be in her Mercedes heading east.

Long ago, Elena had decided she would avoid Vancouver International if she ever had to flee. Instead, she would drive to Calgary or Regina or even Winnipeg and take a flight to Europe. She could access the $5 million she had salted away in Luxembourg anytime she needed through wire transfer. It wasn't as much cushion as she'd planned, but it was workable.

Still, the lure of the prize that would double her assets remained heavy on her mind.

A half hour went by. Elena dried and powdered herself, put on a full-length bathrobe, and relocated to the living room. Her high-rise apartment had a stunning view of downtown Vancouver. The backdrop of city lights was particularly spectacular in this late evening.

Elena sipped the last of her second glass of merlot while listening to Gustav Holst's *The Planets* from the condo's built-in stereo system. Deliciously drowsy, she settled into the sofa's comfy cushions.

She'd just closed her eyes when her cell chimed from the coffee table. She reached for the phone; the display announced a new text. Elena tapped on the screen. It was from Chi, inviting her to dinner the next evening at a Vancouver restaurant.

Maybe she would stick around for a little while longer after all.

CHAPTER 64

Half a world away from Vancouver, it was late morning in Moscow. Two men sat in ornate chairs facing each other over a mini-table that extended from an expansive mahogany desk in the Kremlin office. The president of the Russian Federation preferred the seating arrangement for one-on-one visits to his office. It allowed him to make intimate eye contact with those seeking an audience.

Today the minister of defense occupied the hot seat.

"The Americans are lying," the president said. "You cannot trust them." In his mid-fifties and of medium height with thinning black hair, he was losing the battle of the bulge.

"I agree, sir. Everything points back to them." Almost a decade older and several inches taller than the president, Marshal of the Russian Federation Ivan Volkov remained nearly as slim as when he had commanded a Red Army infantry platoon some forty years earlier.

"What is this new evidence you have?"

"It's from the blood sample that was recovered. First,

we confirmed that the bandage with the blood on it was a standard field dressing issued by the U.S. military. But the same dressing is also used widely in NATO as well as by the military in Iraq and Afghanistan and several other allies of the Americans." Volkov shifted position. "So it could be argued that the dressing came from more than a dozen other countries besides the United States."

"But we know it was them!"

"Yes, and now we have the supplemental evidence to make our case." Minister Volkov glanced down at his notes. "The DNA profile on the blood was most interesting."

"It's American—correct?"

"It's not that simple. The way I understand it is that DNA cannot reveal the race of an individual. However, it can provide 'markers' that tell where the ancestors of a person came from. The technical term used for the blood sample is 'autosomal marking.' The technique was developed in the United States to determine the amount of a person's ancestry from three distinct demographic sources." The defense minister again consulted his notes. "The groups are African, European, and Native American."

"What do you mean by 'Native American'?"

"The indigenous tribes in the United States, various clans that inhabited North America before the Europeans arrived."

"Ah, the cowboys and Indians of Hollywood. I see."

Volkov continued, "For the blood sample in question, sixty-five percent of the autosomal marker was identified as Native American."

"So we've got them!"

"Maybe. The results certainly suggest that the individual is of Native American origin. But the sample also contained thirty percent European and the rest African."

"But sixty-five percent—that's significant."

"Yes, it is."

"Can you refine the analysis any further?"

"It's unlikely. The wounded individual was probably a member of either the U.S. Navy SEALs or the Army's Delta Force. We suspect Native Americans are members of both units but have no way of verifying demographics. The U.S. keeps all personnel matters regarding their Special Operations Forces secret."

The president leaned back in his chair. "I want to keep this to ourselves for now. Continue with the storyline that Chechen terrorists attacked the Sakhalin plant. That will help us on the home front because the people will believe it, which will allow us to continue with our crackdown on those bastards." He rubbed his chin. "What I do not want to happen is for the Americans to figure out that we know they destroyed our plant."

"To keep them off guard?"

"Correct. I want to maintain the element of surprise for your operation."

"I understand."

"When will you be ready?"

"It will be under way soon."

"Excellent. Keep me posted on your progress."

"I will, Mr. President."

CHAPTER 65

DAY 30—TUESDAY

The *Yangzi* slowed as it approached the bottom coordinates, both Caterpillars dialed back to match the waning flood current. It was 12:25 A.M. Other than a southbound tugboat that passed to the port ten minutes earlier, the superyacht had the north end of Admiralty Inlet to itself.

Kwan Chi and Lieutenant Commander Wang Park relocated to the lower deck garage near the stern. Wang opened the thirty-foot-long port-side retractable tender door. With its top edge hinged to the hull nine feet above the waterline, the door extended perpendicular to the water surface. From the south came a whisper of a breeze, which barely ruffled the sea surface. Rippling wavelets splashed against the hull a foot below the open door. Overall, launching conditions were ideal.

"What's next?" asked Kwan. He stood beside the PLAN officer and the Mark 12 Viper. Three other crewmen hovered nearby, ready to respond to Wang's orders.

"We'll use the overhead gantry for the launch."

"What about the anchor?"

"After the unit's in the water, we'll deploy it."

Wang issued directions to his men. They connected nylon straps wrapped around the fore and aft ends of the thirty-inch-diameter steel casing to the lifting hooks of the overhead gantry crane. Twin, heavy steel box beams on roller rails set twenty feet apart made up the gantry system. Wang used a wireless control device to activate the crane system's hydraulic drives. In unison, the dual motors elevated the twenty-three-foot-long Mark 12 about a foot above its cradle.

After Wang verified the weapon was free of its crib, he again activated the control device. Another hydraulic drive system extended the twin steel beams through the open garage door, suspending the Mark 12 over the water surface. After another check, Wang lowered the casing into the water. Although it weighed nearly three tons, its cylindrical volume displaced sufficient seawater to remain buoyant. About one foot of the casing projected above the water surface.

Kwan issued new orders and two crewmen relocated to the opposite side of the garage. At the starboard door a twenty-foot-long rigid-hulled inflatable boat, tethered with a line, bobbed next to the hull. The men climbed into the RIB, started the outboard, and departed. They were alongside the Mark 12 within a minute. They attached a Dacron line to the eye ring welded to the casing's forward end and disconnected the lifting straps.

Wang reeled in the straps and instructed the men, "Head out slowly. Watch the towline and don't foul your propeller."

The boat motored away with the Mark 12 trailing about twenty feet behind. As the weapon moved farther away from the *Yangzi,* another line paid out from the garage deck. The 3/8-inch-diameter galvanized steel cable connected to the aft end of the steel casing with a shackle assembly. The other end of the cable connected to a concrete block resting on the deck near the open garage door. Three feet long on each axis, the cube had a steel eyebolt in the center of its top surface. Another steel shackle linked the cable to the anchor block.

Kwan Chi continued to observe but remained silent.

The cable tightened. The RIB, still under power and over sixty feet away, was going nowhere.

Wang keyed a portable handheld radio. The RIB crew had a companion unit. "That's good," he said. "Get ready to cut power and release the line on my command."

One of the men acknowledged the order.

Wang knelt next to the concrete block and inserted the hook end of another steel cable into the block's eyebolt. The opposite end of the four-foot-long cable connected to the aft gantry's hoist hook. He activated the crane, raising the block two feet above the deck. He triggered a different control and the aft gantry transported the block through the opening until it was clear of the hull.

Wang keyed the radio. "Disconnect the towline."

Kwan joined Wang, standing at his side. They watched as a RIB crewman executed the order. The boat powered away.

"Are you set now?" asked Kwan.

"Yes, sir. All I need to do is trip the release."

Wang stepped to the edge of the opening and reached outward where he removed the safety pin from the

quick release clamp and grabbed the clamp's trailing
tag line. He stepped back into the garage. "Releasing
now," he said. Wang tugged on the tag line, a solid jerk.

Nothing happened.

Wang repeated the effort.

Still nothing.

Wang tried a third pull, yanking the quarter-inch
line with all his might. He cursed.

"What's wrong?" Kwan asked.

Wang's brow puckered. "The quick release clamp
failed—it won't open."

Kwan Chi checked his watch. "We're almost out of
time. What are you going to do?"

"I don't know . . . let me think."

The Mark 12 drifted to within a few feet of the yacht
before the RIB crew towed it away from the *Yangzi*.

The concrete block was back inside the garage. A
crew member removed the defective hook clamp and
replaced it with a short section of rope. He secured the
line to the cube's eyebolt and the aft gantry's lifting
hook.

"Are you ready now, Wang?" Kwan Chi said, agitated.

"Almost, sir."

Commander Wang activated the aft gantry, lifting
the two-ton concrete cube. About a foot and a half off
the deck, the hastily tied double-half-hitch knot connecting the line to the hoist hook slipped. The block
crashed onto the steel deck with a sickening thud. The
impact sent a tremor the full length of the hull.

Wang swore at the sailor who'd made the connection. He retied the knots himself, using bowlines at
each end.

Kwan Chi chose not to comment.

Wang reactivated the aft gantry, lifting the cube. The line held. He extended the gantry's support beam through the hull opening. The concrete anchor dangled three feet above the water.

"Release it!" Wang ordered, addressing the RIB crew who held the Mark 12 at bay. The men again disconnected the towline and powered away.

Wang extracted a knife from his pants pocket and pulled open its four-inch blade. He again leaned through the hull opening and attacked the one-inch-diameter line. The laser-sharp blade sawed through the synthetic fibers. With less than a quarter inch remaining, the line snapped with a sharp *clack*. The concrete anchor plunged into the sea, dragging the Mark 12 Viper with it.

Wang pulled himself back inside the compartment. "It's on the bottom now."

Kwan Chi consulted his watch. "We're over the limit now. Is that going to be a problem?"

"We should be okay."

Before long, the RIB was home and the *Yangzi* remained over the drop site. Wang and Kwan relocated to the wheelhouse. The ship's master reported that the extended loitering had not yet triggered any radio inquiries, likely due to the lack of vessel traffic. The captain also noted that a sweep of the bottom with the ship's high-energy sonar did not detect the Mark 12. As designed, its rubberized anechoic coating absorbed sound energy.

Wang and Kwan both leaned over the main instrument console, studying a digital display. Wang was conducting a new test. The Mark 12 had just responded to a coded underwater acoustic pulse broadcast from a hydrophone mounted to the underside of the super-yacht's hull. The torpedo mine's encrypted return signal revealed its location and operational status.

"How does it look?" Kwan asked.

"It's armed. Not quite as deep as I planned—sixty-three meters. We drifted over the target depression but it will work where it is."

"Very good, Commander."

Kwan turned to face the ship's master. "Captain, you may now proceed to Vancouver at normal cruising speed."

CHAPTER 66

After checking into a mid-range hotel near down-town Vancouver, Yuri and Nick retreated to their individual rooms. Nick captured five solid hours of sleep. Yuri struggled, winning at best two.

They met for breakfast in the hotel's restaurant at half past six and then drove to nearby Stanley Park. Yuri parked the Jeep in a lot near the north end of the park, where they followed a trail to the bridge.

The *Yangzi* was just half a mile away.

Nick eyed his wristwatch: 8:10 A.M. "It's on sched-ule."

"Where do you think they'll dock it?" Yuri asked.

"It's a big sucker. There aren't many marinas around that can handle it. Maybe it'll end up anchoring."

The superyacht was now just two football-field lengths from the bridge.

Yuri said, "I wonder if they can see us."

"Doubt it, but maybe with binoculars."

The *Yangzi* passed under Vancouver's Lion's Gate Bridge, heading eastward in Burrard Inlet. Yuri and

Nick needed to find a new vantage point to continue spying. They walked briskly back to the car.

"Wow," muttered Nick.

"It's impressive all right," Yuri said.

Both men stood on the public boardwalk next to a large marina. The stunning boat harbor was first class in all respects, but what overwhelmed Nick and Yuri was the spectacular mountain range of mid- and high-rise condominium and office towers bordering the moorage basin. The architectural wonders jutted skyward in a maze of slender columns that conveyed affluence and splendor.

Yuri turned toward the water. The *Yangzi* dominated the other 250 boats berthed in the Coal Harbour Marina. Moored at the seaward end of a dock, the superyacht occupied most of the guest pier.

Nick and Yuri leaned against the boardwalk railing while eyeing the ship's starboard flank.

Nick said, "It looks like we have the same problem here as in Seattle. The marina has excellent security. Getting out to the dock may be a problem."

"I agree. Let's get a better look." He pointed to his right.

"Okay."

They walked several hundred feet farther along the boardwalk, stopping near a waterfront park. The new venue provided an improved view of the *Yangzi*. Moored to the floating pier along its starboard side, the superyacht pointed its sleek bow east toward Yuri and Nick.

Nick noticed first. "See that guy standing by the boarding ramp?"

"Yeah."

"I bet you he's some kind of a guard or sentry. He's just hanging out there."

"To do what? It's broad daylight."

"Discourage other marina tenants from getting too curious about the boat and his boss—the billionaire Chinaman."

"You're probably right."

"If there's one on display like that guy, you can be certain there are others aboard that we don't see. Hell, they could have glasses on us right now."

That got Yuri's attention. "Right. Let's keep walking."

They walked into Harbour Green Park, out of direct line of sight to the *Yangzi*.

"My plan is not going to work," Yuri acknowledged.

"I agree. They'll be on us before we get halfway down the dock. There's got to be another way."

Yuri said, "Are your men still in town?"

"Yes—in a hotel someplace around here, still sleeping, I expect."

"Wake them up."

Summoned by Kwan Chi, Commander Wang Park walked into the lounge on the *Yangzi*'s upper deck. Kwan waited, sitting in a chair beside a coffee table. His steward had just delivered a serving of tea. It was 9:25 A.M.

Kwan gestured for Wang to join him.

As Wang sat in a chair, Kwan asked, "Any issues with the Canadians?"

"No, sir. Routine review of passports and visas. Inspection of the bridge and safety equipment. That was it."

"Good."

Kwan Chi and the *Yangzi* were frequent visitors to Vancouver, but it was Commander Wang's first. He was awed at the city's beauty and its palpable riches.

"Tea?" asked Kwan.

"Please."

After Kwan served he said, "I want to compliment you on your excellent work last night. Very impressive."

"Thank you, sir. Overall, it went well." Wang still reeled from the cable clamp failure and then the slipped knot that dropped the anchor block onto the deck.

"So, all we have to do is to wait for the submarine to go by and it will activate on its own?"

"Correct. I programmed the Mark Twelve's computer with the sound print recovered from the Russian listening device. It's unique to that boat alone."

"The *Kentucky*."

"Yes—the *Kentucky*."

"This assumes it will be running on the surface. What would happen if it were submerged instead?"

"There's no history of an *Ohio*-class submerging at that location—maybe the converted ones but not the ones carrying nuclear weapons."

"I understand. But let's say the Americans are worried about an unspecified threat to their submarines and the *Kentucky* submerges in Hood Canal and then proceeds to the ocean underwater. Will the mine intercept it?"

"That's exactly what it was designed for—to attack submerged submarines. However, there are major differences in the acoustic output from a submarine on the surface compared to when it is submerged and operating under maximum stealth conditions. That's why our Navy is so interested in the submerged recordings."

"Again, I understand, but could it work for our situation?"

Wang fidgeted in his chair. He was now going out on a limb. "Assuming the mine's hydrophone detects the *Kentucky* while submerged—which is a huge assumption—the computer might be able to distinguish some of its unique sound signatures like propeller wash and circulation pump activity. That might be enough to trigger targeting and launch the weapon."

"But it's not a certainty."

"No, sir. Based on what we know about the *Ohio*-class, when the *Kentucky* submerges, it would likely cruise past the Mark Twelve without being detected." Wang took a sip from his cup. "Why are you asking about this? Has something changed?"

"No, the mission continues as planned. However, I did receive a communiqué this morning from our operative monitoring the Hood Canal base. One of the other submarines was not at its dock this morning and there have been no openings of the bridge."

Wang frowned, surprised at the report. "Which one is it?"

"Nevada."

"That's a missile boat."

"Yes, and according to our operative, it is not due to deploy for two months."

"It might be undergoing submerged testing in Hood Canal," said Commander Wang. "It's deep and quite long."

"Let's hope that is what's going on, but if it's something else—"

Wang laughed. "How ironic would that be . . . it could have sailed under us this morning while we were deploying the Mark Twelve." Wang thought about it before concluding, "But I don't believe it. My money is on the test protocol. I expect the *Nevada* will return to its berth later today."

"You're probably right."

CHAPTER 67

Maggie and Jessie raced across the undulating terrain, their snow machines screaming and their hearts pounding as they dodged dwarf evergreens and serrated rock outcrops. The pair never envisioned they would have such fun—not with the looming business that waited at the end of their journey.

They had arrived in Fairbanks two days earlier aboard an Alaska Air flight from Portland. They had filled their checked luggage with top-of-the-line REI winter gear and the latest fashions from Nordstrom. Flush with cash and each carrying separate Visa cards with $10,000 of prepaid credit, the couple had no issues with money.

Both stylishly attired, with a first-class hotel and their rented new Cadillac Escalade SUV, Maggie Sinclair and Jessie Martel fit the profile of affluent high-tech millennials out for a late-winter Alaskan escapade. But it was all part of their cover. They shared a third-floor studio in a seedy section of Portland near the industrial sector. Jessie worked as a bicy-

cle messenger. Maggie waited tables at a seafood restaurant.

The Kawasakis tore across the snow. It was easy
running now that they followed the cleared right-of-
way. Jessie and Maggie had been on the go for only
twenty-five minutes but had already covered twelve
miles. The Escalade and the rental trailer remained on
a side road just off the highway about thirty-five miles
north of Fairbanks.

It was twenty-eight degrees Fahrenheit and snowing—just right for the op.

The pair continued northward, running side by side.
It was almost noon. They headed upslope, following
the steep grade of the hillside. Bands of spruce trees,
their growth stunted by the subarctic climate, lined the
hundred-foot-wide cleared right-of-way on each side.
Jessie periodically glanced down at his GPS unit clamped
to the snow machine's console. The first stop was
about a mile away.

Maggie spotted the target first as they descended
into the valley. "There it is," she shouted, her frosty
breath lost in the slipstream.

The snow machines went silent. Snowflakes landing on the exhaust pipes broadcast mini-hisses as they
flashed to vapor.

Dismounting, Jessie trudged through the three-foot-
deep snow until he stood next to Target One. He removed the glove from his right hand and placed his
bare skin on its exterior surface. The insulated cover
was cool to the touch. However, under the foam and
inside the four-foot-diameter steel tube, lukewarm
Prudhoe Bay crude flowed southward at a leisurely
three miles per hour.

Maggie joined Jessie. "Amazing," she said, taking in the elevated pipeline that stretched ahead for over a mile, following the rising slope of the mini-mountain. "It's so exposed and no one is around."

"Except for us." Jessie grinned. "Let's get to work."

It took just ten minutes to install the device. Jessie cut away a one-square-foot section of the nearly four-inch-thick foam insulation from the underside of the pipe. Maggie verified that the batteries were fresh and the internal clock was accurate. She set the timer.

Jessie placed the charge. The magnetized base plate matched the curve of the steel pipe. It snapped into place with a metallic clang.

Jessie armed the bomb with a simple flip of a toggle switch. There was no going back now. At precisely 6:00 P.M. local time, the ten pounds of plastic explosive molded in the form a circular-shaped charge would detonate, punching a ten-inch-diameter hole through the half-inch-thick steel pipe.

Jessie and Maggie remounted their machines and blasted off. Charter members of the Environmental Direct Action Anarchy Network, they had three additional bombs to plant, each one in the base of a valley. It was snowing two inches an hour. If it kept up, their tracks would vanish by the time they returned to the Cadillac.

CHAPTER 68

Kwan Chi and Commander Wang Park were in the PRC's consulate general in downtown Vancouver. It was early afternoon. Summoned an hour earlier by the consulate's supervising MSS officer, they took a cab from Coal Harbour.

"What do the Americans know about what happened?" Kwan said, addressing the supervisor.

"Not much. So far they appear to be treating it as an accident."

"That won't last."

Kwan, Wang, and the supervisor along with three of his staff huddled around a table in a secure conference room. The windowless room was about twenty feet square with plain white walls and fluorescent overhead lighting. A National Geographic map of the Gulf of Mexico, covering the tabletop, was the focus of their collective attention.

"What was their target?" Wang asked.

"We believe they were planning to attack a floating production plant located in this area." The senior MSS officer tapped the map with his right index finger. "It went operational a month ago. The oil wells supplying the plant are in very deep water—almost three thousand meters." He removed a color photograph from a file folder and placed it onto the tabletop. "This is a photo downloaded from the company's website."

"They store oil inside of it?"

"Yes, Commander. According to the website, a converted supertanker is permanently moored over the well field. Oil is pumped up to it and stored in the ship's tanks. When it's full, another tanker comes alongside and fills up. Apparently, this arrangement was more cost effective than a pipeline because of the water depth and the distance from shore."

"That's quite a juicy target," Kwan commented.

"Yes, sir. That's why we believe the Russians were after it."

Wang said, "The helicopter that crashed—where did it originate from?"

"At first we thought it might be Cuban, but we're now certain it was Russian. We believe it took off early this morning from a military base west of Havana. After making the attack, it was supposed to land on a Russian-flagged cargo ship that departed Havana early this morning. The ship is still in the area. It appears to be loitering."

"Searching for crew?"

"Possibly, or waiting for other assets."

"How did we manage to get this information?" Kwan asked.

"Our people in Havana reported the arrival of the naval *Spetsnaz* unit two days ago—supposedly for joint training with the Cubans. They arrived on two Russian military transports loaded with combat gear, including a helicopter. Our electronic eavesdropping station at Bejucal focused its assets on the base."

"Beijing must have suspected something," Kwan said, not letting on that he'd received an earlier briefing on the Russian unit.

"That's right. When the special operators showed up, Beijing speculated that the unit was going to target a U.S. oil installation somewhere in the Gulf of Mexico."

"As a response to Sakhalin?"

"Yes. We were able to track the Russian helicopter for about a hundred kilometers before it dropped below the horizon. It was headed toward the oil storage facility."

"When did it crash?"

"We think about fifteen minutes after losing radar coverage. One of Bejucal's sensors picked up the automatic emergency beacon. It activates on water contact."

Kwan leaned forward, eyeing the chart. "So to pull this off, the Cubans had to be involved, too."

"Possibly. But they could have just as easily been duped by the Russians."

"Improved relations with the U.S.?"

"Yes, sir."

"When the Americans figure it out, and they will, Cuba may once again be on their shit list." Kwan took a step away from the table. "Thank you, gentlemen. I need to speak with Commander Wang, so please leave us."

The MSS supervisor and his aides exited the room.

Kwan faced Wang. "Now we know what they had planned. It was a brilliant idea and a fitting response."

"But it failed."

"Yes, and you of all people know how fragile helicopters can be—even the brutes the Russians make. The crash was just bad luck."

Wang rubbed his wrist with his other hand, reacting to the phantom pain. He had survived an exceedingly hard helo-landing during a training mission early in his career. Six others aboard perished. Wang and another crawled out of the wreck before the flames engulfed the entire passenger compartment. He spent over a week in a hospital recovering from a shattered wrist and third-degree burns to his forearm.

"This is actually a lucky break for us," said Kwan.

Wang cocked his head to the side, not making the connection.

Kwan checked his watch. "Assuming our surrogate operation in Alaska is under way as we speak, the double-pronged attack will truly shake up the Americans."

Wang smiled, putting it together. "And that will mean the immediate deployment of the *Kentucky*."

"Exactly."

Arms around each other's waists, Jessie and Maggie walked down the long hallway that led to their fourth-floor hotel room. Pumped from their afternoon jaunt, they couldn't keep their hands off each other.

Jessie inserted his keycard into the door's electronic lock and pushed it open. Within a minute, they were naked under the sheets of the king-size bed.

Lost in passion, Jessie and Maggie did not hear the door open.

The man stealthily approached the enrapt couple.

He wore a heavy dark parka with a hood that concealed his head. A backpack hung from his shoulders and wool gloves covered his hands. He was in his forties with a slight build and medium height. Of Asian descent, he easily passed as a native Alaskan.

Maggie spotted Joseph first. She shrieked.

Jessie turned around. "What the hell are you doing here?"

Joseph sat on a chair by the desk. "Did you complete your work?"

The couple sat up, covered themselves with the sheets, and leaned against the headboard.

"Yes, it went just as planned," Jessie said. "Why are you here?" he asked again.

"Peter sent me."

"To spy on us."

"Watch your backs."

"No one knows what we did."

"I know. You did well."

Joseph checked his watch. It was 5:48 P.M. He reached for the TV remote and clicked it on. He tuned it to a local news channel, turning up the volume.

"What are you doing?" Jessie said, annoyed at the elevated sound level.

Gesturing toward the live newsreader, Joseph said, "We should know soon if it worked." He pulled off his nylon backpack. "Peter has another assignment for you up here," he announced as he reached inside the pack with his still gloved hand.

"No way," protested Jessie. "We're bugging out tomorrow morning just—"

Joseph pulled the trigger from inside the backpack. The first suppressed-sound hollow-point hit Jessie in the throat, just above the Adam's apple. The second slug plowed into Maggie's forehead between her eyes.

Hands clamped around his neck, Jessie gagged with an awful gargle as blood surged from his mouth and nostrils. He collapsed onto Maggie's still form.

Joseph dialed back the TV's sound.

Laura was miserable. Still bound to the bunk, she could feel her lower back in spasm. It had started as a dull ache but morphed into stiletto-class agony. She remained supine, unable to shift to either side to ease the stress of the restraints.

The only relief occurred during feeding sessions with Maddy and bathroom breaks when she was able to stand for a few minutes. The female tag team that traded off watching Laura ignored her pleas to slacken the bindings.

No longer sensing motion or the faint tremor from the engines, she was certain the boat was again dock-side. But she had no inkling where it had moored.

Laura stretched her spine as much as she could and closed her eyes. Sleep was an impossible expectation, not with the pain. Even more troubling was the uncertainty of her predicament. Her thoughts leapfrogged as she searched for answers.

Where do they take Maddy? Who are these people? What do they want? What's Elena doing with them?

And where's Yuri?

"State Troopers, Fairbanks."

"Ah, I was out hunting this afternoon and I spotted a

couple suspicious characters monkeying around with the pipe."

"Alyeska pipeline?" asked the Alaska State Trooper.

"Yeah, the Prudhoe Bay pipe."

"May I have your name, sir?"

"Nah, I don't want to do that. I just wanna let you know what I saw."

"What did you observe, sir?"

"They were across the valley from me, but I scoped 'em. Looked like they were attaching something to the bottom of it. Then they took off on snow machines."

"Where did this take place, sir?"

"North of Fairbanks. I think it was not too far from one of the pump stations."

"When did this occur?"

"A couple hours ago."

"Can you describe the individuals?"

"A white couple. They looked young to me—twenties. The guy was a big oaf, six foot plus. He had a scraggly beard and long black hair hanging from under his ski hat. The gal was blond, slim, nice looking from what I could see."

"What direction did they—"

The conversation ended. The caller's English was ordinary. His dialect was Alaskan Inuit, since he had spent over forty hours in Beijing with speech experts to perfect his diction and storyline.

The MSS operative masquerading as "Joseph" walked into the hotel bathroom and removed the SIM card from his cell phone. He tossed it into the toilet bowl and flushed. He returned to the hotel room's main section. Jessie's and Maggie's corpses remained in the blood-saturated bed.

Still wearing gloves, Joseph reached in his backpack and removed a one-kilogram brick of Semtex and assorted bomb-making parts—spares from the Alyeska bombs. He laid them on the desktop. He retrieved Jessie's suitcase from the closet and placed the plastic explosive and bomb paraphernalia inside, wrapping them in clothing.

His mission complete, Joseph slipped on the backpack and exited the hotel room. Although he'd already disabled the hallway's closed-circuit security camera system, he kept the hood on and walked with his head down.

Jessie and Maggie's co-conspirator Petruso ("Peter") Teslenko remained in Oregon—but not for long. An East Ukrainian immigrant with a degree in electrical engineering, the thirty-seven-year-old worked for a London-based international engineering company with a branch office in Portland. He designed electronic control systems for water treatment plants. His real vocation, however, was eco-anarchism. His specialty was bomb making. Peter acquired his lethal skills from three years as a separatist fighting the Kiev government. His mentor was a Russian explosives expert.

Peter supplied the bombs. He also arranged for funding. A wealthy benefactor sympathetic to their cause deposited $100,000 into Peter's checking account through a wire transfer originating from an East Europe bank known to service the Russian mafia.

Joseph had posed as the forty-two-year-old son of wealthy Chinese American parents who owned a chain of automobile dealerships in the Bay Area. Appalled at the West's dependence on petroleum, the impostor's stated goal was to import anarchist initiatives to Taiwan.

The Semtex and timers left behind in the hotel room would pull in the FBI and Homeland Security. Most damning of all, the credit cards John and Maggie used to pay for the hotel, SUV, and the Kawasakis left a trail that would point straight back to Peter Teslenko and his pro-Russian affiliation.

The Department of Justice would issue a federal arrest warrant for Teslenko, charging terrorism and a dozen other crimes. But the warrant would languish. Unable to locate Peter in North America, the FBI and the U.S. Marshals would mount a worldwide hunt. But that, too, would fail.

Shipped across the Pacific in a forty-foot container packed with steel barrels filled with toxic waste chemicals, the drum containing the remains of the third founder of the Environmental Direct Action Anarchy Network would join the other million-plus barrels dumped into a mammoth earth pit about twenty miles west of Shanghai.

CHAPTER 69

Yuri and Nick relocated to their hotel. They were in Yuri's room after a shopping spree at a dive shop, marine equipment store, and an outdoor recreational gear retailer. Sprawled across the carpet were half a dozen boxes of diving equipment and other paraphernalia. Nick kneeled beside one of the boxes. He extracted a neoprene wetsuit jacket and held it up.

"This doesn't look like the kind of suit you used for the *Neva*. Will it keep you warm enough?"

"It'll be fine. I won't be in the water that long." Yuri stood beside the bed, connecting a regulator to the valve of a steel scuba tank on the mattress.

Nick tossed the wetsuit back into the box and stood up. He turned to face Yuri. "I thought you were supposed to avoid diving."

"It's been over a year. I'll be okay. Besides, I won't be going deep."

"What about the bubbles—won't they give you away?"

"They could, but I'll be okay."

Nick made his way to the opposite side of the bed and retrieved the Colt .45. He examined the weapon, verifying that it remained loaded. "I think you ought to use two of the bags to keep the water out."

"Good idea. Would you take care of that for me?"

"Yep."

Nick placed the pistol and the extra six-round magazine inside the first plastic storage Baggie. He started to seal it when Yuri said, "Try to squeeze out as much air as you can before sealing it up. I don't want that thing bulging out when I submerge."

"Got it."

Yuri finished examining their purchases and announced, "Everything checks out."

"Good, what's next?"

Yuri spread a chart on the bed. "The *Yangzi* is moored here, at the end of this dock," he said, pointing.

"Right, and that location is about as exposed as it could be, with that public walkway and the marina and all those condos."

Yuri arched his eyebrows. "How do I get in the water without someone seeing me? That's the problem we need to solve."

Tucked into a back corner of a low-rise building east of downtown Vancouver, the restaurant was near the center of Chinatown. It offered no view, but none was needed to attract its clientele. With just a dozen tables and a handful of private dining suites, the eatery rarely had an open table. Only serving dinner, the restaurant specialized in authentic mainland Chinese dishes while also providing an impressive selection of the world's finest spirits.

Elena ordered the Peking duck. Kwan Chi chose the sea bass. They had just finished the main course and were enjoying the last of the Loire Valley sauvignon blanc. A pot of green tea was on the way.

Over the meal, Elena and Chi engaged in casual chat. Elena refrained from peppering him with questions, knowing it was best to wait for Chi to initiate the conversation. After the tea was served, Kwan did just that.

"Have you heard from Kirov?" he asked.

"Nothing since yesterday. What have you heard?"

"He evaded our men."

"I can't say that I blame him, Chi. There was a deal on the table."

"It's still there. We ran into a time issue and had to delay the exchange."

Elena sipped from her cup. "When will you pick it up again?"

"Soon. Our other work here is complete."

"Tomorrow, the next day?"

"I can't be specific yet."

"I take it you want me to contact him again."

"Yes, he made it clear that he will only go through you."

Elena expected the confirmation. "He will want proof of life before he does anything, like the other times."

"I understand."

"Are they still aboard?"

"Yes."

Elena checked her watch. It was a few minutes before nine o'clock. "I could try to reach him tonight and set something up for, say, two days from now. Would that work?"

"Yes."

Elena met Chi's eyes. "I do not wish to pester you, but upon the successful exchange of Laura Newman and her child for the information Kirov is holding, my commitment to you will be fulfilled."

"Yes, my dear, it will. The funds have already been set aside. One call from me and they will be transferred to your account."

"Thank you."

"I've got something interesting here," Nick called out.

"What?" Yuri asked. They were in his hotel room. Yuri sat cross-legged on the bed examining a waterproof bag he'd purchased earlier.

"The boat—*Yangzi*—that's not her original name." Nick sat at the desk, hovering over his laptop. He had spent the last half hour searching the Web for anything he could find on the superyacht.

"What was the name?"

"*Columbia,* I guess after the river."

"Have you checked that name?"

"Working on it now—there are a zillion boats named *Columbia.*"

Nick clicked his way through numerous sites and then muttered, "Son of a bitch."

Yuri looked up from his packing. "What?"

"It was owned by some Southern California real estate developer. He went bankrupt and the boat was sold at auction. It cost a hundred sixty-five million dollars to build, but the guy that owns it now picked it up for ninety-five mil."

"He got a great deal."

Nick clicked on a new link. "Wow," he called out.

"What?" Yuri asked.

Nick turned in his chair, a grin breaking out. "When the *Columbia* was launched, there was tons of press on it—apparently the original owner loved showing it off. I found a write-up in the online archives of one of the magazines that featured the boat. It's loaded with good stuff."

Yuri stood beside Nick, peering down at the LCD screen. "This is fantastic," he said as Nick clicked his way through the gallery of high-quality color photographs of the *Columbia*'s interior and exterior spaces. Key features of the yacht were revealed on each of the six decks ranging from the twin thirty-five-hundred-horsepower Cats on the bilge deck to the top deck's endless pool and bar.

Nick completed the tour and said, "There's more." He clicked another file. "Take a look at this." He stood up, allowing Yuri to sit in the chair.

Yuri studied the image, eyes wide.

Nick said, "There's a naval architect's plan for each deck level. You can blow up the images. They get a little fuzzy, but they still give you a good idea of the layout."

"Incredible," Yuri said.

"This will help, won't it?"

"This is a huge help. I won't be going in blind now."

Yuri scrolled from one deck level to the next while Nick stood by silent. Finally, Yuri settled on the plan view of the second-level deck, identified on the plan as the lower deck. He pointed to the yacht's bow on the laptop's screen and said, "See these cabins here?"

"Yeah. Compared to the other ones they look small."

"They are. I'm sure they're for the crew."

"Okay but what's—"

"That's where I would confine someone, low down in the hull. The smaller the cabin, the easier to keep watch."

Nick squinted at the screen. "There must be a dozen or more."

"Fourteen. Most are doubles with bunk beds."

"You think that might be where she is?"

"That's where I'm going to try first."

Nick again examined the screen. "How do you get to that section of the boat?"

Yuri summarized his plan of attack.

"There's still something that bothers me," Nick added.

"What?"

"Even though you're coming from the water, how are you going to get on that thing without being seen? I'm sure those guards we saw today will be on the lookout at night, too, maybe even more so."

"I'll need a diversion—something to distract them while I slip aboard."

"That's what I thought," Nick said.

"You have something in mind?"

"Yeah, I do."

Nick and Yuri were discussing the op when Nick's cell rang. He checked the display. "It's my guys."

Nick received the report and repeated it to Yuri. "Elena just boarded the boat. She was accompanied by an Asian male. My men think he might be the owner, Kwan Chi. It was dark but they got a couple of good shots with an infrared camera."

Yuri processed the news. *Elena again!* "This doesn't change anything. I'm going aboard tonight."

CHAPTER 70

Laura dozed off just as half a dozen sharp knocks to the cabin door jolted her back to reality. She peered at the doorway. The watcher was already on her feet. She punched in the new code to the door's electronic lock and it swung inward.

Commander Wang stood in the entryway. He ordered the guard to exit, and the twenty-two-year PLAN sailor obeyed. Wang stepped aside, allowing Elena Krestya-nova to walk in, holding Madelyn.

"Hello, Laura," Elena said with a smile.

"Why do you have my daughter?"

"She's such a sweet thing. The women watching her say she's a delight."

"What do you want?"

Elena approached the bunk. "I know you're pissed off, but it's almost over now."

She rested a hip on the side of the bunk. "Yuri's co-operating again. You know how bullheaded he can be. We almost had it worked out the other day, but it fell apart because of a technical glitch. The good news is that the issue has been resolved and we are moving forward again."

"When are we going to be released?"

"Possibly tomorrow but no later than forty-eight hours from now."

Laura wanted to scream—*two more days in this hole?* Instead, she said, "My lower back is killing me—can you get me some ibuprofen?"

"I'm sure they have it aboard. What's wrong?"

"What do you think? I've been chained to this stinking bed forever. I can't turn over."

Elena turned around to face Wang. "Can you get it?"

Wang relayed the request to the guard who stood by in the corridor.

"They'll get something for you right away." Elena eyed the bunk. "I can see how this might be uncomfortable. I will ask for a better arrangement, perhaps a chair instead of the bed."

"Thank you."

"Laura, I want you to know that involving you was not my doing. The FSB—your FBI equivalent—is running the operation. I don't like any of what's happened."

Laura turned away.

Yuri, too, woke from a nap to the sound of someone pounding on his door. He sat up on the hotel bed, peering into the darkness.

"Yuri . . . it's Nick, open the door."

As soon as Yuri let his friend in, Nick grabbed the remote to switch on the TV. He scrolled through the channels until he found the all-news cable channel.

The banner running diagonally across the upper left corner of the screen read BREAKING NEWS. The curvy blond correspondent from Fairbanks was in the middle of a briefing, her image and voice transmitted to New York City via satellite. Visible in the background were a dozen parked pickup trucks and SUVs, most with flashing lights. Portable lighting lit the night sky around the vehicles and snow covered the ground. The reporter continued with her account, addressing an off-screen network anchor:

"John, the amount of oil spilled is unknown at this time, but from reports of bystanders who are on scene, it appears to be a major incident. Two witnesses I spoke with reported hearing multiple explosions several hours earlier. Although we are about half a mile from the pipeline, there is a distinct odor of crude oil in the air. Alyeska is in the process of mobilizing spill-response units from Fairbanks who are expected to be helicoptered soon to the spill sites, which we understand include four separate locations. A state trooper I spoke with would not confirm that this is the work of terrorists, but did acknowledge that the FBI and Homeland Security have been contacted."

Nick muted the TV. "That's bullshit about not knowing if it was a terrorist incident. Multiple explosions and four separate spill sites—give me a break."

Yuri's brow wrinkled. "Alaska again—and oil. Could it be retaliation?"

"Maybe. Someone sabotaged our well in the Arctic and then Sakhalin."

Yuri said, "This is beyond serious—it's going to lead to a war."

"No shit."

Nick and Yuri spent the next few minutes listening to the news report, when Yuri's cell phone rattled on the nightstand next to the bed. He picked it and checked the display. There was no ID.

"Hello," he said.

"*Dobryj večer!*"—Good evening. It was Elena.

Yuri engaged the speakerphone option on his phone and said, "What do you want, Elena?"

Nick perked up when he heard Elena's name. He reached into his pants pocket and removed his smartphone. He engaged an app that turned the cell into a recorder.

"Someone wants to say hello."

A voice came through. "Honey, it's me."

Jubilant to hear Laura's voice, Yuri smiled—the first of his protracted day. "Are you okay?"

"Worn out, but I'm all right. Same with Maddy."

"Have they hurt you?"

"No, but being confined is not easy."

Yuri was about to ask another question when Elena took over. "As you just heard, Laura and Madelyn are fine. And they'll remain fine. This should all be over in the next day or two."

"How so?"

"The exchange will take place the day after tomorrow but not at the airport—that will not work."

"No, I don't trust the FSB or whoever you are working with."

"I'm just the courier, Yuri. Remember that."

"But what about the Chinese players? This whole op seems to be directed by Wang."

"As I've explained before, this is a joint Russian PRC operation."

Yuri turned Nick and mouthed, "You getting this?"

Nick held up his phone.

"I don't want to wait. Let's do it now. Where do you want to meet—downtown Seattle, the Eastside, Everett, Tacoma? I don't care as long as it's a public place."

"We're not ready. I will phone you tomorrow with a time and place."

"When will you call?"

There was a slight delay before Elena responded. "I'll call you at noon."

"All right, but I want to speak to Laura again. Give her your phone."

Laura said, "Yuri?"

"We're close now, sweetie. Just take care of yourself and Maddy. It will be over soon."

"Please be careful."

"I will, don't worry about me."

"I love you."

"I love you, too."

The call terminated and Yuri turned to Nick. "Did you get that?"

"Every word."

CHAPTER 71

At 10:00 P.M. Wang was in the *Yangzi*'s op center with Kwan Chi. Wang had just completed a one-on-one encrypted telephone conversation with his commanding officer in Shanghai. "Sir, it's time for me to leave," Wang said.

"You must be expecting deployment soon," Kwan said.

"We are. With the successful execution of the Alaska pipeline operation, Beijing expects the Americans will increase their defense status, which will likely mean ordering all available submarines to sea."

"Then the plan proceeds as designed."

"It does, sir."

Kwan asked, "What did they decide about Kirov?"

"I've been ordered to wrap up that element of the operation."

"His company?"

"Yes. I'm driving back tonight. My team is waiting." He held up a thumb drive, given to him earlier in the day by the Vancouver consulate's senior MSS officer.

Kwan said, "What about the other underwater recording information he's been offering?"

"I've been directed to abandon it. Beijing decided the risk of prolonging the mission for the hope of obtaining the extra data is no longer warranted."

"Good. We've been fortunate so far; I never liked that anyway—pushing so hard."

"Understood, sir."

"Newman and the child?"

"It's your discretion."

"I'll take care of that."

"Very good, sir."

Commander Wang left, returning to his cabin to assemble his personal gear. A car and driver—one of his *zhongdui* team members—waited in a nearby parking garage.

Alone in the operations center, Kwan considered Wang's assignment. The PLAN special operators would return to Washington State tonight using fraudulent Canadian passports—like the Russians employed. On the way south, they would first stop in Anacortes. The workboat remained moored to a dock on Fidalgo Bay. Wang would install the software on the ship's navigation computer. Although the system was password protected, skilled forensic IT specialists at the FBI or NSA would break the encryption and discover the Russian military program. Designed to aid in the deployment of subsea mines, the software would link Yuri Kirov with the pending attack.

Wang's next stop would occur in Redmond. Kirov had yet to surface. Private security continued to watch over Northwest Subsea Dynamics and Laura Newman's residence.

Undeterred, Wang's team devised a plan to evade the watchers and gain entry to the NSD office building. The operative would tape the thumb drive Wang used to implant the damning code on the workboat to the underside of a locked desk drawer in Kirov's office.

Wang's final task was the elimination of Yuri Kirov.

Kwan Chi also received orders from Beijing.

The *Yangzi* would depart for Hong Kong after his phase of Sea Dragon was implemented. A fresh crew would arrive tomorrow afternoon to make the 5,800-nautical-mile voyage. Most of the ship's crew members disembarked upon arrival in Vancouver. Many had been aboard for months and were due home leave. Just a handful remained aboard now.

During the first leg of the transpacific voyage to Hawaii, Kwan would carry out the MSS's first mandate. Laura Newman would be deep-sixed in the middle of the night.

Upon arriving in Honolulu, and as requested by Kwan and approved by the MSS, baby Madelyn would be surreptitiously dropped off at a local fire station. Kwan was then permitted to return home the rest of the way aboard his Gulfstream.

Beijing's final order presented a greater challenge. Elena Krestyanova had already turned down Kwan's offer to accompany him on the trip to Hawaii due to pressing business elsewhere. Besides, he had grown fond of the Russian turncoat. If the choice were left to

Kwan, he preferred to keep Elena on the payroll. The intelligence she provided was exceptional. Beijing, however, did not see it his way.

Kwan was not yet ready to carry out the directive. It could wait. Right now, he had personal business with Elena back in his quarters.

CHAPTER 72

DAY 31—WEDNESDAY

The president of the United States sat at the head of the conference table. A dozen others joined him in the basement of the West Wing. His national security advisor sat to his left with the director of national intelligence to his side; the secretary of the Department of Homeland Security sat on the president's right along with the FBI director. Deputies and aides filled in the remaining chairs. Also participating via a secure video link was the chairman of the Joint Chiefs of Staff and his boss, the Defense Department secretary. Both men sat in a conference room inside the National Military Command Center located deep underneath the Pentagon. Video cameras and outsized flat-panel television screens at both venues allowed the parties to see each other in high definition.

It was 3:35 A.M. in the White House Situation Room. Instead of his usual suit and tie, President Magnuson wore an open-collar shirt and a pair of blue jeans. The other men in the room sported suits and ties, the three women stylish dresses.

The DHS secretary completed his briefing and the president responded, "So there is no question it was sabotage?"

"Correct, sir. There were four separate charges, all placed in similar locations along the pipeline route over a length of about five miles. Each bomb was detonated in a valley or low spot so that the oil stored in the pipe would drain out through the ruptures."

"Even when the pumps stopped, it would all drain out because of the holes?"

"Yes, sir. The locations were selected to inflict maximum spillage. The pipeline's leak detection systems worked well. As soon as the line pressure drop was detected, the computers shut down the pumps and triggered the block valves. But with so many deliberate breaches, the oil inside the pipe just drained out."

"How much are we talking about?"

"Somewhere around fifty thousand barrels—just over two million gallons."

"That's not as much as the tanker that sank."

"Correct, the *Alaskan Star* had one point three million barrels aboard. About half that spilled."

"What about cleanup?"

"Alyeska's already on it. Their spill-response system is first rate. We'll know more during daylight, but so far the spilled oil hasn't entered into any streams or rivers, which is good news."

"Thank you, Charles."

President Magnuson faced the FBI director. "Bob, has anyone claimed responsibility?"

"Not yet, sir. But we suspect it might be anarchists."

"They're in Alaska now!" the president said, rolling his eyes.

"Probably a splinter group."

"Where'd this come from?"

"One of our informants in Portland—Oregon. She claimed to have heard something big was being planned for Alaska."

"Well, at least it isn't the damn Russians again."

"We'll know more soon, Mr. President."

POTUS next turned his attention to the DOD chief. He peered at the wall-mounted video monitor at the end of the table and said, "Bill, what's the latest on that Russian helicopter?"

"Ah, Mr. President, the Russians have said nothing about the incident, but our listening posts picked up chatter from the Cuban military. They sent two patrol boats to the crash site and recovered several bodies."

"Russian military?"

"That's our take. There was at least one reference to 'commando' in the Cubans' radio talk."

"That freighter still hanging around?"

The Joint Chiefs chairman, a four-star admiral, responded. "Yes, sir. It continues to loiter about fifty miles east of the crash site."

"You're confident that it was a special operations unit?"

"Correct, sir. We tracked the military transport from Saint Petersburg to Havana. It was a naval *Spetsnaz* unit."

"How capable were they?"

"Very proficient—similar to our SEALs."

"What happened?"

"It appears to be a mechanical failure. The Hind was flying low to avoid radar. Something happened, we don't know what. Anyway, it went down quick at high velocity. The crew never had a chance."

An American military reconnaissance satellite tracked the Russian helicopter during its entire flight. The president had already viewed the video recording of the crash.

The Central Intelligence Agency provided the initial lead. A Russian naval officer in Saint Petersburg tipped off a CIA case officer about the elite special operations unit.

"Admiral, do you remain convinced that this commando unit was bound for the Mercury Oil Complex?"

"I do, sir. It was on a direct heading for the converted tank-ship. The helo went down about forty miles short. There was about one point five million barrels stored aboard the vessel."

"An easy target."

"Indeed. Assuming the *Spetsnaz* operators were familiar with the technology, a unit like that would have her in flames in just a few minutes and on the bottom within an hour and still leaking crude."

"That would have been a real disaster."

"A nightmare, sir. Probably worse than the *Deepwater Horizon* blowout."

President Magnuson directed his next question to his director of National Intelligence. "Madison, anything new to report on the Sakhalin incident?"

"It's quieted down considerably, but the Kremlin continues to blame the attack on Chechen separatists. However, we've also picked up chatter about a possible Ukraine connection." She consulted a notepad on the tabletop. "Although the Chechens are well motivated, we are not convinced they carried out the operation. The attack was military-like and carried out flaw-lessly. The Chechen fighters are brawlers—tough to be sure but lacking in precision. The Ukraine military, on the other hand, is well trained."

President Magnuson cocked his head. "Ukraine attacked Russia?"

"We don't know. We have nothing tying them to the attack, or for that matter the Chechens, only rumors reported by our agents plus intercepted communications. There are Ukraine Army units capable of making the attack, but the logistics of carrying it out would have been a stretch for them, and a near impossibility for the Chechens."

"Well, at least they aren't blaming us for it, like they did for that oil well blowout in the Arctic."

The DNI frowned. "Well, sir. I'm not so sure about that. The CIA ran some war gaming simulations based on Russian military protocols. One scenario was particularly troubling. I reviewed it last night, it was to be in your daily briefing today. If a Ukrainian special ops unit were transported to Sakhalin by submarine, it would work."

"Do they have that capability?"

"No—but we certainly do."

POTUS leaned back in his chair, taken aback by the comment. "Russia thinks we assisted Ukraine with blowing up their plant?"

"The simulation suggests that they might be considering it."

The president turned his attention to the national security advisor. "Peter, what about this situation Madison suggested?"

"She called me earlier today and told me about it. With the attack on the pipeline, it suddenly made sense to me. It could have been part of a two-pronged operation by the Kremlin to avenge the Sakhalin attack."

"You think the Russians are behind the Alaska pipeline sabotage as well as blowing up the *Alaskan Star*?"

"We can't discount it at this point, regardless of what the informant in Portland told the FBI. It fits the pattern of escalation."

President Magnuson looked toward the video monitor linking the Pentagon to the conference.

"Bill, based on the current events, what is your recommendation?"

"Mr. President, the admiral and I are in agreement that the Kremlin's intentions are unpredictable. It is likely there may be additional attacks on our infrastructure or even military. The physical attacks could continue or they could switch to cyber or both. Given that uncertainty, we recommend raising DEFCON from four to three."

"That's a big change. It will spook the Russians."

An alert system used by the U.S. military, DEFCON or defense readiness condition, consisted of five levels ranging from the lowest state of readiness, DEFCON 5, to imminent nuclear war, DEFCON 1.

"We agree, sir."

"I'm not comfortable with that—at least at this point."

"I have a suggestion, sir," the admiral said.

"Yes."

"Perhaps the Air Force could remain at DEFCON four but all other forces would transition to level three."

DEFCON 3 required Air Force bombers and fighters to be ready to mobilize within fifteen minutes' notice.

"That sounds better to me. Not so hair trigger."

"Yes, sir. Under level three, we'll be able to get our slower units under way, particularly our ships and subs, and also get our quick-reaction Airborne and Marine units in place."

"All right, Admiral, let's proceed in that direction."

CHAPTER 73

Yuri and Nick stood near the shore, looking northward at the black waters of Coal Harbour. It was chilly at half past two in the morning. Frosty plumes marked their exhalations.

They walked along the boardwalk that ringed the pocket park. Yuri wore his wetsuit under a parka. The duffel bag strapped over his right shoulder concealed the rest of his diving gear.

With no direct vehicle access, they parked the Jeep a couple of blocks away and hoofed it. Although they had Cardero Park to themselves, Yuri could not risk being seen in full diving attire strolling along the public walkway.

"I see why you picked this place," Nick said as he stared at the rock-covered embankment. It sloped downward to the water.

"This is a lot easier than trying to get over a bulkhead or a pier. I can ease into the water."

They spoke in low tones, not wishing to alert any nearby live-aboards. The western end of Coal Harbour Marina was just thirty meters away.

Yuri lowered the duffel bag onto the grass and dropped to his knees.

"What can I do to help?" Nick asked.

Yuri removed the air tank and handed it to Nick. "Hang on to it while I strap myself in."

"You got it."

Five minutes elapsed. Yuri stood beside Nick, decked out with a combination SCUBA tank and buoyancy compensator backpack, a stainless dive knife secured to his right calf, an illuminated compass banded to his left wrist, and a wetsuit hood encasing his head. A face mask and a companion snorkel were temporarily parked on his forehead while a demand regulator and a backup regulator from the air tank both dangled over his chest. Attached to the air tank with cable ties was a waterproof bag stuffed with additional gear. Beneath the wetsuit jacket, Yuri wore a neoprene vest for extra insulation.

To Nick, Yuri looked like he was ready for a moonwalk. "Where's your weight belt?" he asked.

Yuri patted his waist with both hands. "It's built into the BC."

Integrated with the buoyancy compensator were forty-five pounds of lead weights. By pulling ripcord straps on each side, he could easily jettison thirty pounds in an emergency.

Yuri stretched out his six-foot-plus frame. He was uncomfortably warm but that would soon change.

Nick held a plastic bag. "You ready for this?"

"Yes, go ahead and stuff it in."

Nick stuffed the double-ziplock bags containing the Colt .45, extra magazine, and Yuri's cell in the open wetsuit jacket. He zipped the jacket closed, forcing the zipper over the bulge. Yuri reached up to check the seal. He said, "Gloves, please."

Nick helped Yuri slip on the dive gloves. They were a tight fit over the sleeves of the wetsuit jacket.

Nick reached into the duffel bag and removed a dive light and a pair of fins. He handed them to Yuri and said, "I think you're set now."

"I am." Yuri stretched again, testing the various fasteners securing the gear. Satisfied, he said, "Time to go."

"Be careful, Yuri Ivanovich."

"You, too, my friend."

Gripping his fins and light, Yuri waddled to the embankment and descended, stepping from one rock slab to the next. When he reached the water's edge, Yuri stopped to slip the fin straps over the heels of his booties. He eased himself into the water.

In the dimness, Nick watched Yuri swim under the deck of the circular public view pier that marked the seaward end of the park. Before long, Yuri submerged.

"*Udači!*"—Good luck, Nick whispered.

Elena stood next to the arched window wall of the master stateroom, taking in the city lights. She wore a stylish white bathrobe with YANGZI embroidered in scarlet thread over her left breast. She'd just stepped out of the shower—a spectacular arrangement of plumbing that had invigorated her skin with steaming pulsed jets followed by cascading sheets of treated silky water. Her damp blond hair hung straight, the ends brushing the robe's collar.

Kwan Chi remained in the bed fast asleep, lying on his side with just the back of his black mop exposed.

The sex was intense. Chi was a superb lover. He took time to ensure that all of Elena's needs were met—three times—before he peaked. From their prior coupling, she expected that he would sleep soundly for the next several hours.

Too keyed up to sleep, Elena couldn't stop thinking about the money. During nightcaps, Kwan showed her where he'd parked the funds—$5 million U.S. It was in an offshore online escrow account, made payable to Elena's Cayman Islands bank account. Just one click on the Authorization to Release Funds tab from his phone would transfer the funds. No humans involved.

All that remained to guarantee Elena's payday was for Yuri Kirov to hand over the data he had in return for the release of Laura Newman and her child. A simple trade, yes, but still dangerous for all concerned, especially Elena.

She did not trust Yuri. Bullheaded, cagey, and exceedingly creative, he had confronted an impossible situation and pulled off a near miracle. It was not in his nature to back away from adversity.

If Yuri ever learned that Elena was responsible for embroiling him in his current predicament, he would never stop looking for her.

Yuri swam about two meters above the bottom, unhurriedly pumping his legs. Holding his dive light at waist level, he directed the beam downward. The bulk of his body helped shield the luminous sphere generated by the light ray. The eight meters of murky water above Yuri absorbed the residual photons before they reached the surface, preserving his stealth.

To minimize his presence further, Yuri paced his breathing, taking shallow breaths and slowly exhaling. Compared to a typical SCUBA diver, Yuri left a bubble trail that created minimal disturbance when it reached the surface. The bubbles burst with a barely audible spatter.

As Yuri advanced into the gloom, a flounder covered by a lens of silt burst to life just ahead. It scurried away, leaving a muddy wake. Yuri chuckled. *Sorry to wake you up like that, little fellow.*

Yuri checked the compass. He was on course. A check of his watch verified he'd been swimming for about six minutes. It was time to check his bearings. He pitched upward, switched off the light, and ascended. When he broke the surface, he was facing northward. He saw no familiar landmarks. He kicked his fins and pirouetted in place.

A mountain range of glimmering skyscrapers filled his face mask. In the foreground, silhouetted by city lights, was the sleek profile of the *Yangzi*. It was about sixty meters away.

Yuri checked the compass, establishing a new bearing. He released a charge of air from his buoyancy compensator and sank below the surface.

Nick Orlov leaned against the guardrail, peering seaward into the murk from the public boardwalk. He had relocated to the east end of Coal Harbour Marina, near Harbour Green Park. Even in darkness, the sheer bulk of the *Yangzi* dominated all other watercraft in the marina—a massive shadow ringed with subdued lighting.

Nick raised the night vision device that hung from a leather strap around his neck. He'd purchased the Bushnell Lynx binoculars from a Vancouver sporting goods store after Yuri visited the dive shop. Even with most of the superyacht's lighting switched off, the combined monotone green image in the viewfinder revealed dim objects with striking clarity.

"There you are," he muttered after switching on the Bushnells' infrared illuminator, tagging the guard who stood at the top of the gangway in the shadows. He next spotted the roaming sentry near the stern.

Nick lowered the binocs and checked his wrist-watch: 3:05 A.M. It was time. He reached into his coat pocket and retrieved his cell phone. He hit the speed dial.

"*Allo?*" broadcast from Nick's phone after the first ring.

"Are you in position?" he asked, continuing in Russian.

"We are."

"Proceed."

"Yes, sir."

Nick waited, observing the marina's floating walk-way without need of the NVD. He spotted the two SVR officers. Walking side by side, they casually worked their way seaward. One of his men tripped and almost tumbled onto the concrete float before catching himself.

Nick laughed quietly. *Nice move, Pyotr.*

Ordered to mimic a couple of drunks caught up in late-hour revelry, the two men from the San Francisco consulate who'd trailed Elena for the past two days carried out Nick's instructions. Both in their late twenties, the SVR officers carried bottles of Molson and took occasional swigs as they staggered toward the *Yangzi*.

Despite the distance, Nick could hear his men verbally acting out as they approached the yacht's bow.

"Look at the size of that thing," Fredek called out in English.

"Big some bitch all right," Pyotr said, slurring his words.

Pleased with the performance, Nick pulled up the NVD binocs. *Here they come!*

The sentry on the main deck near the ship's gangway stepped out of the shadows. He walked down the gangway and stepped onto the floating pier. The lookout watching the stern headed forward along the starboard side deck to back up his partner.

Nick's impostors now stood opposite the towering bow of the *Yangzi*.

"Some fat cat must own this monster, eh?" offered Fredek.

"I heard it's a Chinaman."

"Chinese own everything around here."

The sentry approached the counterfeit drunks. Although the SVR men were both six-footers, the Asian had half a foot on them and fifty pounds on the larger of the pair.

"Gentlemen, this dock is reserved. You need to turn around and head back to shore."

"Bullshit," Pyotr said. "We can walk out here if we want. I have a boat moored here, too."

The Russian spy's statement was partially true. Earlier in the afternoon, he rented a vacant slip on the same pier, paying two month's rent and a damage deposit in advance for a new boat he had just purchased. An electronic key card that allowed access to the marina was included. There was, of course, no new boat. Having the key eliminated the need to scale the security fencing.

"I'm sorry, sir, but you cannot continue. You need to return to your boat."

"You own this monstrosity?"

Nick looked past his men, studying the other sentry, who remained at the head of the ship's gangway. He checked his watch. The timing was perfect.

Okay, Yuri, now's your chance.

Yuri kicked with both fins, launching his body upward onto the stern platform between a pair of guardrail stanchions. He pulled himself onto the teak planking, and on his hands and knees he surveyed his surroundings. The floating dock to his right remained deserted. Centered overhead on the adjacent bulkhead, the yacht's silver nameplate glimmered in the residual light.

So far, so good.

Yuri pulled off his fins and stood up. Just below the nameplate was a watertight door. It connected with the ship's garage. From the deck diagrams Nick had provided, Yuri knew the hatchway provided access along the lower deck—the ship's second level—through the tender compartment and the engine room to the crew quarters in the bow. He remained convinced that Laura and Madelyn were in one of the crew cabins.

Yuri examined the hatchway and located a recessed handle. He pulled on it but nothing happened. It was secured from inside.

That called for plan B.

While in the water, Yuri had removed his combo air tank and buoyancy compensator, strapping the gear to one of the stern platform's guardrail stanchions. The equipment dangled just below the surface, suspended by a short section of poly line. Yuri knelt on the deck by that line and pulled the tank until it was awash. He detached the waterproof bag from the tank and used another section of line to secure his fins, light, and face mask to the tank's valve stem.

After submerging his gear, Yuri opened the bag and removed a black canvas backpack. He stood and slipped it on. He partially unzipped his wetsuit jacket, reached inside, and removed the Colt .45 from the plastic Baggies.

Gripping the pistol, he cautiously ascended the built-in stairwell on the starboard side of the stern bulkhead. The stairs connected with the main deck on level three—the deck where most of the ship's activity occurred.

As Yuri stepped upward, he issued orders to himself: *Keep your head down and watch for movement.*

After the sentry repeated his warning, Pyotr and Fredek retreated, maintaining their cover as drunks. They were halfway down the dock, still stumbling and muttering gibberish.

Nick maintained his surveillance. The immense Asian kept his eyes on the retreating pair for several minutes before returning to his perch on the main deck. The other sentry stood fast until the disturbance subsided before fading into the shadows near the stern.

Nick checked his watch. The distraction lasted just over five minutes. He hoped it was long enough for Yuri to sneak aboard the yacht.

Yuri crept forward, crouched down along the port-side bulwark of the main deck. He'd just passed the grand salon and was opposite the dining room. He took an instant to peer through a window. Subdued interior lighting revealed both compartments were vacant. The side deck ended amidships with a companionway—stairwell—that ascended to the next deck. Adjacent to the stairs a hatchway opened into the main deck's interior. He worked the door handle, but it would not open.

Now what?

His goal was to reach the bow section one level below his present location. But that was impossible. Two choices remained. Backtrack to the aft deck and try another route along the starboard side of the main deck, or take the stairs to the upper level and search for another way inside.

Yuri climbed the stairs to the fourth level—the owner's deck. Opposite the stairs was a door that led to the interior. He was about to try the handle when he noticed movement from the bow. He retreated into an alcove, pressing his back against a bulkhead.

Someone was walking his way. A guard, he suspected.

Yuri stuffed the pistol inside his wetsuit jacket and rearmed with the dive knife. His training flashed into focus: Attack from the rear. Use the free hand to muffle the mouth while repeatedly stabbing between the base of the neck and the collarbone.

Yuri's heart accelerated. He was on automatic kill.

An errant breeze blew cigarette smoke his way.

Steady. He's coming.

The nightwalker strolled into view, the glowing tip of a cigarette leading the way.

Now!

Yuri lunged forward and cupped his gloved hand over the mouth, pulling the slender body back into the alcove. Just as was he was about to strike home with the knife he spotted the long blond hair.

What the hell?

He wrestled the victim to the deck, pinning the struggling form to the planking with his bulk. During that maneuver, the individual's robe parted, revealing a naked female.

With his hand still clamped over her mouth and the knife poised to shred arteries, Yuri leaned forward so his lips were just an inch from her right ear. "If you want to live," he whispered in Russian, "stop resisting or I'll gut you right here."

Elena complied at once.

CHAPTER 74

"Where's Laura?"

Elena lay on her back with her bathrobe open. "Down below—the lower deck is what I think they call it. She's in a cabin near the bow."

Yuri kneeled over her, straddling her waist with his thighs while holding the knife against her throat.

"How do I get there?"

"There's a lift—that's the only way I know."

They spoke in whispers and in Russian.

"Where?"

"Inside this deck near the middle. I'll take you there."

"What about guards?"

"What do you mean?"

"Where's the guard for this deck—I saw guards below."

"They are not allowed on this level when I'm with Chi in his private quarters."

"Chi?"

"Kwan Chi—the owner."

"Where's he right now?"

"Sleeping."

"How do you know?"

"Because I just left his bed. I couldn't sleep and decided to have a smoke."

Elena's admission did not faze Yuri. He continued the interrogation.

"How many people are on this boat?"

"I don't know—maybe ten or so. Chi told me that most of the crew left already, something about a crew change in a day or two."

"Are they all Chinese?"

"Yes."

"Military?"

"Some of them, I think."

"What about this Chi guy, is he PLA?"

"No, he's a civilian."

"I don't believe you." Yuri pressed the knife tip against her throat, drawing a prick of blood.

Elena jerked her neck aside. "He's with the MSS."

"That's better. Now what the hell is their real mission here?"

"I don't know any details. I was tasked as a liaison only. You know more than I do."

"Where's Wang?"

"I haven't seen him. I don't think he's aboard."

Yuri withdrew the knife and stood up. He offered his other hand. "Get up. Take me to Laura—right now."

Nick remained at his observation post on the public boardwalk, now accompanied by his two would-be drunks. All three SVR officers leaned against the guardrail, gazing seaward at the *Yangzi*. They spoke in low tones.

"Do you think he made it aboard?" Pyotr Skirski asked. The bulky twenty-eight-year-old's stature and shaved bullet-head screamed athlete.

"Probably."

"Who is he anyway?"

"All I can tell you is that he's with military intelligence."

"GRU?" asked Fredek Kocyk. He stood next to Pyotr. Although he was nearly thirty, his lean build and fresh looks suggested a college student.

"Like I've told you both before, he's deep undercover. Let's just leave it at that."

"Okay, just curious."

Pyotr chimed in next. "What about Krestyanova? She must still be aboard—what's her involvement?"

Nick turned about to face both of his charges. "We're not certain at this point, but there's a chance she might have been turned."

"Chinese?"

"Like I said, we don't know, but the MSS might be running her now."

Both men cursed.

"I know her well from a previous op," said Nick. "It's really hard for me to believe that she crossed over. I've got to find out one way or the other."

Fredek said, "Is that what Kirkwood is doing?"

When Nick introduced the agents to Yuri earlier in the day, he had used Yuri's cover name from the *Neva* operation—John Kirkwood—but nothing more.

"Yes, that's part of his mission."

Nick turned to peer at the *Yangzi*. His subordinates remained mute.

Pyotr spoke up a minute later. "I see movement— the middle deck, near the stern," he said, pointing.

Nick raised the night vision binocs. "Son of a bitch!"

"What?" Fredek asked.

"It's Yur—John. He's with Elena."

"How much farther?" Yuri asked.

"It's just ahead, maybe ten meters."

Yuri and Elena were on the starboard deck hugging the bulkhead near amidships. They had been on the move for over five minutes, first heading to the aft end of deck four, where they skirted the luxurious outdoor lounge and hot tub. Yuri followed behind Elena, the Colt .45 clenched in his ungloved hand.

They crept forward, remaining in the shadows cast by the starboard bulwarks and the overhead of the bridge deck. Just ahead was the double doorway that opened into the interior of the upper deck—the main entrance to Kwan's private residence.

Set into an elegant but tough mahogany frame, the laminated glass inserts of the doorway were rated bullet resistant—not to repel invaders, but to resist a rogue wave washing over the deck.

Elena pulled open the forward door and stepped inside with Yuri on her heels. She pointed straight ahead to the elevator and said, "There it is."

Yuri eyed the narrow door within the enclosure.

"How big is that thing?"

"It's for four people."

Yuri noticed the stairway to the right of the elevator. "Where do those stairs go?"

"Same as the lift."

Yuri signaled with his pistol. "I prefer to walk."

"Whatever."

They were just passing the main deck—the ship's third level, headed to the lower deck—when a young Asian female dressed in coveralls trotted up the stairs.

The PLAN specialist froze the instant she spotted Yuri. His hefty frame clad in all black certainly was intimidating. But the wide-caliber barrel he pointed between her eyes instilled immediate terror.

Yuri tipped the barrel of the Colt upward a few short strokes, signaling her to approach.

The woman moved to Elena's side, trembling.

Yuri addressed Elena in Russian, "Use the belt on your robe to tie her hands behind her. Do a good knot because I'm going to check."

Elena scowled as she turned away.

The trio started heading deeper into the hull. Yuri followed the women, his hand still holding the Colt with the barrel pointed at the overhead. Wrapped around his other hand was the tail end of the cloth belt that bound the wrists of his new captive. Without the belt, Elena had to cross both arms over her chest to keep her robe closed.

They were now on the lower deck, standing near the elevator.

"Which way?" Yuri asked, continuing in Russian.

"This way," Elena said as she walked past the elevator and opened a side door. Yuri and his Chinese prisoner followed. Elena pulled open the fire door that provided entry to a narrow corridor that extended forward toward the bow. Cabin doors lined both sides of the hallway.

Elena started down the passage as Yuri commanded in a hushed voice, "Stop, come back here."

Elena complied, closing the door with a confused frown. "What's wrong? The cabin you want is up ahead on the right."

"Keep your voice down. How many of the crew are here—sleeping?"

"I have no idea."

"There's a dozen or more cabins there. How do I know you're really taking me to one Laura is in?"

Elena replied, "The only cabin I know down here is the one that Laura is in."

"The cabins all have electronic key card access. How do we get into the cabin Laura's in?"

"I knock on the door. They keep a guard in there with her."

"Guard—why didn't you tell me that before?"

"You didn't ask."

Yuri glowered at her. He sensed Elena was leading him into a trap. He turned to his new captive, and switching to English he whispered, "Do you speak English?"

"Little English," she said, still edgy.

"How many here, sleeping—now?" he said, gesturing with his hands.

"Sleep now—off duty."

"How many?"

"Chief steward—he in his cabin." She pointed forward.

"Where are the others?"

"Engineer in his cabin." She again pointed forward. "Captain, he in his cabin on bridge." She pitched her head back, glancing at the overhead. "Other crew fly home today."

"What about security?"

She frowned, not making the connection.

"Guards, how many on duty now?"

"Two."

Yuri did the math: seven crew members including the woman and the other guard with Laura—a skeleton crew. That was far fewer than Nick's estimate—good news for a change.

"Where's your cabin?"

"Two cabins forward on port."

"How many in there now?"

"Me only—others gone."

"What do you do here?"

She shook her head.

"Your job—on this ship."

"Assistant steward."

"Are you military?"

She glanced away without comment. Nevertheless, Yuri had his answer.

"Where were you going?" he said, again addressing the young woman.

"To galley—for tea. No sleep anymore."

Yuri suspected she was lying but didn't pursue it. He was running out of time.

"All right, Elena, here's what we're going to do . . ."

They assembled beside the cabin entry. Elena and the captive stood side by side, facing the closed door. Yuri crouched down next to the assistant steward, still grasping her leash.

"Do it," Yuri whispered.

Elena knocked on the door. "Open up, please," she said in English with a raised voice. "I need to speak with Laura Newman again."

The door cracked ajar.

"I need to see the prisoner," Elena said.

The door rotated inward. That was Yuri's signal. He rose from behind and shoved both Elena and the assistant steward through the opening.

Yuri's maneuver was so unexpected that the two women slammed into the guard—another petite female—without uttering a word or even a scream. All three crashed to the deck in a tangle of limbs.

Yuri rushed inside, shoving the door closed.

Still lashed to the bed, Laura stared wide-eyed at Yuri.

CHAPTER 75

Elena and the two female crew members lay sprawled out on the deck inside the *Yangzi*'s brig. Yuri towered over the trio brandishing the Colt.

Yuri winked at Laura. "Hang tight, honey. I'll have you free in a minute." He addressed the two Chinese crew members, "Get up and untie her—now!" He faced Elena. "Sit there and wait."

The youngest of the pair, the one Yuri had captured minutes earlier, translated for her companion. They stood and worked on Laura's lashings.

Laura struggled to stand, her muscles stiff and lower back on fire.

With the pistol still trained on the trio, Yuri planted a quick kiss on Laura's right cheek and said, "Are you okay?"

"I think so." Laura stepped between the two PLAN sailors to check Maddy. She remained in the baby carrier parked on the desk. The commotion woke her and she howled.

Laura picked Maddy up and consoled her. "It's okay, honey, I'm here."

Yuri faced Elena. "Sit in the chair." He eyed the two sailors. "Both of you, on the deck facedown."

As the women complied, Yuri handed the pistol to Laura. "Shoot her if she moves."

With Maddy over her left shoulder, Laura gripped the .45 with her right hand, aiming the semiautomatic at Elena's exposed navel.

Yuri bound the women, using Laura's cuffs. Before long, both females were hogtied and gagged.

"Get up, Elena," he ordered. He bound Elena's wrists behind her back with the belt from her robe. He turned to Laura, "Time to go, honey."

Yuri reclaimed the pistol. With Elena in front and Laura behind carrying Maddy in the baby carrier, they exited the cabin. As he had done with the first Chinese captive, Yuri used the trailing end of Elena's bonds as a leash. He was thankful that Madelyn had quieted down.

They stood at the base of the stairway that led upward to the main deck. Yuri started to push Elena forward, when Laura placed her hand on his shoulder. He turned to face her.

"Where are we going?" she whispered, bewildered by the abrupt turn of events.

"To the stern. There's a dive center there."

"Why?"

"We're going to swim off this thing—it's the only safe way. There should be extra wetsuits in there for you."

"What about Maddy?"

He pulled on a backpack shoulder strap. "Everything needed to keep her safe is inside."

Laura's eyes narrowed in worry.

Yuri broadcast a reassuring smile. "I'll show you soon. We need to go."

"Okay."

It was a calculated risk on Yuri's part. The Web article Nick found had a page featuring the *Yangzi*'s—or *Columbia*'s—dive center, an amenity usually found on superyachts. If he found no dive gear in the compartment, Yuri had a backup plan. He would give Laura his wetsuit jacket and its hood—it would be bulky over the coveralls she wore but it would keep her vital organs warm. The sleeveless rubber vest covering what he wore under the wetsuit jacket would get him to shore.

Inside the backpack were a child-size immersion suit and a plastic inflatable one-person raft. The survival suit was too big for Maddy. Nevertheless, it would keep her warm and dry in the raft.

They reached the main deck, amidships. Yuri oriented himself before directing Elena to head through a nearby interior doorway. They entered the galley. The stainless steel appliances filling the spacious compartment were all top-of-the-line commercial grade.

At the opposite end of the galley a hatchway opened onto the exterior deck. With Elena at his side, Yuri cracked open the hatch and peered aft.

He stepped through the doorway, pulling Elena with him. "Head aft," he commanded.

Laura followed with Maddy.

They walked a few steps when one of the guards walked into view at the far end of the side deck.

Startled, the sentry jerked out a pistol from his shoulder holster and raised it to eye level.

"Get down," Yuri yelled to Laura and Elena. With no other options, he attacked.

Just as Yuri squeezed the Colt's trigger, the sentry fired.

The guard buckled to the deck, hit in the lower abdomen with the first round and then his left forearm. On his stomach, he scurried out of view.

Yuri kept his pistol aimed downrange, admonishing himself for blowing the second shot. His ears still rang from the double reports. Then he noticed Elena on her knees, staring up at him. Her eyes were as wide as saucers, and her cheeks were pale. She rolled onto her side, her hands still tied behind her back.

Huddled on the deck shielding Madelyn, Laura noticed the blood first. "She's been shot."

"What?"

Crawling on her hands and knees, Laura moved next to Elena. She pulled back the bathrobe. "Oh my Lord," she said.

The nine-millimeter hollow-point slug had shattered Elena's left shoulder. Blood pulsed from the wound.

"We can't stay here," Yuri said. "We've got to go."

"We can't leave her like this, she'll bleed to death."

Elena turned her head toward Laura. "Please help me," she whispered.

Laura pressed her palm over the wound just as Yuri gripped Elena's waist and hoisted her limp body up and over his shoulder, legs forward, head rear. With one eye on the aft deck, waiting for the guard's return, Yuri searched for a new escape route. It was a couple meters forward. He gestured to Laura with his gun hand. "We need to get up the stairs."

Laura complied, hauling Maddy in her carrier. Yuri followed with Elena. Blood spattered onto the bleached teak decking of the companionway's treads.

* * *

"*Govnó!*" Nick muttered.

"That was gunfire," Fredek said.

"*Króme shútok.*"—No kidding, offered Pyotr.

The three men remained at their observation post on the public boardwalk. Although the *Yangzi*'s hull partially attenuated the pistol reports, the sharp cracks radiated into the tranquil night air like thunderclaps from a summer mountain storm.

Nick surveyed the yacht with his night vision binoculars. At first, he observed nothing out of the ordinary, but then he spotted the guards on the main deck. The bulky Asian who confronted Fredek and Pyotr had his arm around a colleague, helping the injured man forward along the starboard deck.

"Something's gone wrong," Nick announced.

Kwan Chi was up. He slipped on a robe to fend off the slight chill in his stateroom. Peering through the window at the foredeck, he saw only black outside.

He turned around. The bed was empty and the nightstand clock displayed 3:25 A.M. Elena's dress and underwear remained draped across a bedroom chair. Her high heels sat by a dresser.

Where is she?

The master bath was empty and ditto for his private study.

Kwan walked aft, headed for his private galley, where he expected to find Elena sipping a cup of tea.

As he approached the galley, he heard voices—English-speaking whispers.

What's this about? He pushed open the door.

Elena was on the tile deck lying on her back, her naked body partially covered by a robe. She moaned—low mournful tones. A woman in standard crew coveralls with her back to Kwan was on her knees, leaning over Elena. She held a towel against Elena's shoulder.

Blood was everywhere—on the towel, the robe, and the deck.

"What's going on?" he said in Mandarin.

Laura looked over her shoulder for an instant.

"You!" Kwan shouted.

Astonished at the American's presence, Kwan stepped forward to investigate.

The black shadow lunged from his right. A burst of lightning flashed through his brain. He dropped to his knees and rolled on his side.

Yuri stood over Kwan, the .45 clamped in his hand. A few strands of hair were embedded in the butt of the Colt's handgrip.

"You better tie him up," Laura said. "He's the one behind all of this." She turned back to tend Elena's wound.

Yuri stared at Kwan, who was groaning and reeling from the blow to his temple. Yuri was tempted to kick the son of a bitch in the belly but refrained. The rubber booties covering his feet offered nil protection. He couldn't risk a sprained ankle. Instead, he knelt down next to Kwan and grabbed his arms, flipping him face-down. Using the cloth belt that Laura had removed from Elena's wrists, Yuri bound Kwan's hands behind his back.

CHAPTER 76

Nick outlined his game plan while Pyotr and Fredek helped him lower the dinghy into the water. All three stood on the stern deck of a forty-foot powerboat moored to the same pier as the *Yangzi*. The huge yacht, lit with enough illumination to rival a carnival marquee, was about fifty yards away.

The eight-foot dinghy kissed the water surface as Nick held the bow painter. He turned to continue his instructions. "I just need a couple of minutes, like what you did before."

"But what if they want to see IDs?" Fredek said.

"Just bullshit 'em. Tell 'em you're undercover and heard gunfire. You've already called in reinforcements. Believe me, the crew will be freaked about having to deal with a surprise inspection by Canada Customs and Immigration."

"What about that big sucker?" Pyotr reminded Nick. "He saw us up front and close—drunk as skunks."

"Part of your surveillance op. After you heard the shots, you had no choice but to act."

Pyotr grinned. "Okay, boss. Got it."

* * *

A pulsing tone blared from the overhead. "What's that?" Laura asked.

Yuri looked up at the speaker. "Some kind of shipboard alarm."

"That's not good."

"No, it's not. We've got to go now."

Laura stood, wiping the blood from her hands onto the sides of her coveralls. "She's in bad shape. I don't know if E—"

Yuri cut her off. "Forget about Elena. We're going to have to jump overboard." He handed Laura the Colt and removed his backpack. He had just begun to open it when he heard muffled voices approaching from beyond the galley door. The only word he understood was "Kwan."

"They're searching for him," Yuri said. He leaned over and grabbed Kwan by his bound wrists and launched him upright.

In obvious pain, Kwan grimaced but remained silent.

Yuri gestured to Laura with his hand. She returned the pistol. He marched Kwan to the galley door and pushed it open.

Two men approached from a corridor not far off.

Yuri ordered Kwan, "Tell them to back off—in English. Now!"

Kwan recognized his personal steward and the *Yangzi*'s engineer. "Go back," he said.

Both men halted, each fluent in English.

Yuri stared over Kwan's right shoulder, the muzzle of the Colt tight against the PRC spy's skull. "Retreat to the deck below now," he commanded.

"Do what he says," Kwan ordered.

"Do it—right now or I'll blast his brains out!"

The men backed up, keeping their eyes on Yuri. They passed around a bulkhead and disappeared.

Yuri manhandled Kwan back into the galley.

"Did they go to the other deck?" Laura asked. She'd eavesdropped on the terse dialogue.

"I don't know. Maybe."

Yuri weighed their options. With the crew on alert, his original exit plan was futile. Descending two deck levels while they tried to work their way to the stern was impossible. If they jumped overboard from their current location, they might be picked off like fish in a barrel.

There was only one route left.

Yuri again pushed the MSS spymaster through the galley door, his left hand clamped on to Kwan's bound wrists and the Colt glued to the back of Kwan's head. Laura followed with Maddy.

Yuri verified the corridor remained clear. "Let's go," he said.

"Where?" asked Laura.

"Up."

Nick sat inside the dinghy. He rowed to the seaward end of a floating pier located west of the *Yangzi*. Across the open waterway, he watched Fredek and Pyotr as they approached the ship's gangway. A crew member standing watch on the main deck was already halfway down the gangway. Nick raised his NVD, focusing on the guard. It was the beast they'd confronted earlier. He wasn't brandishing a weapon, but Nick ex-

pected he had a pistol or knife or both concealed somewhere on his body.

The guard now stood at the base of the gangway
blocking entry to the ship. Nick couldn't make out the
interplay between his operatives and the sentry, but the
Asian's body stance, arms folded across his chest,
broadcast defiance—just what Nick expected.

"Good job, boys," Nick mumbled.

"I don't care who you are. You cannot board this
vessel."

"We heard gunfire and we're going to investigate."
Pyotr Skirski inched his way up the gangway with Fredek in his wake. The hulk continued to block their passage.

"You are mistaken. There was no gunfire."

"What's that alarm about?" The shipboard klaxon
continued to wail.

"A false alarm. It will be silenced soon."

"Stand aside," Pyotr ordered.

"You need a search warrant. Until you have it,
you're not boarding."

"Hang up," Yuri ordered. "And turn off that alarm."

"Do what he says," Kwan said.

The *Yangzi*'s captain stood in the pilothouse like the
proverbial deer in the headlights, stunned by the unannounced entry of his boss and the black-clad gunman
from the aft doorway.

* * *

Nick pushed off from the dock and engaged the oars. He cut across the open water in less than a minute, pulling alongside the *Yangzi*'s stern. Just before scrambling onto the stern platform where Yuri had boarded, he caught a distant glimpse of Fredek and Pyotr. As planned, they reluctantly retreated, heading back to shore.

Nick was just about to ascend the stairway to the main deck when a tremor in the stern platform pulsed through his legs. He heard a rumble—a dull tone emanating from deep inside the hull.

They're starting the engines—what's going on?

The cell phone in his coat pocket began to vibrate.

It was Yuri calling.

Yuri, Laura, Maddy, and Kwan were in the pilot-house along with the *Yangzi*'s skipper. The forty-two-year-old master, a PLAN officer, stood at the ship's helm. Unlike the typical yacht, this one had no steering wheel. Instead, a joystick hand control mounted at the center of the jetliner-like instrument panel guided the ship.

Yuri stood behind Kwan, his left hand looped around Kwan's leash and the Colt in his right. Laura was at his side, still carrying Maddy in the baby carrier. She held the cell phone to his ear. It was on speakerphone.

"We were spotted," Yuri said, using Russian. "I had no choice but to shoot the bastard."

"Are you okay?" Nick asked.

"We're fine, but Elena was hit."

"Damn!"

"She was with us on our way out when we ran into a sentry."

"How bad?"

"Shoulder—a real mess."

"You need to get off this thing right now," said Nick. "They just started up the engines—they must be getting ready to take off."

"I'm responsible for that."

"What?"

"We're on the bridge. We've got Kwan and the ship's captain under gunpoint—my hostages. It's the only way I can keep the rest of the crew at bay."

"Why did you start up the engines?"

"We can't stay here. Someone triggered an alarm. Reinforcements could arrive any minute—from the PRC consulate or who knows where. China owns half of Vancouver. I ordered the captain to head into Burrard Inlet. I'll figure out something once we get there."

"Can they hear us?"

"Kwan and the captain?"

"Yes."

"They can hear but they don't speak Russian."

"Are you certain?" asked Nick.

"No."

"Go someplace where you have privacy."

"Give me a minute."

Yuri traded with Laura, the cell phone for the Colt. In English he said, "Shoot them in the legs if they try anything."

Laura kept the .45 aimed at the captives, a round in the chamber and three in the magazine.

Yuri stepped to the far side of the bridge but kept an eye on Kwan and the captain.

He disabled the speakerphone and said, "Okay, what is it you want to tell me?"

"I just managed to sneak aboard this thing."

"Where are you?" Yuri said, startled.

"The same place you came aboard—your diving gear is still hanging over the side."

"Pull it up and stow it on the deck for me."

"Okay."

Yuri said, "There's only a skeleton crew aboard, far fewer than we thought, maybe less than ten. I've got two on the bridge here with us and I left two tied up below. The guard I shot is either dead or too weak to be a threat."

"How many others?"

"Kwan's steward and someone manning the engine room. But there could be more."

"Are they PLAN?"

"Probably, or MSS."

Yuri and Nick schemed for the next two minutes, hashing out the plan.

CHAPTER 77

Nick grabbed his phone and called Fredek and Pyotr back to the floating pier. The SVR officers had made it halfway up the gangway when the guard reappeared—it was the brute again. He rushed down the incline, halting their advance. The resulting verbal barbs between the three provided the distraction Nick had engineered.

Crouched next to the starboard bulwark on the main deck, Nick monitored the ensuing argument.

Remaining low, Nick shuffled forward and stepped onto the gangway. Pyotr upped his vocal assault on the Asian.

"You are hereby ordered by Canada Border Services and Immigration to submit to our inspection. If you refuse, we will—"

The guard felt Nick's footsteps on the aluminum deck and turned. Nick was on him before he could retrieve the pistol from his shoulder holster.

Knocked silly by a vicious whack to the back of his skull, the guard dropped to his knees and fell face forward onto the aluminum deck. Momentum propelled his 260-pound bulk down the gangway's incline. Fredek and Pyotr jumped aside, allowing him to toboggan onto the concrete deck of the floating pier.

Nick and his agents checked the cataleptic Asian. Nick slipped the fish billy into a coat pocket. He had found the salmon bludgeon in the dinghy.

Nick checked the surroundings before addressing his charges. "Help me pick up this prick. We need someplace to stash him."

"Then what?" asked Fredek.

"We steal this bitch and go for a ride."

In the pilothouse Yuri hung up his phone and whispered to Laura, "It worked." He kept his eyes on Kwan and the captain.

With her back to the captives, she mouthed the words, "They're aboard?"

Yuri nodded. He stepped forward and addressed the ship's master. "Time to depart, Captain."

"But we're still tied to the dock."

"No, we are not. The mooring lines have been released."

"But how—"

"Do what he says," ordered Kwan.

"Yes, sir. Departing now."

The captain engaged the bow and stern thrusters and the *Yangzi* crabbed away from the floating pier. About thirty feet away from the dock, the captain switched off the thrusters and throttled up the main engines.

Eighteen minutes after the MSS guard made his frantic cell phone call from the *Yangzi*, a black Mercedes-

Benz SUV roared up to the street fronting the marina. The four-man armed security team from the PRC consulate rolled down the shore-side gangway, defeated the locked gate, and clamored down the main walkway of the floating pier, only to discover that the *Yangzi* had slipped her moorings.

About to return to the consulate empty-handed, one of the gunmen heard feeble moans. He tracked them to a fiberglass dock box near the intersection of the guest dock and the main walkway of the pier.

It took all four to haul the mammoth guard out of the container and deposit his mass into a dock cart. By the time they shoved the overloaded cart up the ramp, the guard had regained enough of his wits to reveal that the *Yangzi* was hijacked.

CHAPTER 78

The *Yangzi* passed under the Lions Gate Bridge and headed west into Burrard Inlet. It was 4:18 A.M.

Nick, Yuri, and Laura manned the bridge. Kwan and the captain were one deck below under guard. The subdued scarlet lighting inside the wheelhouse minimized glare. Yuri sat in the pedestal-mounted captain's chair. Intimidated by the vessel's size, he kept the speed down to a modest five knots. Standing on Yuri's right, Laura monitored the radar screen and the GPS vessel traffic display while holding her daughter. Leaning over Laura's shoulder, Madelyn bobbed her head as she surveyed the new environment. On Yuri's left, Nick scanned the ink-black waters ahead with his night vision binocs.

"Looks clear ahead to me," Nick offered.

Laura looked up from the console. "Same here. No close-by traffic, just a southbound tug and barge in the Strait."

"Good," Yuri said. He was relieved to have successfully maneuvered the huge yacht around the dozen or

so ships anchored in the inlet waiting to offload or take
on cargo in Vancouver Harbor.

Yuri glanced at the electronic navigation console to
his left. The LCD screen displayed the color image of
a Canadian chart of the southern Strait of Georgia.

"We'll stay on this course for another twenty minutes and then head south."

"How long will it take to reach Seattle?" Nick asked.

Laura addressed Yuri, "You still want to use Rosario Strait?"

"Yes, I want to get out of Canadian waters as soon
as we can."

She turned toward Nick. "Late in the afternoon, four
to five o'clock."

"Then what?" Nick asked.

Yuri answered, "I'm not sure—maybe anchor this
thing offshore and take one of the tenders to shore."

"What about our little collection below?"

Joining Kwan and the captain in the upper-deck
salon were the ship's remaining crew. All had surren-
dered without struggle. Fredek and Pyotr stood guard,
armed with Yuri's Colt and the "beast's" pistol.

"I don't know." Yuri had not anticipated the events
of the past hour. His original plan was to find Laura
and Maddy and then sneak them off the yacht without
detection. Stealing the *Yangzi* and holding its crew at
gunpoint would have been unfathomable earlier.

Laura said, "We have to turn them over to the Coast
Guard, maybe the U.S. Navy."

"For kidnapping you?" Nick said.

"No. To protect Yuri."

"What?" echoed both men.

Laura's and Yuri's eyes met. "So much has happened tonight . . . I haven't had the time to tell you what I saw."

Yuri puckered his brow, puzzled.

"A couple of days ago we managed to escape from the cabin. We ended up inside some kind of control center one deck level above where I was held. While I was hiding there, the man you called Kwan and another Asian—a younger man—came inside and held a videoconference. It was in Chinese, but they had a PowerPoint display with lots of graphics."

"What were the images?" Yuri asked.

"Maps, very technical plots, like some of the seismic data Cognition works with but different."

"What else?"

"Many photographs—one of them of you. In your Russian officer's uniform."

"Me?"

"I heard your surname used several times. They also showed photographs of either the *Deep Explorer* or the *Adventurer*. I couldn't tell for sure."

"Do you have any idea who they were speaking with?"

"It was a two-way video setup. The monitor I saw had a room full of Chinese—most in uniform."

"The younger Asian with Kwan, what did he look like?"

"Late twenties, early thirties, athletic build, short close hair, confident."

Yuri cursed and said, "Commander Wang—People's Liberation Army-Navy."

Nick interjected, "Laura, do you have any idea what they were discussing?"

"Something about submarines. They had several photographs of a sub on the surface."

Yuri turned to Nick. "Take the helm for me." He turned back to Laura. "Take me to this control center."

Yuri and Laura relocated to the ops center. Laura parked Madelyn in the baby carrier on a desktop. Still awake, she kept busy looking around the compartment while babbling on.

Yuri tried to access the center's main computer with one of the built-in console keyboards, but it was password protected. The file cabinet on the side of the console was also locked. Undeterred, Yuri inserted the tip of his dive knife between the top drawer and frame and then pried open the drawer, which was stuffed with documents. He pulled out file folders until he discovered the manual. "*Govnó*," he muttered as he opened it.

"What?" Laura said.

"This is bad."

"What's wrong?"

"It's all starting to make sense now," he said while paging through the pamphlet.

Laura was at his side. "What is that?"

"A Russian naval manual." He handed over the inch-thick booklet.

She rifled through the document, ignoring the Cyrillic text. Studying its diagrams, schematics, and photographs, she quickly deciphered the purpose of the manual. "This is a weapon system—I saw some of these diagrams in the slideshow."

"Yes, it's a torpedo mine, what we call the *Gadjúka*—Viper."

"Why would they have something like that on this boat?" Laura said, stunned.

"China's trying to start war between Russia and the United States, and they're going to blame it on me."

CHAPTER 79

Yuri returned to the pilothouse to monitor the helm, now set on autopilot with a southerly heading. Through the windscreen, the predawn sky remained carbon black. Nick was busy examining the Mark 12 Viper manual.

"How the hell did they get this thing?" Nick asked as he turned to face Yuri.

"I don't know, but I suspect Elena was somehow involved."

"How could she ever get her hands on a document like this?"

Yuri hunched his shoulders. "You know her better than me. She's resourceful and cunning, like all of you SVR types."

Nick ignored the barb. "If they have the manual, then they must have the mine—probably paid someone a fortune for it."

"That's the way I see it."

"What are they up to?"

"I haven't figured that out yet. But you can be sure whatever it is, it's bad."

Laura reentered the bridge from an aft compartment with Maddy in the carrier.

"How is Elena doing?" Nick said.

"She appears stable. The bleeding has stopped and she's sleeping, which is good. But she needs to be in a hospital."

"We don't have time to transfer her to shore yet," Yuri said. "That will have to wait for now." He faced Nick. "Maybe you should wake her up and question her about the mine. We've got to find out what they're planning."

"That's not a good idea," Laura said, now at Yuri's side. "She's too weak."

Nick said, "What about the Chinaman—Kwan? We should question him."

"I don't know." Yuri hesitated. "He strikes me as a hard case. This is his op. He won't give it up—would you?"

Nick was about to counter when Laura said, "What is it you're looking for?"

Yuri said, "Based on the fact they have the manual to one of our most secret underwater weapons, I suspect that they also have the actual mine and will soon deploy it."

"To do what?"

"Sink an American ship."

Laura said, "And that will start the war you're worried about?"

"Yes. After all of the trouble in Alaska, I think it just might be the trigger."

"You mean the oil spills?" Nick said.

Yuri nodded. "I think it's all tied together, including the attack on Sakhalin."

"The last I heard, it was Ukraine that was—"

Laura cut in, "What kind of American ship would have to be destroyed to spark a war?"

"Military for sure," Yuri said. "Probably an aircraft carrier or maybe a submarine."

"Like those missile submarines based on Hood Canal?"

"Yes, that would be enough."

"I agree," Nick added.

"The slides of the submarine I saw . . . maybe that's what they're after."

Yuri tilted his head to the side, stunned at Laura's comment.

"What slides?" asked Nick.

Laura ignored Nick as she questioned Yuri. "How do you deploy the mine—the Mark Twelve thing?"

"Drop it overboard from a ship or parachute in from a plane. It sinks to the bottom and waits for the right target to come along. It then fires the torpedo and 'boom.' "

"Would it take long to deploy it?"

"No. With the anchor and the unit itself, it probably would take ten to fifteen minutes, assuming decent weather. Why do you ask?"

"Could it be done with this boat?"

Yuri's eyes narrowed as he considered the question. "Probably. From the place where they keep the tenders and other watercraft. There are overhead hoists that could be used to lift and then lower it into the water."

Laura pursed her lips. "That must have been what they were doing."

"What are you talking about?"

"During the trip to Vancouver from Seattle, the boat stopped for at least fifteen minutes, maybe longer. I wondered what was going on. I thought maybe we had docked somewhere. I heard a lot of racket and then something really loud sent a shudder through the hull. And I also heard some kind of a small boat running around outside with an outboard engine."

"Do you have any idea where this might have taken place?" Yuri asked.

"No. But the boat slowed down a couple of hours after leaving Seattle."

Yuri turned back to the instrument console, signaling for Laura to join him. "Please check the GPS system for me. Maybe we can backtrack the course."

"I'll give it a try."

Yuri, Nick, and Laura stared at the electronic navigation chart of Puget Sound displayed on a wide-screen monitor built into the main console. Superimposed on the chart was the track line of the *Yangzi*'s position for the past seventy-two hours.

Yuri keyed in a new command and the resolution of the chart tripled. He pointed to the screen. "There, in that area. The boat hardly moved for almost twenty minutes. That's got to be the place."

"You think that's where it was deployed?" Nick asked.

"That's where I would put it if my mission were to ambush an American Trident missile sub."

"Sweet Jesus," Laura whispered, turning back to Yuri. "You're right, honey. This was orchestrated to blame you and Russia. They used me to get to you. I'm sorry."

"It's not your fault. They tricked me. I'm the one to blame for being so damn naïve. I should have known something was wrong with what they had me doing."

It was clear to Nick now, too. He switched to Russian. "Yuri, I've got to let Moscow know what's happening. The consequences could be catastrophic for both us and the Americans."

"I know, but not yet."

"Why?"

Observing Laura's growing annoyance over the language barrier, he answered in English. "We need to find the mine and then maybe, just maybe I can neutralize it."

"How?" Laura asked.

"Remotely signal it to shut down. If that doesn't work, I'll dive down to it and manually turn it off."

Laura leaned closer to the LCD display, squinting. She looked back at Yuri. "It's over two hundred feet deep in some places there. You know what the doctor said."

"I'll be all right."

"No, you won't."

"What are you talking about?" Nick asked Laura.

"He's still not recovered from last year. He has residual damage to his central nervous system. Another deep dive could permanently cripple him or worse."

"It's less than one-third the depth of the *Neva*, and it'll be a quick dive," said Yuri.

Laura's face dissolved into a scowl.

Yuri reached forward and advanced the dual throttles. "I'm kicking her up to ten knots." He turned back to Laura. Smiling, he said, "Would you please program the autopilot to take us to Admiralty Inlet—via Rosario Strait?"

Laura keyed in the waypoints.

Nick stepped back from the bridge console.

She's not happy with him at all.

CHAPTER 80

Lieutenant Commander Wang Park was southbound on Interstate 5 passing Marysville when his cell phone rang. He took the call. It was from the Vancouver consulate's security officer—a lieutenant in the PLA.

"Sir, the *Yangzi* was attacked an hour ago. It's been hijacked."

"What!" Wang shouted.

"The intruders came in from the sea. They wore wetsuits."

"How many?"

"Unknown. One of the MSS agents assigned to the ship was left behind on the dock—unconscious. He recovered enough to reveal that the other security officer on board was wounded in a firefight. He's apparently still aboard. Two men on the dock posed as Canadian Customs and Immigration police. They ambushed the officer who was left behind."

Stunned, Wang said, "A coordinated attack?"

"Yes, sir. No question about it. Sea-based and land-based."

"Where's Kwan?"

"Taken hostage."

Wang's stomach flopped as his instant assessment of the tactical situation gelled. *The Americans are on to us—the mission's blown!*

Wang recovered enough to ask, "Is Kwan still on the ship?"

"As far as we know. No one else aboard other than the one officer made it to shore."

"Where's the damn boat?"

"All we know is that it's not at the marina."

"What about GPS? Use the Internet to check the vessel tracking system."

"We did. They turned off the transponder. It's gone black, sir."

"*Tāmāde!*"—Dammit—Wang said. "At first light, I want everyone you can muster searching. We've got to find it."

"Yes, sir. We are implementing that now."

"I want a report from you at least every thirty minutes—understand?"

"Yes, sir. Will you be returning to Vancouver?"

"No. I'm going to stage from here."

Wang ended the call. He checked the dashboard clock: 4:34 A.M. He was about to make another call when his driver spoke up.

"I couldn't help but hear—the *Yangzi* has been hijacked?"

"Yes, and they took Kwan Chi."

The driver, a PLAN special operator, was privy to the mission details. A couple hours earlier, he had assisted Wang with planting incriminating software aboard the workboat in Anacortes. He was also one of the shoot-ers who invaded the Newman residence.

"American military?"

"Probably—operating in Canada without authoriza-tion. Delta or SEALs."

The *zhongdui* sighed. "Do we abort?"

"No."

The commando perked up. "Are we going to take it back?"

"As soon as we locate it, we attack."

"Excellent!"

"What's the plan, boss?"

"We're headed back to U.S. waters."

Nick and Fredek caucused at the forward end of the upper-deck salon. They spoke in their native tongue and kept their voices down. Pyotr was nearby, standing watch. The captives sat on the plush lounge furniture or on the carpet, wrists bound behind their backs.

"What will we do then?" asked Fredek.

"We're not sure yet. Things are still fluid. We need to get out of Vancouver."

"Okay."

Nick changed subjects. "It's time to take care of that 'other' matter."

"Oh—that's right."

Nick and Fredek relocated to a guest suite on the main deck. The guard who had lost the duel with Yuri lay on the queen bed covered by a bloodied sheet.

Nick pulled the shroud away. The Asian stared back with unblinking eyes. He was in his late twenties and his once brown skin had paled to a dull gray. Unlike the rest of the male crew with their short military-style haircuts, the man's thick black mane was long and stylish.

Nick said, "We need to search him."

"All right."

Other than an electronic keycard in a pants pocket and a *Yangzi* photo ID tag fastened to a neck strap, the man carried no personal items.

"He was probably a spook like us," commented Nick.

"MSS?"

"Yes, or Second Department."

Nick pulled the sheet back over the body. "Let's haul him out of here."

Fifteen minutes later, Nick and Fredek returned to the upper-deck salon—Kwan's domain.

After they raided a locker in the garage, Nick and Fredek weighted the body with ten meters of galvanized steel chain. Standing on the stern platform, they eased the corpse into the churning wake. It disappeared in just a couple of heartbeats.

While Fredek conferred with Pyotr, Nick walked forward and entered Kwan's stateroom. Elena rested on the huge bed, lying on her back.

He leaned over. She was asleep, rendered unconscious by morphine Yuri had found in the sickbay.

Laura had placed a towel over Elena's chest to cover her breasts. The dressing on her shoulder was saturated with blood. He gently pulled it away. Elena remained unresponsive.

There wasn't much to the wound, just a pencil-diameter dimple. A dollop of blood oozed from the opening. He used a gauze pad to soak up the fluid and taped a fresh dressing over the bullet hole.

Nick placed his left hand on Elena's forehead; no fever, which was a relief. So far, the antibiotics kept infection at bay. She needed emergency surgery, but it was out of the picture for now.

He wondered about Elena's loyalty—did Kwan really turn her as Yuri claimed? He still couldn't believe it.

Nick placed a blanket over Elena, kissed her forehead, and stepped away.

CHAPTER 81

The U.S. Navy issued the recall notice by text and e-mail. It followed up with telephone calls until each officer and enlisted crew member acknowledged the new orders. One by one, 153 of the ship's normal complement of 172 had made it aboard the USS *Kentucky* at Naval Base Kitsap-Bangor.

Many of the absent sailors were on leave and out of the state. They scrambled to catch military or civilian flights back to Sea-Tac International or Joint Base Lewis-McChord. Later in the day, at 1530 hours, dockworkers would disconnect the gangplank and the deck crew would shed the moorings. The *Ohio*-class ballistic missile submarine would head north on Hood Canal, bound for the deep blue Pacific a hundred miles away. Those not aboard at the sailing would be marooned ashore for the duration of the *Kentucky*'s mission.

SSBN-737 had been scheduled to depart from Bangor in twelve days for its next deterrent patrol until the president intervened. The *Kentucky*'s gold crew now hurried to prepare the boat. Rumors abounded as the crew carried out pre-departure duties.

"We're at DEFCON Three—that's a new one for me."

"It's those damn Russians, they're behind all of this shit."

"This is crazy—no way are we ever going to nuke the Russkis over spilled oil."

"I bet they keep us on patrol for the full seventy days plus the extra dozen for the early start—that will suck for sure."

"You watch, old Spud is gonna show up one minute before we shove off, drunk as a skunk!"

"War is coming, I just know it!"

CHAPTER 82

Yuri and Laura were in the pilothouse. The sun climbed over the distant Cascades, illuminating the jade waters. It was a clear, chilly morning with a faint northerly breeze.

The *Yangzi* proceeded southeastward in the outbound shipping lane, running at eight knots. About an hour earlier, Vancouver Vessel Traffic Control had hailed the yacht over VHF Channel 16. Yuri informed the controller that the ship's AIS transponder had failed and that they were returning to Seattle for repairs.

He stood behind the helm, monitoring the autopilot. Laura leaned against the instrument panel, holding a pair of binoculars to her eyes.

"There it is," she announced.

Yuri turned and peered eastward. A brown smudge with a backdrop of green projected from the inland sea. The landform looked like an island, except it wasn't.

Point Roberts, USA, was a five-square-mile enclave located at the seaward end of a peninsula that jutted six miles from Canada into the Strait of Georgia.

"I can just make out the breakwater," Laura said. "The rest of the shore is too fuzzy."

Yuri turned back to face the helm, choosing not to comment.

Laura thought about the private investigator Deborah Newman hired to check on Ken. Tom Hamilton was going to visit Point Roberts to restart the search for Laura's missing ex. Laura had not heard back from PI Hamilton—and she hoped she never would.

Laura returned the binoculars to their instrument panel housing. She looked aft, checking her daughter. Madelyn was in the portable carrier that occupied part of a bench seat. She chewed on a teething ring, her lower gum enflamed from a new tooth. Laura walked to the far side of the bridge and gazed southward at the approaching San Juan Islands, an archipelago of over a hundred named islands. The scenic view did not register.

Later this morning, the *Yangzi* would sail over the watery grave of her estranged, revenge-seeking homicidal husband.

CHAPTER 83

"What is your target?" Yuri demanded, using English.

Kwan stared down at the deck.

They were alone in the *Yangzi*'s operations center. Kwan, with his wrists still bound behind his back, sat uncomfortably in a chair at the main console. Yuri stood next to him. It was mid-morning.

"Your plan was to sink an *Ohio*-class sub from the onset—correct?"

Again, Wang refused to comment.

"I know you want to start a war between Russia and America, that's obvious now. This whole operation was designed to use me as your scapegoat. Let Russia and America tear at each other's throats while China remains on the sidelines—waiting. But waiting for what? That is the question, Mr. Kwan."

Silence.

Frustrated, Yuri fought the urge to punch his nemesis. "What's Elena's involvement? I know you turned her. How much does she know?"

No response.

Yuri peered at the huge flat panel screen on the forward bulkhead. It displayed the contents of the op center's computer system. Dozens of file names in Chinese characters filled the screen. With her computer skills, Laura had accessed the onboard system, calling up the encrypted files. During that process, she also discovered a mirror drive to the primary. It served as a backup and contained duplicate files of everything.

Yuri gestured at the screen. "What do you think is going to happen when the CIA and the NSA start tearing into these files? They will put you in prison for the rest of your miserable life."

Kwan looked up, meeting Yuri's eyes. "And your woman will be right there, too."

"What do you mean?"

"We know her involvement with you and your submarine—the *Neva*. And so will the FBI."

"Laura was forced to help. She has nothing to worry about."

Kwan laughed.

Yuri whacked Kwan's right cheek with an open hand. "You lousy son of a bitch!"

Kwan kept grinning.

Yuri struck again, using his right fist, propelling Kwan from the chair.

Kwan looked up at the towering Russian. The smirk replaced with a steely stare, Kwan said, "Free me and Laura Newman's secret will remain safe."

"Go to hell!"

* * *

Commander Wang Park chartered a helicopter and its pilot from a company operating at Boeing Field, located south of downtown Seattle. As a walk-in requesting immediate departure, he paid a premium hourly rate. But cost was not a concern. He gladly handed over his credit card.

His stated purpose for the charter was to view waterfront properties for potential purchase. He carried a Nikon that his team had used for surveillance of the Newman residence and NSD's offices. Wang would take photos of Puget Sound shorelines but his real mission was to locate the *Yangzi*—and Kwan Chi. The superyacht remained unaccounted for on the AIS vessel tracking system.

If the U.S. military had snatched the *Yangzi,* as Wang feared and duly reported to Beijing via secure satphone, the CIA would stash Kwan Chi away in a safe house and work on him until he broke. And he would break—eventually.

Wang expected the yacht was currently southbound, returning to Seattle, and hoped it had Kwan still aboard. Beijing ordered Wang to prepare a strike plan to rescue Kwan. If that were not possible, his orders called for the destruction of the *Yangzi* and all those aboard. Wang's *zhongdui* team was already assembling gear and preparing for the assault.

If the *Yangzi* was under way, Wang and his team had a fifty-fifty chance of successfully executing the mission. However, if the *Yangzi* ended up sailing into one of the several U.S. Navy or Coast Guard installations in Puget Sound, the chances of executing a successful attack were nil. All naval bases throughout the region were on heightened alert under DEFCON 3. Beijing warned Wang about the change in U.S. defense posture.

Worse yet, if Kwan had already been ferried away by helicopter or another vessel, attacking the yacht would only destroy evidence. Kwan would still end up spilling his guts to the Langley interrogators. The jackals in Taipei would then discover the ultimate outcome of Operation Sea Dragon—the invasion of Taiwan.

Any way Wang assessed the situation, disaster was imminent. His new job was to serve as the janitor—clean up the mess and get out. An important element of that sanitation effort called for the neutralization of the Mark 12 Viper torpedo mine.

Sinking an American warship now would spark a war—not between Russia and the United States as Beijing had schemed but between the USA and the PRC. China was not ready for that confrontation. It would lose—badly.

The looming consequences of a military defeat and the resulting worldwide condemnation of China's treachery instilled absolute terror in the Communist Party leaders. China's fragile economy would tank, bankrupting the once burgeoning middle class and empowering legions of the underclass. Overnight, the corrupt ruling Party would be squashed.

Wang had to recover the Mark 12 before it launched. But as he sat in the helicopter's copilot seat, watching the seascape race by, Wang had no plan. Never once had the war-gaming scenarios called for disarming and recovering the weapon.

How the hell do we do that?

CHAPTER 84

The *Yangzi* loitered in Bellingham Bay about a mile offshore of Governors Point. Headed southward, the autopilot synced with the engines to generate just enough thrust to match the one-knot flood current. It was 1:54 P.M.

Yuri and Laura manned the bridge.

"I still don't think you should make the dive. It's too risky," she said.

"It'll be okay. It's not that deep." Yuri tried to sound confident.

"Two hundred feet is deep."

"It won't take long."

"You don't even know if it's really there."

"That's why I'm going to check first."

Laura changed subjects.

"Where will they take Elena to get help?"

"The consulate will take care of it. I suppose they have a private clinic someplace in San Francisco."

"Nick must be pulling a lot of strings to make it happen."

"What do you mean, strings?"

Laura smiled. Yuri's English was excellent but he remained clueless to many American maxims.

"Call in favors."

"Oh, I suppose so, but he also has a lot of authority as assistant *rezident*."

Nick and Fredek had departed from the *Yangzi* nearly an hour earlier in the RIB, docking at the Port of Bellingham's guest float in Squalicum Harbor Marina. Elena Krestyanova accompanied them. Capable of walking, she had her right arm in a sling. Underneath her jacket, a fresh dressing sealed the nasty puncture in her shoulder.

Laura said, "She seemed to be in a lot of pain."

"Probably hurts like the devil. Movement causes the bone fragments to tear muscle and tissue."

"She'll need surgery."

"Nick said they would take good care of her."

"What do you think will happen to her?" Laura asked.

"Prison, if she's lucky."

"Do you think she knew what the Chinese were up to?"

"If not directly, she knew it was bad—for both Russia and America."

"You're probably right." Laura glanced at Madelyn. She remained in the portable carrier, her chubby hands spinning a built-in toy.

"How do you plan to turn Kwan over to the U.S.?" asked Laura.

"I'm not sure yet."

Yuri was working on a plan to use Kwan as a bargaining chip with the American government.

"I suggest you start with the FBI," Laura offered. "They have a large office in Seattle."

Yuri offered nothing more.

Laura let it go, knowing he would reveal his plan after he fleshed it out. She again changed subjects. "Who from NSD is coming up?"

"Tom Donaldson. I don't think you've met him. He's a tech, hired a month or so ago. Mid-twenties, nice guy."

"His name sounds familiar."

"He's the one who gave me the salmon."

"That's it."

"Are you going to have him operate the ROV?"

"No. I don't want any employees involved in this mess." Yuri turned to face Laura. "Besides, I'd like you to take the controls of *Scout*, like you did with *Little Mac*. Piece of cake for you."

"Okay," Laura said, smiling. That was one adage Yuri embraced.

Laura broached another troubling subject. "Kwan must know what happened to Sarah Compton."

"Probably, but he's not going to admit anything."

"You still think they . . . you know?"

"She was nothing to them—just an obstruction to eliminate."

Laura was about to ask a follow-up question when she sensed the low-frequency vibration. It resonated within the bridge house. An instant later, she heard the racket—*Thump, Thump, Thump.*

"What's that?" she said, looking through the windscreen.

"I don't know."

Laura stepped across the wheelhouse deck and pulled open a door. She stepped onto the starboard bridge wing. Yuri followed.

The helicopter hovered about two hundred feet away, its cockpit at eye level with the bridge. The furious downwash from the rotors churned the water surface into a mini-maelstrom.

"*Govnó*," muttered Yuri. Over the din he shouted, "Back inside!"

They retreated to the bridge. Just as Yuri pulled the door shut, the helicopter pivoted and continued on its southward course.

As the beat of the rotors subsided, Laura said, "I think we might have just been found."

"I was expecting it."

"What do we do now?"

"Wait for Nick and then continue south."

Twisting in his seat, Commander Wang Park fired off shots from the Nikon as the helicopter proceeded south. He turned back in his seat, facing the windscreen.

I found the damn boat!

It took all morning and then some.

Wang directed the pilot to fly to the airport in Anacortes, where his *zhongdui* team was standing by aboard the workboat *Ella Kay*.

Buoyed by the turn of events, Wang keyed the

Menu button on the Nikon. He called up the digital photos he'd just recorded. He clicked through the images, stopping on a clear photo of the two individuals who'd appeared on a bridge wing. He increased the magnification to its maximum setting.

"*Shǐ dàn*"—Shit—Wang muttered as he stared at the images of Yuri Kirov and Laura Newman.

CHAPTER 85

It was late afternoon. Yuri and Laura were aboard the *Yangzi*'s runabout. The twenty-foot RIB was in the entrance to Admiralty Inlet, about two miles southwest of Whidbey Island's Point Partridge.

Sixteen miles to the north, the *Yangzi* waited offshore of Deception Pass. The shipping lanes to and from Seattle were active with commercial traffic, preventing the superyacht from loitering in Admiralty Inlet. The runabout, on the other hand, was too small to be of concern. It could move about without raising red flags with the U.S. Coast Guard.

Yuri and Laura completed the second transect with the side-scan sonar unit, using the *Yangzi*'s GPS tracking history as a guide. Drifting with the current, they studied the laptop's screen.

"Right there," Yuri said, pointing to the screen. "That's got to be it."

Laura squinted, examining the faint smudge-like image that projected above the flat bottom. "Are you sure? That's not much of a return."

"The casing is coated with acoustic absorbing material to minimize sonar reflections. Without the GPS tracking data to pinpoint the search, you'd never know it was there."

"So it's time to break out *Scout*."

"Yes, I need eyes on it to make sure."

Nick Orlov commanded the *Yangzi*. He was in the wheelhouse with Fredek, who held Madelyn. She was fixated on the myriad multicolor gauges, displays, and LCD screens that populated the instrument panel.

The ship remained offshore of Deception Pass, jogging in a mile-diameter orbit at a couple of knots. Worried about the helicopter sighting, Nick and his men rendered the helipad inoperable by inflating one of the *Yangzi*'s twenty-person emergency life rafts. About the size of a heavy-duty pickup truck with its inflatable roof, the fluorescent orange raft filled up much of the open space of the landing pad.

Pyotr guarded Kwan Chi and the other captives in the salon one deck below the bridge. The three new SVR arrivals from San Francisco, ferried north on a charter jet arranged by Nick's boss, stood watch on the yacht's open decks. Each man carried an AKSU-74 submachine gun borrowed from the consulate's armory. All of the Russians remained in contact by portable radio and were on high alert.

"What is he going to do if it's really there?" Fredek asked.

Nick turned away from the helm to face Fredek. Maddy eyed the radar display. "Dive down and release it."

"Then what?"

"It's supposed to come to the surface, where he'll disarm it."

"He certainly has amazing skills."

"That he does."

"You know him very long?"

Nick turned back to the helm. "We've worked together before."

"He's military, correct?"

"He's undercover."

"I know, you can't talk about it," said Fredek. "Still, he's impressive. And his woman, Laura. Is she an American or does—"

"Leave it alone, Fredek. Their mission is highly classified and must remain that way."

"Yes, sir. Sorry."

Nick couldn't fault Fredek's curiosity. Yuri and Laura were extraordinary individuals. When they teamed together, their combined skill sets produced exceptional results.

Nick glanced at his wristwatch. Almost two hours had elapsed since Yuri and Laura had raced off in the runabout.

Nick was tempted to request a new progress report but decided against it. Still, he worried.

I wonder how they're doing.

The USS *Kentucky* was under way at 1530 hours. Five of her crew who were en route would remain ashore as the sub commenced its emergency patrol. Primed with two dozen nuclear-tipped Trident ballistic missiles, the 560-foot-long behemoth proceeded northward up Hood Canal, shadowed by two U.S. Navy thirty-foot RIBs, each equipped with a fifty-caliber machine gun. A harbor tug cruised a hundred yards off the *Kentucky*'s starboard bow, ready to offer assistance if she were to lose power or steering.

After the *Ohio*-class submarine passed through the drawspan opening of the Hood Canal Floating Bridge, she would rendezvous with a U.S. Coast Guard cutter and two U.S. Navy workboats. With the cutter in the lead and the two-hundred-foot-long workboats positioned on each side of the sub as blockade vessels, the flotilla would navigate through Admiralty Inlet and then head westward along the length of the Strait of Juan de Fuca to the *Kentucky*'s diving station.

Unknown to the crew of the *Kentucky* and the other local security forces was the presence of the Mark 12 Viper. Undetected during a recent underwater sweep by a U.S. Navy patrol craft, the torpedo mine remained armed and tuned in to the unique acoustic signature of the submarine's power plant and propeller.

Designed to ignore other vessel noise in the water column and to track only the approaching submarine by the strength of its in-water acoustic footprint, the Mark 12's torpedo would launch from its containment casing when in range. The weapon's power plant would accelerate the underwater missile to sixty knots while homing in on its target. The 550-pound warhead would punch a two-foot-diameter hole through the bottom of the mono-hulled sub, sending it to the seafloor in minutes.

Laura hovered over the laptop's screen while manipulating the joystick control with her right hand. A dark greenish tint dominated the image on the computer display. Tiny specks flashed as light from the ROV reflected off detritus in the water column.

"See anything yet?" Yuri asked. He sat at the RIB's control station, monitoring the GPS unit while steering and adjusting the power level to maintain a stationary position.

"No, nothing is—wait. It's coming up on something."

Yuri leaned aft, straining to view the laptop's display.

"Take a look." Laura turned the Dell toward him.

Yuri stepped away from the helm and knelt next to her.

"That's it—the *Gadjúka*." He tapped the screen. "That's the steel casing. The torpedo is inside." Having trained with the weapon, Yuri had no doubts regarding its identity.

"So they really did it—the bastards!" cried Laura.

"Yes, they did."

Yuri continued to examine *Scout*'s video output. About the size of a briefcase, the tiny ROV produced high-definition images of the Russian weapon. A pencil-thick fiber optic cable transmitted video signals from *Scout*'s camera to the Dell.

"Descend three meters please."

"Ten feet. Okay."

Yuri made a quick check of the RIB's GPS location. "Hold it," he said. He pointed to the screen. "I need a close-up right there."

"Okay."

Yuri examined the image—a steel shackle assembly.

"Is that the connection you were looking for?" Laura asked.

"Yes. All I need to do is remove the bolt from the shackle and it will float to the surface."

Laura leaned closer to the screen. Digital parameters were displayed at the bottom—camera heading, water temperature, and water depth. "That shackle is a hundred and ninety feet deep," she announced.

"Good, that should work."

"That's still a long way down."

"Don't worry. It'll be a piece of cake."

But she would worry.

CHAPTER 86

"Is it still there?" Wang asked his observer.

"Yes, sir. It continues to patrol the same route."

"Very well. Let me know the instant it departs from the routine."

"I will, sir."

Commander Wang Park terminated the cell phone call. His observer was on foot at a public park at the north end of Whidbey Island. For the past two hours, the MSS operative had monitored the *Yangzi* as it orbited offshore of Deception Pass.

Wang was inside the cargo compartment of a heavy-duty Ford van parked at the Anacortes airport. The driver and another commando were in the front seat. The third team member sat next to Wang. Chockfull of *zhongdui* equipment, the van was the same vehicle used to kidnap Laura Newman.

Located near Anacortes' western boundary, the public airport occupied the flattened crest of a hill. Residential subdivisions surrounded much of its perimeter.

The sun was in full retreat with complete darkness less than half an hour away.

Soon! Wang thought.

He speed-dialed another number. When his call was answered on the first ring, Wang demanded, "Give me a status report."

"Sir, it continues northward, with its escorts."

"What's the ETA?"

"At its present speed and heading, thirty minutes."

"Very well. Continue to track and call me at once if there are changes."

"Yes, sir."

The second observer stood on the ruins of a coast artillery mount at the Fort Casey State Park on Whidbey Island near Coupeville. He had an unobstructed view of Admiralty Inlet. Through binoculars, he observed the USS *Kentucky* and its entourage head northwestward in the outbound shipping lane.

Wang dialed once again. Again receiving a response on the first ring, Wang issued new orders. "Proceed to the target area, but do not approach until I give the order."

"Understood, Commander."

Wang terminated the call with the PLAN officer who had assisted him aboard the *Ella Kay*. The lieutenant remained aboard the workboat. He was accompanied by the chief petty officer who'd served as the workboat's helmsman and four fresh MSS special operators rushed from the Vancouver consulate. The *Ella Kay* proceeded westward down Guemes Channel at ten knots.

With Kirov in control of the *Yangzi* instead of American authorities, Wang adapted. Operation Sea Dragon was in play again. After the Mark 12 sent the *Kentucky* to the bottom, Wang and crew would attack the yacht. He would personally kill Kirov.

Laura kept her eyes on the marker, maneuvering the runabout to within thirty feet of the float. Five minutes before starting his dive, Yuri deployed the guideline.

To mark the approximate bottom position of the Mark 12 Viper, Yuri used the RIB's Danforth anchor and its 100 feet of Dacron line combined with another 150 feet of line borrowed from the *Yangzi*. The anchor line connected to an air-filled boat fender that bobbed on the sea surface. Laura used the float as a marker.

Worried about Yuri, Laura waited anxiously for his return. He had assured her he would return within ten minutes. Twelve had already passed.

Come on, honey, where are you?

The shackle's bolt would not budge.

Yuri was over 190 feet below the surface hanging on to the steel cable that anchored the aft end of the Mark 12 to the seabed another 20 feet down. In near darkness due to the retreating sun and the infestation of particulate matter in the water column, Yuri used his dive light for illumination. The torpedo mine loomed above. Housed inside the thirty-inch diameter by a 23-foot-long cylinder, the weapon hung vertically with its still closed launch hatch aimed at the surface. It angled northward a few degrees, pushed by the ebb tide.

Yuri checked the dive watch strapped his left wrist. He had been under for almost fifteen minutes. *Govnó!*

Yuri pulled on the screwdriver once again, trying to unscrew the pin. He'd inserted the shaft of the driver into the hole at the rounded head of the shackle's bolt.

The pin did not budge.

This isn't working! I've got to try something else.

Reluctantly, Yuri descended.

Laura failed to notice the approaching armada until it was about a mile away. In the fading light of the receding sun, she used a pair of binoculars to examine the collection of vessels headed her way.

"Oh my God," she muttered. "It's the sub!"

On the sandy bottom with his knees clamped to the concrete anchor block, Yuri examined the shackle that connected the mine's mooring cable to the eyebolt embedded in the block. Apprehensive that the nitrogen in the compressed air he breathed had impaired his judgment, Yuri reminded himself of the task ahead—three times.

Insert the screwdriver and rotate it counterclockwise.

Yuri yanked on the driver. No movement.

Yuri again attacked the shackle, leveraging the screwdriver with everything he had.

This time it moved.

Fantastic!

Yuri unscrewed the shackle's bolt from the threaded fitting but the mine remained glued to the bottom. Tension in the anchor cable from the buoyant casing prevented complete withdrawal of the bolt. The bolt's shaft was jammed halfway out, pinned by the pull of the cable.

With one hand clamped to the concrete anchor block and the other grasping the steel cable, Yuri pulled. Nothing.

Yuri rested, preparing for another try, when he heard the muted whine of an electric motor. He looked up, aiming his light at the Mark 12 *Gadjúka*.

Oh God, no!

The launch tube hatch had rotated open.

Although Yuri had not yet heard the drone of the approaching vessels, the torpedo mine's acoustic package had been tracking them for ten minutes. The weapon's computer detected the unique suppressed sound print of the *Kentucky*'s propeller, now just a thousand meters away. It ignored the racket from the two barricade workboats that straddled the submarine. The Mark 12 was seconds from launching as its onboard sensors homed in on the target.

With his gloved left hand grasping the concrete anchor block, Yuri yarded on the cable with his right. He gained half a foot of slack, which caused the shackle bolt to slide away from its housing and drop onto the seafloor.

What happened? Yuri wondered, puzzled at the ease with which the cable had moved. Then he put it together. With the hatch open, the casing flooded, reducing buoyancy, which relieved tension in the anchor cable.

Yuri released the anchor cable. Still vertical in the water column, the mine crept upward. Its velocity was about one-third of Yuri's bubble trail.

The remaining flotation inside the flooded casing was designed to provide enough residual buoyancy to initiate a vertical launch.

It's going to launch any second now!

Laura's gaze alternated between the marker buoy and the advancing flotilla. Yuri had not briefed her on this scenario. Unsure of what to do if confronted by the security forces escorting the USS *Kentucky*, Laura prayed for guidance.

Yuri raced upward to the bottom end of the free-floating Mark 12 casing. With his right hand, he grasped the shackle that he had not been able to open earlier. With his other hand, he reached down and yanked the buoyancy compensator's twin ripcords. Thirty pounds of lead raced to the seabed.

Yuri opened the inflation valve on his BC. He heard the rush of compressed air and felt the fabric in the backpack expand around his neck and the flanks of his abdomen.

By releasing the weights and inflating the compensator while hanging on to the casing, he added extra buoyancy to the lower end of the mine. His goal was to rotate the axis of the Mark 12 from a vertical orientation to a horizontal position.

A nano accelerometer in the torpedo mine's arming mechanism—the same type used in tablets and cell phones to sense screen direction—would interrupt the launch sequence if the mine was seventy degrees or

more from vertical. It was designed to prevent an acci-
dental launch from the mine's deployment vehicle—a
ship or an airplane.

Ignoring the need to make a decompression stop as
both he and the Mark 12 ascended, Yuri hung on to the
shackle.

Where are you? Laura wondered to herself as she
scanned the waters around the RIB.

She had her answer a minute later.

The Mark 12 Viper broke the water surface about a
hundred feet to the south. It was barely awash. Laura
spotted a shadowy mass at the far end of the casing.
Yuri's black hood and face mask were nearly invisible
in the receding light.

Nick Orlov's cell chimed while he stood solo watch
in the *Yangzi*'s wheelhouse. It was 6:05 P.M. and twilight offshore of Deception Pass.

He answered the call; it was Laura.

"We've got it, we're heading north now," she reported.

"Outstanding! How's Yuri?"

"He's on oxygen."

"And the cargo?"

"We're towing the damn thing—it's behind us."

"Great, we'll meet you halfway."

"Nick, there was a submarine. It just went by us. It's
headed westward down the Strait of Juan de Fuca."

"What?"

"It's crazy, I know. But Yuri did it—just in time."

"Incredible."

CHAPTER 87

Yuri and Laura were inside the *Yangzi*'s garage. Yuri had just activated the gantry system to retrieve the Mark 12. The torpedo mine sat on its shipboard cradle.

"What are you doing now?" Laura asked.

"I need to disarm it."

Still in his wetsuit, Yuri was on his knees next to the weapon's control compartment working with a screwdriver. He removed the last screw and opened the inspection port. He reached inside and flipped a pair of switches.

He looked up at Laura. "Done."

"Is it safe?"

"Yes. I disabled the detonator and the guidance system. It's not going anywhere."

"Good. Let's dump this awful thing overboard—it's still dangerous."

"No, we need it," he said, standing up.

"What?"

Yuri explained. He then reached inside his wetsuit jacket. He retrieved his cell phone and began taking photos of the Russian weapon.

CHAPTER 88

Commander Wang Park squatted in the aft compartment of the King Air 90. The twin-engine Beechcraft lifted off from the Anacortes airport. It soon cruised eight thousand feet above the black waters of the Strait of Juan de Fuca.

Wang was horrified that the Mark 12 had failed to launch. The *Kentucky* and its escorts were churning westward toward the Pacific, oblivious to the threat. Wang was more determined than ever to complete the other element of his mission.

Although the King Air's passenger seats were removed in Seattle before heading north, the space was still an awkward fit for Wang and his three companions. Outfitted to the hilt, they wore black combat fatigues, Kevlar helmets, and jump boots. Strapped to their backs were ram-air parachutes with companion reserve chutes. Clipped to chest harness D rings were suppressed submachine guns. Each man also carried a nine-millimeter pistol, extra magazines, and grenades—fragmentation, white phosphorus, and smoke.

Night vision devices were mounted to their helmets.

In the blacked-out cabin, Wang kept his eyes on the target as the plane orbited. They had removed the cabin door in Anacortes. Through its opening Wang's infrared optics detected varying shades of white emitted from the *Yangzi*.

Observing the superyacht, Wang spoke into the microphone mounted inside his helmet. The PLAN lieutenant was on the other end of the encrypted radio signal aboard the *Ella Kay*.

"I can't tell what they're doing," Wang commented. "It looks like they might be trying to retrieve something. The RIB is moored alongside the starboard garage door."

"We can't make out any details from our position. Should we advance?"

"Negative. The ship's radar will detect your approach. Wait for us."

"Understood. We'll maintain separation until we hear from you."

"Very well, we're going airborne now."

Wang switched frequencies, hailing the MSS pilot.

"We're exiting now. Return to Anacortes and wait for further orders."

"Aye, aye, Commander."

Twenty seconds later, the *zhongduis* jumped from the aircraft. Wang went first, followed by his cohorts. Within the blink of an eye, the ink-black night sky swallowed them.

CHAPTER 89

Yuri knelt on the deck of the rigid inflatable boat. He adjusted the controls of the portable device with his right hand. The stainless steel container from Yuri's company was about the size of a toolbox. A black cable from the box dangled over the RIB's starboard side. Thirty feet underwater, the cable connected with another stainless steel gadget that was roughly the size of a gallon milk carton.

Yuri adjusted the controls as the RIB bobbed next to an opening in the *Yangzi*'s side. The overhead doors on both sides of the garage remained open, extending seaward from the hull like a pair of stubby wings. The Strait of Juan de Fuca remained calm as the yacht drifted westward with the waning ebbing current.

The *Yangzi* was a mile southwest of Smith Island. About five miles to the east in the darkness lay Whidbey Island. A rotating high-intensity strobe light from the northeast marked the airport tower at NAS Whidbey Island. The EA-18 Growlers practicing touch-and-go landings at the base broadcast thunder into the night air.

Satisfied with the adjustments, Yuri pressed the transmit key on the NSD hydrophone. A pulse of acoustic energy radiated from the underwater speaker.

Two hundred and sixty-six feet below, *Deep Adventurer* woke up. After resting on the bottom in hibernation mode for four days, the AUV reenergized itself. Within just a minute, compressed air discharged into the buoyancy tanks, expelling seawater ballast. The onboard computer engaged the propeller. She began the ascent.

Wang adjusted a halyard, angling the parafoil a couple of degrees to the left. Descending through the thousand-meter mark, he kept his NVD glued to the target. To his right the infrared strobe lights marked his companions.

At their current descent rate, the *zhongdui* operators would reach the target in three minutes.

CHAPTER 90

"How much longer?" Laura asked. She stood on the garage deck next to the RIB.

"Soon—I hope." Yuri was still inside the runabout, leaning against the starboard gunwale. He peered seaward, using his dive light to illuminate the nearby water surface.

"Couldn't this have waited?" she asked.

"I want the *Deep Adventurer* out of here. There's too much risk for NSD if the American authorities discover what it was doing." Yuri also had another incentive—he'd promised Bill Winters that he would ship the AUV to Barrow.

"How long will it take to reprogram it?"

"Ten minutes maybe." Once Yuri verified the remaining power supply, he would program the submersible to head north to Anacortes. He planned to park the AUV on the bottom in Fidalgo Bay and recover it later.

Laura peered into the gloom. "Nick's anxious to get going. I think he's right."

"Hang on. I should know soon if this is going to work."

With Nick's blessing, Yuri intended to deliver the *Yangzi* to the U.S. Navy—on the proverbial silver platter. After passing through the Hood Canal floating bridge's drawspan opening in the wee hours of the coming morning, Yuri planned to anchor the yacht in Thorndyke Bay. After Yuri and company departed in the RIB, Fredek would make an anonymous cell phone call to Naval Base Kitsap. Using an app on his phone to disguise his voice, he would report that a yacht filled with foreign terrorists was bent on attacking Bangor.

Within minutes, a quick-response detachment of U.S. Marines and sailors would descend on the anchored yacht by air and sea. It would not take long before the boarding party discovered the Mark 12, Kwan Chi, and the remaining boatload of PLAN crew members.

The real payoff would occur later when the attorneys representing Yuri and Laura negotiated with the Department of Justice. The bargaining chip would be the hard drive Yuri planned to liberate from the *Yangzi*'s op center. Although the incriminating evidence was encrypted, Yuri expected that experts from the FBI, NSA, and/or CIA would recover the full details of the PRC's Operation Sea Dragon.

Similar efforts would also take place in Russia. Nick had shipped the op center's backup hard drive to the San Francisco consulate in care of the SVR officer who'd escorted Elena. Also accompanying the agent was a duffel bag filled with cell phones, laptops, and other personal electronic devices looted from the *Yangzi*'s crew.

But not everything was shipped to California. Yuri searched Kwan's stateroom alone. He found Elena's and Kwan's cells along with Kwan's satphone. He sealed them inside a ziplock bag and stuffed it inside the vest of his wetsuit.

"Extra insurance," he explained to Laura.

Laura spotted it first. "What's that?" she shouted, pointing.

Yuri aimed his dive light, capturing the canary yellow bow of *Deep Adventurer* as it crawled out of the murk with the strobe on top of its hull flashing once a second.

Yuri turned away from the spotlight, looking up at Laura with a broad smile. "Right on schedule, honey!"

Wang made some final tweaks to the canopy. He was half a minute out. As planned, his men were in trailing positions, each spaced about fifty meters apart.

Although the helipad on the bridge deck remained blacked out, there was sufficient residual light from the *Yangzi*'s hull to power his night vision optics. The life raft remained in place on the helipad.

Wang's body stiffened in preparation for the landing. He glided onto the teak decking on the starboard side of the raft, managing to stop after half a dozen steps. His parafoil collapsed as the next man swooped in from above and repeated the landing.

The third operator landed on the port side of the raft but while still moving, tripped on an unseen line that secured the raft to the deck. He crashed onto the deck.

The fourth *zhongdui* flared his chute upward to avoid colliding with his fallen colleague.

Wang watched in horror as the commando sped overhead and smacked into the base of the superyacht's mast.

Wang jettisoned his backpack and reserve chute. He raced forward to check on his man.

Nick returned to the garage, taking up position next to Laura.

"How's Maddy?" Laura asked.

"Fine."

"She's going to be hungry soon."

Nick grinned. "We've got that covered."

"What?"

Pyotr had relieved Nick from bridge watch. On his way to the garage, Nick checked on Fredek, who was in the galley standing near the stove. Maddy, cradled in Fredek's arms, expressed herself through gurgles and trills as a bottle of milk warmed inside a water-filled pot resting on a burner.

"One of my guys is feeding her now—baby formula from the supplies the Chinese bought. He comes from a big family, oldest sibling. Lots of experience with infants—bottles and diapers."

"Really," Laura said, arching her eyebrows.

Yuri was still inside in the RIB, leaning over the gunwale working on *Deep Adventurer*.

Nick knelt next to the open garage door. "How's it going?" he asked.

Yuri turned. "Hi, Nick."

"What are you doing?"

"Getting ready to haul the *Adventurer* aboard so I can reprogram it." Yuri reached backward with his arm to massage his left calf. It had been throbbing for the past hour.

"That's great, but we need to get going. We've been lucky so far."

"I know, but I've got to take care of this first."

Updating the AUV's navigation system was a priority, but there was an even more pressing matter for Yuri. Before he sent *Deep Adventurer* to the bottom earlier, he'd booby-trapped the underwater robot as retribution, should Wang and company run a double-cross. But Yuri now needed to disarm the bomb. If the AUV malfunctioned on its trip to Anacortes and popped to the surface, the five kilos of Semtex hidden inside would decimate any innocents who tried to pry open the payload compartment. Yuri could eliminate that risk in about five minutes once he retrieved the AUV from the water.

Commander Wang Park climbed down the stairway from the top deck after checking the ship's mast. Two of his men waited on the helipad.

"He's gone," Wang reported. "Snapped his neck."

Both operators frowned but said nothing.

"How's your ankle?" Wang asked the other operator who'd landed hard.

"I'm okay."

"Can you function?"

"Yes, sir."

"Good."

Wang activated his helmet mike, connecting with his second in command aboard the *Ella Kay*. "We're in position. Commence your approach," he ordered.

"Executing."

With Laura at his side Nick continued to watch Yuri tinker with *Deep Adventurer*, when his cell phone activated. Nick answered. It was Pyotr.

Nick cursed and hung up. He announced to Yuri, "A boat on radar is closing on us from the north. It's been trailing for a while but just sped up. It'll be on us in a couple of minutes."

"Coast Guard?" Laura offered.

"Maybe," Nick responded.

"Maybe not," Yuri muttered.

CHAPTER 91

Wang and his team made their way forward through an interior corridor of the bridge deck. They passed the vacant cabins for the captain and navigator and entered a mini-salon reserved for the ship's officers. The vacant lounge connected with the pilothouse.

Crouched by a glass-panel doorway at the center of the pilothouse, Wang surveyed the bridge. A single occupant manned the helm. While his men stood guard, Wang opened the door and entered, his SMG at the ready.

A three-round burst of suppressed gunfire tattooed helmsman Pyotr Skirski's upper spine. The SVR officer fell forward onto the instrument panel.

Remaining crouched down, Wang advanced halfway into the wheelhouse, when a thunderous torrent of submachine fire erupted from the port side of the compartment. Wang dove for the deck. The storm of nine-millimeter slugs shattered the starboard bridge windows but missed their mark.

Hidden from Wang, the SVR agent standing next to the port bulkhead sprayed the starboard side of the bridge house with a thunderous barrage from his AKSU-74.

After the Russian expended a full magazine, Wang's backup team took the Russian out with multiple rounds to the head and chest.

The zipper-like reports of an SMG on full auto broadcast from an upper deck. The racket penetrated to the garage.

"What's that?" Laura asked.

"Gunfire?" Nick offered.

"*Govnó*," Yuri muttered, still aboard the RIB. With the gantry crane system's fore and aft rail beams over the floating *Deep Adventurer*, he was just connecting the lifting cables. "It's the Chinese—making a counterattack. They want the *Yangzi* back."

Nick withdrew his pistol and turned toward the interior garage bay.

Yuri hauled himself onto the deck and stood up. "Both of you, in the RIB now. I want you to power away from here."

"But Maddy!" Laura screamed. "We've got to take her with us."

"I'll get her. Now get in the boat before it's too late."

Nick started to protest, when Yuri cut him off. "I need the pistol—I'll check on your men if I have time. Take care of Laura."

Nick handed over the Colt.

"Once I have Maddy, we'll get wet. I'm going to swim due south." Yuri held up the compass still strapped to the left wrist of his wetsuit. "When we're in the clear, I'll call you on my cell." He tapped his chest. Under the bulge of the wetsuit was a plastic bag. It contained his cell phone and the phones belonging to Elena and Kwan.

"That'll work," Nick said.

Laura wasn't buying it. "Maddy—in the water? That's crazy."

"I've got it covered. Nick will fill you in. Now please, both of you go—NOW!"

After boarding the RIB, Laura reached up and handed Yuri his diving fins and face mask. "I love you," she said. "Save Maddy—and yourself."

"I love you, too, and I will."

Nick eased the RIB away from the *Deep Adventurer* and gunned the throttle. The runabout powered into the gloom without running lights.

Yuri made his exit.

The *Deep Adventurer* bobbed next to the *Yangzi*, secured by the overhead crane's lifting cables.

The bomb inside remained lethal—Yuri's choice.

With their cover blown, Wang and his shooters descended from the bridge deck to the upper deck expecting trouble. It came when one of the SVR agents guarding the captives moved forward to investigate the racket.

Wang ambushed the man, dropping him in a passageway near the elevator. He and his team approached the salon—Kwan Chi's private lounge.

Familiar with the layout, Wang elected to enter from the aft, using the starboard deck for access. As they moved on the outside deck, he observed Kwan and the

PLAN crew members through the windows. All remained bound and were sitting on the carpet. They also spotted the guard. The Caucasian squatted behind the corner of Kwan's bar. He held a submachine gun with his hand. A baby carrier rested on the deck beside his left knee.

The PLAN commandos made their way to the aft doorway. With his companions again serving as backup, Wang flipped the selector switch on his SMG to full auto and burst through the aft doorway, peppering the bar area with half a mag. He moved forward to inspect the kill but found no body or blood trail. He surveyed the rest of the salon, deciding the guard had moved forward before his attack.

Keeping an eye out for the rogue gunman, Wang greeted Kwan Chi. "Are you injured, sir?"

"No. Get these damn things off my hands."

After Yuri exited the garage through the aft hatchway, he ascended the stern stairs to the main deck, working his way forward on the starboard side. The pain in his left calf surged, slowing his progress. Stooped over, Yuri pulled open one of the double doors that opened into the interior spaces of the upper deck. Still hunched down, he advanced into the lobby area that fronted the elevator and the adjacent stairway. He gripped the Colt with his right hand.

Fredek bounded down the staircase on the opposite side of the lobby with the AKSU-74 in his right hand and the baby carrier suspended by the other.

Startled, Fredek raised his weapon. Yuri countered in Russian. "It's me—don't shoot!"

Fredek lowered his weapon. "We're under attack."

"I've got to get to the bridge—for Maddy's survival gear." He'd parked the backpack on the deck in the aft port corner. It contained the child immersion suit and plastic inflatable raft.

"No way, man. They're following me—they're killing everyone on sight."

Yuri had no choice. He reached forward and grabbed the baby carrier. "We've got to get off this thing now."

"But how?"

"Follow me."

"How many of you are aboard?" asked Kwan Chi.

"Three. The rest of the team will arrive soon by boat." Wang hesitated. "Sir, who were these men that held you?"

"Russians—SVR, I think."

"But how could—"

"Kirov! He's responsible. Find him. I want that son of a bitch dead. And his woman, too."

"Yes, sir."

CHAPTER 92

Yuri and Fredek stood inside the storage locker at the aft end of the garage. Fredek struggled to pull on the immersion survival suit. Fluorescent orange and constructed of thick neoprene, the one-piece dry suit provided cold-water protection from booties to hood.

Yuri assisted Fredek, tugging the chest zipper tight and then pulling the neck flap to complete the water-tight seal.

"That should do it," Yuri said.

"What about you? There are a bunch more of these." He gestured to the lineup of survival suits in the compartment.

"I'll be fine in my wetsuit."

Yuri leaned forward and picked up Madelyn. Tucked inside the shoulder and hood section of the smallest immersion suit he could find, her tiny head peered up at him. She gave a two-tooth smile.

"It'll be okay, sweetie. You just sit tight." He faced Fredek. "Help me secure her."

"Right."

With Madelyn facing Yuri's chest, Fredek crossed

the suit's arms over Yuri's shoulders, knotting the sleeves with a section of line behind his neck. He repeated the same with her legs, tying them together near the small of Yuri's back.

Fredek checked his work. "She's snug as a bug."

"Good," Yuri said while reaching down to make sure Maddy could breathe unobstructed. An instant later, they both heard a dull thud and felt a tremor in their feet.

"What's that?" asked Fredek.

Yuri cracked open the aft hatch. "It's another boat. They're coming aboard on the stern platform."

Yuri dogged the hatch shut and pushed Fredek through the forward hatchway, reentering the garage. He flipped a switch by the hatch, extinguishing the overhead lighting. Since both garage doors were open, they prevented the approaching vessel from mooring alongside, leaving the stern the next best access point.

The *Deep Adventurer* remained moored to the starboard side of the garage, so they relocated to the port side. Standing next to the edge of the open door, Yuri whispered, "Get in now."

Fredek eased himself into the water, slipping feet first over the one-foot-high ledge. He bobbed like a cork in the immersion suit.

"Pull yourself onto it but stay facedown for now."

"Okay."

With both arms extended, Fredek pulled himself onto the ten-foot-long paddleboard. He lay prone with his elbows tucked under his chest. He looked up at Yuri.

Yuri handed Fredek two carbon fiber paddles. Fredek tucked the paddle ends under his chest, letting the shafts project over the board's bow.

Yuri dropped the second paddleboard into the water. He sat down, letting his legs hang over the ledge. He looked down, checking Maddy. "Here we go, sweetie."

Yuri lowered his body into the water. Maddy's hybrid immersion suit added extra flotation, keeping her head two feet above the water's surface. Yuri pulled himself onto the second board. After extending his legs over each side, he sat up. He nodded to Fredek, who floated nearby.

Fredek repeated the same maneuver. Now sitting up with his legs straddling the board, he handed Yuri a paddle.

Yuri aimed his paddle toward the south and whispered, "Head that way, I'll follow you."

Fredek dipped the paddle into the water, propelling his board forward.

Maddy whimpered. Yuri reached down and caressed the top of her head. "It's okay, honey, I'm here."

Yuri's comforting words were not enough. Scared, cold, and miserable from a new tooth that pierced her lower gum, Madelyn Grace Newman wailed full throttle.

CHAPTER 93

Kwan Chi and Commander Wang stood next to the open starboard garage door, gawking at the floating *Deep Adventurer.*

"What is this thing?" asked Kwan.

"An autonomous underwater vehicle—a robotic submarine from Kirov's company. We deployed it to search for the recording devices he planted the year before."

"What's it doing here now?"

"Kirov told me that it would park itself on the bottom when it completed the survey. We were supposed to recover it several days ago."

"So it's just been waiting?"

"Yes. Kirov must have sent the recall signal."

"But why now?"

"I expect he wanted to recover it. The unit is quite valuable."

"To pull it out like the Mark Twelve?" Kwan said. He turned toward the Russian torpedo mine parked in its cradle on the opposite side of the garage.

"That appears to be what he was doing."

"Cast it off. We need to leave now."

"Ah, sir, I'd like to bring it aboard. The technology is quite advanced—we'd learn much from it. Plus, there's a chance it located the second Russian recording pod."

Kwan considered the request.

With his mission aborted, any mitigation Kwan could offer Beijing would bolster his precarious position. Kirov's machine would help in that endeavor.

"Go ahead and bring it aboard, Commander. But be quick about it. We need to head to the ocean now. We've been recalled to Hong Kong."

"Aye, aye, sir. We'll have it aboard and stowed in ten minutes." Wang had an afterthought. "The boat my men arrived in, I wish to scuttle it. There's too much evidence left behind now that the mission is blown."

"Sink it here?"

"No, in the ocean—far from here. It can follow us."

"Very well."

CHAPTER 94

Yuri feared Maddy's squeals would give them away. Bundled within the immersion suit, her cries were somewhat muffled. After bellowing for several minutes, her wails diminished to whimpers and she fell asleep.

Managing to paddle about a thousand feet away without detection, Yuri and Fredek watched the yacht as it drifted, both engines set to idle. It appeared to Yuri that every light aboard was on, creating a lightship spectacle. When he noticed a flurry of activity in the garage, he guessed they had discovered the *Deep Adventurer*.

After dousing the cabin lights, the *Yangzi*'s engines throttled up, and it proceeded westward at ten knots. The *Ella Kay* followed. Yuri and Fredek watched the running lights fade into oblivion.

Yuri extended his hand behind Maddy's capsulated covering. She remained asleep. He reached inside his partially unzipped wetsuit jacket and removed his cell phone from the ziplock bag.

He keyed the speed dial.

"Yuri!" Nick Orlov answered in a flash.

"They're gone. You can come pick us up now."

"On the way!"

Nick and Laura hid behind nearby Smith Island to avoid the *Yangzi*'s radar. Encased in neoprene, Yuri and Nick were immune to radio wave detection.

Yuri turned toward Fredek. "Get the light."

"Okay."

Fredek unzipped the front of his survival suit and removed the beacon. Because the emergency light was water activated, Yuri had placed the unit inside Fredek's suit before sealing it. Otherwise, the flashing strobe might reveal their location too soon. Maddy's suit did not have a light.

Fredek scooted beside Yuri's board and handed over the light.

Yuri yanked the plastic ring, manually activating it. He used his chest to the shield the light from the west.

Twelve minutes elapsed. The RIB homed in on the flashing strobe with the precision of a cruise missile. Yuri, Maddy, and Fredek were assisted aboard, along with the paddleboards. The rigid inflatable boat drifted with the current.

Yuri would not have made it into the runabout without Nick's help. His lower left leg had morphed from stinging pain to terrifying numbness.

"Hi, honey," Yuri said as he embraced Laura, wobbly.

Laura beamed. "Thank you, Lord, for saving all of us."

"Amen to that!"

Propped against the center console, Yuri leaned forward to allow Laura to check her daughter, still cocooned inside the immersion suit. Maddy was awake.

She broke into a beaming smile when she spotted her mother.

"How are you, sweetie?"

Yuri used the hydrophone to recall *Deep Adventurer*, expecting it had been turned loose when the *Yangzi* took off. The underwater acoustic signal would reactivate the strobe light on the top of the hull. But there was no sign of the AUV.

"Maybe they took it aboard?" Nick suggested.

"Or they scuttled it," Yuri said. He sat in the captain's chair.

"Hmmm, that's too bad. I know it's valuable."

"Doesn't matter. What counts is that we're all okay." Yuri massaged his left calf with both hands.

With Maddy in her arms, Laura zeroed in on Yuri's discomfort.

"What's wrong with your leg?"

"I'm half-frozen, it's stiff."

"Are you sure? That could be the bends again."

"I just need a hot shower."

"And a triple shot of Stoli," Nick added.

"Hear! Hear!" agreed Fredek.

Laura grinned. "Let's go home, boys."

CHAPTER 95

Kwan Chi and Commander Wang were in the *Yangzi*'s main deck salon, sipping tea while seated in luxurious leather chairs. It was early afternoon. The yacht was fifty miles offshore of the Washington coast. The seas were mild and the sky clear. They had the spacious and unscathed compartment to themselves as they discussed the mission debrief.

"When will you scuttle the workboat?" Kwan asked. The *Ella Kay* trailed a mile behind.

"Tonight, once we're clear of other vessels."

"What about the mine, can we get rid of it, too?"

"Yes, we'll dispose of it at the same time."

"Good," Kwan said, taking another sip from his cup.

"We've been lucky. If Kirov had contacted the American authorities . . ."

"He couldn't do that. We had the ultimate leverage over him."

"His woman?"

"Yes."

Wang asked, "What happened to Elena?"

Kwan sighed heavily. "The Russians took her ashore. She was in bad shape."

"They'll interrogate her."

"She knows nothing about the mission. Her only connection was Kirov."

"That will help. But the missing backup hard drive—"

"We can only hope that the encryption software works."

"Do we know where they took it?"

"Probably to their consulate in San Francisco."

"Do you think we can get it back?"

"I'm sure Beijing is looking into that."

They sipped in silence for a time. Wang said, "Are you leaving the ship in Ensenada?"

"Yes, my plane will be there." Kwan hesitated. "Would you like to accompany me to Hong Kong?"

"I would, sir, and if it's possible I'd like my other two team members to come along. We've all been re-called—we're too hot to remain in North America."

"Fine, there's plenty of room."

"Thank you."

Wang checked his watch. He drained his cup and stood up. "I've got some work to do, sir, if you'll excuse me."

"What's going on?"

"We're going to run some diagnostic tests on Kirov's robotic submersible. I want to see if it located the other Russian pod. We might have gotten lucky with the recordings."

"That would certainly be good news."

"Yes, sir." Wang hesitated. "Would you like to observe?"

"No, you go ahead. I'm going to relax in my cabin. I'm worn out."

"Very good, sir."

CHAPTER 96

As the RIB raced into Elliott Bay, Yuri's symptoms worsened. The extra depth and extended bottom time, combined with Yuri's unconventional ascent, reignited his previous bouts with decompression sickness.

Laura hailed a cab at the Bell Street Marina and rushed Yuri to the hospital, leaving Nick and Fredek to fend for themselves. In the emergency room, Yuri was examined and admitted. Within an hour, he was in the chamber compressed with air to an equivalent pressure of 165 feet of seawater. The six-hour session in the hyperbaric chamber cost a bundle without insurance, but Laura gladly handed over her AMEX card.

After Yuri recouped in a hospital room for the remainder of the morning, the attending physician ordered a second treatment at a lower pressure. After spending another two hours in the chamber, the numbness in his lower left leg diminished to almost nothing.

To pass the time he read magazines and watched television. The RN accompanying Yuri in the chamber tuned the flat panel TV on the opposite wall to a local station. Yuri ignored the talk show as he perused a two-month-old issue of *Popular Science* magazine.

That changed when a "Breaking News" banner flashed onto the screen. The announcer reported the story:

"We have breaking news exclusive to our station. There has been a massive explosion aboard a yacht off the Washington coast near the Oregon border. A commercial fishing boat reported witnessing the explosion and took these cell phone videos of the incident, which are only available from our station. As you can see, the boat is . . ."

Yuri stared at the screen. The video was poor quality but he recognized the *Yangzi*. The aft end of the ship was gone and the remaining forward section was fully ablaze. The carnage was far worse than he'd expected from *Deep Adventurer*'s "surprise" package.

My God, the Mark Twelve—it must have detonated, too.

The reporter continued:

"The crew of the fishing boat report that the yacht sank minutes after they recorded the video. There's no sign of survivors so far. The U.S. Coast Guard is investigating. Stay tuned for updates on this disaster."

Yuri experienced neither jubilation nor remorse. *It's over—at least for now.*

He sat quietly for the remainder of the session. A few minutes before six o'clock, Yuri walked out of the chamber.

Laura was waiting. Maddy was in a new baby carrier parked in a chair beside her.

Yuri wondered if she'd heard the news.

Laura stood as he approached, her infectious smile breaking out. "Your limp—it's gone."

She doesn't know—I'll tell her later.

Yuri stretched his left leg and rotated his ankle.

"Good as new. Thank you, honey."

Standing on the tips of her toes, Laura leaned forward and kissed him—a lingering, delicious kiss.

ACKNOWLEDGMENTS

Thanks to Mike McCarter for his review of the manuscript. His insightful suggestions and comments were of great value to me.

I wish to thank Cody Hulsey for helping me navigate as an author through the "uncharted waters" of social media.

Thanks again to Todd Wyatt of Carson Noel for his assistance with negotiating the contract with Kensington Books for *The Good Spy* and *The Forever Spy*.

I would like to take this opportunity to express my heartfelt gratitude to Michaela Hamilton, executive editor at Kensington, for her critical review of *The Forever Spy*. Michaela is a remarkable editor who worked with me to improve the story, just as she did for *The Good Spy*. Michaela and her talented team at Kensington are a pleasure to work with.

Finally, I'd like to thank my family for continuing to encourage me with my writing career.

In case you missed the first exciting Yuri Kirov thriller,
THE GOOD SPY—keep reading to enjoy an excerpt . . .

CHAPTER 1

DAY 2—TUESDAY

Kirov plowed into the gloom. The firestorm deep inside his right shoulder raged but he hung on. He'd lost all sensation below the left knee—it was just dead meat. If the unfeeling crept into his other limbs he was doomed for sure.

He focused on the captain's orders: "Get to shore. Call for help and then coordinate the rescue. Don't get caught!"

He was the crew's only hope. If he failed, they would all perish.

The diver propulsion vehicle surged against the aggressive tidal current. As he gripped the DPV's control handles with both gloved hands, his body trailed prone on the sea surface. Hours earlier he'd exhausted the mixed gas supply, which forced him topside, where he used a snorkel to breathe.

The chilled seawater defeated his synthetic rubber armor. His teeth chattered against the snorkel's mouthpiece. He clamped his jaws to maintain the watertight seal.

Shore lights shimmered through his face mask but he remained miles from his destination. The DPV's battery gauge kissed the warning range. When it eventually petered out, he would have to transit the passage on his own, somehow swimming the expanse in the dark while combating the current.

Two grueling hours passed. He abandoned the spent DPV, opening the flood valve and allowing it to sink. He butted the tidal flow until it turned. The flooding current carried him northward.

He swam facedown while still breathing through the snorkel. As he pumped his lower limbs, his good leg overpowered its anesthetized twin, forcing him off course. He soon learned to compensate with his left arm, synchronizing its strokes with his right leg.

The joint pain expanded to include both shoulders and elbows. The frigid sea sapped his vigor to near exhaustion.

While staring downward into the pitch-black abyss, he tried not to dwell on his injuries or his weariness—or the absolute isolation, knowing he could do nothing to mitigate them. Instead, his thoughts converged on the mission. *They're counting on me. Don't give up. I can do this; just keep moving.*

He continued swimming, monitoring his course with the compass strapped to his right wrist. An evolving mantle of fog doused the shore lights he'd been using as a homing beacon. For all he knew, the current could be shoving him into deeper waters.

Maybe at dawn he would be able to get his bearings. Until then, he would plod along.

I wonder where the blackfish are now.

During a rest with fins down and a fresh bubble of

air in his buoyancy compensator, he had heard dozens of watery eruptions breach the night air as a pod of *Orcinus orcas* made its approach. Sounding like a chorus of steam engines, the mammals cleared blowholes and sucked air into their mammoth lungs. The sea beasts ghosted by at ten knots. Their slick coal-black hulls spotted with white smears passed just a few meters away from his stationary position.

The killer whales had ignored him. They had a mission of their own: pursuing the plump inbound silver and chum salmon that loitered near the tip of the approaching peninsula. At first light, the orcas would gorge themselves.

There was no time to be afraid; instead, he marveled at the close encounter. Oddly, the whales' brief presence calmed him. He was not alone in these alien waters after all.

Time for another check.

He stopped kicking and raised his head. He peered forward.

Dammit!

Still no lights and the fog bank oozed even closer.

Where is it?

He allowed his legs to sink as he mulled his options. His right fin struck something.

He swam ahead for half a minute and repeated the sounding.

I made it!